THE GOD PARTICLE

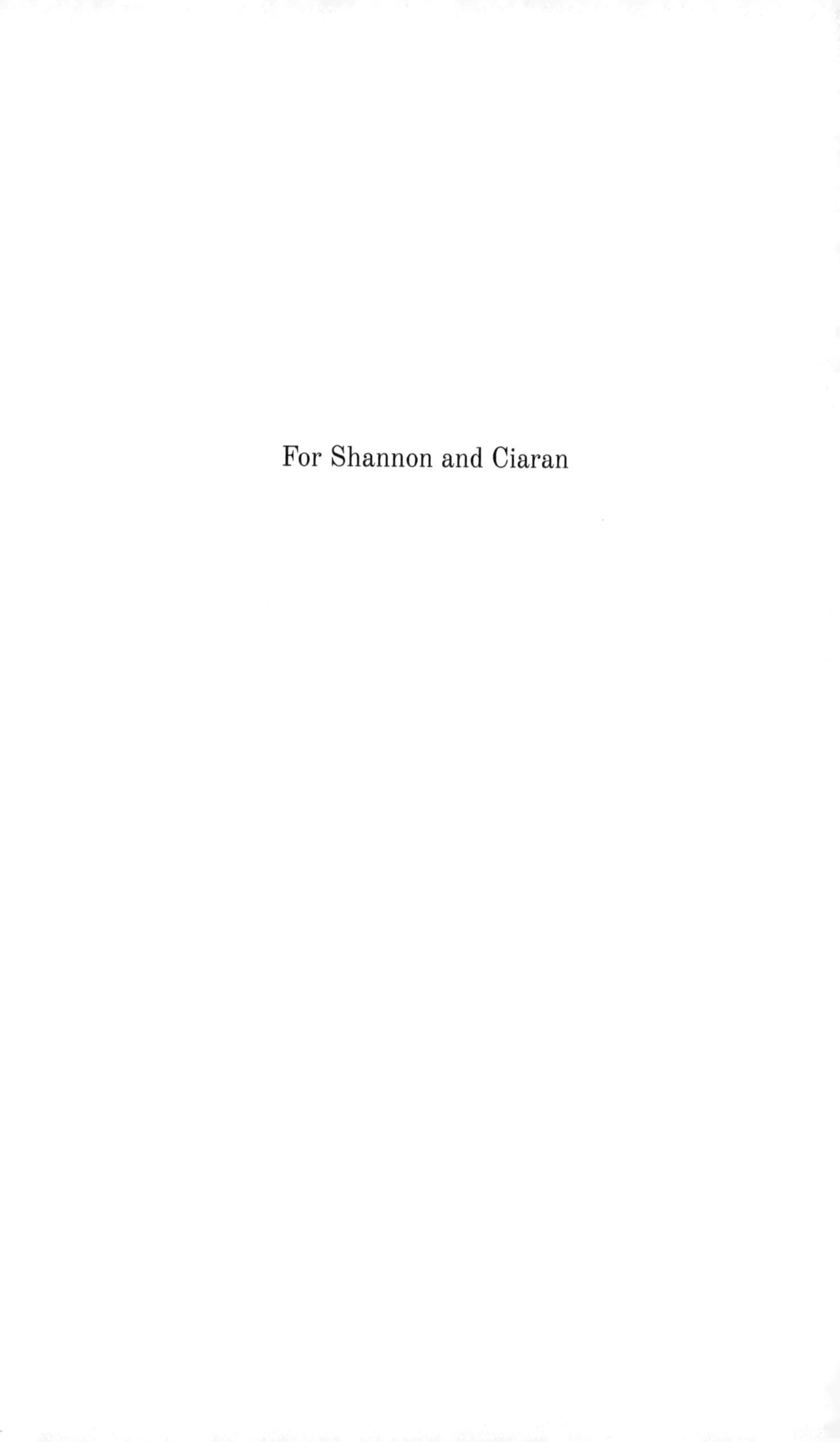

For Shannon and Ciaran

The God Particle

Liam Stirling

Liam Stirling

ISBN-13: 978-1-7397792-4-5
ISBN-10: 1-7397792-4-5

Cover design by: Adrian DKC
Printed in the United Kingdom

First Printing, 2022

Contents

Dedication — ii
Foreword — vii
Genesis — ix

One — 1

Two — 18

Three — 47

Four — 89

Five — 129

Six — 176

Seven — 210

Eight — 236

Nine

256

Ten

281

Eleven

319

Twelve

354

THIRTEEN

389

Revelations 399
About The Author 410
Free Audiobook 411

Foreword

ON 4TH JULY 2012, scientists at CERN, the European Centre for Nuclear Research in Geneva, discovered the Higgs boson, a fundamental particle that gives all other particles mass. I'd always imagined that the scientists were looking for a bosun, who is a member of a ship's crew. It turns out I'm not very good at spelling.

Hercules Leek was born several years before, when I discovered that the French word for "leek" is "poireau". So I imagined Agatha Christie's famous Belgian detective as a leek with a fine moustache and a monocle. But his name is spelt "Poirot", so it turns out I'm not very good at spelling in French, either.

For younger readers, Mao Ze-Dong (China), Stalin (Russia), Pol Pot (Cambodia), Kim Il Sung (North Korea) and Idi Amin (Uganda) are five despotic leaders from recent history who between them were responsible for the deaths of a huge number of their own citizens.

I would like to thank my friends for help with spelling and other foibles.

"The truth that can be told, is not the eternal truth."

Lao Tze

Genesis

A VOICE.

A voice older than Space and deeper than Time.

A voice that resonates across infinity with the deafening roar of absolute silence.

A voice that might say 'Let there be light'. And there would be.

A voice that arcs across Creation and asks, in a slightly puzzled tone, 'What do you mean – *"Have I tried turning it off and then turning it back on again?"*?'

One

AN AGNOSTIC ATHEIST is someone who isn't sure that they don't believe in god. Consequently, in their darkest hour, when the chips are down and their backs are to the wall, the agnostic atheist is usually to be found on their knees offering up prayers to some previously unacknowledged deity.

An atheistic agnostic, by contrast, while generally unsure of their beliefs, is almost pretty certain that they don't involve an Almighty. As a member of this latter group, it is therefore true to say that it came as something of a shock to Hercules Leek that, shortly after his death, he should find himself in Heaven. But this was nothing compared to his surprise at what happened next…

* * *

'*Jeeeeeeeezus*, Moses, LOOK OUT!'

Moses jolted up in his seat and grabbed a little too eagerly at the steering wheel. The huge articulated lorry rocked violently as it swerved away from the verge. Moses fought the skid and somehow managed to wrestle control of the vehicle.

'*OW!* What the hell was that for?' Moses put a hand to the reddening cheek where he had just received a hard slap across the face.

'*FerChistssake* - you're going to get us both killed if you don't pay attention,' snarled Toby.

1

Moses Malone grunted. He reached for a near empty can of Red Bull and poured the last of the sticky sweet liquid into his mouth.

'*GAH!* My tongue still feels like sandpaper!' he complained. 'What I wouldn't give for a shower…and a bed.'

'Just try and stay awake – or we'll both be gonners.'

Moses crushed the can in one hand and tossed it into the steadily-accumulating mound of rubbish in the passenger foot-well. Toby didn't seem to mind this invasion of his space. But then Toby Slate wasn't taking up any more space in the cab than was occupied by Moses Malone himself: for Moses Malone and Toby Slate were one and the same person.

Moses had debts. A few years back credit had been easy, and like so many, Moses had developed a taste for living slightly beyond his means. But changing times had brought an end to easy credit. The years of overspend and accrued interest now added up to considerably more money than he could make as the owner-driver of his rig – even taking into account the various small-scale opportunities for personal gain that came from constantly crossing borders.

He'd tried consolidating his many debts into a single repayment plan. Now, instead of being faced on a monthly basis with a number of bills which added up to a total he couldn't afford, there was just the one big bill that he couldn't afford each month.

Despite his occasional petty law-breaking, Moses didn't regard himself as a proper criminal. Certainly not enough to get involved with some of the more lucrative, but considerably higher risk, opportunities for cross border profiteering which presented themselves to him from time to time. He wasn't that desperate – yet. The problem, as Moses saw it, was that when his truck wasn't moving, he wasn't earning. Up against multi-national transport organisations he simply couldn't earn enough by sticking to legally allotted hours. What he needed was another driver. He just couldn't afford to pay anyone a wage.

Then he'd had a brainwave, and Toby Slate was born. For the record, Toby Slate *had* been born around the same time as Moses, but had sadly passed away within a couple of weeks of his birth. With a bit of creative paperwork, Moses had breathed a new lease of life – if not into Toby himself – then at least into his name. Toby had taken over the tenancy of Moses' flat, and Moses had moved in with his parents. With two addresses, a bit of additional creative paperwork, and a use of stimulants that had long since crossed the borders of the lands of reckless and was now giggling and speeding towards the dusty plains of insanity, Moses and Toby began to share the workload. Alone together in the cab for the long hours on the road they were happy enough in one another's company, and it was not unknown for the pair to while away the time engaged in animated conversation. For the occasional change of company, Moses would sometimes give a ride to the odd lone hitchhiker, who could pose as the second driver if he was ever stopped and questioned by the authorities. This rarely happened – and never to the point where his subterfuge was discovered. Twice as many hours on the road meant twice the miles covered, twice the loads delivered – and twice the income.

If it was a crime, it was victimless.

Until now.

Moses wiped a hand over his face and puffed out a breath. He wound down the window to let some fresh air into the cab and flicked through the channels of the radio, stopping when he stumbled across a tune he liked. He was coming to the outskirts of town.

'Not far now.' He exhaled hard again, and forced his attention back onto the road ahead.

Traffic was slowing for the approach to a crossroads. Moses watched the lights change to red. He had done this journey countless times. He could practically do it in his sleep. There were still a couple of hundred yards to go to the lights and there was a good stretch of clear road ahead of him. If he timed things right, he would arrive at the lights and make his left turn ahead without needing to stop completely. With practiced judgment, he shifted down through the gears. As he slowed, he didn't notice the bicycle pass him on the inside.

Sure enough, the lights had changed to green before the lorry reached them. Moses started to accelerate and flicked the indicators. He spun the wheel hard and swung the lorry through the bend. There was a barely noticeable bump. Moses thought nothing of it, but as the truck straightened into its new course, something caught the corner of his eye. He glanced across at the pavement and saw a man waving frantically at the cab. Standing next to the man was a woman pointing in horror.

Moses slammed his foot to the floor, and, with a bang and a hiss, the air brakes kicked in. To the screeching of eighteen protesting tyres, thirty tonnes of haulage slewed to a stop in the road.

Moses flung the door open and raced to the rear of the lorry. As he rounded the back of the trailer, he skidded to a halt. His eyes followed the black trails of rubber snaking along the road, from his still-smoking tyres through the broken wreckage and twisted metal of what had once been a bicycle. As his brain untangled the scene before him, any colour left drained out of his haggard face and his limbs turned to lead.

In a daze, Moses retraced the tracks of the skid marks, oblivious to the bystanders. He felt like he was moving through treacle, the world silent yet roaring in his ears. The black marks changed to red as Moses approached the heap of crumpled rags lying in the road. A clammy sweat enveloped his face. Reality crashed through the trance that had carried his legs this far. The rags revealed a bloodied and broken body, screaming its inertness.

'Jesus!' gasped Moses.

Then he was sick.

* * *

The hand-written notice blu-tacked to the battered doors of the community centre announces that a meeting is taking place.

To the casual observer, who may chance to push through the doors into the room beyond, 'meeting' might be considered an overly grand description. However, in this unloved corner of this unloved estate, any observer who appears casual is probably only faking casualness as he keeps watch while his mates nick the wheels off your car.

'Well, Mr Dumb-Arse. Are you having this meeting or not? It's not like I've got nothing better to do, you know.'

A look of annoyance flashed briefly across the face of the chairman, followed just as quickly by a smile so ingratiating that a Cheshire cat would have spat with envy.

'As you well know, Mrs Cunningham, my name is pronounced DOO-MA. The U is pronounced OO, as YOU well know, and the RS is silent: DOO-MA.'

The old lady met his smile with a stony look. 'Really? You never struck me as the silent type, and to me you've always been a dum–'

'Yes, all right, Mrs Cunningham.' A shade of pique coloured his voice, but the rictus grin did not waver. Maximilian Augustus Dumars, for that was his full given name and spelling, whatever the pronunciation, straightened a few papers on the table in front of him. 'I hereby call this meeting of the Broadfields Estate Community Litter Patrol Committee to order.'

'Ha!' a contemptuous snort erupted from the old lady.

'Really, Mrs Cunningham! I do hope you are not here simply to be disruptive. The litter on this estate is a grievous problem and one that this committee takes most seriously.'

'Take yourselves seriously, more like,' retorted Mrs Cunningham. 'I mean, you come down here and hold your meetings every week and what changes? I'll tell you what. Nothing. If anything, litter's getting worse, not better. And then there's the graffiti...'

'Graffiti isn't the concern of the Broadfields Estate Community *Litter* Patrol Committee, Mrs Cunningham. The *clue* is in the *name*.'

'That's not very *community* spirited.' Mrs Cunningham fixed Mr Dumars with a determined stare. 'Anyway... Know what I saw last Friday? Over by the bins?'

'No, pray tell us.'

'A fox.'

'Mrs Cunningham, this is a meeting of the Community Litter Patrol Committee. Unless the fox was dropping crisp packets and cigarette butts,' Mr Dumars' smile shifted from ingratiating to patronising, 'I simply fail to see the relevance of your observations of the local urban natural history – however fascinating they may be.'

'You never asked me what the fox was doing.'

Maximilian Dumars sighed. 'And what was the fox doing?'

'Running!'

'Ah, yes, I see. Running... *Running!* Well, Mrs Cunningham,' Maximilian Dumars spoke slowly as though addressing an idiot. 'Running is what foxes do, I believe. I am no expert, but I am fairly sure that foxes have, on occasion, been known to run.'

He looked to his left and right for support and was reassured by the nodding heads of his companions.

'Yes, it appears we agree. Foxes run. Now is that all? Or can we kindly get on with things please? We are all busy people.'

'Really? – I'm a pensioner, you only work part time, and as for those two –' she cast a dismissive glance to either side of Mr Dumars, '– *they* couldn't hold a job down between them if it were made of lead and had an elephant sat on top!'

'We are all busy with our efforts trying to contribute to the community.'

'Don't see much evidence of that.'

'That's because you keep interrupting!' His reddening face indicated that Maximilian Dumars was beginning to lose his cool. Little white flecks of spittle gathered at the corner of his mouth and a small muscle in his left temple began to twitch involuntarily. He took a deep breath and once again straightened the papers in front of him, carefully aligning the corners of the sheets to form a perfectly neat stack.

'This meeting is now in order. I will begin with the minutes of the last meeting.'

'Didn't ask why the fox was running.'

'This is a committee meeting! There is a protocol to follow! At the end of the meeting any other business may be introduced from the floor. We have rules you know.'

Mrs Cunningham was unrepentant. 'Didn't ask why the fox was running,' she repeated.

'This is highly unusual, but since I fear we shall get no business concluded until you have regaled us with every last detail of your story, please, the floor is yours. Tell us, do, why was the fox running?'

'It was being chased...' she paused, dramatically. '...by rats. Loads of 'em. Each the size of a terrier they was. All chasing the fox away from the bins 'cos there's so much rubbish and that's how they get to be so big. And you call yourself the Litter Patrol Committee, but

I don't see much litter patrolling happening and, if you did, you'd see what I'd seen and it's a disgrace. That's what it is. A disgrace.

'Anyway I've said my piece.' Mrs Cunningham scooped up the knitting bag from the chair beside her that was the only other occupied seat in the room. 'I can't see you lot doin' much about it, mind. I was just curious, what with all your meetings and nothing ever getting done.'

She started towards the doors at the back of the hall with an arthritic shuffle. As she reached the door, she paused and turned. 'You know what you lot are?'

'I doubt I could stop you telling us even if I wanted to.'

'You lot,' a smile further split her already wrinkled features, 'you lot are… RUBBISH!' The room went quiet. 'Litter…rubbish…get it?' And with a snort and a final 'Ha!' she shuffled out into the day, leaving the doors to swing closed behind her.

The members of the committee sat in a stunned silence, staring at the doors, almost in expectation that they would suddenly swing open again.

After a long moment of silence, with the three of them still staring fixedly at the door, it became clear that there would be no further interruptions, or indeed, attendees to this particular meeting of the Broadfields Estate Community Litter Patrol Committee.

* * *

Although Hercules had been known to spend a good deal of time pondering the nature of the Universe and the place of himself – and indeed his species – within the framework of existence, he actually gave very little thought to what would happen to him when he died. Not being blessed with any great degree of precognition, he had always imagined that he would live to a ripe old age and that whatever came next might be a matter that could consume his thoughts in his twilight years.

So a turning truck smashing into him as he was cycling to work and mashing him into the tarmac was not only a wholeheartedly unpleasant experience, but also – it is only fair to say – somewhat unexpected.

* * *

The sky is dark and brooding. A gusting wind chases the lighter, lower clouds across the background of their gloomier brethren above.

In a car park, atop the moor, a lone vehicle is parked. It is a battered old van - a mixture of rusting panels that make it difficult to tell what colour it may have been when once, a long time ago, it was new.

Next to the van a large cage has been placed on top of a folding table. The door of the cage is open.

A young man sits on the bonnet of the van, scanning the sky…

Earlier that morning, while it was still dark, Asif had risen, prayed and breakfasted, before packing his favourite birds into his van and setting off to the northeast. The day had been carefully chosen for the weather conditions. The same strong south-westerly wind that would later chase the clouds across the sky above the moor would provide resistance to the birds' flight, slowing them down. Asif's battered old van could only manage a noisy sixty-five miles an hour on the motorway in the most favourable circumstances, and under normal windless conditions it was perfectly possible that the pigeons would beat him home.

Only he wasn't at home. Should the pigeons find him here on top of the moor it would mark a crowning triumph to his months of diligent preparation and planning. This was the final test flight.

Asif had greeted the breaking dawn sitting on a beach, with the pigeons in their travel cage beside him. When he travelled, a piece of old blanket over the cage kept the birds calm. Now he drew the blanket aside to let the first weak rays of the new day rouse his charges. He gave the birds a couple of minutes to adjust to wakefulness and their unfamiliar surroundings, talking gently to them as they puffed and preened inside their cage.

'Yes, my special ones,' murmured Asif. 'This is a historic day; thanks be to God.'

The pigeons cooed softly at the familiar sound of Asif's voice. Asif unlatched the cage and reached inside, gently scooping up one of the birds with a practiced touch. Each bird was wearing a small harness fastened across its back and under its wings, and a soft leather hood fastened under its chin. Asif checked the fastenings of hood and harness and when he was satisfied rose to his feet, planted a kiss on the pigeon's head and launched the bird to the heavens. The pigeon climbed rapidly and circled the beach as it adjusted its bearings.

Asif watched the bird's ascent with a critical eye. Satisfied, he bent to the cage and took out its mate. Again he repeated the checking of harness and hood. Again, satisfied, he planted a gentle kiss on the head of the bird and whispered softly to it, 'Now, my beauty, fly home.'

He flung his arms open, and the second pigeon raced into the sky to join its circling partner. Together the two birds made a final circuit above Asif's head before deciding on a bearing and racing off towards the south.

With a following wind Asif's pigeons could cover ninety, sometimes even a hundred, miles in an hour. Of course, that was with the wind behind them and unburdened by their harnesses and hoods. Although he had made every effort to keep these as light as possible, Asif knew that the added weight only increased the effort the birds had to expend. Flying into a strong headwind, like today, they would be lucky to cover more than thirty miles in an hour. Unlike Asif, who had to follow the roads, they could, however, travel in a straight line.

In theory this gave Asif ample time, even in his less-than-sporty van, to cover the sixty miles to the moor where he hoped to re-join his charges. The moor was twenty miles from the loft that was the pigeons' habitual journey's end. Therein lay the purpose of this experiment. If his craftsmanship was adequate and his calibrations correct, Asif was in possession of the world's first and only directionally programmable pigeons.

As the van droned along the motorway, thick smoke belching from the straining diesel engine, Asif craned his neck to scan the sky. He knew it was a pointless exercise. He should be ahead of the birds, and they would not be following the route of the road – but a combination of nervous excitement and fear of failure kept drawing his eyes magnetically to the sky above.

A little over an hour later Asif pulled into the deserted car park, relieved to find himself alone. Given the weather it was no surprise that there was no one else about: it was not the kindest of days for embracing the great outdoors. Asif sat in the van for a while scanning the sky to the north. Then he got out of the van and found a clear patch of ground, unfurled the prayer mat he had brought with him, turned to the east and began to pray.

When he had finished his prayers Asif checked his watch. It was nearly an hour and a half since he had left the beach. He rolled up his prayer mat and returned it to the van, taking out a flask of hot, sweet tea and a package of sandwiches wrapped in cellophane that had been lying on the seat. He balanced the thermos on the bonnet of the van and poured himself a cup, then un-wrapped the sandwiches and started to eat, munching slowly and occasionally taking a slurp of the steaming tea. A crumb got caught in his straggly black beard. Asif absentmindedly retrieved it with his long fingers and popped it in his mouth, all the while his eyes fixed on the sky to the north.

Finishing his tea, he wiped the back of his hand across his mouth, screwed the cup back onto the top of the flask and returned it to the passenger seat. He unpacked a folding table and the pigeons' cage, into which he placed a bowl of birdseed. From the glove-box, he retrieved a pair of binoculars. Laying the binoculars on the bonnet, he sat down next to them, and waited.

* * *

'That awful woman – I thought she was never going to go!'

Maximilian Dumars' companions nodded in agreement.

'Still, it's nice to have someone actually turn up to one of our meetings,' ventured the smaller of the two.

'Yeah… Nice to see someone showing an interest,' his oversized colleague replied.

'Very civic minded.'

'Even if she is a bit…loopy.'

'And calling us rubbish wasn't very funny.'

'Nah…That was just mean.'

'And I didn't really get why she thinks we need an elephant.'

Maximilian Dumars watched this exchange between his two companions with growing incredulity.

'*Gentlemen!* Enough! Do I *really* need to remind you of our purpose here?'

'It was just nice to have someone show an interest, that's all I'm saying,' mumbled the short one.

Maximilian Dumars sighed. 'How many times do I need to explain to you, Nicholas, that the Broadfields Estate Community Litter Patrol Group is just our front? Our cover –' And then, almost to himself, he added, 'and the only way we get to use this hall free of charge.'

'You mean we're not here to sort out the litter on the estate?'

''Cos the old bird was right.' His much larger companion glanced around the room with a critical eye, from the grubby functional furniture and flickering strip-lights to the peeling paint and cracked panes of wire meshed-security glass. 'It *is* a bit of a mess round here.'

'And it wouldn't hurt if this room had a lick of paint, either.'

'No, Gentlemen, we are not here to discuss the state of the litter on the estate, or even the décor of this hall for that matter. There are more important matters to discuss. There is a more insidious trash on our streets – a tide of detritus that we *must* take a stand against.'

His two colleagues regarded him blankly.

'Immigrants...?'

'A yeah, Boss. All them foreigners.'

'Yeah, coming here - taking our jobs and scrounging off the state.'

'Yeah, schools don't even teach in English. Bloody outrage, that's what it is.'

'Right then,' Maximilian Dumars shuffled his papers, 'now that we're all on the same page, I call this meeting of the Aryan Defence Order to order.'

'League,' interjected the shorter of his colleagues.

'Front,' contradicted the human colossus that was the other.

'Gentlemen, I thought we were in agreement at the end of the last meeting that we would operate under the name of the Aryan Defence Order.'

'I liked League,' said Nicholas – known to everyone who knew him who wasn't his mother or Maximilian Dumars, as Nick.

'I thought Front was better. Besides - it sounds funny, calling a meeting of the Aryan Defence Order to order. That's too many orders. How're we meant to know which order we're supposed to be following?'

'Order – as in Organisation, Chapter...'
'What, are we a book now?'

'Look, we've spent the last six meetings discussing what to call ourselves and getting nowhere. We really need to get past this name thing so we can get on with the important stuff.' The room fell silent. Maximilian Dumars straightened the corners of his already precision-stacked sheaf of papers. The three stared aimlessly around the room, none willing to catch the others' eyes.

Eventually Maximilian Dumars broke the silence. 'OK...Suppose we call ourselves the Aryan Defence Order...League...Front?'

'Yeah,' Nick concurred, visibly rolling the name around in his head. 'That sounds good. I like it.'

'Eugene?' inquired Maximilian Dumars, turning to the enormous figure to his left.

'Works for me, Boss,' nodded Eugene.

'An *excellent* choice.'

The three men looked up. A very smartly dressed man was leaning insouciantly against the wall by the double doors. He was sporting a deep red suit of impeccable tailoring, under which a crisply-ironed purple shirt was offset by a tie of a colour to match his suit. A purple pocket square matching the colour of his shirt rounded off the look. His patent shoes shone like mirrors, and he carried a silver-topped cane. His blond hair was swept back and immaculately groomed, as was his neatly-trimmed goatee beard. Pale blue eyes sparkled like pools of ice. Although his face was apparently untroubled by the wearing effects of time, he carried himself with a confidence and sense of purpose that spoke of an ageless maturity.

None of the three had heard him enter. They eyed the stranger suspiciously. To the protesting squeal of metal on concrete, Eugene shifted his weight in his chairs, ready, at the word of his boss, to eject the interloper.

The stranger held up his hand and strode purposefully forward. 'Please do not be alarmed, Gentlemen,' he began. 'I represent certain –' he paused '– *interests*. My employers are very powerful indeed. And they have noticed you.' The three seated men looked at one another with puzzled expressions, then, as one, turned back to face the stranger. 'They think you have –' he paused again, either for dramatic effect or because he was searching for the right word, '– *potential*. Yes. Amazing potential. They like your politics. Love your style. And they have a proposition for you.'

The three men at the table continued to eye the stranger with distrust.

'But I'm getting ahead of myself. Please – allow me to introduce myself. My name is Mr John. But you can call me Lee. My card,' he reached inside his jacket pocket and with a flourish, produced a business card and proffered it to Mr Dumars. The card was black with silver trim and ornate lettering. It read:

'Very grand, I'm sure, Mr John,' said Maximilian Dumars, coldly, 'but it doesn't really tell us much, does it? "*We Are Many*"?' His voice was heavy with sarcasm. 'Who are "*We*"? How numerous are the "*many*"?' He tossed the card dismissively onto the table. 'There's not even a phone number.'

'Yes, well, as you no doubt appreciate, "*We*" deal with sensitive issues and not everyone is aligned to the cause – *yet*. A certain amount of – ... *delicacy* is called for in such matters, as I have no doubt that the members of the Broadfields Estate Community Litter Patrol Committee are only *too* well aware.' He smiled broadly at them. Although still suspicious, they were nevertheless listening intently, wondering where all this was leading. 'Our missions require a certain amount of – ... *discretion.*

'I can't say too much at this point. Just as you have questions about *us*, I have to be sure that *you* are the men of character my masters have taken you for.

'Suffice to say, they have devised a –' Mr John did *love* his dramatic pauses, '*mission*... For the right souls... Men of the right – ... *breeding...*

'There is a New World Order brewing, Gentlemen, and I am offering the chance to lead the change... To right wrongs... To purge the unclean... To sit at the very pinnacle of power...

'To take your rightful place in history.

'If you are even half of what I have been led to believe, if you are *ready* –' he had them utterly. As he drew out this last pause he saw each of the three men sharing the look of drunkards with their feet at the edge of a very tall building, teetering on the precipice: grounded by fear, believing they could fly. He spoke the last sentence slowly and quietly, a whisper direct to their innermost beings, '– *you – could – rule – the – world!*'

With a loud **clack**, his heels snapped together. In an impressively Pavlovian reaction the three seated men shot to their feet, scattering cheap plastic seats in the process, and flung out their right arms in salute.

Mr John smiled. 'Very well, Gentlemen. I shall leave you to consider my proposal. I *will* be in touch.' And he turned and strode from the room.

Once again, the three men found themselves staring at the double doors as they banged slowly to stillness. They stood this way for about a minute after the door had come to a complete rest. Then the dawning realisation grew that they were three grown men performing a Nazi salute in an empty room to a closed door and, as one, they dropped their arms.

Eventually, Eugene broke the silence.

'Well, that was nice – two visitors in one meeting… That's a record for us.'

* * *

If Hercules Leek was surprised to find himself in Heaven, the scale of his shock was only surpassed by his astonishment at a turn of events that he had truly *never* expected would befall him when he died.

Hercules Leek got a job in I.T.

Two

GIVEN HIS ALMOST TOTAL lack of religious convictions, it came as something of a surprise to Hercules Leek that a brilliant white light should appear as his broken body was ground under the force of the third heavy truck tyre to have passed over it in quick succession.

'What a cliché,' he found himself thinking with disappointment. He was slightly annoyed that he could not have imagined a more original scenario for his impending demise, which actually seemed to be a strangely trivial thing to be worrying about, given the circumstances. He just had time for a quick 'What the...?' and the entirety of his being, his whole existence and all that he had ever experienced, collapsed into a single point of brilliant luminescence and was catapulted into infinity.

* * *

One summer, a group of musicians had banded together and launched a series of pop concerts urging that the governments of the world pledge to "Make Poverty History".

Somehow, this hadn't happened.

As unlikely as it may seem, the exhortations of some well-meaning entertainers had not healed the world. Sadly, it turned out that all the cash that might have been used to meet their worthy goals was in fact needed to ensure the bonuses and pension pay-outs of bankers through the years of recession that followed the bursting of an economic bubble that the banks themselves had created.

So poverty wasn't history. And neither was famine. And while twenty per cent of the world's population succumbed to the epidemic of obesity, elsewhere fifteen per cent starved.

The rains had failed again in northern East Africa and crisis raised its tired head. It wasn't just the drought. Factional fighting and political instability had once again succeeded in turning the possibility of famine into reality.

Those that still had the strength began to congregate in the aid camps, sometimes bringing with them those that would have been too weak to make the journey alone. Sometimes the weak didn't make it. Sometimes the clean water and rations that the camps distributed were what made the difference between life and death.

Sometimes.

When the help didn't come too late.

Doctor Maurice Lacouille swung his legs over the side of his canvas camp bed and pushed his mosquito net to one side. He was still dressed from the night before. He had worked into the small hours of the morning, treating the sick and the desperate. He almost felt guilty for the relative luxury of a tent shared with only a few other aid workers, his canvas camp bed and the mosquito net. It wasn't luxury, but compared to the suffering that he encountered daily he almost felt it was. But he could serve no one – help no one – if he himself became sick. As one of the few trained medical professionals in the camp, and the only doctor, he was badly needed.

He rubbed his eyes and reached for his boots. He checked them carefully for unwanted visitors, only too well aware of the stories of scorpions and spiders that crawled into unattended footwear overnight and lay hidden to sting or bite the toes of the unwary. Finding no lurking dangers, he pulled on his boots, laced them and ran a hand over his stubbled chin. He dragged his weary body upright and stretched. It was time to face the day and whatever fresh trauma it would bring. He pushed the flap of the tent to one side and stepped out into the bright sunlight of the bone-dry landscape.

It took a few seconds for his eyes to adjust to the change in light, but as the landscape came into focus he had to rub his eyes to check that he was not seeing things. He looked again and the sight before him did not change. The population of the camp – which the night before had numbered a few thousand – had grown tenfold overnight.

'Merde!' Doctor Lacouille muttered to himself. 'We are definitely going to need more supplies.'

* * *

Mr John stepped into the open air and smiled. It was not a bright or sunny day. In fact, the sky was grey and overcast and there was a stiff breeze chasing litter across the tarmac like so many fallen leaves. Nevertheless, he reached inside his jacket pocket, produced an expensive pair of sunglasses and, with a little flourish, put them on. He started to stroll across the forecourt in front of the high-rise buildings. He was, he decided, in a very good mood indeed. The meeting couldn't have gone any better.

At the foot of some stairs leading up to a walkway between the tower-blocks a gang of youths in a uniform of hoodies, low-slung jeans and baseball caps was milling about, chatting and smoking. A couple of them were riding BMX bikes in tight circles and figures of eight. Another lad had a large, brindled mastiff on a chain leash. The dog was full of energy, leaping up and snapping at any scrap of litter that occasioned to blow within range of his heavy jaws. With each leap he jerked his owner, who had to lean back and strain to avoid being pulled off his feet.

It was the dog that first noticed Mr John.

The dog stopped its random bouncing and jumped a couple of times in Mr John's direction, emitting a deep, guttural bark. The lad struggling at the other end of the leash followed the direction of his hound's interest and took in the sight of the sartorially splendid Mr John, almost skipping across the forecourt and twirling his silver topped cane as he went.

'Guyz,' he said, alerting his mates. 'Wot the …?'

The boys turned together and watched Mr John for a few moments.

'Gonna' have some fun here, innit?' said one of the lads who'd been sitting at the bottom of the stairs. He flicked the stub of his cigarette across the tarmac and pushed himself to his feet with sinuous, muscular ease. A vicious smile cracked his face. 'C'mon,' he said to his friends, 'Let's show dat clown who rulz dis yard.'

He nodded at the pair on bikes, who immediately broke away from the group and rode over to Mr John. They began circling him, standing up on the pedals of their under-sized bikes, large expanses of their underwear visible above the tops of their low-hanging jeans. They crossed and re-crossed in front of him, pulling an occasional wheelie or bunny-hop; threatening, but never quite making contact.

At first Mr John ignored them, but they matched every slight shift in direction he made until eventually he stopped walking altogether. The youths gathered around him, a wheel with Mr John at its hub. Last to slot into place were the dog owner and the lad that had been sitting on the steps. The dog began to snarl menacingly, drool dripping from its massive jowls and pooling on the tarmac.

To the gang's surprise, it was Mr John who spoke first. It was not so much that it was he who broke the silence. It was more what he said.

'Children, children,' he began. 'I do assure you that under normal circumstances I would utterly condone this kind of behaviour – encourage it even. But today I am a busy man. So if you kindly step aside, I assure you that none of you will be hurt.'

A chorus of disbelief erupted from the lads.

'Wot de…? Iz dis freak real?'

'He dissin' us? Are you dissin' us?'

'Hey, mandem, arksed you a question, Mister!'

Mr John smiled.

'Man, he's bare mental, innit!'

'Time he learned some respect!'

'Yeah, dese our ends!'

'Maybe he tink him Bruce Lee!' One of the lads waved his hands around in mock kung-fu style. 'AAAiiiiyah!' Laughter met his antics.

The youth from the steps was not laughing. He rolled his neck and cracked his knuckles loudly. The laughter stopped abruptly.

'I don't know who you think you are, Mister. You a bare funny man fo' sho'. But as mandem say, dese our ends. Dis our yard, you get me?' It was a rhetorical question. He wasn't expecting Mr John's reply.

'I'm afraid I'm not sure that I do. You know you really are awfully difficult to understand when you talk like that, young man. I mean, it's not even as if any of you are black, "*innit*"?'

There was a collective sharp intake of breath from the crew. All eyes turned to their leader.

'Listen carefully, then,' replied the lad, dropping the patois. 'I'll say this clearly so even *you* can understand.' His voice was cold with menace. 'Give us the cane… and the sunglasses… and Rooney here,' he nodded towards the dog, '*won't* give you a face transplant. Then we'll *think* about letting you go.'

In response to hearing his name, Rooney's snarl deepened and his drew his lips back to reveal a fearsome set of fangs. He knew what was expected of him. His drool output doubled.

'You see, it's so much clearer when you *enunciate*!' said Mr John cheerfully. 'But no, I don't think so. *My* sunglasses. *My* cane. So as I said. Step aside, please. I am not blessed with infinite patience.'

'Right, don't say you weren't warned!'

He nodded at the lad holding the straining dog, who dropped the leash. What happened next was not clear, it happened so very fast. Rooney leapt forward, jaws bared. Mr John waved a hand dismissively in the air. He didn't seem to make any contact with the dog, but the boys quickly edited this part out of their collective consciousness because the fact that he made no contact with the animal made no sense. What was clear to all was that Rooney dropped to the ground, yelping like a whipped puppy, and bolted from the scene.

'Rooney!' cried his owner, 'What'd he do to Rooney, Shanks?'

'I don't know,' replied the ringleader, slipping his right hand behind his back. 'But don't worry; cos now he's really gonna pay.' From his back pocket he had drawn a large flick-knife. He held his right arm straight and low out to the side and clicked the button, his gaze never shifting from Mr John's face. The knife snapped open. 'I'm gonna wet him up. Big time.'

'*Flowers?*' Mr John held his right hand to his chest in feigned surprise. 'For *me*? Shanks, you shouldn't have.'

Shanks looked down at his hand. Sure enough, he was holding a cheap bunch of petrol-station flowers. The lads around the ring looked at one another with shared disbelief. Shanks looked at Mr John and then back down at his hand.

He was holding his knife.

'I don't know what you're pulling here, Mister,' his voice still carried menace, but it had lost its air of certainty. He was losing control, but like a wild animal cornered into a trap, he was ready to lash out in desperation. 'But your mind-games don't impress me.'

It didn't sound convincing.

'You should be careful, you know,' Mr John was clearly enjoying himself a lot more that his adversary. 'I'm sure those things are dangerous.'

'It's supposed to be dangerous – for you.' Shanks seemed to be regaining some of his composure.

'I've heard they've got quite a nasty bite.'

The lad looked back down at his hand. He was no longer holding his knife. In his hand was a small, sandy-yellow viper which, as he watched, was turning its head back towards his hand and bunching to strike. He instinctively dropped it, whipping his hand away from potential danger.

The knife clattered to the tarmac.

Mr John was leaning on his cane. Now *he* was the one with the vicious smile.

'I warned you, boys,' he said, spinning slowly on his heels to make sure that he had the attention of every one of his would-be aggressors. 'I even said "please". I *never* do that.

'Would you listen?' It was Mr John's turn for rhetorical questioning. 'No. You just had to push me, didn't you? Well now I *have* lost my patience and you will all –' he paused before completing the sentence. His voice had changed completely from the good-humoured, clipped tones of Received Pronunciation. The voice that uttered the next words was altogether different. It was an ancient voice that spoke directly to the ancestral memory of primal fears shared by humans from times even before cavemen huddled around fires for protection from the unknown forces hidden in the dark. **'GET - OUT - OF -MY - WAY!'**

He whipped off his shades and repeated his slow pirouette. One by one, as he stared deep into their eyes, the boys' faces turned white. Dark patches soaked across the crotches of seven pairs of low-slung jeans in succession.

Lee John stepped forward in the direction of the gang-leader. The lad stood rooted to the spot, without a flicker of emotion to soften the mask of horror that had frozen into his face. Lee John neatly side-stepped him and strode across the fore-court towards an alley between the tower-blocks and an adjacent row of dilapidated and boarded-up shops.

He was no longer in a good mood. He was fuming.

He reached the mouth of the alley and turned to look back. The lads all still stood in the positions where he had left them. When they came too, there would be seven souls who would almost certainly *never* do evil again – which was such a shame as they had all shown such promise. Now, he thought with disgust, they would probably start going to church. Worse still, he could even imagine them joining a choir. He shuddered at the thought. What a waste! They wouldn't listen to him, and he had been forced to show his true nature. Seven fewer souls up for grabs!

If his inferiors ever found out, they would not be impressed.

He muttered furiously to himself as he walked down the alley. The words were strange and arcane, no language of the human realm. As he walked he began to wave his hands in an elaborate pattern. Weeds that had been fighting for life in the cracks in the tarmac wilted and turned to dust. A discarded apple core began to ooze, rotting down to a slimy stain as he passed. A rat that had been scampering along next to the wall stopped in its tracks. It lifted a paw and sniffed the air. As Mr John drew alongside it the rat keeled over, stiff as a board. By the time he had passed, it was no more than a pile of little bones.

The alley was a dead end. Lee John did not check his stride, but continued towards the wall that sealed it. A small flame appeared, suspended in mid-air. The air filled with heavy, sulphurous fumes. As he approached, the flame grew and spread, as if following the course of an invisible frame.

Around his feet the tarmac began to bubble and melt.

Legion continued into the flames and disappeared in a sigil of fire.

* * *

'Bluds, dat was bare *deep!*'

The gang were beginning to recover.

'Yes. Let's not talk like that anymore, though.'

'Agreed.'

'And let's never mention this to anyone.'

'Agreed.'

'Ever.'

'Fo' sho'...er, sorry. I mean, agreed.'

Silence.

'I've got a really strong urge to do something... righteous.'

'Me too.'

'We could volunteer for the Community Litter Patrol Committee.'

'Nah, that's just a front for a bunch of neo-Nazi losers.'

'Oh.'

More silence.

'Bredren, me bare need some new batties.'

'Er...I thought we'd agreed to stop talking like that.'

'Oh, yeah. Sorry...I really need some new trousers.'

There were general murmurs of agreement.

'I don't know how you chaps feel… but perhaps next time… what I mean is…well, would it kill us to get some jeans that actually *fit?*'

* * *

'Crikey! This is comfort to die for!' Hercules thought to himself. He appeared to be in a large airport departure lounge. The room itself was light and airy, with minimum, but tasteful, décor.

'Lucky me! I must have been bumped to first class.' But he couldn't shake the nagging feeling that he didn't remember having any trips scheduled. And the more he looked around, the less his fellow travellers looked like regular customers of first-class travel.

He realized that a good number of the people around him were either very old, or very young. There were faces of all colours, but common to each was a look of slight bemusement – a shared uncertainty as to where they were and why.

But my! Was his seat comfy! Hercules glanced down – then did a rapid double-take. He looked around the room again, this time not looking at his fellow travellers, but at their seats. Then he looked down again, up again, down again, up again and smiled.

Each and every one of them was sitting on a small, perfectly-formed, white, fluffy cloud.

Out of nowhere, a harp chord rang out. A multitude of screens, that Hercules had not previously noticed, sprung into life. The screens were arranged in squares facing outwards, an arrangement that repeated around the room as far as the eye could see. Whichever direction someone was facing, one of the screens would be in full view. And clearly it *was* a very large room.

The same kindly face filled each screen. Its bearer was a middle-aged man with middle-eastern features – swarthy skin, a pronounced nose and dark eyes which sparkled with good humour.

His black hair and beard were streaked with grey that bestowed an air of dignity. He smiled.

'Welcome.' The voice was smooth, warm and open, like the face from which it came. 'Welcome to you all... Welcome to Heaven.'

In that instant, the reality of recent events struck Hercules. The horrors of his accident flashed through his mind with blinding clarity. His last moments of life replayed like a fast-forwarded video-recording. The approach to the traffic lights... the slow-moving truck... the green light signalling him forward and then... bang! Slamming into the uncompromising solidity of the side of the lorry, his bicycle buckling beneath him and slewing sideways and then a succession of bone-crushing, organ-squishing impacts as he was tossed like a rag-doll through the wheels of the lorry and then...

Hercules was back on his cloud staring at the kindly face on the screen. He glanced around and realized, from the looks on other faces that he could see, that he was not the only one to have just relived a real-death experience. This was obviously a routine part of proceedings. The man on the screen, who had been silent for a few moments as the members of his audience caught up with their selves, now resumed his greeting.

'My name is Peter. I do apologise for the somewhat impersonal nature of this greeting...

'There was a time,' he sighed, 'when we could afford a more... - ...a more *human* touch. Sadly, those days have passed. I'm afraid there are simply too many of you passing through here these days.

'It all used to be scrolls and quills and a personal handshake,' he continued. 'Each soul was weighed individually for its worth. We had the time to take that kind of care. But populations grew and scrolls gave way to ledgers, and when the quill could no longer keep pace with demand, we took the decision to automate. I'm afraid even here in Heaven we've had to move with the times. Mercifully, most of the Hindus and Buddhists recycle themselves – otherwise it would be Bedlam here.

'In the beginning, of course, was The Word… But it quickly became apparent that we would need The Spread-Sheets and The Databases to make things work properly…and now of course it's all about The Social Media and The Big Data…'

He stopped again, a wistful look in his eyes as he remembered other times and other ways. With a slight shake of his head, he brought himself back to the present.

'This is the best we could come up with…It keeps things moving and it keeps you out of limbo. And trust me the loss of the personal touch is a small price to pay to avoid being stuck in limbo. The lesser of two evils, you might say.' Somewhat unexpectedly, he giggled. It wasn't very dignified. He sort of snorted through his nose. 'Sorry – just my little joke… *Evil…* here… in Heaven! The *very* thought!

'Anyway, where was I?' his face straightened. 'Ah yes – slight loss of the personal touch. The good news is that you are the wheat. The chaff has already been sorted. As part of our new fast-track process, souls are now directed in transit, and you are all now here in the admissions hall for Heaven. Your souls have been saved for all eternity.

'No more pain. No more suffering. You've left all that behind, praise unto the Creator. But I'm afraid Heaven is a busy place these days and you will all be given jobs to do. Progress doesn't maintain itself and as for the admin in this place – well, you'll all find out soon enough.

'So now I'd like to hand you over to the Admissions Angels, who will take you to your new posts, and it just remains for me to wish you all a very happy stay here in Heaven. For ever more. Amen.'

Another harp chord chimed, and the screens went blank. The angels to whom Peter had referred now began to appear, and the new arrivals found themselves divided into groups of twelve. For the admissions angels it was a familiar drill. Almost without realising it had happened, Hercules found himself standing with eleven other of the new arrivals. He surveyed the group. They were a mixed bunch.

A young man, dressed all in black and with a number of facial piercings, broke from the others and strode up to the angel that had shepherded the little group together. The angel was carrying what appeared to be a delicate slab of stone about the size and shape of a slim magazine.

'Er… don't think I should be here,' the young man mumbled.

'I'm sorry, what was that?' asked the angel with a benevolent smile.

'I said,' ventured the young man a bit louder, 'I don't think I should be here.'

'And you are?' The angel held up his stone tablet in front of the young man and pressed the edge. There was a sudden flash of bright white light. An image of the young man's face appeared on the surface of the tablet.

'Draven,' said the young man.

The angel tapped the image on the tablet. The image shrunk and some text appeared.

'Ah yes, Adrian,' said the angel.

'My name is *Draven*,' said the young man sternly. 'Draven the Unholy.'

'Yes, yes,' replied the angel. 'That's what I've got here. Adrian Thompson, but it appears you like to be known as Draven the Unholy. And what seems to be the problem, Adrian?'

'DRAVEN!'

'Yes, of course. What seems to be the problem? Why don't you think you should be here, Adri – er, Draven? You *are* dead. You do know that?'

'Yeah, I know I'm dead. It's just I'm not supposed to be *here*.'

'Because...?' prompted the angel.

'Because?! *Because*?! Because I'm a *Satanist*!'

'Oh, I see,' said the angel, running his finger down the edge of the tablet. As he did so the text scrolled down. 'Yes, I'm sure it'll be here somewhere. Ah, yes. Religion – Satanist.'

'But this is Heaven!'

'And you *are* dead.'

'But I worship the Devil.'

'Well, it is nice to have *something* to believe in... Though not,' Hercules felt the angel cast a glance in his direction, 'by any means compulsory.'

'We sacrificed chickens!' The young man was getting more and more agitated.

'Yes, so it says on your file. But is also says that you *did* make sure that they were well looked after beforehand. Regular food and water, that kind of thing.'

'We drank their blood!'

'How and where you source your protein isn't generally a matter that affects your everlasting soul.'

'*BUT I SHOULD BE GOING TO HELL*!'

Even the angel, who up until now had been kind but somewhat dismissive, noticed how upset he had become.

'Listen, Ad- I mean Draven,' the angel slipped a comforting arm over the young man's shoulder. 'I know there is a lot to get used to, what with this being your first day dead and everything, but the fact is this; you may have been a Satanist, but you weren't actually *evil*.

'Yes, you worshipped the Fallen One, and yes, you participated in some arcane rituals, but I'll bet you never succeeded in summoning up an actual demon, did you?'

'Not as such,' admitted the Unholy One.

'No – I didn't think so. It's no surprise. Very few of the old rites are still observed properly. Usually the only way you meet a demon these days is if it wants to meet *you*. In your case it looks like you were just involved in some chanting and some rather odd food preparation. So, you see, you haven't actually done anything that was altogether any worse than the things most other people do. It says here,' he ran his finger down the side of the tablet and the text scrolled down some more, 'ah, yes; it says here that you never forgot your Mum's birthday. You used to do shopping for an elderly neighbour. And your prime motivation for becoming a Satanist was for the social life and because,' he looked the young man up and down, '– as I can see – you have a fondness for the colour black.'

'Whether or not that is a crime against good taste,' the angel, unsurprisingly, was dressed in flowing white robes, 'is a matter for debate. But it's hardly a mortal sin.'

'No, I'm afraid that to get into Hell, short of breaking one or two rules that the Boss is very particular about, you generally have to be unspeakably evil. Hitler, Pol Pot – that sort of thing. It's all down to the forgiving nature of the Lord, you see. You have to overstep the mark by quite a considerable distance to really upset Him, it would seem.'

Adrian/Draven looked sheepish. 'But what am *I* going to do in *Heaven*?' he asked.

The angel looked back at the tablet. 'Well it says here under "skills" that you used to make a terrific cup of tea.' Adrian/Draven flushed visibly. 'And your coq au vin was, by all accounts, par excellence.'

'Well, I had enough practice,' muttered Draven.

'So how about we assign you to catering? Would you give that a try?'

'I s'pose.'

'Good, that's settled then.'

The angel turned to address the group.

'Look,' he said, 'I know this is new for all of you and it's going to take a bit of getting used to. You've all no doubt arrived with certain preconceptions and beliefs,' once more he looked at Hercules, 'or a lack of them – about what it would be like.

'Heavens, there's enough confusion from Christians, Jews and Muslims to find themselves in the same place, and they all believe in the same Creator. So if it's a challenge for them I completely understand that it can be a lot to get your head round if you come from a more esoteric background; although, strangely, most of the animists seem to be pretty open-minded about the whole thing.

'The point is,' he continued, 'that you are all the Creator's children, and whatever stories you've been told or have imagined for yourselves to make sense of existence, this is what happens next and it's pretty much the same for all of you. The beauty is, though, that you will all experience it differently. We put whatever differences we may have had before aside and all pull together, and, in a nutshell, that's what makes it Heaven.

'I wouldn't take the need to get used to change too personally. You'll find that also helps. Even for us old hands, there's often something new to get used to. I mean, you spend centuries perfecting the use of a quill and then, all of a sudden, they give you one of *these*.' He waved the tablet. 'In fairness I suppose you could argue that they've been in development for long enough. After all, the Boss did give a couple of early prototypes to Moses on Mount Sinai.

Now we've all got to use them. Very efficient,' he said, wistfully, 'but sometimes I find myself asking "where's the *soul?*"

'And then I realise the answer's right in front of me,' he brightened up. '*Here's* the soul,' He spread his arms to the group, 'or rather, should I say, souls.' He smiled warmly.

'Anyway... you don't want to spend Eternity standing around listening to me rabbiting on. So come along, follow me, and I shall take you all to your new posts.' So saying he turned and led his little group, including Draven the Unholy, towards a large set of pearl-encrusted gates.

* * *

'You realise that this will be a merit on your copy-book...'

'Yes,' mumbled Legion, shifting uncomfortably from foot to foot like a small child who needed the toilet.

Baalberith swivelled his monitor screen toward Legion so that he could view the Cursed Circuit TV footage of the confrontation in front of the towers of the Broadfields estate. Legion watched impassively as the episode with the gang played out on the CCTV screen in front of him – him strolling across the forecourt, being surrounded, Rooney's attack, the knife, THE STARE. 'Damn, I look good,' he thought.

'...A white mark against your name,' Baalberith continued, bringing Legion back to the present.

'SSss,' mumbled Legion.

'What was that?' demanded Baalberith. 'Did you just apologize?'

'No,' said Legion, defiantly.

'I should hope not. That's *one* thing I will *not* have. If demons were to start apologizing to one another...well that would be the thin end of the wedge, I can assure you. But I'm digressing. This debacle of yours – you do realise I'd be entirely within my rights to promote you over this…?'

Perhaps this would be a good point to explain to the reader something about the structural organisation, or lowerarchy, of Hell. In fairness, "organisation" is a bit of a misnomer. Hell is anything but organised. It is, however, immensely bureaucratic.

On earth, taking the lead from the generally perceived direction of Heaven, mankind has traditionally striven in an upwards direction. There is a framework of language that reflects this situation. Good work is rewarded with promotion. We speak of those above us in the hierarchy as our superiors.

In Hell, by contrast, the direction to aim for is down. Good work is still met with promotion. But this is a punishment. No self-respecting demon should be doing *good* anything. Success, for a demon, is demotion. In Hell your boss is, of course, your inferior…

'Yes,' mumbled Legion again.

'And can you give me one good reason why you think I shouldn't promote you?'

Legion kept quiet. Baalberith, secretary to the Dark Lord himself, was a pompous ass. Despite this, Legion couldn't stand him.

The feeling was mutual. Technically Legion was not an individual demon. He, or rather they, were what is known as a host, a multitude of demonic personalities that all (usually) occupied the same space. For Baalberith, indeed for anyone, this made it very difficult to know what Legion was thinking at any given time. Usually it was fair to assume that Legion *was* thinking what you thought they were thinking. The trouble was that they were also thinking a couple of thousand other things at exactly the same time. It was nigh on impossible to guess which one of all those thoughts was the one that held sway, unless Legion wanted you to know, and since Legion were demons, if this *was* the case, they were almost certainly lying. For Baalberith this made the task of managing Legion something of a major headache.

'Well?' Baalberith glowered at Legion with his two black eyes. It wasn't that he'd been punched repeatedly in the face, although were the opportunity ever to arise to do so there would certainly have been a long queue, in which Legion would not have been very far from the front. No, his eyes were black. The pupils were black. The irises were black. Even the whites of Baalberith's eyes were, well, black.

'Well,' began Legion, 'the truth is...'

The truth was it was all about pride. Being a (collection of) demon(s), Legion just couldn't help showing off if the opportunity presented itself. That was the thing about being a demon. They just couldn't resist temptation. Oh, they could dish it out all right. When it was about being the tempter – well, *no one* could *tempt* like a demon. But when the shoe was on the other foot, when it came to actually *resisting* temptation...

The other thing about being a demon was that when you did something you tended to give very little thought to the consequences. The lads on the estate had challenged Legion. Mere mortals! There was no way his pride was going to let them get away with that. Pride is one of the seven deadly sins, so responding to an urge driven by pride is generally regarded as healthy behaviour in a demon.

But, as in the case of the gang on the estate, pride often comes before a fall. Legion had stared deep into the eyes of each of the lads and, in doing so, had given them all a glimpse into the unholy horrors of Hell. The effect of this, after the initial terror had worn off, was generally to convince all but the most murderous of souls that they should stop misbehaving pronto and refrain from doing bad stuff ever, ever again. Relapses after this kind of treatment were extremely rare.

At the time, when you gave THE STARE, you didn't think about the consequences. You just thought about the terror you were dishing out. It was fun watching the maggots curl up in the heat of your sun. And then you realised what you'd done. The souls that could never be harvested – that had been forever lost to the Dark One. Pride did indeed often precede a fall.

This led to anger. Not normal human anger, but utter, all-consuming, demonic fury. A demon could, quite literally, end up fuming; flaming as well, sometimes. This was proper wrath – wrath being another one of the seven deadly sins. So that was two mortal sins, pride and wrath, committed in within a matter of minutes. It was win-win really.

Apart from the souls that had been lost. Legion figured that taking the lost souls into account kind of made it a score draw.

There was no way that Legion was going to explain all of this to Baalberith. Demons have little respect for one another at the best of times. *Fear* is the currency of hell. But from Legion's very many points of view there was very little in Baalberith that they were scared of. There was only one inhabitant of Hell that could make Legion's blood run cold.

Fortunately for Legion, Baalberith was not a patient demon.

'Yes, well I think you can spare me your truths,' he said. 'Just consider yourself lucky that I'm very busy at the moment – too busy to waste my time with *this*.

'You've had your successes in the past,' admitted Baalberith, begrudgingly, 'but you can't expect to get by on the strength of past misdemeanours forever. You've got to stop going round acting like you're beneath everyone else. It does you no favours, you know. Now, get out of my sight!'

* * *

'Where *are* my manners?' The angel stopped in his tracks, nearly causing a pile-up as the following group came to an unexpected halt. 'I'm afraid my little chat with young Draven quite distracted me. I haven't even introduced myself. My name is Bazriel. But please, call me Barry.

'I should explain was happens next. As no doubt you've gathered by now, once we've passed through the gates I'll be taking you all to the departments to which you have been assigned. As St Peter said, it's pretty busy around here, and with a constant stream of new arrivals it never seems to get any less so. Now come along and you can all start to get settled in.'

They continued to stroll along at a gentle pace, all the while Bazriel chatting amicably like a well-practiced tour guide. Hercules noticed, as they went along, that whilst it certainly felt like they were walking, he couldn't be altogether sure if they were actually moving. He was wondering to himself if there was any way he could test the validity of this observation when Bazriel himself pulled to a halt. The group followed suite. A large pair of doors stood before them. Above the doors, in ornate gold lettering, a sign spelt out 'Catering Department'.

'Right, here we are,' said Bazriel. 'Draven, this will be your stop.' He pulled out his tablet and tapped a couple of times on the screen. 'Also, Kim Na... and Jasmine Hussein... if you would like to join young Draven here: catering seems to be your calling, too.'

A young Korean boy and an elderly Arab lady stepped forward. Together they stood hesitantly in front of the doors.

'Well?' asked Bazriel. 'What are you waiting for?' He smiled encouragingly at them. 'In you go.'

The three smiled back at him nervously and together they pushed on the doors. From inside came the sounds of a busy kitchen. The air filled with heavenly scents. Kim and Jasmine disappeared inside.

Draven hesitated and turned to the angel, 'Bazriel?'

'Barry!'

'Of course... Sorry. Barry. About earlier – I'm really sorry if I bit your head off, so to speak, and I just wanted to say thank you – for everything.'

'Think nothing of it.'

Draven was just about to follow the others into Heaven's kitchen when the angel added, 'Er, Draven?'

The unholy one paused halfway through the door and turned and looked expectantly towards Bazriel. There was a mischievous glint in the angel's eyes.

'Yes?'

'I probably shouldn't say this, but...'

'Yes?'

'Give 'em hell!'

Draven grinned back at him. 'You bet!' he said, and he was gone.

'Nice lad,' said Bazriel watching the doors swing to a close. 'Right,' he continued, straightening up and checking his tablet again, 'where to next? Ah yes... hospitality.'

They set off again. Bazriel continued to chat to the group, but Hercules was now completely distracted in trying to figure out something – *anything* – that might give him an indication of how far they had walked. After a little while they arrived at the Hospitality Department where they parted company with two more of the new arrivals, and Hercules was none the wiser.

The pattern repeated itself with stops at Entertainment ('Mostly singing,' Bazriel had told them. 'Like the X factor but without the why-oh-why factor.'), Gardening ('Eden didn't just plant itself, you know.') and finally Heavenly Resources ('but mostly we just refer to it as HR') where four souls left to embark on their post-mortem careers. Only Hercules was left.

'Right, Hercules,' said Bazriel. 'It's I.T. for you.'

'I.T.?' asked Hercules. 'Are you sure? I was never really very good with computers when I was…well before.'

'Yes, it's definitely what I've got down here: I.T.… Between you and me, I don't think prior experience really counts for much up here. My understanding is that they operate to a different set of recruitment criteria.'

Hercules waited for the angel to continue, but he seemed to have finished his train of thought. 'Such as…?' Hercules prompted.

'I'm sorry, I thought you knew. But how could you, I suppose.' He did ramble a bit, thought Hercules.

'They tend to like people in I.T. who aren't too firmly committed to any particular set of beliefs. It seems to be the one area up here where having too many beliefs can lead to problems.'

'Problems?' asked Hercules. 'What kind of problems?'

'Oh, I'm sure that they'll explain it to you much better than I could. The only thing I really know is that the computers are quite unlike anything on earth, so a lack of prior computing knowledge never seems to be a problem. When you're dealing with Heaven's I.T. system, *everyone* lacks prior experience.'

They walked on in silence for a while.

'Barry?'

'Yes, Hercules.'

'I've noticed that even though it *really* feels like we're walking, it's very difficult to know if we've actually moved anywhere.'

Bazriel stopped and turned to Hercules. He looked deeply into his eyes, as if measuring him. Oh no, thought Hercules, feeling decidedly uncomfortable under the angel's intense scrutiny. My first day in Heaven and I've already upset an angel. He started to wonder what the system for dealing with misdemeanours was. Then all of a sudden, seemingly satisfied that Hercules was worthy of an answer, Bazriel's eyes softened, and he smiled.

'Ah yes, that's one of His paradoxes,' he said. 'The Boss does love a good paradox, you'll find. Most people eventually stumble upon the realisation you've just had, but it doesn't usually happen so quickly.

'Heaven is infinite. But it's also a singularity.'

Hercules looked blank.

'Imagine a single point...'

'That goes on forever.' Hercules completed the sentence for the angel as the penny dropped. 'So we're in different parts of everywhere at the same time.'

'Yes, I suppose you could put it like that,' said Bazriel, looking pleased that his pupil had grasped the concept so quickly. 'And incidentally,' he added, 'it neatly resolves an issue that philosophers have wrestled with for centuries.' He started walking again, taking Hercules, who was still pondering this new revelation, by surprise.

'Which is?' asked Hercules, jogging to catch up.

'The question of how many angels can dance on a pinhead, of course.'

'And what's the answer?'

'Well, I think you'll find that, by and large,' Bazriel winked at Hercules, 'it depends on which band is playing! Ah, here we are. Your stop, I believe.'

In front of them were the familiar large doors. However, instead of the ornate lettering that had been used for the signs of all the other departments they had visited, it appeared that the denizens of Heaven's newest department seemed to prefer

COMIC SANS.

* * *

As he began to wander back to his cubicle, Legion began to reflect on the day's events. The little run in with Baalberith aside, things were going remarkably well. It is true that the Devil makes work for idle hands. There were precious few new arrivals in Hell these days, what with the forgiving nature of the Lord and everything. This meant that an awful lot of the idle hands actually belonged to demons. For ambitious demons like Legion it paid to have many irons in the fire – sometimes quite literally. The danger for Legion was that he was often trying to keep too many irons hot at the same time. But *no one* could multi-task like Legion. Legion was an unstoppable army on the march downwards, and they wouldn't rest until they had reached the very bottom.

Legion's ambitions had been born on the south-eastern shores of the Sea of Galilee, some two thousand years before. For millennia prior to that they had simply been a disorganized bunch of malevolent spirits, causing chaos and suffering wherever they ventured. Blighting crops here, causing tribal conflicts there. But for all their misdeeds they lacked direction and never acted with any real purpose. Then they found Jesus.

Legion had possessed a local man for a bit of a laugh. It was the usual drill – making him run around naked and live among the tombstones of the local cemetery, occasionally jumping out on some poor unsuspecting soul and scaring the wits out of them, that sort of thing. They were quite happily going about their business in this way when who should be the next unsuspecting soul they tried to scare but none other than the Son of Man. *He* wasn't impressed. On the whole He tended to regard demonic possession of his Father's creations in a pretty dim light.

'Name,' demanded the Son of the Almighty.

'Legion,' replied the demons. 'For we are many,' they added smugly, and with absolutely no consideration of the consequences.

This was a mistake.

'Out!' commanded Jesus.

Legion begged with Jesus not to send them straight back to Hell. They knew that this would only lead to inevitable humiliation at the hands of their inferiors, even though they were up against some pretty formidable opposition in the Son of Man. Jesus graciously acceded to Legion's request and instead cast the demons from the man into a large herd of pigs – some two thousand of which conveniently happened to be rootling for acorns nearby.

The thing was that Legion needed to be together in a single body to function with any kind of unity of purpose at all. Legion had since suspected that Jesus knew this all along and had tricked them. Two thousand individual demons occupying two thousand individual pigs had all the coherence of a sack-full of weasels on crack. Ironically, the net result was that, as one, the entire herd of pigs rushed down the slopes of the hill, where they had been foraging, and into the Sea of Galilee, where they promptly drowned.

Legion had found himself back in Hell after all. And the humiliation he suffered at the hands of Baalberith, and his cronies was all the worse for the way in which he had been tricked. He wanted revenge and he didn't care how long it took.

Somewhat upset by his recent run-in with Baalberith, Legion decided that he needed cheering up. Instead of going straight back to his cubicle, he decided to take a detour through the Fourth Circle. That was usually good for a laugh.

Like Heaven, Hell had been moving with the times. The modernisation had involved a grand change management programme that had inevitably called for numerous committees. Legion had been a member of the committee responsible for the redesign of the Fourth Circle. Being Legion, he was used to committee meetings. Most of them took place inside his own head. He knew that letting a committee try to organise anything was a dangerous path to tread. Letting a committee of *demons* try and do anything, what with all the egos and mutual loathing, was an almost sure-fire recipe for disaster. Remarkably though, and against all the odds, the new Fourth Circle was a triumph. Quite possibly it was the only success of design by committee – ever.

The Fourth Circle of Hell was reserved for the punishment of those whose sin in life had been greed. In the past, the occupants of this circle had been forced to push massive weights around a giant circuit. They used these weights as weapons, bashing into one another and hurling abuse as they did so. This was all very entertaining, but the committee agreed that it lacked any real imagination. Certain themes from the old Circle could be retained, they decided, but improvements could also definitely be made.

For starters, the setting of a straightforward circuit was regarded as a bit bland. A few twists and turns were called for. And the background scenery and props could definitely be improved.

So the damned were now condemned to endless circulations through a retail warehouse of affordable self-assembly furniture, with arrows painted on the floor to direct them in an eternal, meandering, mind-numbing loop. Each sinner was faced with countless other souls milling slowly across their path. They still pushed heavy weights, but these were now in the form of wobbly-wheeled trolleys stacked high with heavy flat-packed boxes with which they bashed one another's ankles. Hot wax rained down on the "shoppers" from the million tea-lights that lit the circle.

Here and there, dotted throughout the "store", were "customer service" stands. They were never manned. Alongside them there were thoughtfully positioned plastic boxes that dispensed little pencils in which all the lead had been broken. There were also tissue-thin "shopping lists" that were impossible to write on, and paper tape measures that tore to pieces when rolled out. Conveniently-placed, larger plastic boxes held fact sheets containing the furniture specifications. These were always kept well-stocked – with the details of items that were located in a completely different part of the store. Best of all, to Legion's many minds, was the fact that there were no check-outs. In Hell, when you had passed through the Market Hall, you found yourself back amongst the sofas.

'Excuse me, young man, do you work here?'

Legion turned around to find he was being addressed by a middle-aged woman, teetering on high heels and pushing a trolley stacked with boxes that was twice as tall as she. She regarded him with condescension. He raised a quizzical eyebrow.

'Can you tell me if the Bøløks wardrobe comes in an ash veneer?'

'I beg your pardon?'

'The Bøløks wardrobe... Over there,' she pointed to a square box made of white melamine board. 'Do you know if it comes in an ash finish?' The woman tutted to herself and turned to another passing "shopper". 'Really,' she said loudly. 'Where *do* they find these people?'

Legion looked at the woman. It appeared that her massive sense of entitlement had yet to be touched in any way by her surroundings, which actually quite impressed him. 'Well,' he said, 'if it's an ash finish you want...' With a glance, he set fire to her shoes.

That was the great thing about the Fourth Circle, Legion reflected, strolling away from a smartly-dressed lady who was now hopping frantically from foot to foot in an effort to extinguish her flaming Jimmy Choos; you could always find a way of making someone else's bad day worse.

He wandered past the Shøddi kitchen displays, between the Kråppi and Røtn dining suites and disappeared through a door marked "Staff Only".

Three

THE CAPTAIN OF THE GOOD SHIP the *Good Ship* was not having a good day. By now, his vessel was supposed to be well on the way into her journey down the Red Sea towards the Horn of Africa. Instead, he was sitting in the harbourmaster's office in Suez locked in an argument about supposed irregularities in his paperwork. There were times, it turned out, that sailing under a flag of convenience could prove anything but.

There is a long history of ships sailing under the flag of a nation other than their own. For much of history it proved a cunning way of avoiding the interests of the warships of enemy states. In more civilized times it has proved an equally cunning way of avoiding the bothersome interferences that stand in the way of a healthy profit, such as tax regimes, environmental laws and workers' rights.

This is not to say that everyone takes kindly to vessels operating in this way. Certainly it is beneficial for the owners, who may be practically untraceable, avoid tax and not have to worry overmuch about pay and working conditions on their ships. But to nations that bother themselves with unnecessary esoteric considerations such as safety regulations and workers' rights it can seem that the regulatory playing surface, not unlike the medium on which the ships themselves operate, can be somewhat uneven. To try and redress the balance, various treaties have been introduced which aim to create some international standards. Needless to say these treaties have not all been ratified by the various nations engaged in providing flags of convenience. Subsequently the levels of inspection to which ships operating under flags of convenience are subject have been strengthened under international maritime law.

All of which goes some way to explaining the current fate of the *Good Ship*.

The captain eyed the port official across the desk. It was midday and unbearably hot in the stuffy office. The air-conditioning had packed in. The only fan was on the other side of the desk, pointing towards the customs man. Whatever cooling effect the fan was producing as it buffeted the official with warm air offered no respite to the captain from the stultifying Egyptian heat. Rivulets of sweat ran down his temples. He took a handkerchief from his pocket and wiped his brow.

The captain had been on the bridge of his vessel for twenty hours the previous day as the *Good Ship*, part of one of the twice daily southbound convoys that cross from the Mediterranean into the Red Sea, had made her way down the Suez Canal. When they had reached Suez, he was expecting to be able to proceed without delay. Instead they had been ordered into port. It was not good news. The *Good Ship* was laden with container loads of aid relief for the famine in East Africa and every hour of delay was costing lives.

Over the lifetime that the captain of the *Good Ship* had been at sea, shipping had changed. When he had joined the merchant navy as a young man it had been for adventure: each landfall had been a chance for excitement that countered the monotony of weeks at sea. But over the decades, as his career had progressed and his rank increased, smaller and smaller crews were expected to run bigger and bigger ships in a regime of ever-increasing bureaucracy. As captain, he now seemed to spend most of his time filling out paperwork.

When they did reach dock these days, there was seldom time to leave the confines of the port.

The captain knew there was nothing wrong with his paperwork. This was one of those instances where a strategic greasing of the wheels would miraculously see the irregularities disappear and the *Good Ship* free to continue her journey. Only on this occasion, even if he paid the baksheesh, the *Good Ship* would not be able to set sail. Since they had been forced into port, half of his crew had gone missing.

The *Good Ship*, like so many vessels operating under a flag of convenience, had a two-tier crew. The officers, in this case, were British. The deck crew were Filipino. Merchant ship crews are generally brought together for contracted periods of work. Sometimes this works well, and the ship is harmonious. Sometimes it doesn't.

This time it hadn't.

There had been a change of crew at the start of the current voyage, and there had been friction from the moment they had left port in Marseille. Things had come to a head when, shortly before they had reached the start of the canal at Port Said, the second mate had found one of the deck crew going through some of the officers' personal belongings. The deckhand had offered some feeble excuse, and the rest of his mates had rallied around him. Heated exchanges had nearly led to blows. The atmosphere on board between officers and crew had been nothing short of poisonous since.

In this respect, the halt in the journey was a small blessing. When they had woken in the morning, half of the deck crew, including the foreman, had jumped ship. But this put the captain in no mood to play the official's games. He was damned if he was going to pay a bribe when it didn't make the slightest bit of difference to his ability to leave port.

A fly buzzed lazily once around the room. After a single circuit, it gave up. It was too hot even for flies.

The captain stood up. 'I will have to go back to the ship and radio the Company,' he lied. There was nothing more to be gained in this stand-off. For now, he just wanted to be out of the heat of this office. At least if it was hot on the ship, it was *his* ship.

'By all means, Captain. Then maybe you can sort out the problems with your paperwork and you can be on your way, inshallah.'

The captain smiled grimly. He had the feeling that little short of a miracle would get them moving any time soon.

'Inshallah,' he replied.

***

'Max...? Maxy...? Max...? Is that you?'

Maximilian Dumars let out a deflated sigh. He had been ever so careful as he turned the key silently in the lock and slipped into the flat. After the day he had had, he had hoped his mother would have been too engrossed in one of her mindless TV soaps or 'reality' shows to have heard him coming in, but no such luck. It really was one of those days.

He went into the living room.

'Yes, mother, it's me,' he said, picking up the remote control and turning down the blaring television, deliberately positioning himself in front of the screen as he did so. 'Who else were you expecting from your dazzling social circle?' he added, with unnecessary spite. How even had she heard him come in above the din of the telly, the old bat, he thought to himself.

'Hey! I was watching that. And less of your back chat, young man... Who are you anyway, and what are you doing in my flat? ... Don't cause me no trouble... My son will be home soon. He'll sort you out if you do.'

'I *am* your son, mother. He glared at the old lady as he added bitterly, 'Surely you remember all the joy I've brought you.'

Her eyes flickered briefly with a dim recognition.

'Yes, yes, stupid boy. Give me back my remote so I can get back to watching my program, or it will be bed with no supper. And don't expect I won't be telling your father about your lip when he gets home!'

Maximilian snorted in derision. Neither of them had seen his father since he had abandoned them both when Max was just five. His mother had blamed Max for his father's departure, but kept a candle burning for the man who had deserted them, which for Max led to an upbringing filled with bitterness. Just as he was approaching school leaving age, when he had determined that he would take his below average qualifications and put as much distance between the pair of them as possible, his mother succumbed to the first of many illnesses – illnesses that she blamed on the stresses of raising him as a single mother – and either through misplaced guilt, or just a good old-fashioned lack of imagination, he surrendered his life to being her carer. Now approaching her eighties, with dementia taking an ever-increasing grip on her reality, Maximilian realised that as her end approached she had robbed him not only of a childhood, but also of a life.

Or would have done, if it hadn't been for his calling.

His day at his part-time role at the job-centre today had been just appalling. So many scroungers and ne'er-do-wells looking for a handout from the state, while decent *English* folk struggled to find employment! It was no surprise to find that for Maximilian Dumars immigrants were the sole occupants of the former group, whatever their willingness to take on any job. But it would be unfair to say that Maximilian Dumars only saw things in terms of black and white. He could be offended by a wide range of shades of brown in between as well.

But today had been particularly bad. He had been utterly humiliated by his boss, a *woman*, who had publicly given him a dressing down in front of one of the aforementioned ne'er-do-well scroungers, who she insisted on referring to as a *client*, of all things! He had many of his own words that he would have liked to have used for the so-called "Doctor" Ali, but somehow common sense made him bite his lip.

Before his awakening, this would just have been another humiliating injustice that heaped onto his shoulders and festered in the smouldering depths of Maximilian Dumars' soul.

It was strange to think that only a few short years before, Maximilian Dumars had been so utterly blind to the reasons for his debasement. The Maximilian of then would have suffered his indignities in silence, grinding through the daily attrition of his miserable existence. But then the power of the internet had awoken him to the root cause of his misfortunes.

And yet before the curious Mr John had interrupted the Aryan Defence Order/League/Front's last meeting, Maximilian Dumars would have vented today's humiliations in yet another vitriolic manifesto to share with his co-conspirators and take no further. But Mr John had said that the group had been noticed by powerful supporters – and had the chance to make a difference.

If they were ready…

Well, Maximilian Dumars had just decided that the Aryan Defence Order/League/Front *were* ready – and *would* make a difference. They would grasp the bull by the horns and make the fat lady sing.

And everyone who had wronged him?

They would pay.

Oh, yes. They would pay.

***

Asif had been racing pigeons for as long as he could remember. As a small boy he used to sit at his bedroom window, watching fascinated as the men from the village tended their birds in the coops in their small back yards. As a child from an immigrant Muslim family it was all strange and new to him. His parents, who ran the village store, did not discourage his interest. On the contrary, figuring it may help the growing boy to integrate within a community in which theirs were the only brown faces, they encouraged him.

As soon as he was old enough, Asif began keeping pigeons himself. He would hitch a ride with one of the older men to the release sites for races and, even as a novice, he had enjoyed some success. That only fanned the growing flames of his passion for the pass-time.

But as his skill with his birds and his knowledge grew, rather than giving him a means to integrate with his adopted society, Asif found that it actually highlighted the differences between his heritage and the world his parents had brought him to live in.

The other pigeon-fanciers would often meet at the pub. At first, Asif would sit in the corner nursing an orange juice while the men drank beer. Asif didn't like the smoky atmosphere, and though he shared a bond through the flying of his birds, he felt alone.

He visited the pub less and less, and only turned up to fly his birds in races. The less he tried to integrate, the more he felt shunned by the other fliers. Eventually he stopped going to the meets altogether. He withdrew into a world of his own. He still flew his birds for his own pleasure, as a kind of meditation. He loved to feel the air on his face, a break from the hours he spent in his room, locked in his own world and the answers he found as he surfed the Internet.

Asif stiffened, alert. He slid from the bonnet of the van, grabbing his binoculars as his feet touched the ground. In the distance, to the north, two specks were struggling into the gusting wind. He raised the binoculars to his eyes and swivelled the focus wheel. He scanned the sky in the direction of the specks. Yes – there they were. It was too far to be certain. But he felt sure it was them. Sure it was his birds.

He watched them approach – barely daring to breathe – as slowly, painfully slowly, they grew bigger in the lenses of his binoculars. As they grew he could distinguish the flapping wings, the distinct pigeon shape and, eventually, as they closed the distance, he could even make out the harnesses on their backs.

Asif began to grin. He lowered the binoculars, but otherwise remained motionless as he watched the birds' approach, until a flap-clapping of wings announced their arrival on the table. Soft coos of content followed as they settled into the familiar surroundings of their cage and began to peck at the grain in the bowl that Asif had left for them.

He went over to the cage, reached in and gently took hold of one of the birds. Talking softly, he pulled her from the cage.

'Well done, my lovely.' He expertly slipped the harness and hood from the bird and packed the delicate equipment in a cloth roll pulled from his jacket pocket. He repeated the operation with the other bird and then fastened the cage shut.

For a moment he stared at the two birds through the wire mesh. He breathed in the moment of what he had just achieved. He had directed his birds to a particular location that was not their loft – a location *he* had chosen and programmed for them – and they had arrived without problem. With his special equipment, his homing hoods, he could direct his birds to fly anywhere.

Anywhere.

Asif's time was coming. The pieces were coming together. The chance to deal a righteous blow was in his hands.

And everyone who had wronged him?

They would pay.

Oh, yes. *They* would pay.

* * *

The first thing that struck Hercules as he stepped through the doors into the I.T. Department was the sheer scale of it. The room itself reminded him of the NASA control centres he'd seen on films about the moon landings and footage of space shuttle launches – only multiplied to an almost unimaginable degree. One wall was entirely taken up with huge screens, displaying a multitude of different pieces of information; graphs, tables, images and maps. The wall itself was enormous – the size of several football pitches. Most of the rest of the room was made up with tier upon tier of workstations, all arranged so that the occupants could view the information wall as well as the screens on their desks. The rows of desks were gently curved, so that those at the edges were closer to the main wall and those in the middle were placed further back. Most of the desks had at least two monitors. Some had several more. And the tiers didn't just go up. By some marvel of engineering they also went down and back as well, so the front row was in effect the apex of a giant, gently curving wedge.

A smaller number of desks were placed between the information wall and the banked tiers of workstations, roughly perpendicular to both, but also in a gently curved formation. The occupants of these desks had a controlling view of both the information wall and the ranks of other workers.

Hercules stood for a few moments taking it all in, awestruck.

'Quite mind-boggling, isn't it?' Hercules realised that the question was addressed to him. Standing next to him was an elderly gentleman with grey hair and a grey beard and lively brown eyes, which sparkled behind rimless spectacles. He wore a blue shirt open at the collar, brown corduroy trousers and open-toed sandals, under which he was wearing a pair of grey socks which had holes in them. 'And also quite beautiful in its way.' The pair stood together in silence for a few moments more, sharing the awesomeness of the huge hall before them.

'It's Hercules, isn't it?' said the old man at length. 'I'm Farouk.' He held out his hand in greeting.

'That's right,' said Hercules, shaking the offered hand.

'I'm here to help you get settled in,' said Farouk. 'Show you the ropes, so to speak. As you can see,' he added, 'when you're new to it, this is quite any easy place not to know where you're supposed to be. Come on, follow me. Let's give you the grand tour. Then we'll find a desk for you.'

Farouk led Hercules along a gantry that ran around the edge of the hall and towards the back of the tiers of desks.

'What you see here,' he explained as they walked, 'is only really half of the department. The work we do here is concerned with the software side of things: programming, databases, that sort of stuff. Each section is responsible for a part of the overall systems landscape. As you can imagine, when you are dealing with a computer system that quite literally maps the Universe, things can get pretty complicated if you don't break them down into manageable chunks. Even then it can be a challenge.

'It certainly keeps boredom at bay, though. In theory we're just supposed to be looking after the data and systems. Keeping the machinery oiled and the cogs turning, if you like. In a digital sense. The truth of it is that while we're gathering all these records, we're very often the first to know what's going on…pretty much everywhere, really.'

'So you don't actually *do* anything with all this information?'

'*We*, dear boy, *we* – you're a part of this department now, don't forget. No, we just write the more complicated reports. Beyond that, there are other departments whose job it is to actually *act* on the information we gather – if they can ever be bothered to do anything, that is. Between you and me, it seems that the more we do for them, the less they actually want to do for themselves. Anyway, I'm sure you'll find out all this for yourself soon enough.'

'So what do the other departments do with all the information?' asked Hercules.

'Maintain the cosmic balance, I suppose.' Farouk stopped and turned to face Hercules. He had a very serious look on his face. 'We find it best not to get involved,' he said. 'It only leads to trouble.'

'So I've heard,' said Hercules, recalling his conversation with Bazriel. 'What kind of trouble?'

'Well just because we've got all the *information*, that doesn't mean, apparently, that we see the *whole picture*. At least that's what we've been told. "Just because you know what's what, it doesn't mean you know what's *right*!" … Apparently…' It was clearly a bit of a tender subject. 'The Lord does indeed work in mysterious ways,' said Farouk. 'But sometimes,' he added conspiratorially, 'I think it's just that He can't get the right staff. Anyway, we do our bit and try to keep out of the politics. Ah, here we are.'

They had reached the end of the gantry. In front of them was a door.

'Through here,' said Farouk, 'are the staircases that lead to all the workstation levels. It also houses the other half of the department –hardware. If you ever need to go to any of the other departments, it's back the way we came and through the big doors.'

'I'm not sure I'd ever be able to find any of the other departments,' said Hercules. 'The journey here was…a bit strange.'

'Yes, it does take a bit of getting used to,' agreed Farouk. 'But this is Heaven,' he added with a smile. 'If you really need to get somewhere you'll find it, sure enough.

'Come on, let's go and see the Tin Heads.'

'Tin Heads?'

'Oh, yes sorry – that's what we call the guys and girls that work in hardware. They call us Bit Pushers. There's quite a lot of jargon, I'm afraid. But you soon get used to it. And then you eventually forget you're using it. Anyway, it's this way.'

He opened the door and Hercules followed. On the other side of the door was another gantry that ran back towards the front of the giant wedge of workstations and then turned and ran along at a level that Hercules presumed was the same as the front row of desks. Staircases radiated backwards from this gantry both upwards and downwards, with doors positioned every few meters so that Hercules surmised that each door gave access to a handful of the desks on the other side.

Directly in front of where they were standing, another staircase led down into a massive expanse that appeared to be encased within an enormous glass box. Within this box, numerous figures milled around amongst rows of large cabinets, each carrying a tablet of the sort that Bazriel had possessed. All the figures were wearing white lab coats and what looked like metal sieves on their heads. They were checking the contents of the cabinets and recording details on their devices. In the far distance, Hercules could just make out rows of benches where other lab-coated and metal-helmeted workers were engaged in assembling components. In the very centre of the room there was another glass box which was the size of several hundred of the cabinets combined. Hercules couldn't make out what it contained.

'Impressive, no?' said Farouk.

'It certainly is,' said Hercules. 'But why the funny hats and all that glass?'

'It's a controlled environment,' answered Farouk. 'Some of the equipment is very sensitive to disturbance. It has to be kept within a very narrow range of environmental parameters to operate effectively.'

'What sort of environmental disturbance could there possibly be here?' asked Hercules incredulously.

'It turns out our processing units are extremely sensitive to belief. That's why only the most committed atheists tend to work in the hardware department. And the helmets seem to do a pretty good job of preventing any residual stray beliefs from leaking out of their heads and damaging the equipment.'

'Doesn't being here kind of mess with their stance as atheists.'

'Oh, dear boy, no. An atheist is someone who doesn't believe in God,' explained Farouk, patiently. 'Being here doesn't change that. They don't have to *believe* in God here. Here God is a fact. Come on, let's go and take a closer look.'

He led Hercules down the steps. At the bottom was a rack where rows of spare lab coats hung on hooks. Each hook also had one of the metal helmets hanging from it. Below the lab coats were white, half-sized, rubber wellington boots.

'Better put these on,' said Farouk slipping on a lab coat and reaching for a pair of the boots. Hercules followed suit.

They put on their protective headgear and walked over to the entrance to the hardware section. This involved two sets of doors separated by an airlock. They passed through the first doors, which slid shut behind them. There was a hiss of gas, and the second set of doors opened in front of them. They left the airlock and the second set of doors slid to a close behind them.

Farouk and Hercules stood by the glass wall, watching the workers going about their business. Closer up, Hercules could see that the front of each cabinet blinked and flashed with a multitude of little blue, red and green lights. One of the workers spotted them and waved.

'Ah look, there's Ada,' said Farouk, waving back. 'She can explain a bit about what goes on down here.'

They went over to where Ada was working, and Farouk made the introductions. As she led them between the rows of cabinets, Ada explained to Hercules that they could use their tablet devices to control and monitor the servers which the cabinets contained. Hercules examined one of the cabinets. Behind the flashing lights, it appeared to be empty.

'But there's nothing in the cabinets,' he observed.

'Have you heard of virtualisation?' asked Ada.

'Sort of,' said Hercules, not really sure if he knew what it meant.

'Well, these racks all contain *virtual* servers. All connected by wireless aethernet, naturally.'

'Naturally,' Hercules felt it was just best to play along.

They had reached the centre of the hall. Before them stood the inner glass box that Hercules has spotted from the walkway. In it floated something white and fluffy.

'That's a...' said Hercules, pointing at the glass box.

'That's right,' said Ada brightly. 'Welcome to the Cloud.'

Hercules stared in disbelieving wonder at the perfectly formed cumulus.

'With the Cloud we've managed to take the concept of virtual computing to an entirely different level. Thousands and thousands of virtual servers all effectively joined into one. You see, what we've got here,' said Ada proudly, 'is the very forefront of quantum computing.'

Hercules didn't really see.

'These machines don't just operate with noughts and ones,' she explained. 'They can use everything else in between as well.'

Hercules must have looked blank.

'They don't just calculate the right answer,' Ada smiled. 'With the help of the Cloud, they calculate *all* the answers.'

Hercules wasn't sure this had helped, but he nodded and tried his best to look like he had some kind of clue as to what she was talking about.

'Anyway, we just provide the instruments,' said Ada, modestly. 'It's people like Farouk here that really make them sing.'

'No, no,' said Farouk. 'We all play an equal part. Anyway, Ada, dear girl, we've taken enough of your time. Hercules, I think it's time I showed you where you'll be working.'

They thanked Ada and headed back out through the airlock, replaced the borrowed lab coats and helmets and changed back into their own shoes.

'Farouk, may I ask you something?' asked Hercules as they headed back up the stairs and took the gantry towards the front of the wedge.

'Go ahead, dear boy,' answered Farouk. With a smile he added, 'Just as long as it's nothing to do with the numerical value for the meaning of life.'

Hercules looked puzzled for a second. He shook his head and ploughed on.

'Why do you wear glasses? I mean we're dead, and this is Heaven. There can't be anything wrong with your eyes. St Peter said, "no more suffering". Apart from being dead, I must admit I've never felt better myself. So surely you don't really need glasses, do you?'

'You really are quite logical, aren't you?' came the reply. 'You're quite right of course. Strictly speaking there's nothing wrong with my eyesight. But tell me something; when you were growing up did you ever know a child who seemed to have a grown-up's personality, even though they were still very young.'

Hercules thought for a moment. 'As a matter of fact, there was this one boy I knew at school. He must have been *born* middle-aged.'

'It's not that uncommon,' said Farouk. 'Souls seem to have a way of being that they are comfortable with. My glasses are a bit like that. Here we appear as we are most comfortable - which includes glasses. And even sandals and socks with holes in them, in some cases!'

For the first time it occurred to Hercules that he was not wearing the cycling jacket and work clothes he had been killed in, but was instead dressed in jeans, a sweatshirt and desert boots. He was a bit annoyed for not having noticed earlier. In fairness to himself though, he thought, he had had quite a lot to distract him.

They reached the front of the wedge and turned to follow the walkway along its course behind the front row of workstations. The doors were marked with letters and numbers. The numbers went from zero to ninety-nine for each letter and the letters ascended in alphabetical order. They kept going until they reached the E's.

'You'll be joining us in one of the busiest sections at the moment,' said Farouk as they reached a door marked E91 – Level 0 (#Extensors), where Farouk turned and started up one of the staircases. 'It's just a few levels up from here.'

The stairs were like normal stairs in every respect except for the fact that without needing to move, they were swept up as if on an escalator. The only odd thing about this was that at no point did any part of the staircase appear to be moving. When they reached level 12, Farouk stepped off the stairs. The door was marked E91 – Level 12 (#Extinctions).

'Here we are. Let me introduce you to the team.'

* * *

As Farouk was leading Hercules towards his afterlife as a member of the Extinctions team, elsewhere in Heaven, a conversation was taking place. In truth, there were, at that precise moment, hundreds of millions of conversations taking place all over Heaven, but the one that concerns us was taking place behind a door marked "@Creation". More specifically, it was taking place along a corridor, up two flights of stairs along another corridor and behind another door; this one marked "#Fundamental Particles". The conversation went something like this:

'So, you've released the boson then?'

'Yeah.' There was a moment's silence. 'Sorry… the *what?*'

'The boson. You know; the Higgs particle. The one we got that requisition for. I printed it out for you.'

'Ah.'

There was another pause. This one sounded worried.

'*"Ah"*? What does "Ah" mean?'

'It's just… Well look, someone's spilled ambrosia on the form, and I thought it said…'

'Yes? Go on.'

'What *exactly* is a bosun, anyway?'

* * *

If anything, the information wall was even more impressive when viewed from the front. It was quite mesmerising really. As soon as they stepped through the door Hercules felt his eyes immediately drawn to it. Whichever part he looked at sprang into focus and seemed to expand so that he could see it with crystal clarity. Facts, figures and images raced into his brain.

Farouk put a hand on is shoulder. 'It can take a bit of getting used to.' Hercules was grateful for the distraction. Looking at the wall for just a few seconds had made him feel quite dizzy. 'Don't worry,' continued Farouk, 'it gets easier with practice. Now, some introductions...'

Hercules looked around. The door had opened onto a sort of large, semi-circular balcony. Immediately in front of them was a desk, with two more desks on either side and slightly behind the first. On raised platforms to either side of the door that they had just come through were two more desks. The desks were arranged so that they all had a clear view of the Wall. Three of the desks were occupied.

'Everyone,' said Farouk, 'this is Hercules.'

The occupants of E91 – Level 12 (#Extinctions) stopped what they were doing and looked up. They all smiled at Hercules.

'Over here is Ruth,' Farouk led Hercules to the desk to the left of the door.

'Nice to meet you, Hercules,' Ruth reached over her desk and shook Hercules' hand.

'And in front of her, we have Keith.'

'Alright, laa,' came the greeting in a strong west midlands accent. He too shook Hercules by the hand.

'And this,' said Farouk, gesturing towards a figure standing on his head on the desk to the right of centre and controlling his workstation one handed while upside-down, 'is Vikram. Vikram attained enlightenment while working in a call centre in Bangalore,' he added by way of an explanation. 'As you might have heard, most Hindus and Buddhists tend to reincarnate, so not many come through the Pearly Gates. And usually we don't attract many religious types in I.T., but for Vikram here, it was a kind of logical choice.'

Vikram grinned expansively. 'Please, call me Vik,' he said. Much to Hercules' surprise Vikram also shook him by the hand, while remaining upside-down in a one-handed headstand.

'This is my desk,' said Farouk, pointing to the desk at the front of the balcony, 'which means that you are over here.' He led Hercules to the desk to the right of the door.

'There should be everything you need here,' he continued, waving a hand in front of one of the three screens on the desk. The screen sprang to life. It displayed an image of a white cloud on a blue background.

Hercules sat in the chair behind the desk. 'So what exactly am I supposed to *do*?' he asked. 'The word on the door: it said – um – extinctions?'

'That's right,' said Farouk. 'Actually, we're just one of many sections that are looking after extinctions at the moment. We go up for the next ten floors. I'm afraid it's a very busy arena at the moment. It's quite normal for species to go extinct and even for new ones to be created. It happens all the time. But at the moment there are a lot more species being lost than being created. There are nearly nine million species of living creatures on Earth at the moment, but that number is dropping all the time. At the current rates, the number will halve in the next hundred years or so. That means we're losing about a hundred and twenty species a day. Many of the species lost are never known about. Our job is to make sure they all get catalogued properly.'

He turned to the monitor and tapped the screen.

'The operating system is pretty intuitive,' he continued to explain. 'All you need to do is think about what you want to look at. For example, we could look at a general status screen.'

Accordingly, the screen displayed a map of the world with a large box above it which contained the number eight million, seven hundred and sixty-three thousand, nine hundred and twenty-one. As they watched the one started flickering, turning into a zero and then back into a one repeatedly so the numbers were a bit of blur. The ghosts of both values occupied the space for the last digit.

'What's happening there?' asked Hercules.

'It seems we could be about to lose another one,' said Farouk sadly.

'But why is the number flickering?'

'Do you remember what Ada said about the quantum processors calculating *all* the answers?'

'Yes.'

'Well, this is how the results of that process are displayed on screen. Until something has actually happened it exists as a possibility. The rate of change between the numbers indicates the relative likelihood of an event occurring. Whichever type of creature is currently on the brink, there is a possibility its kind will survive the current threat, but,' the last digit on the screen was now showing more persistently as a zero, with the one only a faint outline, 'as it stands I can't say things are looking very good for it. Let's take a closer look. Actually, why don't you give it a try?'

Hercules looked at Farouk.

'Go on,' Farouk encouraged him. 'Just think about what it is you are trying to do. Let's leave what we've got on this screen. Look for the detail on the next one.'

Hercules tapped the second monitor screen. It sprang to life with the already familiar cloud image. He tapped it again, not quite sure what he was doing, just wondering vaguely about the possibly unheralded life-form that stood at the brink of nothingness.

'Yes that's good, you're getting the hang of it,' said Farouk.

Hercules looked at the screen. The map had zoomed into the tropics: an image of a beetle half-filled the screen.

'Oh,' said Farouk sadly. 'It's the Melodious Stink-Whistler.'

'The Melodious what?' asked Hercules.

'Stink-Whistler. Not everyone's cup of tea, but I'm really rather fond of them.'

'I can't say I've ever heard of Melodious Stink-Whistlers,' said Hercules.

'That's no surprise,' replied Farouk. 'You see, *we* can see from the screen that there are over eight million species on the planet, and yet at last count, only about one and a quarter million have been named by scientists. As it turns out, an awful lot of the unnamed ones are beetles, and many of them are lost before they are even known. But they are all catalogued in the Cloud.'

'So how did it get to be called a Melodious Stink-Whistler?'

'Well that's one of the amazing things about evolution.' Farouk noticed the puzzled look that crossed Hercules face. 'Oh, yes, don't worry; evolution is a perfectly well accepted process around here. In fact, there are quite a few sections of this department working on it at the moment – though sadly rather less than are tasked with our line of work at present.' He paused for a moment.

'Anyway, I was telling you about our friend the Melodious Stink-Whistler. As you may know, many insects use a sense of smell, in particular airborne molecules called pheromones, as a means of communicating with other members of their species. Pheromone signalling can be effective over vast distances and as a result many insects have evolved antennae sensitive even to the slightest hint of a stimulating molecule.

'Acuity of smell is not, however, an approach evolution has taken with the Melodious Stink-Whistler.' Farouk tapped the screen. The image of the beetle began to rotate, giving a three-dimensional view of the insect. 'As members of the recycling brigade of the forests in which they live, they spend all day hidden in the dark of rotten logs, chewing wood. A side effect of the digestive processes that convert chewed wood into fuel for their little bodies is the production of gas. Like miniature cows, feeding stink-whistlers produce a lot of gaseous bi-products - mostly methane, but with a cocktail of more potent ingredients thrown in. In the cramped confines of a burrow in a rotten log, it would be an unfortunate turn of events indeed if the stink-whistler were blessed with any kind of a sense of smell. Fortunately for the stink-whistler, evolution has whittled away its olfactory senses over the ages until it is effectively, in terms of chemical reception, completely blind.'

As Farouk continued to talk various images depicting aspects of the biology of the little creature he was describing appeared alongside the rotating insect on the screen.

'This is no bad thing. A well-developed sense of smell within the rancid atmosphere in the average stink-whistler burrow could easily prove fatal. But just as one potential avenue of communication was lost to these insects, evolution stepped up to the plate once more and blessed them with a remarkable degree of control over the sphincter muscles that regulate the release of gas from their intestines. Forcing gas under high pressure out of their bodies, these remarkable little beetles developed the ability to whistle through their backsides. More amazing still is that, through subtle shifts in posture, stink-whistlers can produce different frequencies of sound. To complement this strange ability, thousands of tiny hairs on the stink-whistlers' legs are tuned to vibrate in the exact range of frequencies of the sounds produced.

'Thus these incredible little beetles communicate with others of their kind – talking through their bottoms and listening with their legs. The sounds reach out to inhabitants of nearby logs and in this way, guided by each other's music, stink-whistlers can meet and mate.'

'Wow! I can see why they are called Stink-Whistlers,' said Hercules. 'But where does the "melodious" come from?'

'Good question. Sadly, the frequency of sound produced by the stink-whistlers is in a range at the very upper levels of human hearing, and so to us would only be audible as a sort of high-pitched squeak. So whilst definitely stinky and a whistler to boot it may well be considered overly generous to bless this beetle with the title of melodious. In fact, there are a number of different species of stink-whistler, but in most of them the whistles are little more than high-pitched farts.

'Yet for some strange reason that has no obvious apparent evolutionary driver – and this may or may not have something to do with His Grand Design – when lowered to a frequency audible to mankind, the repertoire of calls and responses of this particular species appears to be made up exclusively of the melodies of songs by seventies Swedish pop super-group, Abba.'

They both looked at the screen in silence. The zero was becoming ever more solid.

* * *

Legion slid into his chair with his face still a massive grin. He sat back for a few moments, gazing into space and relishing the lingering image that played in front of his eyes of the crazed dance of the posh woman trying to stamp out her flaming footwear.

Eventually the image faded, and he sighed. 'Ah well, better do some work.' He shot a glance at the monitor on his desk. The screen sprang to life with an image of a black serpent coiled around a green apple on a fiery orange background. In the bottom right-hand corner of the screen flashed a red pitchfork.

'Damn!' thought Legion. 'Hellish Resources. What do HR want this time?'

He leaned forward and tapped the icon. The screen went black. Then five words appeared that filled him with dread:

Welcome to the Employee Survey.

Legion had forgotten all about it. It wasn't difficult. Every time a survey happened he tried to push it from his mind. The alarming thing was the regularity with which the surveys recurred. To Legion it seemed that there was a new one every couple of weeks. This was probably because there was.

The surveys were pointless, of course. No one ever told the truth. It was all a point scoring exercise for the lowers-down. The senior demons used the statistics derived from the surveys as grist to the mills of their various inter-departmental feuds. Very often the results were cited as justification for excruciating "team-building" sessions. You had to beware, though. Careful tally was kept of the number of responses received.

The honest thing to do would be not to answer: to be a conscientious objector against the mindless management psycho-babble. But the reality of the situation was that as a demon, Legion had very little conscience. He certainly wasn't honest. He would do what he always did in these situations. He would lie.

He sat up in his chair, squared up to the monitor, took a deep breath and tapped on the screen.

'Thank you for your participation in the Inflammatory™ Employee Survey on behalf of the Management of Hell,' read the screen that followed. 'This is page one of two hundred.' Legion shuddered. Then he steeled himself. He'd survived this sort of thing before, he could do it again. He just had to keep his eyes peeled for the obvious traps. He read on.

"Question 1: Overall Employee Satisfaction. Use the boxes below to describe your response to the following statement (SELECT ONE ANSWER ONLY) – Overall, I enjoy working in Hell."

Below the question were five choices. They read: "Hell YES", "Maybe", "Not Telling", "Maybe Not" and "Hell NO".

Now they're even starting with a trick question, thought Legion. And not even a very subtle one. You weren't *supposed* to enjoy your work in Hell. It was *supposed* to be, well, Hell. If you responded that you did enjoy your work, your inferiors would spend their time trying to make things worse. If, on the other hand, you answered that you did not enjoy your work, your inferiors would suspect that you were lying, and spend their time trying to make things worse. In fact, it was actually a part of your inferiors' *job* to make things worse for you, so there wasn't really much point to the survey. Apart from the fact that it was one of the things that made things worse.

The truth was, Legion really *did* enjoy his work, and he was very good at it. He had some pretty interesting projects on the go, and he had been responsible for developing some delightfully innovative corruption techniques, of which he was justly proud. But he didn't have time to spend all day stuck on question one. He ticked "Maybe" and was just about to go onto the next screen when he decided to tick "Maybe Not" as well, before also ticking the remaining three boxes for good measure. He quickly tapped through to the next screen before he could change his mind.

The next page was entitled "Work – Detail". It listed a seemingly endless variety of questions that could all be neatly encapsulated in the answer to the question on the previous page. Legion held his left hand in front of his eyes, closed them and then ran his right index finger down the screen in a random zigzagging pattern. When his talon brushed the edge of the screen he peeked through the gaps between his fingers to make sure that every question had at least one answer and then quickly tapped through onto the next screen. It was entitled "Environment".

He was just about to repeat the procedure for the previous page when a little alarm bell rang in his head, and he stopped to read the first question. "Are you satisfied with your working environment (temperature, lighting, etc)?" it read. Legion looked around his soulless cubicle. The temperature could be best described as molten. The lighting was generally a flickering orange glow. His chair was diabolically uncomfortable. All-in-all it was an ideal environment for a demon. He clicked "Hell No" and moved on.

A couple of questions later he made sure to tick the boxes that indicated that he had been involved in bullying at least once since the last survey, that it was impossible to voice an opinion without fear of repercussions and that he was frustrated by politics on a regular basis. Those were the sorts of answers that made the bosses happy.

And so it dragged on for page after page. By page one hundred and thirty-five the questions had turned to the "Organisation", which Legion reflected was a funny word to use to describe the way that Hell was actually run.

By page one hundred and fifty, had Legion been alive, he would almost certainly have lost the will to live. He soldiered resolutely on, clicking random answers to questions he was barely reading.

Then on page one hundred and ninety he came across the joke section. There was always one of these. Legion suspected the survey compilers wanted to show that they had a sense of humour, but it was always the same joke, and it hadn't been particularly funny the first time they had used it. The page was entitled "Resignation Intentions". There was a single question "Since the last survey, have you considered handing in your notice? (If yes please use the box below to give reasons.)" Legion did what he always did, ignoring the tick-boxes for the actual question and just typing 'Ha! Ha!' into the "give reasons" box. Once you were in Hell, there was no getting away from it.

But at least the joke question signalled to Legion that he was almost at the end. A few more pages of random ticking brought him to the final screen; page two hundred of two hundred – which bore the title "Anonymous Comments".

As clear as day this was another trap. Although the vacant textbox was supposed to allow demons to provide untraceable feedback, Legion knew from past experience that: 1. this was an outright lie – although the surveyors claimed not to know who submitted which answer they could very easily be persuaded by a senior demon, should said senior demon show an inclination towards finding out (and senior demons had a number of interesting techniques at their disposal, many involving either very hot or very cold stuff and the creative use of various pain-imparting implements, that could make them very persuasive indeed), and 2. It was always fairly obvious from what had been written as to who had written it anyway. Legion considered it best practice in these situations to therefore provide anonymous feedback in the guise of one of his colleagues. Having so many personalities at his disposal he could imitate just about anyone startlingly convincingly. He enjoyed doing so. It totally confused the system and led to endless rounds of recriminations within the department.

In spite of the repetitive surveys and the worst efforts of his inferiors, Legion was *very* good at his job.

The job of any demon is to harvest souls. Granted, God's forgiving nature can make this a difficult task, and one thing that is a nailed-on certainty is that working for other demons in Hell is always going to be a thankless task. Nonetheless there are still opportunities. Human population expansion alone is a statistical guarantee that there will always be a reasonable number of bad apples available to a committed servant of the Powers of Darkness. There may not be as many individual souls heading for the pits as the pearly gates, but the proportions seem to stay fairly constant. Legion had long since elevated the task of corrupting and harvesting souls to an art-form.

Since time immemorial Good and Evil have been locked in perpetual combat. That's the way it goes. For mankind, Evil, in this context, often principally means something that is not familiar to them: something, or somebody, new, different or strange. And it has always been relatively straightforward for demons to prey on this weakness and get people to do evil things to their enemies.

Take water-boarding, for example. In the mind of the perpetrator, it is in fact his enemy, the *recipient* of the water-boarding that is evil. The *water-boarder* is acting on the side of good, because his enemy is evil. If his enemy is evil, the logic follows that the water-boarder must be acting on the side of the righteous. Therefore, the particular sort of water-boarding he is engaging in is morally acceptable. All a demon needs to do is to perpetuate the myth amongst humankind that one's enemies are evil. As long as this belief is upheld it is relatively easy for a demon to exploit – for example by arranging for a bath full of water to be conveniently available at the right time – and reap the resulting harvest of sullied souls.

Interestingly, demons never needed to teach anyone how to do the actual water-boarding itself. Water-boarding is, as are most ingenious torture methods, an entirely human invention. The irony is not lost on the average demon that when a deceased water-boarder finds himself in the pits of Hell, on the verge of drowning in a lake of lava with a demon's foot on the back of his neck, then,

then, all of a sudden, he seems to find the treatment somehow less than fair.

Legion, however, was *not* an average demon. He could appreciate the basic simplicity of the 'my enemy is evil so it's OK' approach and he would also acknowledge that the demon's job was really that of a facilitator: real evil lies in what people themselves dream up to do to one another. But the principle of getting people to do bad things to their enemies all just seemed a bit too – simple. To Legion it lacked – *finesse.*

After his encounter with Jesus, Legion had spent a few years working the Pits as a punishment for his humiliation at the hands of the Son of Man. It was while meeting out just deserts to the damned that he began to formulate his unique approach to the corruption of souls. All too often he'd heard the damned in Hell wailing that they had 'only been following orders'. He didn't want to give anyone this excuse.

Legion considered that rather than relying on the instinctive shedding of inhibitions in the face of an enemy, it would be more *elegant* if he could get people to perform their despicable acts on those with whom they professed to share common beliefs. Of course, it could always be argued that once you engage in wrong-doing towards someone you make an enemy of them, but for Legion it was the starting point that was important.

His first opportunity came not long after he was cleared to resume field operations. The year was A.D. 39 and Legion headed straight for Rome. He'd heard that it was just the sort of place for him to test out his new theories, and before long he found himself hanging around the court of the popular new emperor. Despite, but more likely because of, his spendthrift ways, young Gaius Julius Caesar Augustus Germanicus had been immensely popular with the people of Rome for the first two years of his reign. Then "something" happened that turned him into a deranged lunatic.

Some say he became ill and lost his mind. The history books are not clear on the reason for the change that overtook him. What the history books did record were the numerous murders of family members, the trumped-up trials and executions of rich members of society purely to steal their possessions, and the orgiastic excesses that Caligula, as he was known to notoriety, indulged in until his eventual murder two years later at the hands of his own personal body-guard.

This time Legion returned to Hell in triumph. He knew from the catty comments of the other demons – the overheard whisperings that his techniques were "unnecessary", that he was "showing off" – that he had devised a winning formula.

He returned to Rome shortly after Claudius, Caligula's uncle and successor, had been murdered by his fourth wife, Agrippina (who just also happened to be Caligula's sister). Legion had seen little to work with in Claudius, but there were plenty of other family members intent on plotting, scheming and murdering their ways to an eternity at the business end of a pitchfork.

Top of the list, following Claudius' demise, was his great nephew, Nero – who was coincidentally also the son of Agrippina by a previous marriage. For Legion, imperial Rome had been a welcome breath of foetid air, but even amongst the moral mayhem of the house of Caesar, Nero was special. First, he murdered his half-brother, Britannicus, who may have had a better claim to the imperial throne, being Claudius' son. This quite naturally upset his mother, what with Britannicus also being her son. So he had his mother killed.

All this could seem like quite logical behaviour for a paranoid emperor. To Legion it was one of the little things that made Nero such a pleasure to work on. The mental bruises of his encounter with Jesus still smarted, so when Nero took a passionate dislike to the early "Christians", as they had started calling themselves, Legion was thrilled. When Nero started setting fire to Christians in the gardens of his palaces at night – purely so he could have some light to see by – Legion was nearly beside himself with happiness.

But while Nero's behaviour delighted Legion, the same could not be said for the political and military classes on which Rome depended. Eventually they would tolerate his behaviour no more and in 68 AD Nero was forced to commit suicide to avoid arrest and a sentence of being beaten to death.

Legion regarded the year of civil war and bloodshed that followed, during which, with the right demonic prompting, no fewer than four men adopted the mantle of ruler of the known world, as his "annus mirabilis". In December of 69AD, following the murder of Vitellius in the Imperial Palace, Vespasian became emperor and stability followed.

Legion took a well-earned holiday.

Having broken the golden rule about there being no rest for the wicked – well, if such rules are going to be made you can bet your sweet aunt Jessie that a demon will break them sooner or later – Legion returned to work. For the next few centuries he traversed the globe, refining his techniques and generally practicing until imperfect. He divided caliphates and corrupted kingdoms. He was beginning to get noticed downstairs.

Shortly after the turn of the first millennium, a group of demons – no doubt spurred to action through jealousy of Legion's falling star – began to notice the opportunities that might present themselves to the bad old ways if they could get the Muslim and Christian worlds to properly collide. It took some organising – no doubt made all the harder because the organisation needed to be achieved by demons who, as a rule, co-operate as well as members of a coalition government shortly before a general election – but eventually, at the end of the eleventh century, the first Crusade was launched. Legion felt that the fact both sides worshipped the same God meant that this "revival" of the old ways was actually a subversion of his own techniques, but his inferiors weren't impressed. For a while Legion was yesterday's news.

But it didn't take long for Legion to regain the immoral low ground. He was, after all, a visionary. It was really just a question of working out which one of him had had which vision and what to do about it. If he couldn't claim the discredit for Christians fighting Muslims, he would create schisms in the Christian church. Even after a thousand years his appetite for revenge against Jesus remained undiminished. In reality, any soul was as good as the next to his bosses, irrespective of creed; but for Legion it always *felt* better if there was an element of revenge involved.

Legion's riposte to the Crusades was the Inquisition. What better than a movement which had the goal of saving souls from heresy and legitimised torture to achieve this end? It was such a terrific idea, and the original Papal Inquisition went so terribly well for him that Legion ended up creating franchises of the concept; other demons variously took charge of the Spanish, Portuguese and Roman versions. As Legion handed over control of the blueprints for his model he realised that he was no longer interested in endlessly repeating past successes. From now on, he was all about pushing the boundaries. Once he'd created a winning formula, he could get less imaginative minds to do the donkey work.

As far as Legion was concerned, the ability to create a soul fit for the Pits of Hell without resorting to the illusion of the evil enemy required complete mastery of the arts of bedevilment. He had learnt by experience that very often the person best positioned to inflict the maximum amount of unnecessary suffering on a population was its ruler. Fortunately for Legion, the same qualities of ruthless ambition that fuel a desire to seek positions of power are coincidentally exactly those that lay the psychological cornerstone for the psyche of the average paranoid despot. Legion once again became king-maker.

By the turn of the second millennium Legion hadn't just presided over the creation of some of the most lethal dictators in history – he had written the book on it.

He wasn't directly responsible for the day-to-day management of all the demonic manipulations that resulted in the deaths of millions of innocents, but through the infernal publication of his field notes, observations and suggested worst practices, he had a hand in them all. It was true there were some, like Hitler, who with their "othering" of their enemies, were very much in the thrall of the old-school demons. But five names alone from Legion's hall of fame – Mao Ze-Dong, Stalin, Pol Pot, Kim Il Sung and Idi Amin – between them accounted for the lives of nearly a hundred million of their own subjects. That's twenty million innocents for a single damnation – although they did have staff, all of whom weren't entirely unblemished, but it gives an idea of why Heaven needs the bigger dormitories. And the price Hell is prepared to pay for a single soul.

All this Legion had achieved with old-fashioned tools. These days, his methods were backed up with technology.

* * *

Nore regarded the pitiful shoots struggling upwards through the ashy ground with a critical eye. He had spent the morning repairing the clay ramparts around his vegetable plot in an attempt to slow the rate at which the soil was washed away by the regular downpours.

It was the season of afternoon rains. During the mornings, humid air swept up the valleys from the sea. As the warm, wet air was forced over the mountains it formed into heavy grey clouds as the day wore on. At around three o'clock, with the regularity of a habitual drunk at the door of his local, the heavens would open. The rainstorms were heavy and violent, often with spectacular thunder and lightning. When he was a child and the forest still stood, Nore had been told by the village elders that the thunder was caused by the Thunder Bat, a giant version of the flying foxes that habituated the trees around the villages. The Thunder Bat served the Great Spirit. The sound of thunder was the Thunder Bat stirring in his roost; lightning his fleas hopping to the earth. Now, to Nore, thunder sounded like the anger of the ancestors.

Despite the regular post meridian deluges, the season of afternoon rains was generally considered to be the best time of year for growing crops. The rest of the year it rained from dawn to dusk – usually through the night as well.

Nore eyed the massing clouds with concern. The rains had been heavier than he could ever remember, and even with the low retaining walls he spent most of his time maintaining, it seemed that the vegetable plots retained their fertility for shorter and shorter amounts of time. While the trees had stood, they had held everything in balance; soil nutrients, water cycles, life itself. To Nore it felt that with the forest gone their life was slipping away like the goodness from the soil that was being washed down to the sea.

Nore sighed and chopped in frustration at the clay by his feet with his machete. There was a dull thud and a gentle hiss, followed by the most revolting smell. Nore gagged reflexively and staggered away from the spot, coughing and with his eyes streaming.

He knew instinctively what his machete had struck; there was no mistaking the smell if you had smelled it before. Nore had hit a stink log. The tribe knew all about stink logs. Well, that's not strictly true; they didn't know *all* about them. They knew that they were logs and that they stank. They didn't know why they smelled so bad, because no one had ever been able to stay close enough to one for long enough to break it open without losing their lunch and passing out. But they did know that they were remarkably useful for starting a fire. Even though the wood of stink logs was often rotten, soft and saturated with water, for some reason they burned like a Roman candle. Even on the wettest day, in the midst of the most torrential downpour – which was something of a speciality of the weather in this part of the world – anyone with a stone and steel for a spark, who could hold their breath really, *really* well, was only seconds away from a roaring blaze. And, more often than not, no eyebrows.

Fire had always been a comfort in the life of the tribe before they had lost their forest. After a hard day's hunting it was always good to get back to the village huts and dry out in the warmth of a fire. Sometimes you didn't even make it back to the village at night. If you were forced to spend a night under the forest canopy, finding a stink log was almost certainly a guarantee that your night away would not be too uncomfortable.

Now they used fire to clear scrub to try and grow vegetables. Fire had become bitter-sweet. Nore reflected, from a safe distance, that it was a long time since he had last seen a stink log. He hawked and spat into the ground to try and rid himself of the lingering taste. He was surprised the normally incendiary timber had survived the scrub clearance, but its buried location must have protected it.

The gathering clouds had darkened the sky. Nore untied the bandana he wore around his neck. He took a deep breath and, hold-ing the cloth over his nose and mouth, he picked up his machete and gingerly crept back to where the stink log lay submerged in the mud. When he was close enough he leaned forward and, using the end of his machete, managed to clear away some of the clay that covered it. He could tell it was a good-sized log, some three feet long by a foot across. Nore figured that if it was going to rain as hard as he thought, he would have to stay out through the downpour and do his best to protect his crops and garden from the worst ravages of the weather. Maybe the stink log was a blessing from the gods. He would light a fire and at least he would have a bit of comforting warmth.

Nore backed away from the stink log and spent a few minutes gathering as much other wood as he could find. When he was satisfied that he had enough to keep him going for a while, he once again took a deep breath, held his bandana to his face and carefully approached the stink log, this time carrying a bundle of small sticks which he placed delicately on top of its exposed surface. He backed away from the log and retrieved his machete, picked up a piece of flint from the ground and returned to the log for a final time.

Nore struck the flint against the flat of his machete. A shower of sparks leapt towards the stink log. There was a blinding blue flash and with the briefest of sizzling sounds Nore's eyebrows disappeared.

A few minutes later, as the first fat drops fell from the pregnant clouds, Nore had a comforting blaze going, oblivious to the ultimate price of his warmth. In the log below his fire, the last surviving Melodious Stink-Whistler was farting its final "Waterloo". Its soft bodied grubs had already succumbed to the heat of the flames.

As the conflagration finally breached the lair of the last stink-whistler it exploded in a blue fireball. The very final whistle it gave was not a tune penned by Benny and Björn but the hiss of steam escaping from the joints of its chitinous shell.

* * *

'No,' said Farouk, shaking his head gravely as the final digit on the status count turned to a solid zero and any lingering trace of the one disappeared, 'it's gone. And such a shame,' he waved his hand at the details screen and the image of the stink whistler which had occupied a central position now shrunk into a small box that repositioned itself in the top right of the monitor. The beetle's image was stamped through with red letters that read – "EXTINCT". The bulk of the screen was now a bullet point list of facts about this life form that was no longer.

Farouk turned to Hercules. 'Sometimes I find myself going through the files on the endangered lists. I just think that *someone* should find something out about the species that are being lost before they go. I don't know why I do it, for all I've told you about how we shouldn't get too involved. But very often it's just so hard not to care. I know it's all part of His grand design, but to be honest I've really no idea what that can be.

'You see this?' he pointed to the fact sheet. 'This little beetle that we've just lost that no one, it seems, cared very much about – it says here that the logs where it makes,' he paused and corrected himself, 'sorry made, its burrows are from the tree whose bark the locals used to use to combat malarial symptoms. It appears that the beetles' digestive processes concentrated and transformed the anti-malarial properties of the molecules which occurred naturally in the wood into something altogether more potent, which they excreted as small white pellets. The natural drug contained within the pellets, while totally innocuous to humans, is, or rather would have been, totally lethal to the parasite that causes malaria. But I'm afraid the little stink-whistler's secret will die with it. Now no one will ever know.

'I must admit that I think it's a little unfair,' he added with a hint of pique, 'that it is only we, who are powerless to intervene, who should be the ones that get to care about it.'

'Didn't we have our chance to make a difference, though?' asked Hercules, 'When we were alive, I mean?'

Farouk paused thoughtfully for a moment and then smiled wistfully at Hercules, his composure regained.

'You're right, dear boy. Of course you are right,' he said. 'If only we knew then what we know now. But how could we, eh?'

It was not a question that needed an answer.

His next one did.

'Anyway, all this excitement has given me a raging thirst. Do you fancy a cup of tea?'

* * *

Legion tapped the "Submit" button on the last page of his survey and sat back in his chair with a mixture of relief at having finished and devilish delight at the "anonymous comments" he had just sent in. Abaddon would certainly be very cross when he found out what Baalberith apparently thought of him.

Now that he had dealt with the employee survey, Legion could turn his mind to more important matters. For a while he had been working on a little personal project that was really destined to put the cat amongst the technological pigeons.

Ever since Heaven and Hell had begun their respective automation drives some decades back, a technological arms race had been raging between the white hats of Heaven and the black hats of Hell. Legion saw himself as more of an interested amateur than a bona fide player in this particular theatre of the eternal struggle. Nonetheless, amongst his many personalities were some of the most devious plotting minds within the whole of Creation. And if any of them saw the opportunity to contribute to the fray, there were yet others of his personalities that would positively *insist* that it was their immoral imperative to do so.

A few years back, some of the black hats had developed a technique for disrupting the systems of their seraphic foes by clogging them with unwanted messages. They had called this technique Beelzebub's Anti-Celestial Onslaught of Nonsense, or BACON, for short.

Once the white hats had realised what was happening, they responded by building a firewall around the entirety of Hell's computer systems. It was, literally, a wall of fire that completely encircled Hell. Since the demons themselves were immune to fire, this didn't stop *their* comings and goings; but somehow it halted their digital malevolence in its tracks.

Legion, however, had found a loophole. Not only had he found a loophole, but he had devised a new kind of attack that gave him the chance to make up for his episode on the Broadfields estate.

He opened a drawer on his desk and pulled out an Underworld Storage for Badness drive, which he slid into a port on the side of his monitor. He waved his hands in an arcane pattern to access the program where his virus was stored. As soon as he had opened the program, his monitor screen began to blister and hiss as the malign code sought to wreak its havoc. Very carefully, Legion coaxed the code across the screen and into the USB drive. As soon as the virus was safely in the drive, he whipped it out of the port it was attached to, put a lid over the end, slipped it into his pocket and headed out of his cubicle towards the firewall.

Usually when he crossed hell, Legion would stop here and there to take in the suffering and maybe lend a hand with a bit of light torment. Not this time, though. He could feel the corrosive force of his virus writhing and thrashing about in the drive in his pocket. He would have to be quick. He decided to take the tube.

The tube was the fastest way across the circles of hell, but if he could possibly manage it, Legion always avoided travelling this way. It wasn't that it was hot, smelly and crowded, although it was all of these things. Legion enjoyed the heat, and smelly and crowded meant that there was suffering happening, which also tended to make Legion happy. What he couldn't stand, was the shuffling. For the souls whose eternal punishment was perpetually to ride the Underworld, the end of the line meant a slow shuffling transfer across the platforms for the return journey. And falling in behind the dead-eyed multitudes always made Legion feel uneasy.

Today he didn't have time to be held up. He barged his way through the throng and pushed his way on to the waiting carriage. A beeping noise forewarned of impending departure, while bodies were still struggling to cram themselves onto the tube. There was a whoosh, and the doors slid closed. The edges of the doors had been sharpened like guillotines. For the unfortunates that had not managed to get themselves entirely clear of their paths, this sadly led to a somewhat inevitable loss of face. Or arms. Or hands. Whatever was in the way, really.

Legion had made it relatively safely into the crammed confines of the carriage. Next to him was a particularly large, sweaty demon who was holding on to the overhead rail for support. Unsurprisingly, the demon had BO that, at the very least could strip paint from a distance, but in reality was probably the starting point for several major pandemics. Legion knew this because the weight of people behind him was pushing him forwards so that his nose had nowhere to go but directly into the raised armpit of the aforementioned demon. Luckily for Legion, demons only breathe for show, but nonetheless his eyes were streaming when, a few minutes (that definitely seemed to have lasted a lot longer than normal) later the tube reached the Wall and he burst, gasping, from the carriage and onto the platform.

He raced from the platform to the Wall itself, which surrounded the edges of Hell like a flaming cocoon. Legion headed towards the spot where he had last seen his loophole.

He had to hunt around a bit. He knew the rough location of the loophole he had found, but the wall was a fluid creation, change being at the very heart of the nature of fire. Legion cleared his minds and focussed. Slowly and methodically he scanned the flickering orange and yellow before him. He tried to blank the drive in his pocket from his minds as he fought to concentrate on the wall, even though the drive was beginning to get really hot. As a rule, a demon wouldn't notice the temperature if he was sitting on the sun. He really didn't have much time.

One thousand nine hundred and ninety-nine minds redoubled their efforts on the job in hand. (There's always one, isn't there?) Then Legion saw it: a tiny spec of black amidst the fiery hues.

Very carefully he reached into the wall and caught the edge of the loophole on the tip of a pointed talon. Gingerly he drew it towards himself. Working with the very tips of his nails he started to tease gently at the edges of the loophole, painstakingly making it bigger as he delicately drew it open. When it was big enough to get a finger into he started to use two hands, working away until he had manipulated the loophole to a size he could reach his arm through. He dragged the loophole to the edge of the firewall and adjusted its position so that it ran from where he was standing to the other side of the wall. He peered into it. There was a clear run of black to the outside world. He pushed his arm through the hole until he could feel cool space on the other side.

His trousers were beginning to smoke. It was now or never. He reached into his pocket and pulled out the drive, tossing it from hand to hand to avoid having to hold it in either for too long. He flicked off the cap which fell to the ground glowing white hot. As fast as he could he pushed his hand through the loophole. When he could feel his hand in the space on the other side he pushed a button on the drive and felt the recoil as the virus rushed from the drive and into the aether.

Four

ASIF'S PARENTS had been pragmatic in their approach to their faith. His father had attended mosque on Fridays, and prayed as regularly as his business of running a small shop had allowed. They had observed the feasts and fasts, and his parents had even scraped together the money to perform hajj, as was their duty. But life was a constant struggle to make ends meet, and the more Asif watched his father accept the hardships that came his way, without malice or blame, the more he began to think that his father was weak.

Asif had grown up to a background of the struggle between the western and Islamic worlds. He had not been born when the American war-planes had bombed Baghdad in the first Gulf War. But as a small boy, following the 9/11 attacks on the United States he had witnessed the crusader response, first on Afghanistan, and then the second war in Iraq. The more he watched, and the more his father reacted in the role of the pragmatic peace-maker, the more Asif grew to despise him.

* * *

It had been about a year before. Legion was sitting in his cubicle, which on that particular day was a blandly uniform shade of grey. The temperature was an uncomfortable normal. All this was in honour of the fact that there had been a recent catastrophic accident on the set of the season finale of "In da House" – a hugely popular, and utterly inane, reality TV show.

The observant reader will remember that the admissions department of Hell was generally not a busy place on account of the forgiving nature of the Lord. The observant reader may well find themselves therefore wondering how an accident on a reality TV show could lead to such a sudden increase in activity therein. The observant reader should be directed to two words in the earlier sentence – Reality TV – and remember this: even a benign and forgiving Creator has Her limits. The accident had claimed the lives of all of the contestants as well as its pair of immensely successful, cheeky-chappy, northern double-act presenters. As a consequence, the admissions department of Hell was practically full-to-bursting with the sudden influx of Z list celebs, whose eternal punishment, for the rest of time, was to be treated to agonizing levels of indifference.

Legion cracked his knuckles and squared up to his monitor. He snapped his fingers in front of the screen to launch his anti-social media app and his Foes-book™ logon screen appeared. He muttered a dark incantation and his home page opened up. He was looking for someone to fork; maybe even make some new fiends. There was always room for fresh blood in Legion's circle.

Through Foes-book™, Legion was able to connect to the internet of the mortal world. Sometimes, he would simply take the opportunity to partake in a little light trolling, but this was a skill in which he quite often felt outclassed by his human counterparts. He could be left lost in admiration for the callousness with which humans felt able to dismiss one another's feelings when afforded the security of anonymity. The trolls seldom realised that their anonymity did not extend to the infernal regions, but then there was always going to be plenty of time for introductions later.

Legion's happiest hunting grounds, though, were the extremist sites. In the early days of the internet, the denizens of the dark side had had to work night and day to ensure that on-line you were never more than three clicks away from pornography, hatred, or better still, both. Then human nature had taken over and it had suddenly become a lot less of a struggle, particularly now that everyone seemed to take it for granted that it was the norm, and this was the way the internet operated.

The hard-core users of these sites were not really what Legion was looking for. They already had their beliefs, prejudices, and perversions and more often than not, already came with demons on their backs. This was why it was so important that people could still be easily, sometimes even accidentally, directed to the right kind of site. If innovative corruption was what you were after, you needed to start with an *innocent*.

Sometimes demons would try to steal souls from one another, in an attempt to look bad to their bosses. Legion never really liked this approach. For example, with an established extremist, you knew what you were getting. You could watch them grind out the hatred, but the flavour of that hatred was always going to be after the fashion to which it had already been cast. When you started with an *innocent,* by contrast, you could plant the thoughts you wanted, and tune the hatred to your own exact specifications. It was almost musical. Let the angels keep their harps. This was better.

And so it was that Legion had first noticed Asif.

Being something of an amateur coder, Legion had managed to make some underhanded adjustments to his Oggle™ search engine, of which he was justifiably rather proud. With a few artfully inserted demonic sub-routines, he could, at any given time, access a list of the most vulnerable souls to corruption that were currently logged on to the mortal internet. It provided him with a full bio for each person, should he want to investigate the detail of an individual. But quite rightly, the feature of which he was proudest was that each name was accompanied by a custom-built emoji that expressed their state of vulnerability and subsequent potential for evil.

Asif's emoji practically leapt off the screen at him. It was by far the most perfect mix of confusion, innocence and subliminal rage that Legion had ever come across. In fact, when he had been designing the emoji to express this particular combination of emotions, Legion had not believed that it would ever actually be used; but the set would not have been complete without it.

Almost physically bursting with excitement, Legion tapped on the icon.

The screen blinked, and went dead.

'No!' cried Legion, resorting to the time-honoured method of fixing faulty technical equipment everywhere and giving the monitor a sharp whack on the side: nothing. He hit it a few more times from various different angles: still nothing.

This could not be happening! A once in a lifetime chance was slipping through his fingers. He paced his cubicle frantically. The search modifications to Oggle™ were uniquely his, so there was a fair chance that he had a small window of opportunity before any of the other demons noticed Asif's potential. He had to get his system up and running as quickly as possible. There was only one thing for it. He reached for the telephone on his desk. He would have to call Technical Support.

He rummaged around on his desk for the scrap of paper on which he'd written down the number for Technical Support the last time he'd needed it. With a great deal of forethought, Technical Support only provided their contact numbers on their website pages. The chances were, if you needed Technical Support, you couldn't access their website.

After a few minutes of bad-tempered flinging bits of paper around the cubicle, Legion stumbled upon the scrap he was looking for. He held it reverentially in his hands and laid it carefully on the desk, before taking the telephone from its cradle and dialling the number.

'Thank you for calling Technical Support,' Legion was greeted by a recorded voice. 'Your call may be recorded for monitoring and training purposes. To help us direct your call, please chose from one of the following eighteen thousand four hundred and seventy-three options now:

'If you are happy with our service, press one now;

'To be put on hold, press two now;

'To report a fault on the line you are calling from, press three now;

'If you have the wrong number, press four now;

'For more options, press five now...'

Legion stared in his handset in horror. He remembered it had been bad the last time he had called, but it had been nothing like this. There had obviously been a major system downgrade recently.

'...To report a sudden loss of purpose,' the voice droned on, 'press twenty-nine now...

'...To return to the start of the list, press thirty now...'

He mashed his fingers against the keypad in desperation. As if to prove that miracles can and do occur, and are not purely the preserve of the mortal, godly sphere, Legion found himself connected.

'You've been transferred to hardware support,' said the recorded voice. 'This system operates on state-of-the-art voice-recognition software. Simply state the part of your device that is experiencing problems.'

'Monitor,' said Legion.

'I'm sorry,' said the voice, 'I do not recognise "minotaur". You did say "minotaur", didn't you? Please answer "Yes" or "No".'

'No,' said Legion, as clearly as he could.

'I'm sorry,' said the voice, 'I do not understand. Please try again.'

'Oh for God's sake,' said Legion.

'There is no need to use offensive language, sir,' the tone of the recorded voice had become decidedly frosty. 'May I remind you that your call may be recorded for monitoring and training purposes?'

'How can they train you? You're a recording!' exclaimed Legion, exasperated.

'I'm sorry,' said the voice, 'I do not understand. Please try again.'

Legion thought he would try a different track. 'Screen,' he said.

'I see no reason to scream, sir,' said the voice.

'Aaarrghhh!' cried Legion.

'Thank you, sir,' said the voice, 'Your call is being transferred now. Thank you for calling Technical Support. Your call is important to us. Please hold the line while we try and connect you.'

The line at the other end started ringing. You had to take your hat off to whoever had been responsible for this system, Legion reflected. If he had been their boss, they would definitely be down for a demotion. The ringing on the other end stopped. In the brief pause that followed, Legion was about to speak, only for his ear to be filled with the strains of a performance of Greensleeves by what was at best a primary school recorder group, but could well have been the Hell Philharmonic Orchestra.

Even for Hell, Legion figured that deploying speakerphone would result in unnecessary levels of noise pollution, so he resorted to holding the phone at nearly arm's length. He drummed his talons on his desk and swivelled around in his chair as the music squealed on. Just as he was beginning to think that this was all a waste of time, the music was interrupted by yet another voice recording.

'Thank you for holding. You are currently in a queue. Technical Support is currently experiencing an unexpectedly high volume of calls. Your position in the queue is – one million, thirty-nine thousand two hundred and ten… and a half. You will be connected to the next available operator as soon as one becomes available. Thank you for your patience…'

Patience was something that Legion had just run out of. He hurled the telephone handset at the monitor on his desk. The handset struck the monitor squarely in the centre of the screen and both handset and monitor exploded into flames.

Legion watched the small conflagration with a self-congratulatory smile of satisfaction.

Without warning, a group of imps burst into his cubicle, dwarfed by a large red bucket carried between them. As a well drilled unit, they hopped onto the desk and doused the flames with the sand that the bucket contained.

The lead imp strode to the front of the desk, pulling, as he did so, a small notepad from his back pocket with one hand and a pencil stub from behind his ear with the other. He drew himself up to his full six-inch height, tutted officiously, licked the end of his pencil and stood with the pencil hovering over his pad.

'Oh deary, deary, *deary* me,' he said. 'H'unlicensed fire in a cubicle… destruction of h'I-T property…We 'ave been a naughty boy, 'aven't we?'

Legion looked at the diminutive figure in disbelief. 'Unlicensed fire? *Unlicensed* fire?' he said. 'This is Hell! The whole place is ablaze most of the time.'

'Ah, yes,' replied the little imp. 'But them's *licensed* fires. *H'unlicensed* fires is an altogether different kettle of bananas. 'Elf and safety, you see – though I can't say I cares much for 'Elfs myself, on the whole – untrustworthy blighters, you see?'

Legion wasn't sure that he did.

'When fires is used in the pits for torture,' the lead imp explained, 'it's all done under your "controlled conditions", isn't it? Can't have people getting 'urt h'unnecessarily, now, can we?'

'But I thought that was the whole point of torment,' said Legion. ''Urting, I mean hurting people.'

'Ah yes, but that would be the *necessary* element of people getting 'urt, wouldn't it? There's nothing *h'unnecessary* about torment.'

Legion shook his head. This was all a bit hard to follow. 'I suppose,' he said.

'And then on top of the fire,' the imp continued, 'we've got the destruction of property.'

'But the computer was already broken!'

'Very difficult to prove – I should think – seeing as 'ow you appear to 'ave set fire to the h'evidence. No, I'm afraid I'm going to 'ave to write you a ticket. Name?'

Legion's default reaction to figures of authority, regardless of the size or shape they came in, was to lie. Remembering that he was actually in a hurry to try and locate the precious soul he had spotted, before his I.T. problems began, Legion fought back his worse nature and decided to tell the truth.

'Legion,' he said with resignation.

The little imp was about to put pencil to paper when he paused. He eyed Legion suspiciously.

'Not *the* Legion?' he said. '"We are many" – *that* - I mean *those* one...s?'

'I guess so,' said Legion cautiously, wondering where this was leading.

'Oh, I say,' there was suddenly a complete change of tone to the imp's voice. 'This *is* an 'onour, sir – or should I say, sirs.' He turned to the other imps behind him on the desk. 'Lads, you'll never believe it. We're only in the presence of my all-time demonic 'eroes.

This 'ere is Legion.' The group of imps all looked appreciatively impressed.

'All that stuff you did in Rome. You must've 'ad a blast! And the H'inquisitions: pure genius!'

Legion didn't quite know what to say. 'Well, yes I guess it was fun at the time.'

'There's your book, too. Me and the wife've both read it. She's a massive fan, as well. 'Ere, I say: I couldn't get your h'autograph, could I? It would make 'er day.'

He held out his pad towards Legion. Legion looked down at the tiny booklet and took a piece of paper from his desk. 'I think it'll be easier for me if I use this,' he said. 'Whom shall I make it to?'

'Oh, if you could write "To Muriel, with loathing" that would be grand.'

'And what about the ticket you were going to write me?' said Legion, holding the autographed piece of paper just out of the little imp's reach.

'Ticket? What ticket?' said the imp, innocently. 'Me and the boys were just in the neighbourhood, and we thought we'd pay a little social visit to one of the giants of demonic misdeeds. There's no need for any talk about tickets.'

Legion held out the autograph towards the imp. Just as the little figure stretched out a hand to take it, Legion snatched it back out of reach once more.

'What about my monitor?' he said. 'Can you help me get a replacement?'

'What are you h'insinuating?' said the head imp.

'I know all about imps,' said Legion. 'You get everywhere. Surely you must be able to get me a replacement monitor. It's a bit of an emergency. If you must know,' he leant forward and lowered his voice, flattering the imp that he was sharing a confidence, 'I was seriously up to no good when it stopped working.' He straightened up. 'In a roundabout way that's what led to the fire.'

The lead imp turned to his team. The tiny figures on the desk converged into a huddle. Occasionally a little head would break out and glance at Legion before returning to the circle. After a minute of highly animated whispering, the group broke up and the head imp returned to address Legion.

'Right,' he began. 'Me and the boys think we *might* be able to be of h'assistance, but we figure that one bad turn deserves h'another – if you get my drift.'

'What do you want?' asked Legion.

'Simple really,' said the imp. 'Just put in a few bad words for me and the boys with our boss.'

Legion scratched his chin. 'I could say you were overbearingly officious,' he said.

'And..?'

'Unnecessarily bureaucratic?'

'That's the spirit. Anything else?'

'Overzealous, intrusive, pushy and rude?'

'Now we're cooking.' The little imp spat in his hand and held it out. 'Sirs, I believe we have ourselves a deal.'

Legion extended a talon, which the imp shook vigorously. He then signalled to his team, who hopped off the desk as a unit and disappeared at speed from the cubicle, carrying the broken monitor and phone with them. Legion handed his autograph to the imp leader. The scrap of paper on which it was written was almost the size of the diminutive demon.

'This will look lovely on the wall at 'ome,' said the imp, holding up the piece of paper proudly.

Almost immediately, the rest of his crew reappeared, carrying with them a shiny new monitor and handset. In a blur of motion, the crew set about clearing the remnants of the sand back into their bucket before setting the new monitor in place on the desk and switching it on. When they had finished it was as though the clock in the cubicle had been turned back to before Legion's technical problems had begun.

Legion looked at the tidy desk, impressed. 'It's against my bitter nature to say it,' he said, 'but thank you.'

'Think nothing of it,' said the imp leader. 'Now, if you'll be so good as to h'excuse us, the boys 'ere 'ave a h'inkling of where we might find an dreadful and wanton h'abuse of departmental h'I-T h'equipment,' he winked at Legion in a manner that can best be described as – well – impish, 'and possibly a h'unlicensed fire that needs putting out.'

With this, his crew hoisted their large red sand bucket to their shoulders and the entire troupe rushed from the room.

When they were gone, Legion turned to his new computer and quickly logged back into his Foes-book™ and called up the Oggle™ search results. He breathed a sigh of relief when there, at the top of the page, was the special icon that represented Asif. Crossing his fingers against any further technical mishaps, he tapped on the icon. This time, the bio opened without problems. Legion steepled his fingers and leant forward to read the words on the screen, savouring each little detail of Asif's background and persona, as his demonic brains pondered on how he could put this information to the best possible use.

Legion had already begun to monitor a group of white suprema-cists in east London. They were developing, slowly but surely, into what he reckoned could one day become his ultimate suicide squad; the weapon through which he finally would have his revenge on the Creator and His boy. From this point of view, it wasn't really nec-essary to set another plot in motion. Humans, to Legion's minds, were remarkably adept at accepting what they regarded as necessary evils. If things panned out as planned, his little plot with the fascists would be all the necessary evil Creation would ever need. It was, however, always good to have a plan B. Asif was a purely *unnecessary* evil. And if he didn't get to end Creation, he could always start a war instead.

As Legion absorbed Asif's story – the clash of cultures and faiths, the unbalanced relationship with his father, the growing sense of injustice, his pigeons – the germs of a plan began to form in his head. He switched his attention to what Asif was doing now, and opened up a window on his screen that showed a view of the browser that Asif was currently operating. Legion almost fell off his chair with excitement. This was too good to be true. Asif was currently absorbed in a conspiracy theory website that purported to explain how the 9/11 attacks on America had been orchestrated by agencies within the United States, possibly with support of the Israelis, as a means of turning the west against Islam and justifying the subsequent attacks on Afghanistan and Iraq.

Belief in conspiracies was always a good start. It was definitely material Legion could work with. When people started believing in conspiracies, they became oddly unquestioning with their faith. They would readily give credence to "facts" that "everybody knew" that had somehow been "covered up" by the powerful, almost inevitably for "their" own sinister ends. Legion marvelled at the ease with which logic was very often ignored in such cases, but it didn't bother him overmuch. In his unscrupulous way, he considered this ability of the human mind to park its rational functionality a gift from God. He figured this was his Creator giving him something to work with. Legion was familiar with Jesus' story about talents. He'd be damned if he wasn't going to use his. He'd be damned anyway, but that was just the way he was made.

Legion realised that Asif was angry and confused, and he was looking for someone to blame. With blame he could create a rationale for his suffering, and better still an enemy on which the blame could be pinned.

The fact that the boy was engaged in an "investigation" into the way that American and Israeli agencies had conspired to mastermind the attacks on New York and Washington meant that the enemy was easy to define. To comply with his own rules of *finesse*, what Legion had to do now was to convince Asif that the best way to hurt his enemy would be to plunge a dagger into his own heart.

Legion traced the history in the cache on Asif's browser. It was clear that he was more engaged in the train of thought that suggested that the 9/11 attacks were actively orchestrated and supported from within the United States, rather than merely "allowed" to happen by interested parties. Legion's mind raced. If he had had a heart, his pulse would have quickened. This was what he was born to do. Almost without needing to think about it, a plan was crystallizing.

Legion watched as Asif's mouse moved across the web-page, hovering over a link to more information on the subject. This was perfect! With a little of the right kind of direction, Legion would create his very own lone wolf. And he had just the job in mind.

His first task was to isolate Asif. Asif had already begun this process on his own, so it was just a case of ensuring he kept up the bad work that he had already started. He also needed to protect him from other demons. Legion couldn't risk this opportunity being wasted by some ham-fisted, rock-brained pit-pusher. The second of these tasks simply meant that for a while Legion would have to keep a close eye on his new protégé. This was no real problem. His pet fascists were likely to be a slow burning project and he had some other ducks to line up on that front, so he had the time to spare. As far as isolating Asif went – he knew how to do that.

He quickly inserted a hidden link onto the web-page that Asif was browsing. It led to one of Legion's own special sites: a site that contained purportedly top-secret details supporting the conspiracy theories with evidence so damning that anyone who came across it would fear for their very lives. Legion had learnt that nothing isolates a paranoid mind quicker than the belief that it is in possession of privileged and dangerous information.

It was something of a hobby of his, creating back stories to perpetuate the various conspiracy theories that circulated the web. Sometimes he would release them into the wild, but for some reason he had kept this one back. He was glad that he had; Legion knew that the information on this particular site was, to the right mind, psychological dynamite. It was also total rubbish.

Legion watched Asif's browser screen as his mouse passed over the hidden applet. The link tip flashed up on the screen and the movement of the pointer stopped abruptly. Legion watched as it slowly retraced its route across the page, searching for the hidden link.

Legion had found that it added to the experience if, once one of his links had been activated for the first time, it was then restricted to a couple of pixels in size. This suddenly made it difficult to find, which exaggerated the sense of privilege and conspiracy associated with following it. After a couple of misses, the searching pointer hit the jackpot and the link tip flashed up again.

'Go on, click it,' Legion muttered under his breath.

The pointing finger of the mouse cursor sat still on the screen.

'Go on,' urged Legion. 'What are you waiting for?'

The mouse clicked.

'Gotcha!' A thin smile spread across Legion's lips.

* * *

The captain of the *Good Ship* sat in his office, staring disconsolately at the piles of paperwork that buried the surface of his desk. This wasn't the life of adventure he had dreamt of as a small boy. It certainly wasn't what he had expected, when as a teenager, he had stepped up the gang-plank to take up his first post at sea. He was used to the ever-growing demands of bureaucracy that he had to deal with. What depressed him most was that this voyage was supposed to be for a good cause and right now the very gods seemed against its progress.

There was a knock at the hatch. It was the Chief Officer.

'There's a fellow here who says he needs to speak to you. Most insistent he was. I'm sorry, Captain, but I can't for the life of me think why I agreed to bring him up here, other than the fact he's so very strangely persuasive. Shall I show him in?'

'Go ahead, Jenkins,' replied the Captain. It seemed an odd situation, but right now and with the way he was feeling, what was there to lose?

The Chief Officer ushered in an extremely fit looking individual of indeterminate age and nationality. It was the damnedest thing, thought the captain. There was definitely a person there but even when looking directly at him, he wasn't able to make out even the simplest detail of his face. Inscrutable, the captain thought to himself; must be Chinese. Then immediately afterwards he started to worry that this might be a bit racist.

The stranger extended a hand towards the captain.

'Thank you for agreeing to see me sir,' he said. As the captain shook the stranger's hand he noticed a peculiar sensation of heaviness envelope his own.

'Not at all,' the captain heard himself saying. 'What can I do for you?'

'I'd like a job, Captain.'

'Very well, do you have any experience?'

'I was born to do this job, sir.'

'Yes. That's not exactly the same thing as having experience, is it? What's your name, sailor?'

'Boson, sir.'

'Not your rank, I said what is your name.'

'Boson, sir. That is my name – Boson.'

'You weren't kidding when you said you were born to do the job, were you?'

'No, sir.'

'Dare I ask your rank?'

'Bosun, sir.'

'So that is indeed, both your name and your rank.'

'Aye, aye, sir. Bosun Boson, sir.'

'Very good Bosun Boson. Here's the deal. We're stuck here, full to the gunnels with aid for East Africa that is going nowhere because the port officials want a hand-out. On top of that, half of my deck-hands have jumped ship. If you can find me enough crew to get this ship moving again, the job's yours. Do you understand?'

'Aye, aye, Captain.'

Bosun Boson stood to attention, turned smartly and strode from the office. The captain leant back in his chair and exhaled hard. 'Jenkins!' he called out.

'Captain?' The Chief Officer poked his head around the doorway.

'Where exactly did our visitor come from?'

'I couldn't exactly say, Captain. I found him wandering around on the deck and he said he had to see you as a matter of urgency.'

'I see. And what did you make of him?'

'Very difficult to say, sir. I believe the word is inscrutable, sir. Then again, they all are – from that part of the world, I mean, aren't they, sir? I'll say this for him, though, sir. He's certainly very persuasive.'

'So it would seem, Jenkins. I have a feeling that I may have just offered him a job...'

'Very good, sir.'

'...On the condition that he can find us a full complement of crew.'

'Do you think he can do that, Captain?'

'I've no idea, Jenkins. But he certainly *was* very persuasive. I suppose we will just have to wait and see.'

* * *

'Come on, everybody,' said Farouk. 'Tea break.'

'Surely we don't need to eat and drink?' Hercules queried. 'Being dead and everything, I mean.'

'Need to? Heavens, no. But it's hard to break the habits of a life-time. And you really have to try the nectar and ambrosia they serve in the canteen – although I'm more of a tea man myself. Besides, it'll give you a chance to meet the team.'

The team did not need a second invitation to a break. Keith and Ruth rose from their chairs and Vikram, who had shifted from his headstand into a sort of upside-down lotus position, unfolded from his contortions and lowered himself from desktop to floor. The five of them headed through the door and down the moving staircase.

Farouk led them down the gantry that he had recently brought Hercules along, but to Hercules' surprise they kept going past the door through which they had first entered the wedge.

'I thought you said that we had to go back through the main doors to get to the other departments?' he questioned.

'Usually, yes. But the canteen is something of a special case. Every department has a door that opens into the canteen. I guess with all the comings and goings, it just made more sense that way.'

They had arrived at the end of the walkway. Vikram held the door open, and they all filed through.

By the standards of all the rooms he had encountered so far, Hercules was surprised to find himself in what appeared to be a small coffee shop. There was a counter for ordering drinks and food and a collection of comfortable looking sofas and a variety of other chairs and tables. It didn't look like you would get more than fifty people in at one time. From what Hercules had seen of Heaven, there was no way that this canteen could accommodate all the souls that might, at any one time, fancy a cuppa.

'Wow,' he said, 'it's a lot...'

'Smaller than you were expecting?' asked Farouk. 'Look again.'

Hercules did as he was told. At first he didn't see anything different, but then suddenly, like a magic eye picture coming into focus, he saw that this small coffee shop was a cell in a huge and perpetually repeating hive of similar venues. It made him giddy.

'That's enough,' said Farouk. 'I think you'll agree it's easier if you stick to what we in I.T. like to call "a single version of the truth".'

Hercules looked around again, and saw the room as he had first seen it. The knowledge of the endlessly repeating rooms was still there, but now that he no longer had to look at them, he felt much better. They went to order some drinks.

'Hello, Hercules.' Behind the counter was a familiar face.

'Oh – hello, Draven.' Hercules turned to his new colleagues. 'Everyone, this is Draven.'

'The Unholy,' Draven grinned at four puzzled faces.

'We arrived together. Draven's a Satanist,' explained Hercules. 'Draven, these are my new friends from the world of I.T.'

Everyone said hello.

'So, Draven, how are you settling in?' asked Ruth.

'It's alright, as it goes,' replied Draven. 'The work's pretty easy, mostly making cups of tea. It's amazing, really, we can make just about any dish you can imagine, and some you couldn't imagine unless I told you about 'em first and even then you probably wouldn't believe me – but mostly what people want is a cup of tea.

'I suggested a bit of thrash metal as background tunes might liven the place up a bit, but the boss said to wait and see so I don't suppose he was too keen on the idea really. There's generally lots of comings and goings though – people to chat to, that sort of thing, so, yeah, I guess it's OK. Anyway, what can I get you all?'

Keith ordered a hot chocolate with lots of whipped cream and a flake and a large chocolate muffin, joking that the best thing about being dead was that he didn't have to count calories. Vikram asked for a glass of water. Farouk and Ruth both opted for tea. At the insistence of the team, Hercules ordered a bowl of ambrosia and a cup of nectar.

They settled down into a couple of sofas arranged around a low table. Draven came over with their orders on a tray and began to lay out their food and drinks on the table; Keith's hot chocolate and muffin, Vikram's water and the cups of tea for Ruth and Farouk. Finally, with a flourish, he laid out a goblet containing a golden liquid, a spoon and what looked like a bowl of ice-cream in front of Hercules.

Hercules realised that four pairs of eyes were watching him expectantly. He picked up his bowl of ambrosia and sniffed it. It smelled pleasant, but not remarkable. He was, however, aware of the four pairs of eyes that were following his movements intently. He lifted a spoonful of ambrosia towards his mouth. All he could hear was four people holding their breath.

He put the spoonful of ambrosia into his mouth. He was dimly aware that four people had relaxed and started breathing normally.

The ambrosia, rather than having a specific flavour, was, quite literally, a taste sensation. As it melted on his palette, he was transported with the feeling of a walk through a flower filled meadow on a warm summer's day while a gentle breeze caressed the stems of the plants, making them dance. He took another spoonful. It tasted of diving into the crystal clear, blue waters of a pristine tropical reef, surrounded by iridescent fish that glowed with all the colours of the rainbow.

'How's the ambrosia, Hercules?'

'Wow. It's incredible.'

'Food of the gods, you know. Try the nectar.'

He took a sip from the goblet. As the nectar touched his lips he felt as though he'd gone his entire life without a drop of water – as though he'd lived his whole life with a raging thirst that was so all consuming that he didn't even know it was there.

'Refreshing, isn't it?'

Hercules realised that his four colleagues were still watching him, but now they were all grinning broadly.

'Unbelievable,' said Hercules. He paused.

'There's a "but", isn't there?' said Vikram.

'Well, it *is* very lovely,' said Hercules, 'but...'

'Yes?'

'I couldn't just have a cup of tea, could I?'

His colleagues all burst out laughing.

'Of course,' said Farouk, when the laughter had subsided a bit. He waved over to Draven and signalled for another cup of tea to be brought.

'It was the same for all of us,' said Ruth, reassuringly as she wiped tears of laughter from her eyes. 'I mean, you have to try it and everything, but it is just a bit *intense.*'

'You can say that again,' said Hercules.

'You should have seen your face when you were eating that ambrosia,' said Keith, still chuckling. 'Proper spaced out you looked, man.'

Draven brought over a mug of tea for Hercules. He blew on it and took a sip. It tasted refreshingly normal.

'Anyway,' said Farouk, 'what's your story, Hercules? What series of unfortunate events brings you to our midst?'

'It's all a bit stupid, really,' said Hercules, feeling slightly embarrassed. 'I undertook a lorry on the approach to a set of traffic lights. He was turning left, didn't see me, and after I'd finished being mashed through the tyres of the truck – whoosh –' he made a flying motion with his hand, 'and I was sitting on a cloud.'

'This is unfortunate for you indeed,' said Vikram. 'I too am the victim of careful driving.'

Hercules looked puzzled. 'Don't you mean careless?' he asked.

'Oh no,' said Vikram. 'The driver that ran me down took most special care to avoid a holy cow that had wandered into the road.'

There wasn't really a lot to say to that. Hercules learnt that Ruth had been a victim of the Nazi holocaust and Keith's mortal span had ended with a hang-gliding accident. To Hercules the whole discussion felt a bit like arriving at university and talking about "A" levels; something that no one was really comfortable with, but everyone wanted to get out of the way so they could move on.

He turned to Farouk. 'What about you, Farouk?'

'Well, I'm the old man of the bunch,' said Farouk. 'My mortal days ended over nine hundred years ago. The year was four hundred and ninety-two in the calendar I grew up with, ten ninety-nine in the Christian calendar. I was among the garrison protecting Jerusalem when it was overrun by the knights of the first Crusade. I was decapitated in the slaughter that followed the breach of the walls of the city. Quite dramatic at the time I suppose, but it was all a very, very long time ago.'

'Wow,' said Hercules. 'So how did you come to end up working in I.T., if you don't mind me asking, that is?'

'Not at all, dear boy. Well of course, when I first arrived here the notion of I.T. was still a very long way off indeed. But there has always been a records department and that's where I started, though needless to say it was very different in those days; all quills and ledgers and if you ever wanted to retrieve a piece of information…well let's just say we were lucky that time was never an issue. It kept us busy. Over time we developed a very efficient filing system and I suppose you work with what you've got and get used to a certain way of doing things.'

'When did all that change?'

'Well I suppose the real catalyst was the Great War at the start of the last century. There'd been wars before, of course. And slaughter. But usually it was one event. One big battle or disaster and then things returned to normal. When the killing started in 1914, nothing had ever happened on that scale before that just kept going on and on. A couple of days into the first Battle of the Marne and you couldn't move around here for all the new arrivals. And it only got worse from there. We muddled through, somehow, but it was fairly obvious that things had changed for ever and even the powers-that-be recognised that they could no longer rely on the old processes.

'Fortunately – if one can ever draw a silver lining from such devastating human tragedy – there were some pretty creative young minds among the new arrivals of the time. They, and some of the brighter sparks already among us, got together and built our first computer – the Automatic Processing Engine, or APE as it was commonly known. I think Darwin was responsible for the name. He was on one of the early steering committees, and he's always been a bit of a mischief maker. I think it tickled him to think of the souls of mankind being directed by an APE.

'Of course, APE wasn't anything like the Cloud that you saw earlier. But it was an important first step on the path that led to what we have today. When they were building APE, the workers over in records were offered the opportunity to be a part of the new department and the rest, I suppose, is history.'

Hercules nodded. There was clearly so much to learn. On the plus side, as Farouk had already pointed out, time was no longer an issue. He was just about to ask if any of the angels had anything to do with I.T., when he was interrupted by the wail of a siren. Above the door that led back to the department a blue light was flashing.

Hercules' companions leapt to their feet.

'Come on,' called Farouk, who was already halfway to the door, 'it sounds like there's an emergency in the department. We'd better go and see if we can be of any assistance.'

* * *

The team burst back through the door to find the department in pandemonium. More blue lights were flashing. Through the glass walls of the hardware section, Hercules could make out the Tin Heads, who had been so orderly in their circuits of the server racks before, dashing around in mad panic.

As they raced along the gantry towards their section, sirens wailing in their ears, Hercules glanced down in the direction of the Cloud. What he saw made him stop in his tracks. He had to shout to the others to get their attention over the noise of the sirens.

'Farouk, Ruth, guys…Look!' he pointed down towards the Cloud in its glass case. Although it was difficult to make out much more than the colour from this distance it was clear that the case no longer contained a little white fluffy cloud. The contents of the case were now the colour of thunder and lightning was arcing back and forth within the glass.

'What's going on?' yelled Hercules.

'I don't know,' Farouk yelled back. 'We've had BACON attacks in the past, but this looks like something far more serious. Come on. Let's get back to the section and see what's happening there.'

The five of them began to run again, along the gantry and across the front of the wedge till they reached their staircase. Together they sprinted up the escalator and crashed through the door to their section where what they saw stopped them all dead in their tracks.

The entire information wall, the monitor screens on their desks and on all the other visible desks were displaying the same image; a yellow smiley face.

Farouk was the first to break out of the trance. He ran over to his desk and touched a monitor. Nothing happened. He tried the next one. It was the same. Taking their lead from him, the rest of the team snapped into action and rushed to their desks and followed suit. None of the screens responded. They all looked at one another with rising panic...

Just then the main doors of the department burst open. In flew a dozen angels. Each was carrying a person. The angels deposited their passengers on the gantry and flew back out the way they had come.

'It must be serious,' shouted Farouk. 'It's the Guardians.'

'The who?' shouted Hercules.

'The Guardians!' yelled Farouk, just as the sirens fell silent. His voice echoed through the hall.

Most of the Guardians had rushed off towards the hardware section as soon as they had arrived, but one of them headed for the supervisors' area at the front of the hall. He was dressed in a tunic and sandals and had a thick head of hair and a full beard.

'Who's that?' asked Hercules, relieved no longer to be shouting.

'That? That's the leader of the Guardians,' said Ruth. 'He's called Aristotle.'

'What, *the* Aristotle?'

'If you like, I suppose he must be. Anyway, hush up. It looks like he's got something to tell us.'

'Ladies and Gentlemen,' began Aristotle, 'it appears we have something of a problem.

'Many of you will be familiar with the spate of BACON attacks we experienced some time ago. We seemed to have solved that with the firewall around the Other Place, but it now seems that they have somewhat upped the ante. We are under what appears to be a new kind of attack, which, because of the way it is working, we have decided to call a Demonic Denial of Souls – or DDoS for those of you who love a good acronym. Some malicious code has entered into the logic gate that we have been using to direct the recently departed to their appropriate destination with the effect that all souls are currently being diverted to limbo.'

'Have you tried turning it off and turning it back on again?' a voice called out from the back of the hall. There was some sniggering.

'Yes, yes, very good,' smiled Aristotle, 'you all know I appreciate a good joke, but I'm afraid my very presence here should be enough to indicate to you all that this really is no joking matter.'

* * *

Legion had had a lot of fun developing Asif's paranoia. Over the weeks and months that followed the first hijacking of Asif's browser, Legion devoted a good deal of his time to the development of his protégé. The deeper Legion led Asif into the inner realms of his own fears, the more the young man shut out the world around him. His parents watched him becoming more and more withdrawn, but they were unable to get through the barricades he erected to keep them out. He went to prayers regularly, still disappeared onto the moors to fly his birds from time to time, but he spent more and more time locked in his room and attached to his computer.

Asif's parents worried about him, but they told themselves that all parents worried about their sons. Sometimes he would flare up about injustices against Islam, but then who didn't feel that they were unfairly singled out these days? He had always been vocal in support of his beliefs. Wasn't this a good thing? He was regular at mosque, but he didn't associate with some of the more zealous young men that congregated there. He spent a lot of time online, but they told themselves that perhaps he was just studying. He still had his pigeons and flying them meant he got fresh air. Maybe they were worrying about nothing...

Over time, Legion had guided Asif towards the best the internet had to offer in terms of conspiracy theory. Under Legion's careful guidance, Asif would endlessly prowl the forums and chat rooms under his adopted username – Al Thi'b, the wolf; always watching and reading, never participating. Early on, Asif had decided for himself that he did not want to *talk* about what needed to be done. He would *do* it. His search was not for conversation, but preparation. As he searched and searched, two questions burned in his mind. 'What?' and 'How?'

Asif's reluctance to participate on the forums was frustrating for Legion. He could drip-feed Asif all the dangerous secrets in the world, but it didn't help him if he didn't actually know what Asif was thinking. The only way he could find this out was by communicating directly, but Asif never seemed to want to engage. Legion, however, had an advantage. The "secrets" that Asif had been fed, which only the two of them knew – Asif because no other person had seen the sites that he had visited and Legion, quite simply, because he had made them up – meant that Legion shared a bond of common knowledge with his prey.

Every so often, Legion would hijack Asif's surfing sessions and direct him towards one of the many sites he ran through Foesbook™. It was here that Legion eventually made his breakthrough. Whenever Asif was in a chat room, Legion supplied the rest of the personalities. He had enough to spare. He was sure that given time one of them would strike the right note.

So it was one day, several months into Asif's corruption, that "the Sheik" was discussing with some of his acolytes how the September attacks on New York and Washington and the later attacks on London were orchestrated by members of the American and British intelligence agencies; at first to justify, and then to perpetuate, their mythical "War on Terror". The collapse of Tower Seven at the World Trade Centre was clearly a controlled explosion, orchestrated to destroy evidence hidden in the offices of the intelligence agencies that occupied the building. In common with the other users of this particular chat room, Asif had seen the requisitions for the explosives and the schematics that detailed where they should be planted to bring the building down on itself. Legion knew this, because he had written them. It was a work of fiction of which he was particularly proud. Many conspiracy theories had focused on the collapse of Tower Seven. Only Asif had seen Legion's irrefutable "proof".

The group were expressing their outrage at the duplicity which had resulted in such oppression for the followers of the Prophet, praise be unto him, at the hands of the crusaders. The crusaders must be made to pay. They would bathe in the blood of further attacks. The foot soldiers of jihad would deliver apocalypse into the cities of the infidels.

Asif was watching the conversation unroll in front of his eyes, when he was struck by an epiphany.

Al Thi'b > You are wrong.

He had typed the sentence, before he even realised he was doing it.

Sheik > How so, Al Thi'b?

The Sheik's prompt reply startled Asif. He had spent so long being careful not to show his hand. But he had broken cover now. And this community was clearly very well informed; they knew the type of explosives that had been used and where. He was fired up – he pressed on.

Al Thi'b > The crusaders attacked their own people to create unity against Islam. We must use their own tactics to defeat them.

The response was immediate.

Sheik > Not here. Private chat. Dark Web.

Asif had already become familiar with accessing the more hidden extremes of the internet. Through a protocol known as TOR – the Onion Router, which layered the routes of network traffic like the skin of an onion making users impossible to trace to prying eyes, he could access the "Dark Web". With the privacy of an anonymous connection, Asif unburdened himself. All of his repressed emotions, his carefully guarded secrets and confusion were vented to this stranger who called himself the Sheik. Asif finally felt that there was someone who understood him – a wise soul who could guide him. The Sheik let Asif explore his thoughts without judgement. The Sheik's encouragement of Asif to express himself freely led to a hardening of Asif's steely resolve to make a difference. He would deploy the tactics of the crusaders against them. He would plan a spectacular attack against his own faith.

Spectacular to Asif meant only one thing. He would attack the most holy of cities, Mecca. To maximise the outrage, the perfect time to do so would be when the city was at its busiest – during the annual pilgrimage, the Hajj. The Muslim world would be appalled at the scale of the sacrilege he would perpetrate. Their response would be total a unification of the nations of Islam against the Crusaders of the West. He would succeed where the Caliphate had failed.

Legion was delighted. Asif's inventiveness in devising and justifying such an act of evil against people of a shared faith almost made it seem a shame that he was planning to destroy Creation. He would just have to enjoy such moments while he still could.

Asif may have decided what he was going to do, but the 'How?' still remained. And in it he saw a very clear problem. No follower of the Prophet, he reasoned, would ever consider attacking the Hajj. Blame would almost certainly point elsewhere, but there was always the danger that enough sectarian violence occurred across the Muslim world that the blame for an attack *could* be apportioned to factional differences. There would need to be a smoking gun that pointed from the west. The attack would need to be carried out in such a manner, or with such specific weaponry, that there could be no question as to its origins.

It turned out that the Sheik knew of just the right kind of weapon.

***

A second Guardian trotted down the gantry towards the supervisors' platform. He was dressed in a long dark coat, a white shirt open at the neck and breeches with long white socks. His shoes each bore a large silver buckle. As he jogged along the locks of his shoulder length hair bounced with the rhythm of his strides.

'Hey, isn't that...?' said Hercules, pointing at the jogging figure.

'Newton,' said Keith, matter-of-factly.

Newton tapped Aristotle on the shoulder and whispered something to him. Aristotle turned to face the wedge.

'The Cloud itself appears to be undergoing an episode of precipitous climatic interference,' he announced.

This statement was met by an uncomprehending silence from his audience. Aristotle surveyed the tiers of workstations in front of him.

'Really?' he asked. 'No one?' he pleaded. There was still silence. He turned to Newton, who shrugged. 'Very well – have it your own way,' he conceded. 'The Cloud is raining.'

This announcement was met by gasps and a general worried murmuring from the massed ranks of the department. Aristotle appeared happy that he had his audience's attention again.

'Obviously the longer this goes on, the smaller the Cloud is going to get.' Aristotle continued gravely when the murmuring had subsided a bit, 'And the smaller the Cloud, the less systems power we have. It really is vital that we reverse this process as soon as possible. The alternatives are – unthinkable.

'Unfortunately it seems that we have lost control of all of the consoles. And with all the water sloshing around I'm not sure that if we tried to power down we would ever be able to bring the systems back online. Besides, we must also entertain the notion that this attack is part of a planned assault on our infrastructure and the Enemy is actually trying to get us to turn everything off. We really are in a most awkward predicament.'

There were more murmurings. The section wasn't used to this.

'This is very bad,' said Ruth, turning to Hercules. 'When the Guardians have turned up before, they've swooped in, flicked a few switches here, pressed a few buttons there and everything's been back to normal in no time. I've never seen Aristotle looking so concerned.'

Aristotle held up his hands to appeal for quiet. 'I suppose what I'm saying,' he said, somehow looking smaller, 'is that we are open to suggestions. In the meantime, unless anyone has any brilliant ideas, might I propose that you all try to access your workstations in whatever manner you see fit?'

There was a stunned hush in the hall.

'Really, ladies and gentlemen,' it was Newton who was speaking now. 'Time is of the essence. Whatever you can think of; try it now.'

The silence was replaced by the sounds of thousands of wheeled swivel chairs gliding into position. This was followed by quite a lot of cracking of knuckles.

In section E91 – Level 12 (#Extinctions), Vikram, Keith, Ruth and Farouk squared up to their monitors, concentration etched onto their faces.

'Er, excuse me, Farouk?' Hercules was feeling very lost. So much had happened in the short space of time since his death. If he never really expected to find himself in Heaven, he definitely never expected to find himself in Heaven and so scared.

'Yes,' Farouk replied curtly, his eyes not shifting from his monitor, his look of deep concentration unbroken.

'What should I do?' asked Hercules.

'You heard the man; unless you've got any better ideas, try and access your system.'

'But how?'

'Think!' Farouk almost snapped, but it was more the stress of urgency that accented his reply than anger. 'I've shown you how these machines work. You have to think your way in. Come on! It doesn't sound like we have much time!'

Hercules looked at the monitors on his desk, then at his four colleagues, faces straining with the mental effort of the seemingly fruitless task of trying to unlock their terminals. On the information wall the grins of the ubiquitous yellow smiley faces were growing ever broader.

'OK,' he thought. 'Here goes nothing.' If he wasn't going to be of any real help, he could at least achieve the same level of uselessness as everyone else. He put his hands on the screen.

Immediately he felt a jolt, like touching an electric fence. He recoiled from the screens. Around him the others were still locked in their grim communions with their own terminals. Beads of sweat were running down Farouk's creased temples.

'Countermeasures,' grimaced Farouk through gritted teeth. 'The program can feel that we are trying to get in and it's fighting back. It's a sign we must be making a difference. Don't give up now!'

Hercules raised his hands to his screen once again. This time he was ready for the kick when it came. He rode the jolt of pain that shot along his arms and down through his body to his feet.

When the pain subsided, Hercules realised that he couldn't see anything. The world around him was perfectly black. Or was it perfectly white. It could have been a colour, or a total lack of it. Whatever it was, it was clear that he could not even see his hand in front of his face. He lifted a hand to within a few inches of his eyes: nothing. He moved his hand back to the screen: nothing. He turned his head left and right, up and down. Everything was the same shade of – nothing.

He could still feel; his body, his arms held out in front of him, the screen his hands were touching. He could vaguely hear noises around him, but he could see nothing. It wasn't the darkness you get when you close your eyes and sometimes coloured blobs dance across the back of your eyelids. It wasn't darkness. It was nothing – a clear and absolute void. A void that would make the gaps between stars seem bustling and crowded.

In his mind, but only in his mind, Hercules sat down. An outside observer would still have seen his body standing in front of his terminal, hands outstretched to the screen on the desk before him. But in his mind he slumped cross-legged to the floor and buried his face in his hands. He'd quite simply had enough. As if dying wasn't enough for one day, now he found himself in a new job and completely out of his depth as the I.T. systems of Heaven came under some kind of diabolical cyber-attack. And now, to top it all, all he could see was nothing. He was fed up and he wanted to go home, only he knew full well that he didn't, in the human terms he was only so recently used to expressing everything in, have one anymore. He wanted a way out.

'Hercules!'

He was vaguely aware of people calling his name.

'Hercules! Hercules!'

There were definitely people calling his name. There was more than one of them. He roused slightly within his mind. The voices sounded vaguely familiar.

'Hercules!' He could definitely recognise Farouk's voice now. 'Hercules, can you hear me?' There was urgency in Farouk's voice.

In his mind, Hercules began to nod. As he did so he felt his own head, the one that existed attached to his body rather than just in his mind, nod also.

There was some relieved sounding chatter. Hercules couldn't make it out clearly. Then he heard Farouk's voice once more.

'I don't know what you are doing, Hercules, but it seems to be working,' he said. 'You've got a small door at the bottom of your screen. I don't know how you got it to appear, but it's definitely there. Does any of this make sense to you?'

Hercules nodded vaguely and felt his head nod.

A door.

A way out.

But he couldn't see anything. How would he find the door amidst all of this nothing? He began to cast around, felt the panic rising in his throat once more. He was trapped in a body that couldn't see. Then a thought struck him. He hadn't been looking for the door when it had appeared on his terminal. He had given up trying and had just thought about what he wanted: a way out.

Something, something that wasn't nothing, caught his mind's eye. It was in his peripheral vision, he wasn't sure it was there, but it was so unlike all the nothing that definitely was there – if something that is the absence of anything can actually be anywhere, that is. A way out. He thought about it some more. Surely a way out of where he was now would only take him back to the pandemonium of the I.T. department. They were supposed to be fighting the virus that was attacking their systems. He didn't need a way out. He needed a way in – a back door.

The something that had been hiding in his peripheral vision leapt forward at a terrifying pace. Hercules found himself standing in front of what looked very much like the back door to his house. He knew it couldn't be, but he supposed that if he had to imagine a back door, the one that he had known for the last fifteen years was probably as good as any. He was mostly just relieved to be able to see something again, even if only within his mind.

He faced up to the door and tried the handle. The door was locked. That didn't matter – he knew where the key would be. It would be where he always left it. By the side of the door was a small collection of potted herbs. Hercules lifted a pot containing thyme. Sure enough on the saucer under the raised pot there was a key. Hercules' mum had always told him it wasn't a safe place to leave a key. Right now he was glad he'd never listened.

The key slotted into the keyhole on the door. Hercules turned the key and tried the handle again. The door began to swing open. As it did so, Hercules could hear the sound of running water.

He looked down to see water splashing on the floor. A tap had been left running in the kitchen sink and the overflow was flooding the house. Hercules strode across to the tap and turned it off. He was just about to pull the plug out of the sink when the doorbell rang.

Hercules sloshed his way to the front door. It wasn't locked. He opened it. On what looked like his former driveway, but clearly wasn't, stood Farouk and Ruth along with a number of other people who Hercules assumed must also have come from the department.

'Well done, Hercules!' began Farouk. 'And thank God you're OK. You had us worried for a moment there – we thought we'd lost you. But when we saw you'd got that door open, the Cloud stopped raining and we got some system function back. It's allowed a few more of us to get into the program. This lot are here to start the clean-up.' He gestured to the gathering crowd. 'Ruth and I are here to take you back.'

'Shouldn't we stay and help?' asked Hercules.

'Dear boy, you've done enough already. I had no idea you were such a talented programmer.'

'To be perfectly honest,' replied Hercules, 'I don't think that had anything to do with talent. I just wanted a way out. And then a way in.'

'Modest as well,' smiled Ruth. 'Come on, there are some people who are dying to meet you.'

* * *

The Sheik had taken his time in bringing Asif into his full confidence. Too much too soon, reasoned Legion, and Asif might become suspicious. Following the initial contact, he deliberately kept their encounters short and sporadic. He hinted at things without any great revelations. This had the desired effect on Asif, who became ever more fervent in his longing to become a partner in this special knowledge.

After some time, the Sheik began to hint that he knew of the whereabouts of a weapon that Asif might be able to use to carry out his attack. Asif had visions of wreaking megatons of destruction, but the Sheik made it clear that he was thinking of an altogether subtler agent of doom. The problem with large bombs was that they were big and heavy and difficult to transport. There was also a risk associated with gathering the materials – and none of this would give them the strong association with a western government that they both agreed the weapon needed to have. There was enough errant nuclear material in the wrong hands these days that even an irradiating "dirty bomb" could not be reliably blamed on a particular source. The Sheik, however, had come across something that could be delivered in a tiny payload and was uniquely tied to the government responsible for producing it; it would, nevertheless, cause unparalleled human damage. The only problem the Sheik foresaw was in devising a suitable mechanism whereby the weapon could be delivered.

Al Thi'b > I could take it; I long for martyrdom.

Sheik> No – your insights are too valuable to our cause. We must find another way.

Al Thi'b > What about someone else?

Sheik > There is no one else I trust with this.

There was a lengthy pause while Asif contemplated the flashing cursor in front of him. Then an idea struck.

Al Thi'b > How much weight are we talking?

Sheik> No more than a couple of grams.

Al Thi'b > What about pigeons?

Sheik> ?

Al Thi'b > I fly racing pigeons. Maybe they could deliver the package.

Sheik> Pigeons? Are you sure?

Al Thi'b > I think they could do it, yes, inshallah.

Sheik> How will you get them to go to the right place?

Al Thi'b > I'll have to work on that.

Sheik> Let me know when you have done. Don't contact until you are sure.

And with that the Sheik went silent. Asif was left wondering if he *could* do it. His mind was racing. Had he just made a fool of himself? Had he made a boast that would be impossible to support? He knew his birds could find their way back to their loft when released anywhere around the country. He was confident they would even return from the continent if released there – some of the races involved just that, even though he had never been able to afford to take part when competitions started overseas. But this was different. This did not involve his birds finding their way back to their home. This required them to be directed to a target; a target that was completely unknown to them.

Asif began to spend his time on the internet with a new goal in mind. He knew that scientists had long believed that pigeons made use of the earth's magnetic fields to navigate. When Asif had been racing his birds, they had been timed using specially designed pigeon racing clocks, which worked in conjunction with leg rings that were attached to the birds. When a bird arrived back at its loft, Asif would race to get the ring off its leg and into a special slot in the clock. That was the time that the pigeon was deemed to have finished its race. In reality races were often won and lost in those few frantic seconds as owners tried to catch their bird and remove the ring from its leg. Although he no longer took part in the races, Asif was aware that electronic methods were becoming more common to record birds' arrivals. They were even using tiny GPS devices to monitor the pigeons' exact movements.

Asif began to wonder if he could put any of this information to use. The GPS could relay information of a bird's location, but it wasn't a means to direct it. A microchip might identify a bird and alert a reader, but this was of no help in actually targeting a flight. On top of all this, the exact mechanism by which the earth's magnetic field was used to navigate was only poorly understood. It was hopeless.

But then Asif's luck began to change. In one of his surfing sessions, he stumbled across a paper describing some very precise manipulations of flight direction carried out in laboratory by a scientist called Professor Vieleteufel. The cunning professor had cleverly wired up a large aviary to create an environment in which he could control the strength of a magnetic field by varying the electric current supplied to the wires. Using an equally ingenious harness device to allow birds the sensation of flight while not allowing them to go anywhere, he had demonstrated a precise relationship between strength of field and the directional adjustment that it created. The paper provided detailed data on the strength of the magnetic fields used, the distances at which the flying birds experienced those fields, and the degree of deviation from the flight path that resulted.

Asif was exhilarated. He set about calculating the power that would be needed to create the same strength of magnetic field if the wires were placed in direct contact with the bird's head. Up close, a much smaller current would be needed to produce the same effect as a cage wired to create a field. Extrapolating from the professor's data, Asif was able to calculate that a series of wires running from a small watch battery should be able to generate the strength of field he required. He began to conduct his own experiments.

Asif bought a micro-GPS system and began releasing his birds with little wire mesh helmets hooked up to small battery-powered circuits. When his first releases made their way back to the loft, he quickly learnt that the thin wires were too fragile to maintain the circuit when unsupported. He began experimenting with various materials. Eventually he settled for a kind of soft leather that he fashioned into little caps in two layers with the wires sandwiched between them.

As soon as the wires were contained within the supportive structure of the little flying helmets, the pigeons began to struggle to find their way back to the loft. Asif was thankful for his foresight to invest in the GPS system, as it helped him locate stray birds on more than one occasion. However, despite the help he had from professor Vieleteufel's data, generating the correct directional adjustments was fraught with difficulty. All sorts of variables seemed to come into play – atmospheric conditions, the amount of charge in the battery – that had an impact on the consistency of the sensitive electric fields in the flight caps.

Once more fate smiled on Asif. He chanced upon a French company on-line called Le Gion, which specialised in the sale of high-quality micro-components. They even, quite coincidentally, had circuit diagrams for an arrangement which, with a few tweaks, would provide *exactly* what he was looking for. He placed an order for several sets of the required components immediately.

* * *

As Legion took the delicate components from the drawer in the desk in his cubicle and dropped them into a small anti-static pouch, he paused wistfully. He was going to miss all this. He really was enjoying himself. All the same, he reflected; he was sworn to revenge against the Creator, and revenge he would have. And what better revenge than ending Creation?

Nonetheless, he was determined to have fun right up to the end. He scooped up the collection of anti-static bags, dropped them in an addressed envelope, added an invoice, and sealed it. He tossed the envelope into his "Out" tray with a sigh and left his cubicle to tour the Circles. He was off to enjoy some gratuitous torture while there was still time to do so.

Five

'I HEREBY CALL this extraordinary meeting of the Aryan Defence Order/League/Front to order.'

Maximilian Dumars, Eugene and Nick were gathered once more in the Broadfields Estate community hall. True to the general rule of their meetings that their previous rendezvous had been the exception which proved, there was no one else present. Nonetheless, the three of them spent a couple of minutes staring at the door. Just in case.

Eventually Eugene broke the silence. He sounded slightly puzzled. 'Aren't we doing the bit about litter?'

'No, Eugene, we are *not* doing the bit about litter. The litter patrol group is our front, remember?'

'I thought we were the Aryan Defence Order/League/*Front*,' said Nick. 'I thought that was our front.'

'*We are* the Front. The litter patrol group is *our* front. Is that clear?'

There was silence. Being silence, it didn't contain the sound of tumbling coins.

'Good, well I'm glad we've got that sorted out... Now to our agenda...'

'Pretty sure I'm a bloke.'

'Me too, Boss, last time I looked. I pee standing up and every-thing.'

'Yup, fairly sure our 'genda is male.'

'Although I'm pretty sure these days it's not always so straight-forward.' Eugene's brow was wrinkled as he wrestled with the complications of modern living. 'I mean; I keep hearing that a lot of people don't even seem to know what they are... 'course, each to their own, but I think all this "buy" business is a bit weird... it doesn't seem right that your 'genda should be something you can just pay for.'

This time it was Maximilian Dumars who delivered a puzzled silence. His silence was, however, broken by the sound of a penny dropping.

'Agenda, gentlemen: as in "the reason for our meeting". Not gender: as in "male", "female" – or otherwise. Although I'm glad to hear you are both so in tune with yourselves. It's reassuring to know that the fate of the New World Order rests with such sharp intellects as yours.'

Nick and Eugene beamed at each other with pride, both genu-inely sure that they had just been paid a compliment.

A puzzled frown crept across Eugene's face. 'Anyway, Boss,' he asked, 'why *are* we having this meeting? Don't we normally only get together on a Tuesday afternoon?'

'*This,* Eugene,' said Maximilian Dumars, 'is an *extraordinary* meeting: in the light of the last meeting's extraordinary events – and our extraordinary visitor.'

'Mrs Cunningham is not that bad, really. I mean she does smell a bit of cat food, but show me an old lady that doesn't.'

'Not her, you imbeci...' Maximilian Dumars bit his tongue. He needed his co-conspirators on side. 'I was referring to the mysteri-ous Mr John.'

Nick and Eugene exchanged glances.

'Oh – him.'

'Yes – him.'

'I dunno, Boss. He gave us the creeps. There was something -' Eugene looked at Nick for support. Nick gave him a small nod. '- something, well, a bit nasty about him.'

Eugene looked relieved that he had aired his and Nick's concerns. Nick looked slightly worried. They both watched Maximilian Dumars closely for his reaction. They had expected an explosion. The initial calm of their leader's reaction threw them both off balance.

For a moment he didn't say anything. He steepled his fingers, as if in prayer, and half closed his eyes. He stayed like this for what seemed like an eternity to the increasingly uncomfortable Nick and Eugene. When he had finished processing his arguments in his head, his eyes opened, and he slowly lifted his gaze to face his colleagues. He rose to his feet to address them.

'Gentlemen,' his voice was calm, but there was a steely determination in his eyes, 'we are talking about the creation of a New World Order.' The fires of passion had been lit and his despotic world view was bubbling under the surface. Nick and Eugene had seen him like this before. When he got on his soap-box, Maximilian Dumars was quite the orator. But this time there was a difference. They could both sense that something had shifted in their leader. There was a new level of intensity about him. 'When the Führer set about the creation of the Third Reich, was he not beset by attacks from all sides?'

Nick and Eugene looked at one another. They both shrugged and nodded.

'It took a will of steel to meet the challenges he faced,' Mr Dumars continued, 'and it will be the same for us. However much we wish it, a New World Order will not be achieved by being *nice*. Besides – people are stupid. They don't know what's good for them.

'If more people stood up for what is *right*, this country wouldn't be in the mess it's in. The so-called politicians in Westminster call it a diverse and integrated society. *I* say it's taking away jobs from our citizens and polluting our culture. Immigration is costing us our jobs, our council houses, our neighbourhoods. It's filling our schools with children that can't even speak our language and ruining *our* children's education. It's bleeding our health service while at the same time infecting the population with dirty foreign diseases. It's clogging the courts with terrorists who bleat about their human rights. It's a cost, my friends, which *our* society can no longer bear.

'Fellow members of the Aryan Defence Order/League/Front, let me ask you a question. Is a doctor being *nasty* when he cuts out a tumour - even though what he has to do certainly isn't very *nice?*'

Eugene and Nick looked at one another once more.

'Not really, boss.'

'He's doing what needs to be done, isn't he?'

'Exactly!' Maximilian Dumars had them on side. 'We must do what needs to be done. We are the doctors. Society is the patient, and we must cut out the cancer before it spreads. And with the help of Mr John that is exactly what we are going to do.'

'Well, when you put it like that...'

'I guess you're right, Boss.'

'Of course I am. You both know I am. Now, how did Mr John say we were to contact him?'

'He didn't, Boss. He said he would be in touch.'

Somewhere between the full stop of Eugene's sentence and the closing speech marks, there was a gentle cough.

Three heads whipped around in synchronisation towards the door. Leaning against the wall and looking as insouciant as ever, was Mr Lee John. He was without his cane. This was because in his left hand he was carrying a large briefcase, and, in his right, a large wooden box with a carrying-handle on the top.

'That was quite some speech, Mr Dumars. It seems my bosses were right about you. But then, they are never wrong. Anyway, Gentlemen, have you reached a decision?'

'Yes we have, Mr John,' said Mr Dumars.

Legion watched him with interest, knowing the question that Maximilian most wanted to ask but wasn't going to was – 'How long have you been standing there?', closely followed by 'And how did you get in without us hearing you?'

'And…?'

'We're in.'

'Excellent. I never thought for one second that you wouldn't be. You realise from this point that there can be no turning back. My masters would be most – displeased.'

There was something about the way he said it that carried just the hint of the shadow of a suggestion that causing Mr John's masters displeasure would be quite probably the last thing that any-one should ever want to do. And, almost certainly, it would be the very last thing they ever *did*. Mr John walked over to the table and put down his case and the box.

'It would be unfair to send you on this mission without giving you some kind of idea of what you are being asked to do. In fact, you are *so* crucial to our success that I have been instructed that you are to be fully briefed. You are about to share in a knowledge only afforded to a privileged few. Gentlemen, welcome to the Inner Sanctum.'

Mr John stroked a gloved hand across the lid of his wooden box. 'But first, Gentlemen: a daemonstration.'

'I think you mean demonstration.'

'Thank you, Nicholas,' Mr John fixed him with a stare that Judas Iscariot, encased for eternity in a block of ice in the ninth circle of Hell, would have considered frosty. 'I know *exactly* what I mean.'

Nick and Eugene were right. There *was* something about Mr John: something the human brain was just not programmed to deal with. Sometimes the mind encounters something *really* scary, something that is *sooooo* terrifying that the brain simply ignores it, because if it acknowledged the absolute terror of what it was perceiving it would run screaming through the back of the skull waving its arms madly, without even bothering to shut the braincase behind it. And in fairness to Nick, a daemonstration *is*, in fact, very much like a demonstration, only – as he would shortly find out – a good deal messier.

Nick gulped. 'I'm sure you m-m-must,' he stuttered, which he thought was odd as he never usually struggled with any of the words in his limited vocabulary. And then his subconscious added a word that his conscious mind found even stranger, since it had no idea why he used it. It said, 'Sir.'

* * *

Ruth and Farouk led Hercules along the drive outside the house that clearly wasn't his house but looked just like it. As they crunched across the gravel, his mind began to feel the pull of his body calling him to return. He looked at Ruth. She smiled encouragement and the Hercules of his mind was suddenly whipped from the familiarity of his unfamiliar surroundings and into darkness.

He became aware of himself once more, mind and body reunited, standing in front of his workstation with his hands held out to the screens. He could feel the monitors and feel that his arms were touching the screens, but he could see nothing. A wave of panic rolled over him. The he realised that he had his eyes screwed tightly shut. So tightly shut that the muscles of his face were aching with the effort. He began to relax and slowly opened his eyes.

As his vision adjusted to the light he could see that the image of the yellow smiley no longer dominated the displays and the information wall. Most of the monitors had returned to their normal states, although one or two yellow spots were still visible. But even as he watched these were popping like bubbles, one after another, as normality slowly returned.

'Welcome back, Hercules,' he recognised Keith's accent. 'You did alright there, our kid.'

'Yes, well done, young man. We all owe you a debt of gratitude.' Hercules turned to find that Aristotle and Newton were standing by the door of their section.

Aristotle strode forward and shook Hercules vigorously by the hand. 'Hercules,' he said, '– it's a fitting name for a hero…'

'Well, I'm not really sure what I did…'

'Well, you're a hero to us and this department, young man. Come and show your colleagues that you are OK.' As he was speaking, Aristotle put an arm around Hercules' shoulders and ushered him towards Farouk's desk at the front of the balcony. From here they were visible to most of the wedge.

As they came into view a cheer went up that rippled out from section E across the department. There was even the sound of cheering and applause coming from far below in the lower tiers. Aristotle touched one of the screens of Farouk's desk and suddenly Hercules found himself looking at his own image, and that of Aristotle next to him and the rest of Section E91 Level 12 in the background, blown up to massive proportions on the information wall. The cheering and applause doubled.

The giant image of Aristotle on the screen beamed goodwill while Hercules managed a nervous smile and a self-conscious wave.

After the applause had rolled on for a little while Aristotle held up a hand for quiet.

'Ladies and Gentlemen,' he began, when the cheering had died down to the occasional whoop and whistle, 'today we have had a lucky escape. We are blessed that young Hercules here was on hand.' The cheering restarted, accompanied by the sound of drumming on desks and stamping feet. Aristotle allowed this to continue for a few more seconds before he held up his hands for quiet once again.

'I don't need to tell you all that we have never before suffered an attack of the intensity of the events of today. But I will tell you this: We shall dedicate a team to analysing the malicious code which breached our systems, and we shall create an antidote that ensures that the same thing never happens again. You can rest assured that a full investigation will be launched into how the perpetrator – or perpetrators – managed to breach the firewall.

'In the meantime, I urge you all to be particularly vigilant as you go about your work. Until we fully understand the scope of the attack, we have no way of knowing whether it will happen again. But at this moment in time, a great crisis has been averted. I am proud of the efforts of each and every one of you. Well done, team.'

The room erupted into applause. Aristotle put his arm around Hercules' shoulder once more and led him towards the back of the station.

'So…how long have you been with us?'

'Er, it's my first day actually.'

'Your first day? Incredible, absolutely incredible,' Aristotle turned to Newton, who had been waiting by the door. 'Hear that, Isaac? It's the boy's first day here, and he managed to find a back door into a diabolical virus. Absolutely incredible, I say.'

'You've served all of us very well,' said Newton, bowing deeply.

Hercules felt embarrassed. Two of the greatest minds of science saying such flattering things to him when he himself still didn't really understand what had happened.

'It was probably beginner's luck,' he ventured.

Aristotle looked at Newton and they both laughed. He then turned to Hercules and his face became very serious. 'However you did it, you managed something that the rest of us were unable to achieve at the time. You have done very well: very well indeed. If you ever need anything, you just drop by the Guardians' Department and look me up, you hear?'

'Yes, thank you.'

'Thank *you*, young man. Thank *you*.' Aristotle shook Hercules warmly by the hand once more. Then he turned to his companion. 'Come on, Isaac, we must go and start to try to get to the bottom of this.'

Newton opened the door and held it for Aristotle. 'Don't forget,' said Aristotle, turning to Hercules for a last time. 'Anything. Any time.'

* * *

Mr John snapped open the clasps on either side of the large wooden box and removed the lid. He reached inside.

'Allow me to introduce you to…Schrödinger.'

He gently lifted a small, fluffy and, needless to say, ridiculously cute white kitten from within. Schrödinger mewed softly, blinked his saucer-like blue eyes and yawned a big kitten yawn.

'Aah, he's lovely,' gushed Eugene. 'Can I hold him?'

'No, I think not. Schrödinger is here to help assist with our little experiment. I think for the moment it would be best to maintain a degree of – scientific detachment. I'm sure you will have plenty of opportunity to bond later – one way or another.'

He gently replaced the kitten back in the wooden box and turned his attention to the case. He slid it across the table-top and stood with his hands resting on the fastenings. He paused.

'I'm sure you gentlemen are familiar with the CP violation.'

The brief silence that followed contained the real answer. The members of the Aryan Defence Order/League/Front did not, how-ever, like to appear ignorant, particularly in front of the fancy-pants Mr John. They could have helped themselves achieve this by sticking to the maxim that it is better to be silent and be thought a fool than to open your mouth and confirm it. But Nick and Eugene were still riding high from their boss's earlier confirmation of their status as intellectual giants. They guessed. It is said that great minds think alike. Having a great deal in common in the way they thought, it was not that surprising that they guessed the same thing. It is also said that fools seldom differ.

'We were just talking about it before you came in, as it happens...'

'It's a bloody disgrace and I don't know how they get away with it.'

'A violation: an utter vio-bloody-lation of the sovereignty of our national borders. They shouldn't be allowed in the country in the first place.'

'What have they done now, the bastards?'

Maximilian Dumars had been watching Mr John's slowly raising eyebrow as this exchange progressed. It was time to try and rescue some dignity for the Aryan Defence Order/League/Front.

'Er, which *particular* aspect of the CP violation would you be referring to, Mr John?' he asked.

What a phoney, Legion thought to himself. Not a clue what I'm talking about, but he acts like he does. He couldn't help but feel a little admiration for the man.

'Please,' he said aloud, 'call me Lee. We are colleagues in the cause now, after all. The *particular* aspect of the CP violation I was referring to is the natural imbalance between matter and anti-matter that is observed in the Universe.'

His audience were not scientists. It would be fair to say that they were not, as a rule, given to any activities that might stimulate their mental capacities. They had very few interests between them beyond their shared moral outrage at the way they perceived immigration to be ruining the country. In this respect they were lucky that the tabloid press habitually fed them enough sensationalist stories to fuel their prejudices. The large print and pictures helped, too.

'When the Universe was created,' Mr John continued, 'it contained equal amounts of matter and anti-matter. You know what happens when matter and anti-matter collide?'

'They go bang, don't they?' Eugene had seen Angels and Demons at the cinema. He might not have been a great intellect, but he had an encyclopaedic knowledge of films that contained large explosions. He hadn't actually understood the plot, but he remembered the bang.

'Exactly. Which is precisely what should have happened with the equal quantities of matter and anti-matter formed in creation: they should have annihilated one another.' And then, Legion thought to himself, I would never have had to put up with humiliation at the hands of Mr Holier-than-thou. It wasn't a particularly good insult to level at the Son of Man and he knew it. There were cockroaches that were holier than Legion. There were amoebas with a better developed sense of morality.

'Somehow though,' he continued aloud, 'enough *matter* survived to create a universe that is, to all intents and purposes, almost entirely made of the stuff. This violation of what physicists refer to as CP symmetry underlies the creation of a universe composed predominantly of matter.'

'Oh, *that* CP violation,' said Eugene.

'Yeah,' Nick chipped in, 'we thought you meant the *other* one.'

Once again Mr John's eyebrow began its involuntary arch. He decided to let it slide. 'But the story doesn't end there. Observable matter only makes up about five per cent of all the energy in the universe.'

'What else can there be?' asked Maximilian Dumars, sceptically.

'The beauty of it is that no one really knows. Whatever it is, it is stuff that is not easily observed. For this reason, scientists have labelled it as "Dark Matter" and "Dark Energy". Their calculations suggest that some twenty-three per cent of the Universe is dark matter and the remaining seventy-odd per cent dark energy.

'But when I say no one really knows, I really mean the conventional body of scientific knowledge. This is not the same thing as everyone. The organisation I represent is hugely powerful, even if does operate somewhat – underground.'

It was time for some flattery.

'Organisations like ours have always had the best minds. This is why your group has been singled out. You may remember that although it was the Americans who won the race to the moon, they did so with the know-how of the Führer's rocket technicians. To-day the minds of the right will serve the soldiers of the right. Only today our focus is not the ability to journey into space but a voyage of discovery into the fundamentals of creation. Our scientists have found something beyond dark matter...'

Their faces were screwed up in concentration, but bless them, thought Legion, they still didn't have a clue what he was talking about. It didn't matter. This was all about the drama. He slid the releases on the case fasteners and the hasps snapped open. Slowly he opened the lid.

'Gentlemen, I give you...'

The case opened to reveal three cylindrical containers of progressively increasing size. Each of the containers was made of a black metal that was carved with patterns of strange glyphs and sigils. The smallest was the size of a matchbox. Next to it was a container the size of a coffee cup. The third was the size of a thermos flask. There was also a small lead box.

'...Dark Anti-Matter.'

In the eternal battle between Heaven and Hell, there are certain long-established rules of engagement. One of these regards letting good and evil struggle for supremacy in the world of human affairs without involving any of the extraordinary properties of materials found only in either supernatural location. It is generally accepted that the souls of humankind have enough of eternity to come to terms with these sorts of substances after their deaths. Whichever way this works out for them. Legion, however, was a demon and as such he had scant regard for rules of any kind, irrespective of how long established they were, and the parties involved. He had taken advantage of the chaos caused by his virus attack on Heaven to smuggle the Dark Anti-Matter out of Hell unnoticed.

'So what does it do then?' asked Maximilian Dumars. Each of the vials had a glass panel inlaid amongst the glyphs which acted as a window through which their contents could be viewed. A strange emptiness was visible. The cylinders appeared to contain less than nothing.

'Are you familiar with Heisenberg's uncertainty principle?' Legion knew full well that the honest answer was 'no'. He was also learning that the members of the Aryan Defence Order/League/Front shared some of his own personal issues with honesty.

'That Heisenberg,' said Nick, adjusting his spectacles, 'he can never make up his mind. What *is* he like?'

'Heisenberg's uncertainty principle concerns the apparently contradictory properties of certain fundamental particles. It started with the observation that it is possible to determine either the position or velocity – that is speed and direction of travel – of a particle but not both simultaneously. The principle extended into other areas of subatomic physics. For example, in certain circumstances light appears to behave as a particle, and yet in other experiments it displays properties which would be best explained if it was a wave. Obviously waves and particles are completely different entities.'

'Obviously,' all three members of the Aryan Defence Order/League/Front chimed in unison. It had to be said for them; they did have a lot of front.

'This is where our little furry friend comes in,' said Mr John. On cue, a small fluffy head appeared over the edge of the wooden box. Mr John gave the kitten a friendly tickle behind the ears. 'To investigate this apparent duality in nature, Schrödinger proposed what he would have called a Gedankenexperiment – a thought experiment.'

'Wow! That's one clever kitten.'

'He speaks foreign as well.'

'The Schrödinger that I was referring to,' explained Mr John, patiently, 'was an Austrian physicist. This kitten is named in his honour. More pertinently to our immediate situation, our little feline friend is going to assist our own more practical experiment.'

'Oh.'

'Schrödinger reasoned that if particles displayed duality in their nature, then the things that were made of these particles would be subject to the same duality. This would naturally include all living things. So in Schrödinger's original thought experiment an imaginary cat was placed in an imaginary box with an imaginary vial of poisonous gas. A small amount of radioactive material was also placed in the box. Above the vial of poisonous gas was a hammer linked to a radiation detector. If the radioactive material decayed then the detector would release a lever, causing the hammer to drop, smashing the vial and killing the cat. The radioactive material had a decay rate that would involve one particle decaying, on average, every hour. A single particle of radioactive decay would be enough to trigger the Geiger counter and a potential unfortunate sequence of events for the imaginary cat.

'Schrodinger stated that after the cat had been in the box for about an hour, after which time there was a statistical likelihood that a particle had decayed and the poison been released, there were two possible states that the cat could occupy – dead and alive. Without opening the box, given the duality of the nature of the particles from which the cat was made, the cat must exist as *both* a live cat and a dead cat. Only when the box was opened would the act of observation collapse reality into one or other state.'

'Two simultaneous states of existence...' mused Maximilian Dumars, 'I've never heard such far-fetched nonsense.'

'If it was a *thought* experiment,' Eugene said, very slowly picking his way from one word to the next as his brain completed some kind of mental dot to dot, 'then he could have just *thought* there was an alive cat and a dead cat at the same time. I mean, sometimes I dream I'm a potato and cook myself as chips.'

Nick and Maximilian Dumars both looked in mild surprise at their colleague.

'An excellent point, Eugene,' said Mr John.

Nick and Maximilian Dumars both looked with considerably greater surprise at Mr John.

'I myself have never found the idea of a thought experiment particularly satisfactory.'

'You're not going to put the kitten in that box with some poisonous gas?' Eugene sounded worried now.

'Hell, no…' Mr John watched as Eugene visibly relaxed. 'I thought I'd use some of the Dark Anti-Matter. Don't worry, Eugene. There's a perfectly good chance that this will be quite uneventful.' Mr John took the smallest of the Dark Anti-Matter vials from his case and placed it in the wooden box with Schrödinger. 'Besides,' he continued, 'we're not *entirely* sure what to expect. There is a principle of *uncertainty* at stake here, don't forget.'

He then took the small lead box from his case. 'This box contains a tiny quantity of a radioactive material called francium. I'm afraid I don't have the patience to wait around for an hour for a particle to decay, so I've chosen something that's a bit more un-stable. Francium has a half-life of twenty-two minutes.' He looked at the blank faces staring at him. 'This means that after twenty-two minutes the amount of radioactive material has halved. What with getting here and all the talking we've been doing, there can't be very much left at all. But we should be able to expect that there will be a decay event within, say, a couple of minutes.

'As you can see, I've rigged the Geiger counter and hammer as described in Schrödinger's thought experiment and I can tell you that it was certainly a lot easier for him to imagine than it was for me to build. But it's done. So let's see what happens.'

Before Eugene and Nick could protest he had placed the lead box in the wooden case with the kitten and the vial of Dark Anti-Matter and, in a swift movement, removed the lid of the lead box and replaced the lid of the wooden one, on which he snapped the fasteners shut.

'This box is insulated against background radiation, so the Dark Anti-Matter will only be released if the radioactive material within the box decays.'

'I don't wish to be rude, but...' said Maximilian Dumars.

But that is the universally accepted way of signalling that you are going to be, thought Legion to himself. A bit like pre-empting a racist comment by saying 'I'm not a racist, but...' – although this was something that Maximilian Dumars would never have said. He was proud he was a racist.

'...but is there a purpose to all this? You said you were going to give us a demonstration. So far all you've done is spout a load of dubious – I hesitate to use the word – *facts* about imaginary and seemingly unprovable concepts. I thought we were here to change the world.'

'And so we are,' replied Mr John in his most honeyed tones. 'But please, indulge me a little. I have gone to some trouble to arrange this little *daemonstration* for you, so humour me, please. The kitten has been in the box a short while now. Tell me, bearing in mind what I have told you: is Schrödinger dead or alive?'

'Well, according to what you have just said, he is both?'

'And do you really *believe* that? How about you, Eugene? Nicholas? Do you really *believe* that our little Schrödinger is currently dead *and* alive? He is in the box with some radioactive material primed to release a substance that might do God knows what to him and you *really think* that he exists in two states?'

They all looked at the box.

'Let's look inside,' said Eugene.

'I'm afraid we can't do that,' said Mr John. 'That goes against the rules of the experiment. It will collapse the potential states of existence into one or other reality. I'm asking you what you *believe*? Without looking in the box.'

'Well...' began Nick.

They all looked at the box again.

'...given that there is a hammer that has to break the vial if it is released, we would have heard the sound of it dropping if Schrödinger were dead.'

'Very good!' said Mr John. 'But I'm afraid the box is quite adequately soundproofed and when I checked the hammer mechanism I found that from the outside it is quite noiseless.'

They all looked at the box again.

'Anyone else?' asked Mr John. 'That radioactive material is quite unstable, you know. Of course, it may have all decayed before I put it in the case...'

They all stared at the box.

A deadly hush descended on the hall as each of the members of the Aryan Defence Order/League/Front wrestled with the concept of Schrödinger's fate. Strangely they were all perfectly unmoved by the human cost of Hitler's final solution, but the threatened existence of one tiny kitten...

Through the silence the ticking of Mr John's expensive wristwatch became evident. As they each puzzled their brains, the ticking seemed to grow louder and more insistent. Each and every one of the seconds that passed carried with it an opportunity for the radioactive decay that would trigger the Geiger counter that would release the hammer that would smash the vial that would...

'We've got to have a look!' said Eugene, pressing forward.

'Ah, ah, ah,' said Mr John holding out an arm to stop him reaching forward for the case. 'This is a *thought* experiment, Eugene; admittedly one that I have brought to life for you. The kitten could be alive, dead or both. I want you to tell me, what do you *believe?*'

'I believe,' said Eugene slowly, '*thatwereallyreallyreallyneedtoget-thatkittenoutofthebox!*'

He lunged for the box.

The box exploded.

It was just the box which exploded: blown to shrapnel the size of dust in a cloud that billowed out in apparent slow motion. In the microsecond that followed the four observers could clearly make out a rather surprised looking kitten sitting in the centre of the cloud of wood dust that was unfurling like a fog.

Then the kitten exploded.

Rather than the dust particles to which the wood of the box had been reduced, the kitten was transformed into something altogether – wetter. For such a small animal there was a surprisingly large amount of it. And considering the near perfect sphere of the expanding dust cloud, it was strangely – directional. One moment there was a wide-eyed and bemused fluffy little kitten and in the very next Eugene, Nick and Maximilian Dumars were inundated in a red tsunami as though they had each been subject to an attack by a bucket of coloured paint. Oddly Mr John, who was standing between them, remained unspattered by even so much as a drop.

The other items from the box – Geiger counter, hammer, lead box and the vial itself – must also have been pulverised. As they wiped what had recently been Schrödinger from around their eyes, the members of the Aryan Defence Order/League/Front found themselves staring in what can be best described as, and quite justifiably was, shock. Shock at the empty tabletop before them that turned to disbelief as they simultaneously perceived the miniscule empty dot spinning at the epicentre of the recent explosion. Almost imperceptibly small, it would have gone unnoticed were it not for the fact that it drew the senses like iron filings to a magnet. It would be difficult to describe the spinning dot in terms of what it was, unless those terms could take into account the fact that it wasn't. The dot spinning before their eyes was the very absence of anything concrete or familiar.

As they watched it rotating, the closest particles of box dust started to get drawn into the vortex of its spin. The dot began to suck and draw at the trailing edges of dust. As the inner cloud began to get caught in the draw of the revolving mote it became apparent that it was exerting a force that opposed the expansive force of the original explosion. For a second, the dust cloud paused, just short of enveloping Mr John and his lab partners. Then, as more and more of its core began to get caught in the force of the inner cyclone it started to collapse back inwards. Like a three-dimensional plug-hole, the collapsing dust cloud was sucked into the void.

As if things could get any stranger, the force of the dark anti-particle then began to exert its effects on the liquid formerly known as Schrödinger. Even as they watched the diminishing dust cloud, Nick, Eugene and Maximilian Dumars began to experience the very strange sensation of being unsplashed by the fluid form of an ex-kitten. Viscous droplets began to join the spinning maelstrom, until they were all, for the most part, once more untainted. To the observers, what followed was similar to watching an inflated balloon deflating. If the balloon involved happens to be red, liquid, and spinning at about a thousand revolutions a second. Before their eyes, all that had been of the box, its contents and the small white kitten collapsed into the dot of nothingness which then vanished.

'I've always maintained that if physicists were to stick to physical experiment rather than simply allowing their minds to wander, there would be a lot less room for "uncertainty",' Mr John cheerfully interrupted the stunned silence. 'Well, Eugene,' he continued, 'you had your chance to bond with Schrödinger, but I'm sorry to say that it seems he didn't take to you.' Three open-jawed faces turned to him. Clearly there were many – albeit relatively simple – thoughts trying to compete for the processing power of their brains in an attempt to help the owners of said brains make some kind of sense of what they had just witnessed.

'What you have just observed,' it was no use letting them try to work it out for themselves, 'is the effects of a single particle of Dark Anti-Matter. That was all that the small vial contained. I think you will agree that it is quite a powerful discovery...' The Aryan Defence Order/League/Front was still, in varying degrees, stunned. Mr John knew how to bring them back into focus. '...and in the right hands, an extremely powerful weapon.'

It was just like flicking a switch. The lights instantly went on behind three pairs of eyes.

'We all know, Gentlemen, that this country needs cleansing. But what then? What of the hordes that will simply mass on the borders, looking for a way in to exploit our beloved society? And what about our brothers abroad. Gentlemen, you are not the *English* Defence Order. You are not the *British* Defence League. *You* have set your sights on a nobler goal. *You* are the *Aryan* Defence Order/League/Front.

'If we push immigrants out of these shores, we will be inflicting them on our European brothers. This would be doing half a job. Aryans should stand together. We should not only seek to cleanse these shores. We should cleanse all the homelands of Aryan people. We should cleanse – *Europe*.

'There is a groundswell of support for the Right. The time is ripe for action. You shall be the fulcrum about which the pendulum swings.'

'How *exactly* do we achieve this noble end?' asked Maximilian Dumars.

'Yeah,' said Eugene, his eyes glazed with a combination of what he'd seen and what he was imagining, 'what're we going to blow up?'

'Oh, there will be a chance for fireworks, Eugene, don't worry about that, but our plan as a whole requires a little more subtlety.

'As you Gentlemen are no doubt aware, the Even Bigger Hadron Collider has just come online at the CERN facility in Switzerland. It is an upgrade on their previous Large Hadron Collider and promises previously untold power for accelerating sub-atomic particles. I propose we carry out another experiment of our own.'

'Yeah,' said Nick pumping his fist.

'Yeah,' echoed Eugene.

'*What?*' Maximilian Dumars wasn't going to pretend. 'How on earth is that going to help us achieve anything?'

'We, or rather you, are going to hold the governments of Europe to ransom. You will go to CERN and hijack the Hadron Collider. Once you have the Dark Anti-Matter racing around in the accelerators, the governments of Europe will be forced to meet your demands.'

'Why do we need to go all the way to Switzerland to do stuff?' asked Eugene, earnestly. 'It sounds a bit foreign to me. Why can't we just stay here and make things go bang.'

'Really, you are on *fire* today, Eugene!' Mr John beamed. 'You are indeed correct; Switzerland does represent a certain amount of foreign. The reason you have to go there is quite simple. This Dark Anti-Matter is both extremely powerful, and extremely rare. The two containers I have hold the entire amount of it that our scientists have managed to isolate. The larger one will destroy a city and a good deal more besides. But if you succeed in getting it into the EBHC, the boost it will get from the accelerators will give it enough energy to vaporise – Europe. I should think that you can realise that the governments will have no alternative but to cede to your demands.'

'But won't it just blow up the accelerator?'

'Yeah, and us? 'Cos I don't want to be splashed like poor little Schrödinger was.'

'The core of the EBHC contains a near perfect vacuum. Particles are held away from the sides of the equipment by some very powerful magnets. Once the Dark Anti-Matter is in the collider you will be perfectly safe.'

'Exactly how are we going to get the stuff into the accelerator? None of us are physicists.' Maximilian Dumars was torn between the temptation of indescribable power that was offer and the almost obvious insanity of the mission. To just about anyone else on the planet, it would have been obvious that the mission was lunacy. Mr John had chosen his subjects very carefully indeed.

'You will meet our contact in Geneva,' reassured Mr John smoothly. 'You will be provided with everything you need to take control of enough of the facility to put the plan into action. All you need to do is get to the linear accelerator where the material can be introduced to the collider. The rest can be controlled by this.' He pulled a USB drive from his pocket. 'It contains all the programming sequences to control the collider once the anti-matter has been injected into the accelerator.'

'And why should anyone believe us? It can't be very widely known about, this Dark Anti-Matter of yours. How do we know that just getting the stuff into this collider thingy is going to be enough to have the governments of Europe trembling on their knees?'

'That is where the smaller of the two remaining vials comes in,' he had all the angles covered. 'You are quite right, Max. You will need to get their attention. The smaller vial contains a thousand particles of Dark Anti-Matter. You can imagine the effect it will have. It is enough to atomise a large building. I'm sure I can leave the choice of target for that to you. It'll give you a chance to – express yourselves.'

'And when they agree to our demands?'

'Why, then you will have the world at your feet. By the time the deadline for their complicity passes you will have the governments of Europe behind you. America will follow. Together, Gentlemen, we launch the New World Order from here.

'Or more precisely, Geneva... Your plane leaves at three.'

* * *

Steam filled the little bathroom. Asif washed himself thoroughly, pouring water over his head three times, letting it flow over his body. He then poured water three times over each shoulder, passing his hands over his body so that no part of it remained dry. He was preparing for his mission.

When he had finished washing, he towelled himself down and crossed the landing of the small, terraced house into his bedroom. His freshly laundered clothes were laid out neatly on the bed. Before he donned his shalwar kameez he put on a vest he had made himself especially for this journey. Sewn into the sides of the vest were two pockets – one on each side – tailored to house his two trained pigeons. He had spent the weeks before practicing carrying the birds around in it, getting them used to the strange environment and fine-tuning the design. Snug and warm close to his body, and unable to flap their wings, the birds had actually adapted remarkably well to this novel form of transport. He could successfully carry them around for most of the day without them getting restless. He wouldn't put them in the vest for now, though. He would leave that until the last moment: give them as much fresh air as possible before the ordeal that lay ahead.

He finished dressing and put on his kufi. Then he cast an eye over the rest of his kit that was laid out neatly on his bed. He had all the normal things that one might need for a week away: changes of clothes, a wash kit, passport and plane tickets. Also laid out on the bed were his pigeon harnesses and the homing hoods.

Asif had checked and rechecked the co-ordinate adjustment that he had programmed into the hoods at least a hundred times. The trial flight had been a success but on this trip there was no margin for error.

He carefully packed the items one by one into his small, wheeled suitcase.

Each item was meticulously folded and gently placed into his luggage, which was small enough to be taken onto the plane as hand baggage. Asif didn't want to be hanging around in airports waiting to be reunited with his equipment, and he certainly couldn't take the chance that he might arrive at his destination without it.

When he had finished packing, he picked up his case and stepped out of his bedroom onto the landing. He paused for a moment by the door to his parents' room. It was still locked from the outside, with the sliding bolt and padlock he himself had fitted. For a fleeting moment a feeling hit him that might even have been regret; but as soon as he felt it, he brushed it aside and started down the stairs. They had paid the price for his struggle. They would be rewarded in heaven.

Once his birds and luggage had been securely stowed in his van, he returned to the front door of what had been, for many years, his family home. He double locked the door. Whatever happened next, he knew he was never coming back. He didn't want his absence to invite people in, though. He sat in his van, reflecting on the journey that had brought him this far...

* * *

When the Sheik had first outlined his plans for this mission, Asif had begun to think that he might perhaps be crazy. Legion began to notice subtle indications in some of his responses that Asif might not be totally on board with his scheme.

Al Thi'b > What?? Are you crazy???

Sheik> Trust me.

Al Thi'b > But a place like that will be crawling with security!! It would be lunacy to even try!!!

Sheik> I have made preparations. I have an agent on the inside.

Al Thi'b > All the same - it is not you taking the risks!

Sheik> I trusted you with the pigeons. Now it is your turn to trust me. Remember, we are servants of a higher purpose.

Legion had to concentrate really hard while typing the last sentence. He was almost overwhelmed by the impulse to write "lower purpose". The temptation to do so very nearly got the better of all of his many personalities. As has been noted before; resisting temptation even for a single demon can be a devil of a job. Somehow, though they managed to resist the urge and stay in character. After all, they reminded their selves, it was important not to let the charade slip now. They had come too far…

* * *

The rain had slowed by the time Asif left the motorway near Gloucester in favour of the A roads that continued south towards Wiltshire. Asif found himself driving across Salisbury Plains under leaden skies. He was heading for Porton Down.

As home to the most sensitive and secretive research carried out by the British military, the facilities of Porton Down have long been surrounded in a mist of rumour and theories of conspiracy. Government ministers have gone so far as to say on record that they are not fully aware of everything that occurs at the establishment. If Ministers of State are not fully informed, then the chances of reliable facts coming into the public domain are slim indeed. Where stories have come to light, often many years after the events themselves took place – such as the tests of nerve agents on army volunteers in the nineteen-forties and 'fifties – they point to operations undertaken in circumstances of, at best, a certain degree of moral ambiguity.

For Legion, though, this truly was a blessing. Rumour and hearsay were some of his most valuable weapons. It has been said that ignorance is the sharpest tool the "Great Deceiver" has in his arsenal for Armageddon. It served Legion's purposes that Porton Down was an establishment where it seemed that almost any evil was possible. If government officials didn't know what *was* a part of official research, then they almost certainly didn't know what *wasn't* a part of that research, either. It was all very well that something was deniable on the grounds that you didn't know that it was going on, but this made it very difficult to deny with any confidence something that you didn't know *wasn't* going on.

As far as Asif was concerned, the fact that he was on a mission to steal a deadly virus from Porton Down meant that it had to have been produced there. It could only have come from this one place – the product of the satanic government of this country that sought to destroy his Muslim brothers and sisters. So when the virus was used to do just that, it could only have come from one source – there could only be one culprit. The way Asif saw things, once the culprit had been unmasked, the survivors of his faith would finally unite behind him and rise up together against the Infidel.

Legion knew, rather more practically, that the virus in question – the one that Asif was about to steal – was indeed the product of a satanic establishment; but when Legion referred to the great Satan, he had rather a different figure in mind than the mullahs who railed against the leaders of the West. The fact that it was not, strictly speaking, a product of Porton Down, was irrelevant. It was enough that it was to be *taken from* there.

* * *

Asif turned towards the sprawl of buildings that squatted on the rolling slopes of the down. Ahead, a manned military checkpoint controlled access to the facility beyond. He swallowed hard. There was nothing that he could do now that would not look suspicious, except for keep going. His mouth was dry, and the sound of his racing heart filled his ears. He exhaled hard a couple of times to try and calm down. He watched the speedometer of the car, urging himself to resist the temptation to slow below a normal approach.

As he rolled up to the security checkpoint he took a couple of deep breaths. Armed soldiers were milling around a small gate-house. He was already lowering his window as one of the military policeman approached.

The soldier gave him a dutiful acknowledgement.

'Pass, please, sir,' he said, holding out a hand.

Asif reached inside his jacket. He was scarcely breathing as he handed it to the MP. The policeman studied the pass and scanned it through a chip reader. He scrutinized Asif.

'Down from the ministry for the day, are we sir? Visiting the DSTL?'

'That's right,' replied Asif. To his brain his voice sounded loud and cracked. He was sure that the MP suspected something.

'And what is the purpose of your visit?'

Asif looked at the man. He turned around to watch as another soldier wheeled a contraption with an upward facing mirror around his car, sliding it under the vehicle at strategic points to check for bombs. His heart was racing again, and his throat was dry. He turned back to the policeman by his window.

'I'm s-sorry,' he fought to control his voice. 'I really don't think I'm allowed to tell you that.'

The soldier looked hard at him. Asif smiled feebly back. The soldier was a straightforward man. He'd never felt really comfortable in the company of the scientists that worked on the site. Ministry visitors were no better. To him they all seemed a bit too – complicated.

'No, I don't suppose you are,' he said at length, handing Asif back his pass. 'Your level of clearance is a bit above my pay grade to be honest, sir. Best I don't know. I'm not sure I'd be able to sleep at night if I did.'

Asif took the pass back from the policeman with a puzzled look. His fear had evaporated. He was now fighting the urge to burst out laughing.

'Yes,' he said solemnly as he slipped the pass back into his jacket pocket. 'Best you don't know.'

The soldier signalled to a colleague in the gatehouse and the red and white barrier blocking the route was raised. Asif closed his window and pulled forwards. As the gatehouse receded in his rear-view mirror he slapped the steering wheel in delight and began to grin broadly. The Sheik truly had been good to his word. The first stage of his mission was complete – he had made it onto the site. But he didn't allow himself to get carried away. Compared to what was to come, that was the easy bit.

Asif has been well briefed where to go. As he drove between the various laboratories and offices that made up the complex, he tried not to worry about the people he saw making their way between buildings. The Sheik had taken great pains to reassure him of the fact that due to the secretive nature of their work, workers at the facility were not encouraged to fraternize. He could use this to his advantage – it would be easy for a new face to pass unnoticed. Still, all too suddenly he found himself in front of a laboratory building that he had memorised from pictures. He swung into the car park outside and pulled to a standstill.

For a few moments, Asif sat in his car just looking at the building. This was it. This was where he would find the weapon that the infidels had developed, and he would use it against them. Actually, his plan was to use it against those of his own faith. This was a minor technicality. It would be a blow against the kuffar: it would unite his religion against the West. The unknowing sacrifice of the faithful was necessary for this jihad. Not only was it justified... It was right.

Asif reached down and checked his sock. He had fashioned a small garter in which nestled the three tiny containers that had been in a package he had received a couple of days before. He was ready. He stepped out of the car, not bothering to lock the doors behind him, and strode towards the lab.

Automatic doors slid open at Asif's approach, and he found himself in a modern, minimally furnished reception area. A stern-looking receptionist sitting behind a large, curved desk looked up as the doors slid closed. With a single glance she had taken in his un-habitual efforts at smartness and her look managed to convey the impression that though seated, *she* was actually looking *down* at him. Asif noted the look and it only served to fuel his determination. He strode purposefully forward. The receptionist raised a single, fiercely-plucked eyebrow.

'Yes,' she said brusquely, 'can I help you?'

Asif fished in his jacket pocket and pulled out his pass. He handed it to her. The receptionist passed it in front of a scanner on the desk and turned to a monitor screen to view her visitor's details. Her eyes flicked across the screen, she glanced up at Asif and then back down at the screen. Her expression changed completely.

'I'm so sorry, sir,' she flustered. 'I didn't mean to be rude. We don't usually get many visitors here, and when we do we tend to get a lot of notice. And if you don't mind me saying, sir, you're very young to have the level of clearance that you have.'

Asif pressed the advantage that her confusion gave him. 'It's Janice, isn't it?'

'Yes, sir.' The receptionist looked confused that her visitor should know her name. Asif silently thanked the Sheik's preparation.

'Well, Janice, you are right, I am young. But the level of clearance I have been granted is a consequence of the exceptional skills I possess, which make me an invaluable servant of my country. You would do well to respect that.'

'Yes, sir. Of course, sir,' Janice replied meekly. The stern demeanour that had greeted Asif when he walked in had vanished completely.

Asif stared hard at the receptionist. He was enjoying her discomfort and he was feeling pretty pleased with himself that so far he hadn't even had to tell an outright lie. That was about to change.

'My superiors suspect that there has been some leakage of secrets, possibly even sensitive material, from this laboratory. If even the smallest amount of the – special – products of a place like this were to fall into the wrong hands, it would represent the gravest of possible dangers to national security. I have been sent to try and source the leak.'

Janice looked at Asif. 'This all sounds like it should be a secret,' she said, suspicion creeping into her voice. 'Why are you telling me?'

'We've been watching you, Janice,' once more the receptionist looked nervous. 'We know you are not involved...' a wave of relief swept across Janice's face '...which is why you are going to help me.'

Janice put a hand to her chest. 'Me?' she sounded surprised. Asif was really shaking up her day.

'You *do* love your country, don't you Janice?'

'Yes, of course.'

'So you will help me, then?' But it wasn't really a question.

'I suppose…'

'I need a "yes".'

'Perhaps I should just check with my boss.'

'Janice,' Asif was now the stern one. 'I think you know that my security clearance far outstrips your boss. *You* have been cleared to assist in this operation. Only you. It is imperative that you do not communicate to anyone about what I have told you. Of course, I can always go back to my superiors and tell them that you would not assist me and the whole cost of this operation will be blown. Not to mention the threat to the nation. So I'll ask you one last time. Are you going to help me?'

'Yes.'

'Good. Our investigation has narrowed down the source of the leak to one of the laboratories on the lower basement level of this building. Someone on that floor is putting the safety of the country at risk. We have CCTV footage and computer logs, but there is nothing conclusive – so I need to do a sweep of the floor and see if I can find any evidence. What I need you to do is to keep an eye on anyone that works in that area and let me know if you spot anything suspicious: Anything at all.'

He handed her a plain business card with a phone number on it. 'The minute you see anything you think I should know about, call this number.'

Janice took the card. 'And right now?' she asked. 'What do you want me to do now?'

'Nothing,' said Asif, heading toward the door that marked the start of the restricted section of the building. 'Just act like I was never even here.'

He waved his pass in front of a receiver by the door and the door clicked unlocked. 'Can you do that?'

Janice nodded uncertainly.

'Just remember,' said Asif with one hand on the door handle, 'the security of the nation is depending on you.'

Janice nodded again, more resolutely.

'Good,' said Asif and he pushed through the door into the corridor beyond.

The door shut behind him and he paused for breath. So far, so good. But there was still a way to go. At least now he was in an area that could only be reached with security clearance. He was relying on anyone he met from now on assuming that, because he was there, he was supposed to be there.

At the end of the corridor there were lifts. Asif pressed the down button. A few seconds later there was a ping and the doors to one of the two lifts opened. Asif stepped inside and pressed the button for the lower basement. It wasn't difficult to know where he was going. Etched onto the control panel for the lift, next to the letters LB that indicated lower basement, was a symbol consisting of three interlinked, incomplete circles in a triangular arrangement on top of a fourth circle which sat in the centre of the symbol – the international warning for biohazards.

Asif had been given very precise instructions as to what his target was…

* * *

Sheik> The Ministry of Defence claims to be researching vaccines for deadly diseases, but in reality they have been using new genetic engineering techniques to develop a super virus.

Al Thi'b > How do you know all this?

Sheik> From the same contact who will ensure your safe passage through the facility.

Al Thi'b > What is this virus?

Sheik> The scientists have discovered that by blending the genes of different diseases, the virulence of even the most dangerous pathogens can be increased many times over. The most successful of these so far is a mix of Ebola, Chickenpox, and Flu. It has proved almost a hundred percent lethal in the live tests that have been carried out so far.

Al Thi'b > They've actually carried out live tests? On human subjects?

Sheik> The government has very little real concern for the old and the homeless. They are rarely missed.

Al Thi'b > Amazing. And all this time they send their soldiers to war to kill Muslim brothers based on imaginary weapons of mass destruction! They disgust me.

Al Thi'b > What are the effects of this virus?

Sheik> Messy.

Al Thi'b > ???

Sheik> Infection occurs very rapidly. Within minutes victims are sneezing and bleeding from any thin tissues - eyes, ears, nose, lips etc. Then the fingernails fall out. Shortly afterwards the victim develops a rash of incredibly itchy spots, which of course they cannot scratch. It's not clear whether they die from the assault on their immune system – or from extreme frustration.

Al Thi'b > It sounds diabolical.

Sheik> You have no idea. (Legion somehow resisted the urge to add a "LOL") *The virus can be inhaled or spread through contact with infected blood or blisters.*

Al Thi'b > They are monsters. Mecca will be destroyed.

Sheik> Indeed. But the survivors will be united.

Al Thi'b > Will there be any survivors?

Sheik> Not among the infected. But these super-viruses are not very stable - they cannot survive for very long outside of a human host – unless frozen or kept in a pressurized environment. If no new infections occur within half an hour, the virus will be dead. Once there are no more hosts for the virus to infect the area will soon become safe again. The danger zone should be restricted to the pilgrims in and around the Great Mosque, as long as that is where your pigeons deliver their payload. It is unlikely that anyone infected by the virus will be able to travel very far in the short period before they become too ill to move.

Al Thi'b > How will I transport the virus then?

Sheik> I will send you some special containers. They are built to withstand a high internal pressure, but they are small enough for your pigeons to carry. Don't worry, the samples you need are miniscule: tiny, but deadly.

Al Thi'b > And you are sure these containers are safe?

Sheik> Perfectly. But you will need to test that the virus is still viable before you proceed with the main mission. We know that the containers are safe, but we have not been able to test if the virus will still be viable – for obvious reasons. You will need to find a test subject that you can keep isolated for a few hours. Can this be arranged?

Al Thi'b >...

Sheik> Remember the cause.

Al Thi'b > I'll think of something. Where do I find the virus.

Sheik> It's in a lab on the lower basement level of the building. There is a bio-security cabinet in the level 4 lab where they keep the samples. The cultures are retrieved inside the cabinet by a computer-controlled robot.

You are looking for the Ebola x Chickenpox x Flu samples. They may be coded by abbreviation – "ECF" or something like that. I'm afraid it's the one thing we have not been able to find out – the way the viruses are coded on the database. What we do know is that there have been experiments with various strains which have different levels of effectiveness, which are categorised alphabetically. The one you want, the deadliest strain, is variant 'L'.

* * *

The lift doors slid open. Asif was at the end of a short and well-lit corridor. The brightness of the overhead lighting was accentuated by the white walls and pale grey floor. Ahead of him was a set of glass sliding doors, etched with a larger version of the biohazard logo. To one side was another digital card sensor. Above it a sign declared "Level 4 Bio-security Cleared Personnel Only". Asif held his pass to the sensor. The red-light LED turned green, and the doors slid open.

Asif stepped into the room. A peg rail ran around the walls of the room with several sets of clothing hanging from them. Asif had been given extensive briefings from the Sheik not only on the layout, but also the procedures of the lab.

He undressed, hanging his suit from one of the pegs and placing his shoes neatly on the bench below. Naked, but holding on to his three small containers and the gas canister he had been sent, he walked through to the next room, which was a shower-room. Here he scrubbed himself with the disinfectant under the hot jets of water. After his shower he dried and went through to the next room where there were more pegs, but also railings hanging from the ceiling. From the railings hung a number of blue, full personal-protection pressurised suits – looking to Asif like the macabre aftermath of a lynching of a clan of oversized smurfs. The pegs held sets of less extreme protective clothing – mostly white gowns and jump-suits. On a rack, pairs of sterile boots of various sizes were neatly arranged. There were also boxes of protective latex gloves, masks, goggles, and even boxes of sterile pants and socks. Asif dressed in one of the white jumpsuits, equipped himself with a facemask and goggles, double gloved his hands and stepped through yet another set of sliding doors into the corridor area beyond.

Like the exit from the lift, the corridor was brightly lit and light-coloured. Leading off the main corridor were a number different laboratory areas. Asif approached the first. The top half of the lab-oratory door was glass, and he could see through it. Through the window he could see two scientists, dressed in protective gear and seated at workstations. They were both watching a third scientist, dressed in the fully bio-secure blue personal protection suit, who was carrying out some kind of work in an isolation chamber that was visible through a window from this laboratory. Neither of the scientists noticed Asif as he slipped down the corridor outside.

Asif stopped to look through the next lab window. There were no people in this room. Instead the walls around the lab were stacked floor to ceiling with animal cages. A large macaque noticed Asif, banged on the wire front of the cage and screeched. Asif froze in shock. He stood rooted to the spot for a few seconds, scarcely breathing. Only when it became obvious that there was to be no human reaction to the noise of the monkey, he relaxed and hurried on.

The next door revealed an empty lab. Asif double-checked up and down the corridor, and slipped inside. The lab was dominated by a large glass and steel cabinet. A number of circular holes had been cut in pairs into the cabinet between chest and waist height. Each hole contained one of a pair of long gloves, through which a scientist working on the outside of the cabinet could manipulate materials within.

Asif peered inside. Beyond the reachable working space was a large metallic chest of drawers. In the corner was a robotic arm. At the side of the cabinet, below a label marked "Autoclave" was a small door. Beneath the autoclave, was a steel trolley on which a number of small trays containing specimen handling tools had been laid out. Asif carefully placed his three precious containers and his gas bottle on top of the tools in one of the trays.

The containers could be opened by unscrewing them along a join in the middle. This he did now, and laid the separated parts back on top of the tools. He took the tray to the autoclave, opened the door, and placed the tray inside. He pushed the single button on the autoclave, and a warning light came on as the device fired into life and began the sterilisation process.

The rest of the room was barely furnished, but there was a desk with a computer on it. Asif went over to it. He hit a key on the keyboard and the screen flickered to life. The screen displayed a single text entry field, accompanied by the label: "Search Catalogue".

Asif typed in "Ebola x Chickenpox x Flu" and clicked the mouse cursor on the "Go" button.

The mouse cursor changed to a whirling wheel graphic for a few seconds, and then turned back to the normal cursor arrow. Below the "Search Catalogue" box some text appeared. It read:

"Search Results for: *Ebola x Chickenpox x Flu.*

Sorry. No Matches"

Asif tried again, dropping the *xs* and searching for "Ebola Chickenpox Flu". The wheel whirred for a few seconds. It updated the search results but still been unable to find a match.

Then Asif remembered what the Sheik had said about a code. He tried again, searching for "ECF". Once more the wheel whirred for a few seconds, but again the computer returned with its apologetic failure.

A sudden thought struck Asif. "Flu" and "Chickenpox" were not very scientific terms. He wasn't sure about Ebola, but he thought that was probably the name of the virus as well as the disease. "Flu" – well, he knew that would be called "Influenza" by scientists. But what was the virus that caused chickenpox? Like most children, he had had the disease as a boy. He remembered the awful itchiness of the spots and his mother admonishing him for scratching, telling him he would be scarred for life if he continued to rub at the irritations on his face. She had even gone so far as to make him wear socks on his hands. He scratched around in the recesses of his memory. What *was* the virus called? He couldn't have come this far to fail now.

Varicella! There could almost have been a trumpet fanfare and fireworks. The word practically exploded in his brain. That was it, he was sure of it. That was the name of the virus that caused chickenpox - Varicella. He went back to the computer. In the search criteria he entered: "Ebola x Varicella x Influenza". The cursor whirred but still there were no matches.

Desperate now, he tried the code: "EVI" and clicked on "Go". The little wheel turned and turned. Asif thought the computer must have stopped working. He was just about to break down in frustration when the screen refreshed and instead of the search page, displayed a list of matching terms:

"Search Results for: *EVI* (12 Items returned)

    EVI-A
    EVI-B
    EVI–C..."

Asif scanned down the list:
        "EVI-G…"
And kept going:
        "EVI-L"

There it was! With his hand shaking with excitement, he hovered the cursor over the "EVI-L" text and clicked the mouse button. Behind him, in the cabinet, the robotic arm sprang to life. With a whirring of servos, it swung round to the chest of drawers at the back the cabinet. One of the drawers slid open apparently of its own volition, spewing forth icy vapour. The chest of drawers was in fact the freezer in which samples were kept. The robotic arm retrieved a small vial and swung towards the front of the cabinet, placing it on the bench in reach of the gloves. The drawer slid shut.

The autoclave had finished its cycle and a light by the internal door illuminated green. Asif slipped his hand into the glove nearest to the autoclave, opened the door, retrieved his items from within and placed them on the workspace.

He laid out the six halves of his three small canisters with some difficulty. Manipulating the tiny items with gloved hands through the glass wall of the cabinet was a tricky task. It took all of Asif's patience simply to prepare the workbench before him. He had spent the night before practicing joining the small parts together while wearing woollen gloves. This was much more difficult. Beads of sweat began to gather on his brow as his forehead furrowed with concentration. If simply laying out his tools was this difficult, he began to wonder how he was going to manage to transfer the virus.

He turned his attention to the vial. At least this was a manageable size. He unscrewed the lid and tipped the gently smoking container to view the contents. Inside was a kind of white powder. He placed the vial back on the bench and picked up a spatula in one hand and one half of one of the tiny containers in the other.

Holding the half canister over the vial so that should any spillages occur, they would fall back in, he scooped a tiny amount of powder with the spatula and carefully deposited the virus into the little half container. When this was done, he placed the spatula on the bench and picked up the matching half to the small container. He paused and steadied his breathing. Ever so carefully he brought the two halves together and screwed them tightly shut.

It was not easy, but his practice had paid off. He repeated the process with the other two canisters. A couple of minutes of deep concentration later, and he had all three laid out on the bench in front of him.

Each of his little containers had a screw fitting on one end that allowed attachment to the valve on the gas bottle. Asif had also practiced joining the canisters onto the gas hose while wearing his woollen gloves, until he felt that he had some degree of mastery over the operation. Even so what had proved awkward the previous evening now seemed almost impossible. Taking a deep breath, he tried to join the first. It was extremely fiddly just orientating the canister and the hose so that they lined up with one another. Slowly he brought his hands together. The canister and the hose were not quite perfectly aligned, and as he pushed the hose forwards his hand slipped slightly and the container dropped onto the workbench and rolled towards the back of the cabinet.

Asif cursed and stretched forward. It was just out of reach of his gloved arm. He took his other arm out of its glove and leaned sideways to try and extend his reach further into the cabinet, but it was no use. The little canister remained tantalisingly out of reach. He was sweating heavily now. Asif looked at the surgical tools laid out on the workbench. He picked up his spatula and stretched his arm forward again. Ever so carefully, so as not to push his target even further out of reach, he managed to manoeuvre the little container back to where he could pick it up. He sighed with relief.

Refocusing, he re-attempted the operation of joining the hose to the canister. This time he was successful. When he was sure that the connection was secure, he opened the valve and watched the needle on the pressure gauge creep up. One hundred and sixty atmospheres was what he had been told to fill the canisters to. He could scarcely believe the little container could withstand such force. But once more the Sheik had proved true to his word. As the needle touched the magic figure, Asif closed the gas tap.

Buoyed by his success, Asif managed to repeat the process of pressurizing the other two canisters without further incident. He scooped up the tools he had used and put them back into their tray, which he returned to the autoclave. At the other end of the cabinet there was a bath of disinfectant solution, which connected to another bath on the outside. The level of the liquid was such that there was no space for air to pass between the inside of the cabinet and the lab outside, but items could be placed in the bath on one side and retrieved from the other. Asif put his three little canisters into the interior bath and then removed his arms from the cabinet gloves and retrieved them via the exterior.

He had done it! He had his weapon. He went over to the computer. Next to the "EVI-L" virus entry on the screen was a list of actions. One of them was "Return to storage". Asif clicked on the button. The robotic arm swung into action. The freezer drawer slid open. The vial was replaced into the freezer, the drawer slid closed, and the robot arm returned to its sentry post. Asif hunted around the computer screen and found an option to "Return to Search". He selected this, and the screen displayed the search page it had first shown when he came into the lab. He swept the room with his eyes. There was no trace he had ever been there. Satisfied, clutching his three precious containers tightly in his hand, he hurried for the exit.

He slowed, carefully skirting the labs he had passed on the way in, but no one was alerted to his presence. He reached the inner changing room and stripped off his protective clothing, dumping it in a contaminated clothing bin. He rushed into the shower and scrubbed himself well. A few minutes later he was changing back into his own clothes and heading for the outer door of the lab.

The tension as Asif waited for the lift to come to the lower basement floor was almost unbearable. He was so close to success – but he was not yet home free.

There was a ping, and the lift doors slid open to reveal an immaculately dressed, tall blond man carrying a silver-topped cane. Asif almost started from shock. Following his conversation with Janice this was the first human he had come face to face with since gaining access to the lab. The blond stranger smiled and stepped forward. With an expansive sweep of his arm he gestured Asif into the lift. Asif managed a slightly puzzled 'Thanks' and stepped past the stranger. As the doors closed and the lift began its ascent, he almost sunk to his knees as the adrenalin surged through his system. Somehow he managed to hold it together.

'Nearly there,' he told himself.

The lift reached ground level. Asif swept into the corridor and waved his pass at the exit doors. They slid open. He breezed through the reception, turning towards Janice and motioning for her to call him, without breaking his stride. The building doors slid open, and he stepped into the fresh air with the sense of relief of a prisoner being released from jail.

* * *

On the lower basement level the blond gentleman approached the sliding doors of the Bio-Security Level 4 lab and stepped through them. They hadn't opened.

He continued through the outer changing room, but didn't un-dress. He passed through the shower room without scrubbing. Nor did he change into protective clothing in the inner changing room.

He sauntered down the corridor, nonchalantly twirling his cane. He passed the lab with the scientists. His shadow crossed the door-way to the lab, mirrored by a mask of panicked terror on the face of the scientist in the bio-suit. A hairline crack had suddenly appeared in his visor, and was spreading rapidly across the glass.

The visitor continued past the lab full of animals. The animals cowered in their cages.

He went into the room recently vacated by Asif. He looked around with an air of quiet satisfaction. He wandered up to the specimen cabinet and peered inside. A look of irritation flashed across his handsome features. Sitting all alone in the middle of the bench was a small gas bottle. A hand reached through the glass of the cabinet, picked up the gas bottle and tapered fingers closed around it. As the fingers clenched into a fist there was a flash of flame. When his fingers unfurled, the bottle had gone.

He withdrew his arm and turned his attention to the computer. With one of his elongated fingernails he entered "EVI" into the search box. When the results displayed he selected the "L" strain and watched with a look of mild amusement as the robotic arm performed its little dance to deposit the vial on the workbench. He walked back to the cabinet, once again passed his hand through the glass, and picked up the vial. There was a hiss as his fingers closed around the super-chilled metal.

He pulled his hand back, still holding the vial. He held up the little pot to examine it and a wicked smile spread across his lips. Then he turned on his heels, slipping the container into his pocket as he did so, and headed for the door. As he passed the computer he waved a hand in front of the screen. The search results for the twelve strains of EVI crumbled and vanished.

He made his way back towards the exit in much the same way as he had come in – strolling as if he were promenading on the seafront rather than negotiating passage through a potentially hazardous environment. The animals continued to cower. The scientists were busying themselves with an emergency decontamination procedure. He reached the lift and pressed the button. Shortly afterwards there was a ping and the lift doors slid open.

Legion stepped into the lift and selected a button that Asif would have sworn had not been there before. It was labelled, simply, "Down".

* * *

Asif snapped from his reverie. He turned the key in the ignition and the engine chugged into life and belched a black cloud of smoke from the exhaust.

He pulled away from the kerb. Asif was going to Mecca.

Or rather, his pigeons were.

* * *

After all the excitement of his first few hours in the department, Hercules was hoping that maybe now things would begin to settle down into some kind of routine.

He sat in his chair and swivelled a few full circles for fun. He felt he needed to do something that didn't involve any drama for a while. He spent a few minutes gazing at the information wall. It was true: it did get easier with practice. It also really helped not to be too attached to any of the things you were looking at. As soon as you fixed on a particular piece of information and really thought about it, the underlying detail would be exposed and expand at such an alarming rate it gave you vertigo. But if you just observed, at a high level – skimmed the facts with detachment – well; that felt like flying.

Hercules flew through a universe of data and marvelled at Creation.

Like the ambrosia and the nectar, though, there was only so much that he could take before he felt the urge for something a little plainer. He mentally alighted gracefully from the information wall and turned his attention to his desk.

Somewhere out there, there was probably another species on the verge of oblivion. He was a part of the team that would dignify each passing creation with a record of its existence. Hercules reflected to himself that were the Department a newspaper, his section would be the one handling the obituaries.

He tapped his first screen and called up the general status display. The map of earth appeared, along with a number in a box that now read eight million, seven hundred and sixty-three thousand, nine hundred and twenty. Hercules was staring idly at this figure wondering what to do next when he noticed something that sent a shiver through his core.

'Er, guys,' he said, his eyes not shifting from the screen. 'Er, guys,' he repeated, 'I really think you need to come and look at this.'

'What is it now?' said Keith with a grin. 'Have you just discovered the recipe for ambrosia?'

Keith, Farouk, Ruth and Vikram all gathered around Hercules' desk and looked at the screen that held him fixated. The grin instantly disappeared from Keith's face. There was the ghost of another number behind the species total, but this one digit was large enough to encompass the whole figure that currently held precedence in the status summary. It was still only faint, but strong enough to be clearly visible.

It said simply:

8,763,920

Six

'WHAT DO YOU THINK it means?' said Hercules, his eyes still fixed on the screen in front of him.

'I'm not sure,' replied Farouk, 'but whatever it is, it can't be good. Here, let me try something...' He tapped the second monitor on the desk. 'We don't usually dig around too much in others' parts of the system, but when needs must...' There was a delay. He turned to Hercules. 'It can take a bit of time to connect to the other networks – ah, here we go.'

A list of information formatted in a similar manner to the status box on Hercules' screen was displayed. Next to each species count was a thumbnail map. Each arrangement of lands and oceans was unique, and each box displayed its own unique counter. To Hercules, all were unfamiliar. But they also had a more worrying feature in common. As Farouk scrolled down the list it became apparent that each total was being shadowed by its own ominous, ghostly zero.

'What are all those maps?' asked Hercules.

'You didn't think Earth was the only planet that supports life, did you?' Keith replied with a question of his own.

'Well, it always seemed mathematically unlikely, I suppose. But how come there aren't any – well, aliens, I guess – how come there aren't any aliens here?' It certainly wasn't that Hercules thought it impossible that other planets supported life. So much had happened to him in such a short space of time that he was almost beyond being surprised any more. But if there *were* aliens, then it followed that they would more than likely be subject to the cycles of life and death, which in turn meant there must be some in Heaven. On balance, he thought, if you were going to bump into an alien anywhere, Heaven was as likely a place as any: if not more so.

'Departments tend to be run along planetary lines...' Keith explained.

'Well, it's clear from all this,' said Farouk, breaking off from scrolling through his list, and ignoring Keith completely, 'that whatever is going on, it's a threat to more than just life on Earth. It looks like all of Creation is being affected.'

'You don't mean?' Keith and Ruth shared a look of concern.

'Surely it can't be,' said Vikram, shaking his head from side to side.

'What?' said Hercules. 'Can't be what?'

Farouk looked at him with great seriousness. 'The End of Days, Hercules: an end to the Multiverse and everything in it!'

'But I thought the Universe was supposed to keep going for billions of years yet.'

'And so the Cloud was predicting until very recently. Something must have happened that's changed all that. I suspect someone's not playing by the rules.'

'There are rules?'

'Yes, between the forces of good and evil. It's all part of maintaining the cosmic balance.'

'So it's OK then. We report it, and leave it for the higher powers to deal with.'

'You may also remember that I told you that *they* are not always very responsive to the information we provide them.'

'But you also said we shouldn't interfere.'

Farouk leaned forward onto the desk and paused for a few seconds.

'I've seen too many things lost,' he said, 'witnessed too much destruction at the hand of mankind. Each time there was a group of people who sat around and thought there would be time to act, and before they could agree what to do, it was too late: the same story – endlessly repeating. Well, I will not stand by and let the same thing happen to the whole of Creation. Besides, if this is as serious as we suspect, it will mean the end for us too.'

'What, even Heaven will end?'

'Everything.'

'I'm with you, Farouk,' said Ruth.

'I also am enjoying my job,' said Vikram.

'Well, it *is* Heaven here,' said Keith. 'What about you Hercules?'

'What can *we* do?'

'I propose that we take advantage of the good impressions you've been making, dear boy,' said Farouk to Hercules. 'I suggest we go and pay a visit to the Guardians.'

* * *

Farouk and his crew left I.T. through the main doors. Hercules once again found himself in the timeless, empty surroundings that existed between the departments.

'So what exactly are the Guardians?' asked Hercules as they began to walk. 'I mean, you've told me that Aristotle is their leader and I know Newton is one of them, but how many more of them are there? And what do they do?'

'The Guardians basically represent the intellectual might behind the organisation of Heaven,' explained Farouk. 'You can probably appreciate something of the sheer scale on which things operate around here by now. Oh, before the Guardians, there was the Grand Design, of course. But, you see, the problem with grand designs of any sort is that they are very often painted with broad brush-strokes. It is principally the Guardians who have provided much of the detail.

'When they were alive, they were some of the finest minds ever to have inhabited Earth: Aristotle and Newton you've met, obviously, but Einstein, Darwin, Galileo, Jabir ibn Hayyan, da Vinci, the Curies – they're all in the Guardians Department now. They spend most of their time philosophizing and debating; "What is the sound of one wing flapping?" … "If a tree falls down in a forest and no one hears it, does that mean everyone's dead?" … And then there's the big one, of course…" What is the meaning of death?" Sometimes they perform experiments. Basically they do pretty much what they used when they were alive. Habits of a lifetime, I suppose.

'But when there is a big organizational challenge – like the circumstances that led to the building of APE, and the subsequent upgrades to develop the Cloud – well, the Guardians are nearly always involved in one way or another.'

'So do they have anything to do with the process of maintaining the cosmic balance that you talked about before?'

'Not as such, no. That's really the realm of the angels – and the Boss, obviously. The trouble with the angels, as I see it, is that while they are in fairness often very nice, not ever having been human themselves, they quite often go about things with too much of an air of detachment – well, to my mind, anyway.'

'Yeah sometimes they give the impression that our concerns are all a bit beneath them,' Keith chipped in. 'I mean, they *can* fly and all, so in a way I suppose we often *are* beneath them…'

'I find that often they only really light up when they're talking about the great celestial battles of the past and future,' added Ruth.

'It makes me wonder if to them we aren't all just a part of a great big game.'

'For me it's slightly different,' said Vikram. 'As a Hindu I was long used to the ideas of gods and demons fighting their battles and going about their business in the heavens, for mortals to be swept along in the tides of their actions. My moment of enlightenment came when I realised that whatever it is that *they* do, the responsibility for how *I* respond rests entirely within my own hands.'

'Which neatly sums up our situation,' nodded Farouk. 'If we can't rely on the angels to sort this out, we're going to have to try and do something about it ourselves.'

'Like what?'

'Well, that is where I'm hoping the Guardians will be able to be of some assistance. Ah – here we are.'

In front of them loomed the familiar format of departmental entrances, with two large doors above which a sign bore the legend "Guardians". One of the idiosyncrasies of heaven, Hercules was beginning to notice, was that the distance between departments was uncannily matched to the length of the conversation that took place while journeying between them. It was no doubt, he reasoned, one of the unique properties peculiar to the infinite singularity.

'One thing before we go in,' said Hercules.

'Yes, what is it?' asked Farouk.

'Won't we need some kind of evidence? I mean all of this is a bit much to take on our word. Shouldn't we have brought some kind of report to show them?'

'Don't worry. The Guardians are big fans of gadgets. It was they that pretty much built the I.T. systems from scratch, don't forget. Most of them have got Tablets, if they haven't invented something newer. They're all connected to the Cloud. Don't worry about evidence, dear boy. They will be able to access everything we've seen.'

'Ah – OK.'

'Right: Any more questions? Anybody? It's important that you all know what you're letting yourselves in for and if you come with me, you do so of your own free will. We may be about to seriously ruffle some feathers.'

'We're right behind you,' said Ruth.

'One hundred per cent,' said Keith.

'I also am with you,' added Vikram.

'Hercules?'

'It doesn't really sound like we've any alternative. I'm in.'

'Good,' said Farouk. 'Let's do this.' And with that he pushed on one of the large doors and led the group through and into the domain of the Guardians.

Hercules had more or less given up setting any kind of expectation as to what he would encounter next. So it was pleasant, but not really a surprise, to discover that the Guardian's Department was a large and sunny park.

There were paths and lawns, trees and benches and a large boating lake that was fed and drained by a gently flowing river. Some people were strolling along the paths, others playing games. Some were sitting around chatting, while yet others were simply lying on the grass and gazing into space. It looked much like any urban park on a warm summer's day: if on that particular warm summer's day all of the visitors to the park had attended in the attire of different nations, from different periods in history.

There were also the sheds. Dotted here and there among the trees were countless garden sheds. Some large, some small, but all somehow unified in conveying an air of dignified purpose.

A Frisbee landed at their feet. A moustachioed gentleman with a shock of grey hair, who was dressed in a sweater, a pair of grey flannel trousers and slippers with no socks came jogging over. He stooped to pick up his Frisbee and then paused to take in the I.T. crowd.

'I'm sorry,' he began. 'Can I help you? You're not from this department, are you?'

'Er, no, that's right; we've come to see Aristotle.'

'And you are?'

'We're from the I.T. Department,' said Farouk. 'I'm Farouk. And this is Ruth, Keith, Vikram and Hercules.'

'Aristotle said we should come and see him if we ever needed any help,' added Hercules.

'Ach ya, Hercules,' said the Guardian, 'the saviour of the Cloud. Your reputation precedes you, young man.' He gave a low bow.

'I think I was just lucky, really,' said Hercules, blushing slightly. 'Anyway, can you tell us where we can find Aristotle, please? We need his help with something, and it really is quite important that we see him as soon as possible.'

'Of course, I quite understand. Let's see. I'm fairly sure that there is a debate taking place at the theatre about now. Aristotle wanted to test some theories about the recent attack, so that's probably the best place to start. I was thinking of wandering over there myself as luck would have it. Come along, I'll take you there myself.'

Their guide waved to a couple of others of the Guardians with whom he had been playing his game of Frisbee. He called over to them: 'Neils! Max! I'm going to head over to the theatre. There are some friends of Aristotle's here and we're going to go and see if we can find him. Do you vant to come?'

'That's alright, Albert! You go on,' one of the others called back. 'But leave us the Frisbee if you're going.'

Albert Einstein looked down absent-mindedly at the Frisbee in his hands. 'Ach ya, of course, the Frisbee,' he said, and with a skilful flick of the wrist he sent it in a graceful arc across the lawn where Niels Bohr leapt like a salmon to pluck it from the air.

'Ya, Ya. Very educational, the flight of a Frisbee,' he said to no one in particular. 'Now tell me, young man,' he turned to Hercules as he began to stroll off across the lawn, motioning to the gang to follow him, 'how does a new arrival go about hacking a demonic virus?'

'Well, I think I was feeling a bit – well I'd call it homesick but I'm not sure if that is appropriate. This is my home now, after all.'

'Ya, ya – but it has not been so for very long, and it does take time to adjust. Sigmund often refers to the phenomena in new arrivals. He calls it "life-sickness". Not only is it quite common, you can be reassured that it never seems to last very long. People soon adjust. But this is very interesting; how did your life-sickness help, do you think?'

'Well, I wanted a way out, and I guess something in my subconscious created a door, but then I realised a way out was no good and that I needed a way into the virus program, and I'd heard the phrase back-door before... and the next thing I knew, there I was stood outside my house. Only it wasn't my house. But because it was like my house I was able to get in because I knew where I keep – sorry used to keep – the key. And because I was inside I was able to let the others in. And they took it from there really... I'm sorry, am I babbling?' Hercules had more or less been able to cope with meeting Aristotle and Newton, but now he was recounting his day's events to Albert Einstein, he found himself more than a bit awestruck. If Einstein noticed this, he chose to ignore it.

'Not at all, this is very interesting. You should meet Sigmund. And Karl. They would be fascinated by your story. It is quite extraordinary that life-sickness should have such a strong effect on the subconscious soul so as to be able to create a portal into such a powerful piece of malicious code. Really... Fascinating... But that's enough of me picking your brains. Why don't you ask me a qvestion?'

'Wow!' Hercules thought to himself. It's not every day of your life, or even death for that matter, that someone like Albert Einstein gives you the opportunity to ask them a question. Here was one of the greatest minds ever. He didn't want to appear a fool: but there was nothing he could think to ask. He looked around desperately for inspiration. 'What are all the sheds for?' he blurted out.

'What a fine qvestion,' replied Albert. 'A qvestion based on observation. These are the best sorts of qvestions…Well, as you may have been told; this department is given over to some of the more inventive souls of humankind. The sheds are the beating heart of the department. There seems to be a Universal law that states that sheds act as a kind of magnifying lens for the creative output of an individual. It's actually a deeply fascinating area of metaphysics. I'm currently preparing a paper on this very subject in my own shed, as it happens. And to think, most people just use them to store lawnmowers.'

As they had been walking and talking they had come to the edge of a deep depression. The gently sloping sides of the hollow formed a large natural arena. The slopes of the descent had been carved into deep steps, creating a huge open-air Greek-style theatre of the sort Hercules had seen in travel brochures and on archaeology programs on the television. At regular intervals around the arena were stairways of smaller steps that provided an easier means of ascent and descent than the larger tiers.

Though not by any means full, there was a good crowd of people sitting on the steps of the lower levels. On the stage area were a few more figures. Hercules could make out Aristotle among them, distinctive even from a distance with his mop of hair, bushy beard, tunic and sandals. His dress was not unique amongst the debaters – it seemed that the theatre was a popular venue with the ancient Greek and Roman population of the Guardians' Department, although they by no means represented all the people who were there. To one side of the stage area stood a large, curved, brass horn on a stand.

They started to descend one of the stairways and Einstein began waving his arm in big sweeping arcs at the figures on the stage. One of them noticed him, and nudged Aristotle, who looked up. When he saw the group making their way down the auditorium a look of recognition crossed his face. He waved back and began to make his way up through the rows of the audience to meet them.

'Hello, Albert,' he said when they were within a few rows of one another. 'You appear to have met my friends from the I.T. department.'

They crossed the last rows that were separating them, and Aristotle proceeded to greet each of them with a warm, bear-like hug.

'So what news?' he asked. 'What brings you here to our little slice of Heaven? Nothing trivial, I hope, judging from the looks on all of your faces. For a team that has just averted a near catastrophe, I must say you are all looking extremely serious.'

'It seems it may be a case of out of the frying pan and into the fire, I'm afraid,' Farouk replied. 'Have you got a Tablet handy, Ari? There's something we need your advice on.'

Aristotle turned and called to a group sitting on the steps a few rows closer to the stage. One of the seated party got up and leant across to hand Aristotle the device. He tapped the screen.

'So what am I looking for?' he asked.

'Pull up a general status for species count on earth,' instructed Farouk.

Aristotle did as he was bid. A frown crossed his face. 'Oh dear,' he said. 'That is rather sad.'

'Now pull up the same report for all the other life-supporting planets,' urged Hercules.

The list appeared on the screen. To the members of the I.T. team crowding around the tablet it was apparent that in all the status boxes the species counts had become a margin of a shade paler, while the zeros had all taken on a proportionally darker tone.

'What?' said Aristotle in disbelief. 'All of them? You know what this could mean...?'

'The End of Days!' said the I.T. team in unison.

'Perhaps the DDoS attack was a diversion after all. You were right to come here. This is beyond serious.'

'What are you going to do?' asked Hercules.

'We must convene the council,' replied Aristotle. 'But while we're waiting for everyone to get here, we should see if we can uncover some of the facts behind this disturbing possibility for the future. At least for the moment it seems that we have some time on our side, though how much I couldn't say. Come on,' he said. 'Follow me.'

He led them down to the stage. The current debate was still in full flow. An earnest looking young man in the habit of a Franciscan friar was occupying centre stage and extolling the virtues of avoiding unnecessarily overcomplicated explanations for things. At least that's what Hercules guessed he was doing. He might have been a bit clearer if he had chosen to use simpler language, and fewer layers to his arguments.

'I'm sorry, William,' said Aristotle, striding into the centre of the stage. 'You'll have to excuse me, I'm afraid, but I'm going to have to stop you there. Something of the utmost importance has come to light. We must convene the council – immediately.'

The monk looked a bit crestfallen at having been interrupted, but then almost instantly cheered up. 'Can I blow the horn, then?' he asked eagerly.

'Please, be my guest, Brother Ockham.' Aristotle made a sweeping gesture with his arm towards the horn at the edge of the stage.

'Oh, goodie, I've always wanted to do this,' he said with a big grin to Hercules and his friends. He quickly crossed the stage towards the horn as though he was worried that someone might suddenly think better of letting have the responsibility. Carefully lifting the horn from its stand, he raised the instrument to his mouth, drew in a big breath that caused his chest to puff out, pursed his lips and blew. The sound that arose from the instrument was entirely disproportionate to its size and that of the friar blowing it. It sounded more like the fog-horn of a large ocean-going cruise ship than a brass trumpet. The natural acoustics of the theatre acted further to amplify the sound so that the very heavens rang.

The friar blew until his face went red. His eyes began to bulge, and his hue changed slowly from crimson to purple. Hercules thought he was going to burst. Eventually he could blow no more and spluttered to a halt. The note had been given a life of its own and continued to reverberate around the department. Eventually it slowly began to diminish in volume. When the last echoes had finally faded, Aristotle turned to the assembled crowd.

'Ladies and Gentlemen,' he began. Hercules realised that the shape of the arena also amplified the human voice. Speaking at a normal level, Aristotle's voice easily filled the theatre. 'Our friends from I.T. here,' he indicated towards Hercules and the others, 'have brought some very serious news to our attention. To save myself from repeating it all, I will save the exact explanation until the rest of our brothers and sisters have joined us. In the meantime, we could well use the time waiting for them to arrive in doing a little research. Please could I urge any of you who have a Tablet with you to search for any cosmic anomalies that may have occurred since the Cloud came under attack? I realise that it is unlikely that there will be any direct evidence. What we are looking for are hints and traces. I realise we could be talking in terms of needles in galactic sized haystacks, but I've no doubt that if anyone can find them, that person is among us. Now get cracking, we need results.'

Aristotle's announcement was met with a chorus of murmuring as Guardians huddled into groups around those with Tablets, and the effort of uncovering some kind of clue into the cause of the impending extinction of everything began.

'What do we do now?' asked Hercules.

'We wait,' replied Aristotle, 'until everyone's here. Once the trumpet has sounded, they're usually quite prompt. Look – people are arriving already.'

Sure enough, the rows of steps down to the stage were filling up as incoming Guardians took their seats. Still more were appearing around the edges of the theatre. After a short while the arena was packed, and the last stragglers were taking their seats in the upper rows. Aristotle addressed the gathering.

'Fellow Guardians,' he began, 'I have convened the council in response to news of the most serious nature that has been brought to us from the I.T. department. As you are all well aware, there was a recent diabolical attack on our computer systems. I am afraid to have to tell you that defeating this threat appears not to have brought about the end of our troubles. These good souls here have uncovered a prediction by the Cloud of the gravest concern. It seems that a *total* extinction event is one of our possible horizons.'

Aristotle paused for his message to sink in. To say his audience were a bright bunch would be an understatement of the obvious – like saying it would take a long time to count the grains of sand on a beach by hand, one by one. He didn't need to wait for them all to be on the same page. By the time he had finished speaking, most of them had finished the book. His problem was not that of getting his audience to understand the issues. Among so many geniuses, there were a large number of extremely well-developed egos involved; and that had been the case even before Sigmund Freud had turned up and started explaining his model of the psyche to them.

'So, we're talking the End of Days,' called out a voice from the auditorium. 'What is the life of a universe if not solitary, poor, nasty, brutish and short?'

'Oi, Hobbes! You said the same thing about the life of man,' another voice called out. 'I consider looseness with words no less of a defect than looseness of the bowels.'

'Brilliant, Calvin! And I suppose you are going to tell us that all of this was predestined…'

'Gentlemen,' interrupted Aristotle, 'the purpose of this council is to try to resolve the issue at hand, not antagonise one another. I should add at this point that while we were waiting for you all to arrive some of those who were present at the earlier debate have taken the opportunity to try and track down any recent cosmic anomalies. Has anyone found anything yet?'

There was some low murmuring, the sound of a lot of very intelligent people embarrassed at having been set a problem that they had not been able to crack easily. Then a voice spoke up.

'I'm not sure if this could be something…?'

'Yes, Erwin, speak up so that everyone can hear you.'

'Well, I've found out that a kitten disappeared.'

There were hoots of laughter from the assembled crowd.

Aristotle held up his hands for calm. 'I'm sorry, Erwin,' he said, 'I know we're in very vague territory, but I fail to understand the significance of a cat going missing.'

'That's precisely my point. It didn't go missing. It disappeared.' Any merriment that had existed moments before evaporated. 'It stopped being – but it didn't die. Look,' he held up his tablet screen. It was too small for any but the closest Guardians to see, but his evidence was clearly enough to win over these individuals and a wave of acceptance rippled out from there. 'Before the attack, here is the kitten's life track, but when we get power back to the Cloud – well, it just *isn't.*'

'But there isn't anything in the Cosmos that would cause this total removal of energy from the Universe,' said Albert. 'Not unless...'

'Unless what?' asked Hercules.

'The other side must be cheating! They must have used the cover of the virus attack to smuggle some un-fundamental particles out of Hell,' explained Albert. 'The rules of engagement strictly prohibit such behaviour. That would be like us using ambrosia to solve world hunger. Granted, there was that one incident a long time ago with the manna, but this is an entirely different proposition: using Dark Unenergy to destroy the Universe!'

This time it was an excitable murmur that buzzed around the arena. It was all very well to follow the Divine Plan, if indeed there was one, but nobody was happy with the thought that this should allow the other side to cheat, and get away with it. These opinions soon found voices.

'We can't let them get away with that!'

'Injustice anywhere is a threat to justice everywhere!'

'We need to stop them!'

Aristotle spoke up again. 'Evil really does bring souls together. I believe we have a consensus view that we do not stand by and let this go unchallenged.'

There was a chorus of approval.

One of the Guardians rose to his feet, waving his fist. 'All that is necessary for evil to triumph is that good souls do nothing!' he cried.

There were more cheers.

'So what are our options?' asked Aristotle to the gathering. 'Erwin, do we have a location for the kitten before it disappeared? That might give us a starting point.'

'It looks like it was on a housing estate in the east of London.'

'Thank you. Clearly we can surmise, as Albert has explained, an agent – or agents – from the Other Side have managed to smuggle some un-fundamental material out of the Other Place. That would be the logical explanation for Schrödinger's kitten. It does seem unlikely that the loss of a single feline on its own is going to precipitate the End of Days, so I think we can assume that whatever they've been up to so far has only been a trial. This would suggest that they must have more dark material. The problem is that we do not know how much they have, or what they plan to do with it.'

A voice from the audience called out. 'If I know demons, they'll try and tempt a mortal soul to do their dirty work for them. It's all about corrupting souls with demons, isn't it?'

'Very true,' answered Aristotle, thoughtfully stroking his beard. 'This does give us a possible avenue for action. Against demons alone we would be fairly powerless without the help of angels, and it's really anyone's guess as to whether they would want to get involved. But against men, we may have a chance. What we really need, so to speak, is a body on the ground.'

'You're not suggesting ghostly apparitions, are you?' a voice called out.

'Heavens no, I believe we need a more physical presence.'

'How, exactly do we, the spirits of the dead, achieve that?'

'One of us will have to go back!'

This time there were gasps of incredulity as Aristotle announced his plan. Murmurings of 'You can't leave Heaven!' and 'It's not even possible!' reverberated around the arena. One Guardian, clad in the tunic of an ancient, arose from his seat on the steps. 'You cannot step into the same river twice,' he announced.

'Yes, Heraclitus, I am well aware of the metaphysical implications of what I am suggesting. But I would ask this question: can anyone propose an alternative?'

An expectant silence filled the arena. Each Guardian was expecting the next to come up with the brilliant solution that would provide an alternative to Aristotle's scheme. As the silence wore on, it became apparent that this was not going to happen. Eventually a voice piped up, 'So how do we go about getting a soul back into its body?'

'Well, as you all know, everything in space is moving relative to one another, so it is impossible to provide a definitive position for the stars and planets within the universe. This has always hampered the possibility of time travel. Were one to be able to travel back purely in the time dimension, one would arrive in a point of space where one's planet was yet to be. This would be something of an inconvenience, to say the least.'

'Ya, ya,' said Einstein, nodding, 'this is true.'

'Because everything in space is moving, absolute motion is impossible to detect,' continued Aristotle, 'even though I used to think differently. It is only possible to detect relative motion.'

'We do know all this,' called out a Guardian.

'I do apologise,' said Aristotle, 'I was trying to bring you on my train of thought. Anyway, all of what I have said, and many of you proved, in your day, holds true within the Universe. But we're in Heaven! This is an infinite singularity! We have something that we never had on Earth: we have a fixed point to measure from. With the computing power of the Cloud we can calculate the exact when *and* where to send our volunteer! Ideally it'll be someone we don't have to send too far back. We want someone who we can get as close to the timelines of whatever's going on now as possible, and as close as possible to the location of the vanishing kitten.'

A fresh round of murmuring broke out. Hercules noticed that a lot of the obviously more senior Guardians looked quite pleased to have been ruled out as candidate volunteers by Aristotle's criteria.

Among some of the more modern looking individuals there seemed to be some heated debates going on. Hercules turned to Farouk. 'No one seems very keen to go,' he observed. 'I would have thought that there would be someone who would leap at the chance. I mean, yes, there's the whole fighting baddies and possibly demons to worry about, but it's another chance at life. And it doesn't exactly look like the future is too rosy here, anyway.'

'There's something I'm guessing you don't know,' Farouk said. 'No one wants to go because they all know it's a one-way ticket. That's assuming the Cloud gets the calculations right of course. After the business with His son, the Boss got quite cross. He made a rule, and I'm afraid it's one of the ones He's very particular about. If you leave, you can't come back.'

'Even when you die – again, I mean? I assume that would happen eventually.'

'Certainly. Only *that* time it would be a downhill ride and an eternity of …' he shuddered. 'After having been in Heaven, I can't imagine that a soul would cope very well in Hell, even before the torment began.'

Aristotle too had been watching the developments in the crowd.

'Friends,' he appealed, 'happiness – nay the very future – depends on ourselves. Is there not one among us who will take up this challenge?'

The debating resumed frenetically as recent Guardians created lavish arguments amongst themselves as to why they would go if only they could but for the pressing reason that prevented them from doing so that was lost in their words but clear on their faces – 'I really, really, *really* don't want to.'

Suddenly a section of the audience fell silent, eyes turned to the stage. As surrounding Guardians noticed the spreading silence they too followed suit and turned their attention back to the centre of the arena.

Hercules had stepped forward.

'I'll do it,' he said. 'I'll go.'

* * *

Aristotle looked appraisingly at Hercules. 'You really are becoming quite the hero,' he said.

'I'm not sure about that,' Hercules replied.

'Men acquire a particular quality by constantly acting in a particular way,' said Aristotle. 'I've said it before, and I'll say it again. You become just by performing just actions, temperate by performing temperate actions – a hero by performing heroic actions.'

'It's just you said you needed someone who hasn't been here very long...' Hercules didn't feel particularly heroic, but it was clear if no one did anything they would all just end up sitting around waiting for the end. '...Someone close to the timeline of whatever is going on. I fit on that count, and I have been feeling a little – life-sick was the word Albert used. Anyway, because I've not been here so long it'll probably be easier for me to cope with not being in Heaven than someone who has gotten more used to it. There might be a bit of a problem though.'

'Oh yes?'

'Well I don't know exactly just how useful my old body will be. When we parted company, it was being mashed through the wheels of a juggernaut. I think it might be a bit of a mess, I'm afraid.'

'I see. Well as luck would have it I happen to know just the person who might be able to help us with that.'

'Oh. OK. There *was* one other thing.'

'Yes? What is it?'

'How *exactly* are you going to get me back?'

'Hercules, my young friend; you are surrounded by a collection of the finest minds ever to have lived. I think you can rest assured that you are in safe hands.' Aristotle turned slightly towards Einstein, and said in a low corner, out of the side of his mouth, so that Hercules very nearly didn't hear it 'We're going to need some kind of accelerator, right?'

Albert nodded almost imperceptibly and mouthed a silent 'Ya.'

Aristotle faced the congregation of Guardians. 'Ladies and Gentlemen, fellow Guardians, Friends. It would appear that young Hercules here is determined to make a habit of putting us to shame.' He smiled warmly at Hercules. 'He has bravely and selflessly agreed to undertake this mission.'

A cheer swept through the crowd. The newer Guardians applauded with that particular level of enthusiasm that can only be fuelled by utter relief.

'Obviously we need to arrange for transportation, and calculate the co-ordinates of his destination. This will require all of our efforts. Albert here will take charge of transportation. Since it was the I.T. department that brought this situation to our attention, I would like to ask Farouk and his friends to head up the effort of calculating the trajectory and co-ordinates of the destination. Farouk, would you be so kind?'

'It would be an honour.'

'Excellent! I ask each and every one of the rest of you to provide whatever assistance you feel is needed to make this undertaking a success. Our own futures demand that we do not fail.'

Roused by this speech, another cheer went up, but it soon turned into the sounds of Guardians rising from their seats and heading out of the arena to do what Guardians do best, which is solving problems. Einstein had gathered a group around him, and they were deep in discussion. A further group had engaged with Farouk and the members of the I.T. team.

Aristotle put an arm around Hercules's shoulders. 'Really this is a brave thing that you are doing,' he said. 'I am full of admiration. But I will not embarrass you further. We have the problem of your broken body to address. And I have something of my own which may be of use to you. Come on, I need to introduce you to a friend of mine.'

He led Hercules up the steps away from the stage and out of the theatre. They walked together through the park in silence. Gone was the air of gentle relaxation that had greeted them when they first arrived in the department. There were still groups of Guardians dotted around the place, but each carried with it an air of purpose; the determination to complete the part of the task to which it had been assigned.

The sheds, too, had been transformed. Before, they had simply been an apparently random collection of garden buildings. Each was now the bustling epicentre of its own project. There was the sound of a lot of hammering, and the occasional small explosion. Hercules derived a certain amount of comfort from the sudden outbreak of purposeful activity: from the explosions, less so.

'You are *sure* they know what they are doing?' he asked Aristotle.

'I've told you before, my young friend, that if it can be done, it can be done by the Guardians.'

Hercules wasn't sure that this actually answered his question.

'What if something goes wrong? I was told that the Cloud calculates *all* the possible answers to a problem. What if they choose the wrong one?'

'My dear fellow, what's the worst that can happen? It's not as if we can kill you?'

'No, but I could just end up floating around in space.'

'Well, I wouldn't worry too much about that one either. If you *do* find yourself floating around in space it will mean that we have failed, and *that* will almost certainly mean the end of the Universe. I would have thought that it will all be over in a couple of days, a week at most.'

'Thanks. I do hope that was not meant to be reassuring.'

'Even the gods enjoy a joke, Hercules.' There was a twinkle in Aristotle's eye. 'Anyway, if it's reassurance you want, we've come to the right man...'

They had reached a small shed that stood some way apart from the other buildings and more popular features of the park. From the outside it was slightly ramshackle, and the one window was boarded up from the inside. A sooty chimney poked through the roof. The door stood slightly ajar, but nothing was visible beyond the gloom of the interior.

'...he practically *invented* the bedside manner. Now where is he? Hippocrates? Hippocrates? Where are you, you old goat?'

Aristotle turned to Hercules. 'I'm afraid he can be a bit – erratic, sometimes. Hippocrates! I've got a patient for you.'

A head popped out from behind a nearby clump of bushes, like a startled rabbit. It had a bushy beard – similar to Aristotle – but the owner of this beard had let it grow somewhat unkempt. Bits of twig and the odd leaf were lodged in the tangled growth of facial hair. Beneath the bald dome of the head a pair of intelligent, but slightly wild-looking, eyes gleamed with excitement.

'A patient? For me? Do you know how long it's been?' In a flash, the look in the eyes changed from excitement to suspicion. 'Wait a minute, Aristotle,' Hippocrates said, 'this isn't one of your little "jokes" is it?'

'I'm deadly serious, my old friend; although the seriousness of his condition might be a test even for your considerable skills.'

The face visibly relaxed, and its owner stepped from behind the clump of bushes. Like Aristotle, he was dressed in a tunic and sandals, although his clothes looked like they had recently been dragged through a hedge, backwards; which fitted with the fact that they just had.

Hippocrates approached the pair of them. 'Is this the patient, then?' he asked, indicating towards Hercules. 'Really, you've no idea how long I've been waiting for this,' he said, rubbing his hands together, gleefully. 'Two millennia!'

He grabbed Hercules firmly but gently and put two fingers to his wrist. He looked up for a few seconds, counting in his head.

'No pulse,' he said, 'but then I wouldn't expect one!' He tipped Hercules head back and pulled the eyelids of his left eye wide apart.

'Not much of a call for the profession in Heaven, you see,' he switched to repeat the examination on the other eye. 'Everyone's so god-damned healthy all the time.' He pulled Hercules' mouth open and peered around inside.

'Tongue out,' he ordered. Hercules did as he was told.

'Say "Ah".'

Hercules said 'Aaah'.

Hippocrates gently closed Hercules' mouth. His shoulders sagged. 'You've tricked me again, Ari, haven't you?' he said. 'There's nothing wrong with him.'

'Well of course there's nothing wrong with *him*. *He*'s not the patient. Well, not directly, anyway…His body is.'

'How can that be possible? We haven't had dealings with the mortal plane since…since "the Ban" was imposed. I've had next to nothing to do ever since.'

'You could always join in the debates, you know, Hippocrates. It's not as if we have restrictions on the right to an opinion. But that's a different matter. The point is; we've just held a council in the light of certain grave news…'

'I heard the trumpet.'

'...Yes, well, if you'd have managed to turn up, you would know that the End of Days is threatened, and we suspect that agents of the Other Side are planning to use un-fundamental material to bring it about.'

'That's cheating!'

'Which is exactly the conclusion arrived at by the council; which in turn is why young Hercules here has volunteered to return to Earth and try to thwart their plans.'

'Volunteered, you say?' Hippocrates looked Hercules up and down. 'Does he know the consequences?'

'Indeed he does, which is what makes his actions all the braver. Not that we would ever send someone without them knowing what they were letting themselves in for. But we do have a little problem, which I'm hoping you can help us with. Hercules, perhaps you had better explain.'

'I think my mortal body might be a bit useless,' Hercules told Hippocrates. 'You see, I got run over by a lorry, and I think I left it in a bit of a mess.'

'Run over – that does sound rather careless of you. So how much damage are we talking?' Somewhat disconcertingly for Hercules, the subject of a potentially mangled corpse had cheered Hippocrates considerably.

'Well, I'm no medical expert,' replied Hercules, 'but I did hear a lot of snapping sounds...some loud squishing...a few pops...'

'Ahhh...broken bones...organ damage...plenty of haemorrhaging...probably both internal and external...Hmmm...I think I've got just thing for you.'

He pushed through the door to his shed and disappeared inside. They heard sounds as he struggled to remove the boarding from the window. There was a clatter, and Hippocrates reappeared at the door. He beckoned them in.

'Come in, come in,' he said.

Hercules and Aristotle stepped into the cramped confines of the interior of the shed. Light from the un-boarded window and open door revealed a bench that ran around three walls of the small building, above which were shelves packed with glass jars and bottles containing myriad different substances. Below the benches the space was filled with neatly labelled drawers. The bench surfaces were cluttered with an assortment of pestles and mortars, test-tubes, racks, alembics and other bizarre-looking instruments. Taking up most of the floor in the centre of the room was a shiny brass still.

'Now, let me see…It's here somewhere,' said Hippocrates, running his finger along one of the shelves of bottles. 'Ah, yes. Here we go.'

He gently drew a glass bottle down from the shelf and passed it to Hercules. Hercules took it carefully and held it up to examine the contents. It held a small amount of clear liquid, above which danced an iridescent flame.

'Thank you,' said Hercules. 'What is it?'

'It's a distillation of nectar,' explained Hippocrates. 'Absolutely marvellous stuff; cures just about anything and everything. I call it the "Holy Spirit".'

Hercules watched in fascination as the dancing flame changed from yellow to blue to red. 'And you're absolutely sure this will work?'

'You've heard of Lazarus?'

Hercules nodded. 'So what do I do with it? Do I drink it?'

'Oh heavens, no, don't do that. You'd be incapacitated for weeks,' replied Hippocrates, 'and I'm speaking from personal experience here. I drank some once and was out for months.' He scratched his head. 'It could have been years, actually. No, you don't need to drink it. Just sprinkle it on your, er – corpse; just before you step back into your body. That should do the trick.'

'It sounds pretty dangerous,' said Hercules.

Hippocrates grinned. 'Extreme remedies are very appropriate for extreme conditions,' he said in a manner that was a touch too enigmatic for Hercules' liking. Hippocrates put an arm around Hercules' shoulder.

'You really do have no idea how good it feels finally to be of some use after all this time,' he said as he ushered Hercules towards the door. 'This really is a tremendously brave thing that you are doing for all of us.'

When they were back outside the shed once more, he shook Hercules warmly by the hand. 'Really,' he said, with great earnestness, 'thank you, Hercules. Thank you. And the very best of luck!'

Buoyed by good humour from his newly rediscovered sense of purpose, Hippocrates then announced that he was off to see if he could be of any more help elsewhere. He strolled in the direction of the centre of the park, whistling to himself and picking twigs and the odd leaf from his beard as he went.

'Amazing,' said Aristotle as they watched the ancient doctor depart. 'He has lived as a virtual recluse for centuries. I think it's no exaggeration to say that your death has given him a completely new lease of afterlife. Now, come with me. I have a gift of my own for you which may well prove useful.'

After a short walk, they arrived at Aristotle's own shed. It was a neat pine construction, built on a slightly raised platform with a veranda at the front which could be reached from a small flight of steps. Aristotle bade Hercules have a seat and briefly disappeared inside. He soon returned and joined Hercules, sitting on the steps of the veranda and gazing out across the park. Around them Guardians were going about the business of preparing Hercules' transportation. Eventually Aristotle broke the silence.

'You know,' he said, 'when I was alive, the world, in all its infinite complexity, seemed a much simpler place than it does today. Don't get me wrong, I'm all for learning. Oh – I know I haven't been alive for a long, long time. But I hear things. The new arrivals always have some fancy new-fangled theory that they bring with them.

'When I was alive, I was certain that the earth stood motionless at the centre of the universe. It gave me a straightforward way to understand Creation... if we existed at the centre of it. Of course, all the clever souls that followed managed to show the flaws in my simple thinking. With what I know now it is difficult to understand why I ever really thought the Universe should revolve around humankind. Advance is brought about by people correcting the mistakes of others, after all, so in my defence I was the one making the mistakes that provided the platform for improvement. Nowadays we accept that the Universe is expanding, galaxies are whizzing apart from one another – movement between objects can only be described in relative terms.'

Aristotle produced something from the folds of his tunic. It was a glass sphere, about the size of a golf ball. Inside something was moving at such a speed that it was impossible to discern what it might be, the rapid spinning turning it into a blur. Together they watched the hypnotic motion within the transparent globe.

'It turns out, though,' said Aristotle brightly, 'that as much as I was wrong, I was also right. There is no fixed point in the Universe. This is true. But Heaven, it seems, *is* a fixed point. Even though it is also infinite, it is a single point of reference for the whole of the Universe.

'Just as earth has a magnetic field, so Heaven is subject to a similar phenomenon. Over the time I have spent here I have studied the properties of the belief field in Heaven extensively. Certain materials are more sensitive to it than others...in the same way that iron responds to magnetism on earth, but a piece of sandstone is unaffected.'

He held up his glass sphere. 'It's difficult to make out, but this contains a small angel feather. It's one of the most sensitive materials in the presence of a belief field – responsive to a fraction of a cred…that's the unit of measurement we have devised to assist our studies of the phenomenon. Of course, here in Heaven, the field is equally strong all around us; hence the blur. But if you take this device outside Heaven it would give you a fix on the infinite singularity. That's the theory, anyway. In the absence of any strong belief fields, it would allow absolute detection of motion by showing your movement relative to Heaven. For this reason, I call it the Motion Observable Relative to an Absolute Location Compass.'

Hercules joined the letters of together in his head. 'So it's a sort of M-O-R-A-L compass, then.'

Aristotle smiled. 'Yes, I suppose that is a bit less of a mouthful. I want you to have it, Hercules. I said that in the absence of a strong belief field it allows absolute motion to be detected. The feather is attracted to the divine and repelled by evil, you see. I'm guessing that right now on earth, the strongest field of evil that currently exists is being generated by the persons who are attempting to destroy Creation. You may not be able to get back here after you leave, but the M.O.R.A.L compass should be able to help you locate the perpetrators of whatever diabolical plot is afoot. Whichever way the compass is pointing – well, just head in the opposite direction.'

He passed Hercules the compass. Hercules watched the spinning blur. 'What am I going to do when I find them, Aristotle?' he asked.

'That's for you to work out. I'm afraid I can't tell you what you are going to encounter, and when the opportunity comes I won't be there to help you right this injustice. But I can give you this piece of advice: Anybody can become angry – that is easy; but to be angry with the right person and to the right degree and at the right time and for the right purpose and in the right way – that is not within everybody's power and is not easy. But looking on the bright side; if you fail – well, no one will have the chance to be cross with *you* for very long!'

* * *

The captain of the *Good Ship* regarded the assembled deck crew before him. He couldn't work out which he found more astonishing: the fact that bosun Boson had managed to persuade most of the deserting Filipinos to return to their posts, or the fact that he had complimented their numbers with some new crew members that meant that the *Good Ship* was now, once again, fully manned.

Not only that – the Filipinos, who had been at best antagonistic and at worst belligerent throughout the journey across the Med, now all seemed to be strangely acquiescent and well-behaved. And to round off the strangest day that the captain could remember, he had just been contacted by the port authorities who had informed him that the mistake with the paperwork had, in fact, been of their making and that the *Good Ship* was free to weigh anchor and proceed with her journey at her earliest convenience. Miracles, it seemed, *did* happen.

'Well, Boson,' said the captain, 'it appears you have managed to fulfil your part of the deal, so now it is up to me to fulfil mine: Welcome to the crew of the *Good Ship*, bosun.'

'Thank you, sir,' replied the newly appointed bosun. 'I promise you won't regret this, Captain Higgs.'

* * *

Farouk approached Einstein, who was busy overseeing the finishing touches to his transportation device.

'Albert, can I have a word?'

'Ya, what is it, Farouk?'

Farouk handed Einstein his tablet. His brow was creased into a frown. 'We've run and re-run the programme to get the co-ordinates,' he said, 'and the best accuracy we can get is this.'

Einstein examined the screen. There were a series of numbers. The worrying feature was that a set of constant digits was alternating with another set of numbers in a seemingly random sequence.

'I don't know if it's something to do with the virus attack…that the Cloud is not yet back up to full power, perhaps?' said Farouk.

'What do you estimate are the chances that these numbers are wrong?' asked Einstein.

'We've had an update on the extinction files. At the moment the chances of us having the right co-ordinates are about the same as the chances of the Universe being destroyed.'

Einstein looked at him with shared concern. 'Then none of us will have very much to worry about for very long.'

* * *

Aristotle and Hercules were still sitting on the steps outside his shed when a breathless Newton came jogging up.

'It's all ready,' he said. 'We've finished building the transport.'

'Well, young man,' said Aristotle turning to Hercules, 'I guess this is your cue. Are you quite sure you want to go through with this?'

'I don't see that there's any alternative, is there?'

'We'd better go and find out what my colleagues have prepared for you then. Lead on, Isaac!'

Newton led them back towards the centre of the park, past the sheds and boating lake until they came to a large expanse of lawn. Laid out around the perimeter of the lawn the Guardians had assembled some kind of monorail track. Every few inches, wires led from the track to headsets that were laid out neatly on the grass, both inside and outside the circuit. At one end of the circuit, two short spurs led off the main ring. One of the spurs of track was terminated in some hefty buffers. On the other sat a large florally-patterned armchair, which had been adapted to sit on the rail and fitted with a harness seat-belt.

Large numbers of Guardians were milling around, while others were sitting on the grass, waiting. Gathered by the armchair, Einstein was deep in conversation with some of the other Guardians. Farouk and the rest of the team from I.T. were with them. Newton led Hercules and Aristotle over.

'I see you've been busy, Albert,' said Aristotle as they approached, eyeing the construction with a look of bemused interest. 'Isaac says you're ready for launch.'

'Ya, ya,' replied Einstein. 'We have the co-ordinates, and we have the transport. All we need now is our volunteer.'

Hercules looked at the patterned armchair. It hardly looked like a bona-fide celestial transport system. He didn't know what he *had* expected, but he was fairly sure it *hadn't* involved chintz. 'How does it work?' he asked.

'Ach – still the enquiring mind,' beamed Einstein, happy to have a chance to explain his invention. 'We need to get you back to your exact point of death.'

'That bit was worrying me. Surely time has passed since then. I thought time travel was impossible. I thought the nature of the speed of light as a constant prevented it.'

'Very good,' smiled Einstein. 'But we are not of the physical world anymore, are we? You are, of course, right. Nothing can travel faster than the speed of light. Luckily for us, that is exactly what you are in terms of the material Universe, nothing...no thing. So, we can get you back,' he continued happily, 'but to do so, we need to get you to travel faster than the speed of *thought*.'

'How are you going to do that?'

'We will use a belief field to accelerate you. You see those headsets?'

Hercules nodded.

'Each on will be worn by a Guardian. They are wired up to allow the creds generated from each wearer to be fed into the circuit in qvick succession, which will push your transport around the circuit qvicker and qvicker until we have achieved thought speed – and beyond.'

'And then?'

'And then we send you smashing into the buffers!' Einstein smiled at the worried look on Hercules' face. 'No – I'm kidding! The buffers are to stop the chair. If our calculations are correct, when you break the thought barrier you should be catapulted through the dimensions back to within a few seconds of your death. Of course there will be a cost. All that you see in this park has grown from the beliefs of the Guardians. With the effort to send you back, some of the colour will go from our lives. We will lose some trees and flowers…some ducks from the pond…maybe a few sheds…But this is all nothing compared to the sacrifice you are making.'

Hercules wasn't too sure he liked the way everyone kept on going on about his "sacrifice". Nor was he going to question the "if" of the calculations being correct. He already knew what the answer would be.

'Don't worry about the accuracy of the co-ordinates, Hercules,' said Farouk, as if reading his mind. 'We've had the Cloud working on nothing else since the end of the council.'

'Thanks, Farouk, I know you won't let me down.' Farouk looked slightly embarrassed, but Hercules seemed not to notice.

Farouk gave Hercules a warm hug. 'Good luck, dear boy.'

'Good luck, Hercules,' Ruth, Keith and Vikram each bade Hercules farewell.

'Well, I guess this is it then,' he said.

'Ya, ya,' said Albert. 'Let's get you strapped in. Isaac, can you arrange our colleagues into position.'

As Newton went to organise the ranks of Guardians into their headsets, Hercules climbed into the armchair and was helped into the harness.

'Is the seatbelt strictly necessary?' he asked, as it was buckled across his lap.

'We don't want you to fall out before we get you up to speed,' came the reply. 'It would just mean that we had to start all over again. Now...any famous last words?'

'Is it too late for someone else to take my place?'

Aristotle and Einstein grinned at one another and together they pushed the armchair forward along the track. As it joined onto the main circuit, Hercules felt a gentle jolt as the power of propulsion came not from manual effort, but from the thought-field that was being generated by the rows of Guardians to either side. Instinctively, Hercules gripped the armrests of the chair.

The chair floated forward, and he began to relax. The sensation was not unpleasant, as he watched the rows of faces slipping by at a modest pace. He even had a chance to exchange waves with Hippocrates who he saw hooked up to a headset. But as he reached the end of the first circuit, the force pushing him forward began to increase noticeably. He could still make out the trees and green of the grass, but the Guardians gathered at trackside become no more than a blur. He felt himself being pushed down hard into the armchair. He gripped at the armrest once again. This time he could feel his fingers biting into the upholstery. His head was heavy on his neck; he couldn't move it to look around. As he travelled faster and faster his eyes became useless for feeding him any kind of information about his surroundings. Everything was a giddy blur. His ears roared with the space rushing past. The only thing he could feel was the metronomic passing of laps of the circuit. In his head he heard a tick for each lap that completed. At first as he sped forward, the laps ticked like seconds on a clock. As the number of laps increased the ticks came closer and closer together, like the sound of a table-tennis ball dropped onto a hard floor; well-spaced at first, but getting closer together until the sound merged into a continuous stream.

Hercules was squashed down into a single point of existence.

And then everything went black.

Seven

THE NEXT THING he knew, Hercules found himself looking at a familiar place from an unfamiliar vantage point. He was standing on the pavement alongside his habitual cycle route to work. It occurred to him that he couldn't remember ever having set foot on this spot, even though he had passed it on a near daily basis for the last five years.

He looked back down the road towards the traffic lights that were a stone's throw from his current position. The lights had just turned to green, and the traffic was flowing both ways along the thoroughfare. As he watched the cars slip by, he noticed a familiar figure pull up to the junction from the right on a familiar bicycle, wearing a familiar yellow cycling jacket. He heard the guttural thrum of the diesel engine of an HGV working though the low gears...

* * *

Moses Malone was tired. His mouth was dry from too many energy drinks and his eyeballs itched. His skin prickled and he really needed a shower. And a good sleep.

* * *

Hercules shuddered as he watched the truck smash into his former self. He winced as he witnessed body and bike spun through the tyres of the lorry like a rag doll in a washing machine, reliving each bone-crushing squish.

* * *

Moses slammed his foot to the floor, and, with a bang and a hiss, the air brakes kicked in. To the screeching of eighteen protesting tyres, thirty tonnes of haulage slewed to a stop in the road.

Moses flung the door open and raced to the rear of the lorry. As he rounded the back of the trailer, he skidded to a halt. His eyes followed the black trails of rubber snaking along the road, from his still-smoking tyres through the broken wreckage and twisted metal of what had once been a bicycle. As his brain untangled the scene before him, any colour left drained out of his haggard face and his limbs turned to lead.

In a daze, Moses retraced the tracks of the skid marks, oblivious to the bystanders. He felt like he was moving through treacle, the world silent yet roaring in his ears. The black marks changed to red as Moses approached the heap of crumpled rags lying in the road. Clammy sweat enveloped his face. Reality crashed through the trance that had carried his legs thus far as the rags revealed a bloodied and broken body, screaming its inertness.

'Jesus!' gasped Moses.

Then he was sick.

* * *

Hercules stood motionless on the side of the road as he observed his spirit rising up from the inert body. He watched in fascination as it hovered for a second above the remains of his mortal self before being catapulted into infinity through a point of light.

It was time for action.

He crossed to where the body lay, reaching, as he went, for the bottle in his pocket that Hippocrates had given him. He looked down at his crushed and bloody corpse, and at the vial with its many-hued dancing flame. He seriously hoped this was going to work; his body really was a total mess.

Ever so carefully, Hercules removed the stopper and sprinkled the contents over the inanimate carcass at his feet. As the liquid spread out, the body was engulfed in dancing, iridescent flames. Clutching the M.O.R.A.L compass in one hand, and the empty bottle of Holy Spirit in the other, the soul of Hercules Leek stepped back into his corpse.

* * *

Moses Malone finished retching and wiped his mouth on his sleeve. He forced himself to turn back to look once again at the devastation he had wrought. He fought the knots in his empty stomach as he gazed at the human road-kill that he had authored.

The body convulsed. Moses began to heave again.

The body sat up.

Moses Malone fainted.

* * *

Hercules Leek sat up. He looked down at his hands to see that he was still holding the empty bottle and the compass. He slid these into the only intact pocket of his cycling jacket and then gingerly felt his body and limbs with his fingers. He was gratified to discover that he encountered no pain. Much of his clothing was ripped to shreds, and he was covered in blood, but he was alive! And all in one piece.

He looked at the tangled wreck of his bike and then his gaze fell on the prone figure of the truck driver lying in the road. There, thought Hercules to himself, was an accident waiting to happen.

He pushed himself to his feet and walked over to where Moses lay unconscious on the tarmac. At first his steps were hesitant, as his brain recalibrated the unfamiliar effects of gravity on mass, but as he approached the prostrate figure his co-ordination rapidly returned. He squatted by the motionless trucker and slipped his arms under Moses' arms and across his chest. With a grunt he managed to overcome the body's inertia and dragged it to the pavement. He rolled Moses into the recovery position and collapsed, exhausted, on the kerb. At least now they were both out of the traffic.

A couple of cars that had been waiting at the traffic lights on the main road had witnessed the accident. The drivers had pulled over and were in the process of putting up warning triangles and directing the early morning vehicles around the wreckage in the road.

'Are you all right, mate?' a man with a dog on a lead asked Hercules. 'That was some tumble you took. You're lucky to be alive.'

One of the car drivers came jogging over. 'How badly are you hurt?' he asked. 'I've called an ambulance. It's on its way.'

'I really don't think that's necessary,' said Hercules. 'It's mostly superficial. I think he just fainted because he thought he'd hurt me worse than he had,' he said, indicating towards Moses. Hercules looked down at his arms. Beneath the caked blood there wasn't so much as a scratch. He hoped he could explain it away as a few bad grazes. He didn't have time for a lot of questions; he needed to get cleaned up and then try and work out how he was going to find the agents of the Other Side.

Beside him on the pavement, Moses Malone began to stir.

'Hello there,' said Hercules, 'you've decided to re-join the land of the living then?'

Under his ashen face, Moses Malone looked confused. 'I saw you lying in the road – I thought…I'd…killed you.'

'Just a few grazes,' said Hercules, cheerfully. 'I think my bike came off a bit worse though.'

They both looked at the twisted heap of metal and rubber that still lay in the road.

'It's a bloody miracle you survived,' said Moses. 'You must have a Guardian angel.'

'Something like that,' said Hercules with a wry smile. 'Listen, I'm OK – but actually I'm in a bit of a hurry. We can't leave that wreckage in the road, and it's not going to be very easy for me to move in that state. We couldn't put it in your cab, could we? And then maybe you could drop it at a tip for me? If you could do that, I don't see much point in waiting around for an ambulance. We're both OK, no real harm done; and they'll only want to get the police involved.'

Moses Malone couldn't believe his ears. A couple of minutes before he was facing the prospect of having caused a death, and now his victim was offering him the chance to drive away as if nothing had happened. Toby Slate drew a sigh of relief, too.

'Yes, of course I can do that,' they said in unison, eager to be on their way before Hercules could change his mind. Moses hauled himself to his feet. 'Well, if you're sure,' he said.

The pair of them gathered up the main parts of the wreck of Hercules' bike and piled them into the passenger side of the lorry's cab.

'Are we good, then?' asked Moses, keen to be on his way before the authorities became involved. 'I can't give you a lift anywhere, can I?'

'That's OK. I'll have to go home and get cleaned up, it's only a short walk from here.' Hercules shook the truck driver by the hand. 'See you – and drive safely.'

'After this…You've no idea.' Moses turned and climbed into the cab. The engine of the lorry rumbled into life and with a hiss as the brakes were released, it pulled off down the road.

Hercules watched the vehicle that had caused his death until it was once more just a part of the early morning traffic. He turned to the small crowd that had gathered on the pavement, including the drivers that had pulled over to help.

'It was very kind of you all to stop,' he said, 'but as you can see – I'm fine. A bit scruffy now perhaps, but OK. I'm quite sure that I don't need that ambulance, but thank you all for your concern. I'm running late for an appointment, so I really must go home to get cleaned up.'

The group gave a kind of collective shrug, and started to disperse. There was clearly going to be no more excitement here this morning. The drivers of the cars collected their warning triangles and returned to their vehicles. Hercules set off along the pavement.

As he reached the junction and turned right, he realised that one of the people from the crowd was walking alongside him. It was the man with the dog. Hercules now observed that he was scruffily dressed in shades of brown that had as much to do with deeply ingrained dirt as any fabric dying process. His grey beard was streaked brown with nicotine, and he wore a woolly beanie hat that seemed at odds with his ancient sports jacket. What he had taken to be a lead for the dog was actually a piece of string. The hound was just as scruffy as its master, but seemed to be a good-natured animal as it trotted along the pavement.

'That was some trick you pulled off there,' said the man.

'I beg your pardon?'

'Your accident,' said the stranger, 'I saw the whole thing. You were dead; at least if you weren't, by rights you very soon should be. You went under the tyres of that truck four times – I counted. I heard the pops and the crunches; and yet here you are, right as rain, as if nothing happened. Some kind of bleeding miracle to have survived that.'

As the man spoke, Hercules caught a faint but distinct whiff of alcohol. It was very early to have been drinking.

'I think you must be mistaken,' he said. 'Clearly I'm not that badly hurt; I just got knocked off my bike and skidded along the road a bit.'

'Rubbish!' said the man. 'Proper mangled, you were. And yet somehow here you stand now, talking rot to me. What's your secret?'

'Secret..? There is no secret. Look, there were other witnesses. How come you're the only one who thinks I should be dead?' He didn't know why he felt the need to justify himself to this stranger, but there was something that unnerved him about the abrupt frankness of his interrogation.

'People don't know what they see.' The man spat in the gutter. 'Most of 'em walk around half asleep at the best of times; they see what they can cope with, or their brain finds a way of telling them a story that doesn't upset them. Me – I'm different: I see what I see, and I speak as I find. And what I saw back there was a feller getting squished all flat while his bike got all smashed to pieces and yet now here I am talking to the same feller as if nothing happened. And before you ask, yes I have had a drink this morning, but you try spending just one night on the streets and tell me that a wee tot doesn't make the whole thing feel just a little bit less awful, and no me having a drink doesn't in any way change what I saw. I saw what I saw, and what I want to know now is if you're going to tell me the truth about what happened, or are you going to insult us both by continuing to lie to me?'

Hercules stopped walking and looked at the man, who also stopped walking. The dog took advantage of the break in their per-ambulations to sniff around the pavement and cock his leg against a lamppost. As Hercules looked into the stranger's eyes, he realised that whatever the outward appearances, he was dealing with an individual who was clearly accustomed to detecting when he was being fed a line. Hercules wondered what affect the truth would have. He figured he had nothing to lose; he would be harassed all the way home, otherwise.

'You are right,' he said at length. 'The lorry did kill me...'

'I knew it,' said the man, triumphantly. 'Didn't I tell you, Mungo?' he tugged playfully at the string leash, '"There's no way anyone could survive that!" I said.' He turned his attention back to Hercules. 'So if you're dead, what are you? You don't look like no zombie – not that I've ever seen one.'

'I didn't say I *am* dead,' said Hercules, 'I said the lorry killed me. It's complicated. I died and went to Heaven and while I was there I discovered that there is a demonic plot underway to end the Universe and so I volunteered to come back to Earth to try and stop it.'

The man looked at Hercules suspiciously. 'It sounds like nonsense,' he said. 'But it also sounds like you are telling the truth. How come you're not all squashed? You weren't moving at all for a while before you sat up.'

'They gave me an elixir. The man – or maybe I should say soul – who gave it to me called it the "Holy Spirit".'

The man slapped his thigh and laughed explosively. 'I've heard it all, now!' he exclaimed through his chuckles. He stopped laughing abruptly.

'Woss your name, son?'

'Hercules. Hercules Leek.'

'You're really *not* lying, are you?' the man said at length. 'You *really* believe what you are telling me, don't you, Hercules Leek. Which either makes you crazier than my mate half-baked Pete or it means that the Universe will be destroyed in – how long did you say?'

'We're not sure, but the feeling was it was no more than a few days.'

'And how are you going to find these demons? Isn't that a job for angels?'

'By all accounts the angels weren't that bothered – but it seems that the demons have *people* doing their work for them; it's them – the people, whoever they are – that I've got to stop. One of the other souls gave me this, to help find them.' Hercules pulled the M.O.R.A.L compass from his pocket. It was the first chance he had had to examine it when the angel feather wasn't a blur. The feather hung stationary in the globe and glowed a sort of ultra-white – a white that was not produced from a mixture of other coloured light, but a white that was made only of pure white light. As the globe moved in Hercules' hand, the direction indicated by the feather remained constant.

'Wow! That is something! I've said I see what I see and now I think I've seen it all. A couple of days till the End of Time, eh, Mungo. I can't say I'll miss sleeping out in winter. Almost makes me think I should stop you from trying to stop them, the thought of another winter sleeping rough. But no, if a man's on a mission to save the Universe, I think he should get a fair crack of the whip. It'd be wrong to stop you before you've started.'

Hercules looked at the stranger. He didn't really feel threatened, but he suddenly realised he'd taken a huge risk in opening up. 'Are you going to tell anyone?' he asked.

'Ha! Me? Who listens to me? People don't even *see* me most of the time, let alone listen to a word I have to say. If I were to start gabbling on that I'd seen a bloke come back from the dead who'd been to Heaven the very best I could hope for would be a night or two in the cells.'

He paused, thoughtfully. 'Of course, I'd have to be properly drunk to create the right *ambience*...

'Come along, Mungo,' he said, cheerfully tugging at the string. 'We've got work to do.'

Hercules watched the pair of them head off. He looked at the feather in its glass globe. It held its bearing, but he had no way of knowing how near or far he was from his quarry. How on earth was he going to find them? He looked down at the bloodied rags he was wearing. First things first: he needed to get cleaned up. He set off, along the pavement and towards his house.

* * *

Hercules crunched up the short gravel drive to his front door and felt in his pocket for his house keys. His pocket was torn, and the keys were not there. They must have been lost in the crash, and in his eagerness to get away from the scene of the accident he had completely forgotten to check. Not to worry. There was always the back door.

He climbed the gate at the side of his house and went round to the back door. As familiar as they had been when he hacked the virus, there were his herbs in their pots. He lifted the thyme, retrieved his spare key and let himself in.

He carefully placed the M.O.R.A.L compass on the kitchen table, grabbed a bin bag from under the sink and went upstairs to the bathroom. His ruined clothes went straight in the bin bag as he undressed. Then he stepped into the shower.

As the water flowed over him it carried the blood and dirt from his death. Eventually the grime and gore had been rinsed away and the water ran clear, but Hercules just stood under the hot water, with his eyes closed in the hope that the strain of all he had been through would wash away too. The water flowing over his body did come as some relief, but his brain never relinquished a single fundamental thought.

He was on a mission. The fate of Creation rested on *his* shoulders. It was madness. He had no real idea what he was going to do, but something, *anything*, was better than just sitting around and waiting for the end of everything. He had to try, didn't he?

A few minutes later he was sitting on the edge of the bed wondering what to do next. He didn't know where he was going to end up, but he reasoned he had to be as prepared as he could for any eventuality. He tried to work out what this meant in practical terms. Money was obviously a good starting point. His wallet was on his bedside table.

He wondered what else he might need. His passport might come in handy. He just didn't know, but it was better to be safe than sorry. When it came to packing clothes that was a lot easier. What had Aristotle said? A couple of days, a week at the most. Hercules slipped his passport and wallet into his jeans' pocket, stuffed a couple of changes of underwear and a spare jumper in a small rucksack, grabbed his toothbrush and some toothpaste from the bathroom on his way past, and headed back downstairs.

In the kitchen he put the kettle on to boil, then went and got the phone from the living room and called his office. He did a plausible impression of someone with a heavy cold, which he figured was probably more believable on balance than telling them that he had died and come back to life and was on a mission to save the Universe but would probably be back in next Monday. If there was one.

He made himself a mug of tea. Taking a half empty carton of milk from the fridge, he gave it a sniff. It was passable but not the freshest. He added a splash to his tea. He looked at the carton for a couple of seconds and then poured the rest of the milk down the sink. If he *did* save the Universe, he didn't want to come home to a stinky fridge.

Cradling his hot mug in his hands, he sat down at the kitchen table and stared at the compass that remained where he had placed it. The feather inside had not budged. Erwin Schrödinger had said that the kitten that had disappeared was last recorded in east London, and Aristotle had said that the "due south" of the compass would most likely point towards his target, but was the most sensible approach really to head to east London and wander round with the compass in the hope that he might stumble across something?

He sipped his tea and continued to stare at the angel feather. In the silence he could hear the tick of the wall clock in the kitchen, a slow and steady countdown. He continued to sit and watch...and sip at his tea...and think.

The feather began to twitch...

* * *

Mr John had proved to be uncannily well organized; he was certainly very well informed. In addition to providing the Aryan Defence Order/League/Front with tube tickets to get to Paddington, tickets for the Heathrow Express, and boarding passes for the flight to Geneva, he had also produced passports for Eugene and Nick. Neither of them had ventured very far outside London before, let alone abroad. They'd heard that travel broadened the mind. That sounded dangerous.

Mr John had given them a slip of paper bearing a phone number and an address in Geneva, which they were to go to on arrival. The phone number was for the event of an emergency. He also gave Mr Dumars a bundle of notes, a mixture of Sterling and Swiss Francs, for expenses. They were instructed to travel light; all the equipment that they needed, including the Dark Anti-Matter, would be provided when they reached the safe-house. Transporting the Dark Anti-Matter with them, explained Mr John, was too risky. He had "channels" through which he could assure that it would reach Geneva safely.

All that remained was for Maximilian Dumars to return to his flat and get his own passport. Compared to his colleagues, Mr Dumars was a seasoned globe-trotter: he had once visited Calais on a day trip – an experience that had confirmed to him that everything south of Dover was filthy, disgusting and, worst of all, foreign. He didn't speak the language and he didn't like the food. It was all foreign muck. He much preferred simple British fare – like curry. The passport had remained in a drawer ever since.

Nick and Eugene waited outside the tower block while their leader went up to his flat.

'That wasn't right what he did to that poor little kitten.' Eugene was still disturbed by Mr John's daemonstration.

'It wasn't pretty,' concurred Nick, 'but it certainly brought home the power of that Dark Anti-Matter stuff. It sort of proves – the fact that our side discovered it, I mean – what I've always said. That our side is more advanced, brain-power-wise. And it wasn't like he actually knew what was going to happen. There was *uncertainty* involved, you know.'

'Oh, he knew what would happen alright.' The lure of promised power was having a noticeable effect on Nick. He was walking a little taller, acting a little bolder, and talking a little louder. But Eugene wasn't fooled; he had known Nick too long to start thinking that he had suddenly become an expert physicist. Besides, even Eugene knew that "brain-power-wise" was a clumsy use of language. Everyone knew the correct way to say it was "in brainyness". But Eugene had other things on his mind than engaging in semantic arguments with his friend. Besides, he wasn't totally stupid. As committed neo-Nazis he knew that both he and Nick were firmly anti-semantic.

'What worries me,' he said, 'is what he's *really* got planned for us.'

'Power and glory, gentlemen, that's what; power and glory. And we would be fools to walk away from this opportunity.'

The pair of them turned. Maximilian was approaching, brandishing his almost-unused passport. He was in no mood to brook any dissent from his troops.

'This is our moment, Eugene. This is the chance we have been planning for. This is our destiny, and we must seize it. We must stride forward and take our place in the history books. Besides, we were promised uniforms. You've always said we should have a uniform, haven't you Eugene?'

Eugene did like a uniform. In his time, he had applied, unsuccessfully, for just about every job that he could think of that would have given him the opportunity to wear one. Soldier, fireman, traffic warden, nurse: the weight of all the rejections had been one of the things that had driven him to join the Aryan Defence Order/League/Front. If it wasn't for all the rejections, his innate racism and the fact that Nick was his best friend, he may never have joined.

'Yes, Boss,' he said simply.

'Very good,' Maximilian Dumars smiled paternally.

They set off for the underground.

* * *

The battered, rusting van chugged along the inside lane of the M1 motorway, heading south. Asif was making steady, if unspectacular, progress. The traffic was flowing and the regular road-watch bulletins on the radio carried no news of any hold ups ahead. He had been on the road for a couple of hours and was just over the halfway point of his journey. A signpost indicated services ahead.

He decided to pull over and check on his birds. He could afford the delay – he would still be at the airport in ample time to make his flight.

* * *

Hercules watched the minute twitching of the feather for a few seconds, at first unsure of what to do. An idea struck him, and he rushed into the living room and hunted through the bookshelf for a large road atlas of the British Isles. He retrieved a plastic compass from a drawer that was a relic of holidays a few years earlier that he had spent walking in the peak and lake districts.

He returned to the kitchen and opened the road map to a page that showed his hometown. Using the normal compass, he aligned the map on the table to north from the compass bearing. He then positioned the M.O.R.A.L compass over his hometown on the map. The angel feather was pointing almost due west. Hercules cast around for something with a straight edge, settling for a wooden chopping board that was on the worktop. This he placed on the map to the eastern side of the M.O.R.A.L compass so that its edge aligned with the axis of the shaft of the angel feather. He hunted around for something to write with and found a biro that didn't work which he chucked in the general direction of the bin out of frustration. With another pen that did work, he etched a thick black line on the map using the edge of the chopping board as a guide.

He ran out of page where his pen met the M25. A blue arrow indicated the page number where the map continued. Fortunately, it wasn't the adjacent page. Hercules moved the chopping board and M.O.R.A.L compass to one side, turned to the page where his line would continue, and tore it out. He repeated the process for twice until the path of the bearing encountered the sea. He laid out the torn pages in order. Without needing to continue the line in ink, he could see that it travelled across London until it hit the coast at the Thames estuary.

Schrödinger's kitten had disappeared in east London. That was his only solid point of reference: but somewhere along the bearing he had marked was an individual or group of people who wanted to destroy Creation.

The movements of the feather in the M.O.R.A.L compass were almost indistinguishable. Hercules reasoned that if his quarry was mobile, they must be some distance away for the fluctuations of the pointer to be so small. His obvious course of action was to head into London. In all likelihood, the closer he got to his target, the more pronounced the movement of the feather would become. At least he hoped that's how it worked.

He stuffed the torn pages from his road-map and the normal compass into his bag, slipped the M.O.R.A.L compass into his jacket pocket and headed out of the back door, locking it and replacing the key in its hiding place beneath the herb pots.

Feeling a bit lost without his bike, he walked to the bus stop at the end of his road. There wasn't another bus to the station for another twenty minutes: he decided not to wait. Twenty-five minutes of brisk walking later Hercules was sitting on board a Great Western train bound for Paddington station.

Being after the morning commute, the service was largely deserted, and Hercules was alone in his part of the carriage. He pulled the M.O.R.A.L compass from his jacket pocket and sat watching the feather as the countryside slipped by his window. Its movements, though still small, were becoming more pronounced – although it was impossible to know how many of the changes of direction were now as a result of Hercules' own. But the fact that, as the distance to the capital shrank, so the agitation of the feather increased, was enough to suggest that the gap between Hercules and those he sought was closing.

* * *

Asif had passed Luton and was fast approaching the M25. The traffic had grown heavier the closer he came to the London orbital, but it was still moving freely. Asif's van had been incapable of reaching the national speed limit for a good portion of its life even before he had become its owner, so all he prayed for was that the traffic would keep flowing. So far, God was answering his prayers.

* * *

Mr Maximilian Dumars did not like to ride the tube. He considered himself a man of the people, it was true, but whenever he took the underground he had cause to reflect on how many of "the people" he actually couldn't stand. Obviously there were the blacks, the Asians, tourists, and anyone he suspected of being even a tiny bit foreign. But it didn't stop there: the uncommunicative atmosphere of the average tube carriage gave him the opportunity to prejudge almost every single one of his fellow travellers and assign them attributes that would be justifiable grounds for the retribution he would mete out when power was finally his.

This one had too many tattoos; that one too many visible piercings: both obvious signs of moral lassitude. The gentleman in the smart suit was obviously a member of the Zionist banking fraternity who had brought the world economy to its knees and yet still reaped astronomical bonuses awarded at the expense of the public purse. Where Maximilian Dumars could find no obvious characteristic on to which he could project his prejudices he fell back on his old stalwarts and suspected homosexuality if there was the slightest opportunity to do so, and paedophilia if there was not. With so many miscreants and perverts around, it was no wonder that the country was going to the dogs. It was lucky that the Aryan

Defence Order/League/Front would soon be in a position to put things right.

His mood wasn't helped by the excited chattering of Nick and Eugene next to him.

They might have been the backbone of the Aryan Defence Order/League/Front, thought Maximilian Dumars to himself, but they behaved like children. When he had a larger staff, he would see to it that Nick and Eugene had a chance for an early retirement. He would have to make sure, he told himself, that they were well taken care of. In the same way, he reflected, that Hitler had taken care of the leader of the Nazi party's paramilitary wing, Ernst Röhm. The sort of taking care that belonged in an episode remembered in history as the "Night of the Long Knives". The sort of a night for which there wasn't a morning after for many of those involved.

The tube pulled to a halt. Maximilian Dumars watched the name of the station become visible through the windows of the slowing carriage. They had arrived at Paddington.

'Come on,' he said curtly, 'snap out of it. This is our stop. We're getting off here.'

* * *

Hercules sat with the M.O.R.A.L compass cradled in his hands as the train rattled east towards the capital. He was heading towards a meeting with who-knew-what kind of adversaries. The only certainty was that they were hell-bent on the destruction of the Universe. If Hercules succeeded in his mission, Creation would be saved, but his own immortal soul would be condemned to eternal damnation. If he failed, everything would simply cease to be.

Logically, Hercules realised that the Universe itself may well end in eternal nothingness anyway, and from a personal perspective eternal nothingness was almost certainly preferable to an eternity at the wrong end of a pitchfork. But emotionally – *emotionally* it seemed wrong that it was happening now; and Hercules was damned if he was going to sit by and let it just happen – which was ironic, since if he succeeded in stopping the destruction, he was *definitely* damned. Rarely – he thought – had there been such a good example of someone being damned if they did and totally and utterly annihilated along with the entirety of creation if they didn't.

The train had passed through Ealing and was well into the final leg of its journey. Hercules looked at the glass ball in his hands. The feather, which had become progressively more animated throughout the journey, was now positively restless. Hercules still had no real sense of the distance to his target, but he had a definite sense of rising tension as the automated passenger information system announced that they would shortly be arriving at London Paddington Station.

The train pulled to a halt and Hercules alighted onto the platform. Once he had hurried to the ticket barriers, he moved out of the way of the general flow of other passengers and held the compass still so as to get a proper bearing.

The shaft of the feather was pointing upwards, occasionally jerking to a slight change of angle; Hercules followed the tail of the feather that was pointing obliquely past the floor at his feet. At first he could not make sense of the downwards direction that was indicated. Had the Guardians miscalculated? Was he up against beings of the Underworld, rather than just humans? With a sense of rising panic, he looked up, in roughly the bearing that the tail of the feather indicated. The penny dropped as he read a sign that hung above the station concourse, along with an arrow pointing in a direction that continued along the bearing of the compass in his hand. It said "Underground".

Hercules hurried across the concourse to the entrance of the tube. When he got to the steps, he checked the direction of the feather again. The tail still pointed down, but was now at an angle to one side of the escalator. Hercules stepped onto the right-hand side of the escalator and began the descent to the tube, all the time keeping an eye on the M.O.R.A.L compass, which he kept shielded from onlookers. As the escalator carried him down, the feather slowly aligned with his direction of descent.

Hercules was focussing so much on the device in his hand that he was barely taking any notice of the people around him. But out of the corner of his eye, someone coming up the up escalator was simply too big not to be noticed. What made this human colossus stand out even more than he would have done otherwise – and given his size it would certainly have been difficult to ignore him under normal circumstances – was that he was engaged in animated conversation with a man who appeared to be no more than half his size. The smaller of the two men was two or three steps ahead of his companion on the stairway, and yet his line of sight was still no higher than the giant's chest. Even with the advantage of the extra steps, the smaller man was craning his neck upwards while the taller man reciprocated in the opposite direction. Hercules watched them pass in fascination, and even noticed the extraordinarily grumpy looking gentleman who followed behind them before he turned his attention back to the compass.

He stared down in disbelief. The feather was now pointing the opposite way! The shaft of the feather was now definitely pointing down the escalator: which meant that he needed to go up. He moved to the left and rushed down to the bottom, taking the steps two at a time. He reached the base, turned abruptly and began to climb quickly up the return flight. As he reached the middle of the ascent he slowed. A thought struck him. Supposing the human giant he had just seen was one of the opposition. What if he wasn't even human? If that was the case, he was quite sure that he didn't want to walk straight into his enemies. A person of that size would be difficult enough to stop, let alone anything less human.

Hercules arrived back at the top of the tube entrance and looked out across the station concourse. If the tall man was indeed one of the people he had to intercept, he shouldn't be too hard to follow. Sure enough, as he scanned the station, the Goliath was not difficult to spot – Hercules spied him along with his diminutive companion, and the cross-looking man from the escalator, checking platform details for trains on the station information boards.

The M.O.R.A.L compass was pointing directly away from them – or towards them in the sense that Hercules was navigating by. To be sure, he began to walk around the perimeter of the station concourse. It was easy enough to keep the head of the giant in sight. As he moved, so did the feather so it continued to point towards the same group. Hercules strolled over to within earshot.

'There we go, Boss, platform 6 is the next one; leaves in ten minutes. Can we get a burger now, I'm starving?'

'I've told you already, we'll eat at the airport after we've checked in.'

Hercules looked up at the board. Platform six was the Heathrow Express. He hurried off to buy a ticket. He didn't know where they were going, but he was glad that he'd had the foresight to bring his passport.

* * *

The Heathrow Express had sped through Hayes and Harlington station and was following the sweep of the track south that led to the tunnel where it would disappear under the M4 and the runways of the airport. At the same time, a battered, rusting van was making its own way off the motorway towards the main cluster of buildings at the centre of Heathrow that housed terminals one to three.

The van was truly on its last legs now, coughing black smoke whenever Asif applied pressure to the accelerator. But it had done its job. He followed the signs for the Terminal 3 short stay car park. He wasn't so much parking the van as abandoning it.

He turned into the car park and followed the ramps up past the busy lower levels until he reached a floor that was less heavily occupied. He managed to find a group of three empty spaces in the corner and pulled the van into the middle bay. He turned the key and took it from the ignition, then sat for a few moments listening to the pings of the cooling engine. He focused on his breathing, taking long steady breaths and concentrating on trying to relax the heart that had started pounding hard in his chest. The slow breaths had a calming effect, and he reminded himself he was on a holy mission. He would be protected.

It was his destiny.

* * *

The Heathrow Express pulled to a halt in the station below terminal five and its payload of holiday makers, business travellers and end-of-vacation tourists spilled onto the platform. Among them were the members of the Aryan Defence Order/League/Front and Hercules Leek.

Hercules had stowed the M.O.R.A.L compass in his jacket pocket as he knew who he was following now: his current objective had become to trail them unobtrusively while he worked out what he was going to do. Except for the grumpy one, who was carrying a well-worn, brown briefcase, they didn't appear to have any luggage between them. Hercules didn't really know how the un-fundamental material would be transported, but if they were carrying it, there was nothing to indicate that this was the case. Hercules realised that he could not act until he was sure that he would be able to neutralise the source of diabolical destruction with which they had been supplied.

He hung back while the three men he was tailing headed towards one of the hanging boards displaying flight departure information. Figuring that it would also be a perfectly natural direction to be heading in, were he not following them, Hercules followed.

As he walked over towards where they stood, the one with the briefcase was in the process of retrieving some papers from within. His taller and shorter companions were clearly excited about their journey.

'Well, Boss, which one is our flight?'

'Can we use one of those machines to check in?'

'Can I push the buttons?'

'I've already explained,' said the one holding the papers, 'we've already got our boarding passes. Our sponsor has already taken care of that for us. Whatever you think of Mr John, you certainly can't fault his planning so far. If everything else goes this smoothly I'm sure it won't be too long before we are toasting the success of our little operation.

'Let's see, our flight number is...' Maximilian Dumars squinted at the paper in his hand. Something struck him that was odd. His boarding pass had his passport number printed on it. He could understand that Mr John had provided the other two with their passports, so would naturally have had access to *their* numbers, but how had he got hold of his own?

'Boss?'

'Patience, Eugene! Ah yes, here it is – it's BA734.'

The taller and shorter members of the trio immediately switched their attention to the departures board as they searched for the magic number. As their eyes scanned the list, their lips moved.

'There it is, Boss,' said the short one, triumphantly. 'BA734 – Geneva – 15:05. It's right at the bottom. There's no gate number or anything!'

'Which gives us ample time to get through the security checks,' said the man to whom the others both referred to as "Boss".

'Then can we get a burger?'

'Yes, then we can get something to eat.'

He led them off towards the queues for the security screening that stood between them and the departure lounge. Hercules was already at one of the staffed check-in kiosks.

'Hello,' he said to the lavishly made-up member of staff behind the desk. 'I need to get to Geneva as something of a matter of urgency. Is there a seat on any of the flights leaving this afternoon?'

'Let me check for you, sir?' said the check-in attendant turning to her computer. She tapped a few keys and clicked the mouse a couple of times. 'There's a flight just after three that's not very full. Is it just yourself travelling, sir?'

'That would be perfect – and yes it is just me.' He handed her his passport.

'And do you have any luggage to check-in?'

Hercules dropped a shoulder to show his rucksack. 'Just this,' he said. 'I can take it as cabin luggage.'

'And will there be a return date?'

'No,' said Hercules, 'I don't know how long I'll need to stay for yet.'

Hercules had always fancied the idea of turning up at an airport and buying a ticket to God knows where, just on the spur of the moment. When the check-in attendant told him the price of the ticket, he realised instantly why this fantasy had always remained just that. Still, he reflected as he handed over his credit card – you couldn't take it with you...

The attendant took the card, processed his payment and handed him back the card and his receipt. Then she printed out a boarding pass, which she handed to him along with his passport.

'Have a nice flight,' she said.

'Thanks,' said Hercules, tucking his boarding pass and passport into his inside jacket pocket. He made his own way towards the security gates.

The next piece of the puzzle had slotted into place. He knew where he was going. But what would he find in Geneva?

* * *

While Hercules was procuring his seat, over in terminal three, Asif was shuffling forward in one of the queues that snaked back and forth to the airside security checks. The heat from the little bodies of his hidden charges warmed his sides, but he still felt enveloped in a sense of preternatural calm. He was, after all, doing the work of a higher power. He would be protected.

He reached the final switchback and took one of the shallow plastic boxes from the stack by the rolling bench top that ran alongside the front line of the queue. He took off his jacket and neatly folded into the tray. He then lifted his small case onto the conveyor and opened it to pull out the clear plastic bag containing his toiletries in their all-smaller-than-one-hundred-millilitre containers that he had prepared at home. He placed the liquids bag on top of his jacket, closed the case and used the tray to push it along the rollers towards the security gate.

When he got to the end of the conveyor, he lifted his bag and the tray across to the automated belt that fed into the X-ray scanner. A security official ushered him through the metal-detecting security gate. He knew there was nothing metal about his person and wasn't worried that he would set off the alarm. Sure enough, the detector remained silent. The security officer turned his attention to the next person in the queue and Asif went to stand by the exit of the X-ray machine and await his luggage.

From his position by the conveyor belt, Asif could see the monitor of the X-ray machine. He watched as the scanner operator stopped the belt with his case centre screen. He could clearly see the small wires of the homing hoods, around which he had thoughtfully wrapped some in-ear headphones. Among the tangle of cable, the smaller wires of the pigeons' flight equipment were invisible to the scanner operator. Nothing else in the case registered as unusual. The belt jerked into life and the case appeared through the plastic flaps that guarded the exit to the machine and slid down the slope to the waiting Asif.

No one paid him a second glance as he extended the handle and wheeled his little case through to the departure lounge. That was it. He was through!

A little smile played at the corner of his lips. It wasn't just the pigeons and their homing devices that the security checks had missed...

Eight

BA FLIGHT 734 had reached the end of the runway. The captain gunned the engines.

'Wow!' exclaimed Eugene.

The pilot released the brakes, and the plane began to thunder down the runway.

'Whoa!' added Nick.

The plane lifted into the air and started its steep initial climb to gain altitude. As the plane ascended, two adult male voices rang out in unison:

'WHEEEEEEEEEEeeeeeeeeeeeeeeeeee!'

* * *

Ten minutes later, Egypt Air flight MS778 bound for Cairo, following the same pattern, climbed into the sky. Asif's pigeons might have been going to Mecca, but he was not. When his birds arrived there, the Holy City would be far too dangerous a place to be, and this was no suicide mission. Asif's business, launching the birds towards their target, could be achieved safely from the other side of the Red Sea.

* * *

The engines of the plane droned as it flew on through the cloud. To Hercules, looking out of the window, it was almost impossible to tell if they were in motion. The high cloud outside the window enveloped the plane in a white shroud that meant there was no way of knowing that they were actually moving. It reminded him of his trips between departments in Heaven. Aristotle would have choked at the thought that it could be so impossible to detect motion.

The plane began to bounce as it hit a patch of mild turbulence. Strangely, for someone who did not really enjoy flying, Hercules found this reassuring. It reminded him that he was mortal again.

The cabin communications system crackled, and the Captain's voice announced that they had passed the half-way point in the flight and would soon be beginning the descent toward Geneva. A few rows ahead of Hercules, Eugene began to snore.

A thundering cadence filled the cabin. Heads popped up as curious passengers tried to pinpoint the source of the noise. The looks of anger and hostility soon disappeared when they took in the figure of the suspiring giant. Each soon sunk back into his or her seat with a look of chastened humility. No one wanted to wake the bear.

As the plane began its descent, the cloud began to thin. Eventually the surrounding whiteness gave way to actual views and Hercules gazed out of the window at the returning world. Below, a river snaked across the countryside. In the far distance, where the land met the sky, a brilliant crimson strip of the early evening horizon faded into dark blue. Above a half moon was visible.

Hercules gazed at the fiery red of the distant sky. Was this an omen, he wondered: a portent of his destiny? At least if he was facing Hell, it would mean that there was still a Hell to go to. His mission would have been a success. It was an odd way to find solace. In the light of his previous existence, going to Hell was a strange thing to be worrying about. A day ago, it would never have crossed his mind as something to cause concern. Of course, that was before he had died.

The plane began to vibrate as it started to descend more steeply. The cabin crew readied for landing. Nick had tried to wake his friend when the plane came down through the clouds and there was a view out of the window, but his attempts had been in vain. He'd even resorted to punching Eugene on the arm a couple of times, as hard as he could, but it had all the effect of a fly landing on a wardrobe.

Hercules watched the waters of Lake Geneva slip beneath the plane. He gazed at the roads and buildings below and wondered where they were headed. He had heard no mention of any un-fundamental material, and only the cryptic reference that the large one had made to their "being in charge" had given him any indication that there was any motive behind the journey they were making. If it was the End of Days they were presiding over, they wouldn't be "in charge" for long. He wondered if they knew this.

Hercules' ears popped as the descent entered its final phase. The pilot banked out over the lake before lining up with the runway. There was a bump and a shudder, and the roar of reverse thrust as the pilot brought the plane to a trundling standstill.

They had arrived in Geneva.

* * *

Hercules followed the Aryan Defence Order/League/Front and his other fellow passengers off the plane, across the jet bridge and down a flight of stairs into the terminal building of Geneva's Cointrin Airport. As they trudged along the shiny stone floors towards passport control, Hercules could hear Eugene berating Nick for not having woken him.

'I can't believe you didn't try and wake me,' he said in a sulky voice, 'I bet the landing was the best bit and all. Probably better than the take-off. You can be really selfish sometimes, Nick. I thought you were a mate.'

Nick looked in exasperation at his friend. 'But I did try to wake you!' he exclaimed. He turned to Maximilian Dumars for support. 'Tell him, Boss!'

'You were quite oblivious to his best efforts to rouse you,' Maximilian Dumars confirmed in an emotionless voice. 'I trust you are well rested now, Eugene.'

'Apart from missing the landing – it wasn't a bad nap, I suppose.'

'I'm so pleased to hear it.' Maximilian Dumars' voice was heavy with sarcasm. 'Remember, we are here on business,' he hissed, 'and I will not have you dozing off whenever you feel like it. From here on in, you need to focus!'

Eugene looked sheepishly down at his feet. To Hercules, who was watching them as he followed a few yards behind, it was crystal clear who was in charge of the group. Eugene might have had the muscle, but he reacted to Maximilian Dumars like a scolded child.

'Sorry, Boss,' he mumbled. 'It won't happen again.'

'See that it doesn't.'

They were coming to the end of the wide corridor they had been walking down. Ahead was a small booth with two desks, manned by border officials. They had reached passport control. The passengers from their flight began to file through. As each of them stepped forward and handed their passport to the officials, their photos were checked, and they were waved on their way.

Hercules was close to the back of the queue. He watched the three members of the Aryan Defence Order/League/Front pass the checks unhindered. He didn't want to make it too obvious that he was following them: he was happy to hang around at the back of the waiting file of passengers.

Eventually, it was his turn at the booth. He handed over his passport, open at the photo page. The young border guard took it and glanced at the page, then looked up at Hercules' face. He had half closed the passport, and was just about to hand it back, when he stopped abruptly. He opened the passport again and scrutinized the bearer page more closely, then looked up once again at Hercules' face.

'I'm sorry,' said Hercules. 'Is there a problem, Officer?'

The official looked up at him without speaking. He turned to his colleague in the desk next to him and whispered something in French. Hercules didn't catch what he had said. Then he turned to Hercules and said, 'Excuse me, monsieur. Would you kindly wait 'ere for un moment?'

'Certainly,' said Hercules, a bit flustered. 'Can you tell me what's wrong, please?'

The young man said nothing, but slipped out of his chair and out of the booth, taking Hercules' passport with him. He crossed the corridor and disappeared through another door, which had a mirrored window in the top half.

Hercules was alone with the remaining customs officer. All the other passengers had passed through the checkpoint. It was bound to be something trivial, he told himself. He mentally checked off the things that he thought might be causing his detention. His passport had definitely not expired; he was sure of that.

It was probably all just a misunderstanding.

* * *

Hidden from view, behind a one-way mirror, a tall, blond and impeccably dressed man watched the scene at the checkpoint in the corridor with interest. The young customs official approached him, waving the passport.

'I sink we 'ave got 'im, Monsieur Jean.'

'Well done, Bartholème. Your vigilance has almost certainly saved the city.'

'What 'as 'e done?' asked the customs official.

'Nothing…yet,' replied the well-dressed man. 'And with your help, we will keep it that way. He belongs to a highly dangerous and committed bunch of terrorists. We, at Interpol, have had his cell under observation for a while now. We believe this is a reconnaissance mission for a forthcoming "spectacular".'

'Should we not have let 'im through and just followed 'im? Surely his comrades will become suspicious now.'

'You are sharp, Bartholème: and I shall be telling your superiors as much.' The young official straightened and puffed out his chest at the praise. 'Agitating his comrades is exactly the response we are looking for. His mission will be blown, for sure. Unfortunately, we don't know who this one is working with. Maybe when they realise he has been apprehended they will get desperate and break cover.'

'So what should we do wiz 'im now? Hand 'im over to ze police?'

'Oh, no, that won't be necessary. Put him in a holding cell for – I don't know, twenty-four hours should do it,' the well-dressed man waved his hand casually. To the highly trained and efficient border guard whose attention for detail had been responsible for Hercules' arrest, it seemed an odd way to behave. He looked at the Interpol officer suspiciously. But then, he figured, at the rarefied atmosphere of command that the stranger was used to, such behaviour may well have passed for the norm. The Interpol man appeared to notice the way that the guard had looked at him. 'Twenty-four hours;' he said sharply, 'that will be long enough to get them worried. Stick him on a plane back to England after that.'

'Very good, sir!'

'Just remember, this is a matter of extreme secrecy and sensitivity; I singled you out for this task because I've read your record and it is one of exemplary service…' the guard beamed at the flattery, '…and you have repaid my faith with your vigilance. But remember, the fewer people that know about this the better. Here is my card. Let me know the flight you have put him on. Our agents at the other end will take it from there.'

'Yes, sir!'

The guard saluted smartly and turned back towards the door.

Damn! Legion thought to himself. He had to be more careful. He'd noticed the officer becoming suspicious when he'd become too casual. One of the advantages of being a multitude of demons was that he had a personality for all occasions. The problem with this was that sometimes the wrong personality started to emerge at the wrong time. The right ones had regained control just in time.

He watched in satisfaction as the passenger from the plane stood uncomfortably by the passport control booth. Legion didn't know who he was, but there was something about him that the demon found discomforting. He had been planning the Aryan Defence Order/League/Front's mission for longer than he cared to remember. He would not have a random mortal mess it all up now! Still, there was little that the stranger could do to interfere from within a holding cell at the airport.

Legion turned on his heels and strode down the corridor. He had a very busy night ahead of him. When the corridor turned at a right angle to follow the perimeter of the building, Legion kept going straight on. He melted through the wall and into the early evening.

* * *

Hercules smiled weakly at the official in the cubicle. The officer returned his smile with a blank stare. Hercules felt the guard was looking right through him. He knew he had done nothing wrong, but the indifference of the guard almost made him feel guilty. He shouldn't feel guilty, Hercules told himself: he was on a mission from God! Well, not directly, he reminded himself. They had acted without sanction. If he was here on Heaven's behalf, it wasn't an official mission. This was a black op – which suddenly seemed an inappropriate way to be carrying out the work of the Immortal Kingdom. He was a deniable asset: only no one who was currently alive needed to deny anything, and he certainly didn't feel like much of an asset. It was all unravelling pretty fast.

The first border guard reappeared through the door by which he had previously exited. Hercules breathed a sigh of relief. It would all be sorted out and he would be on his way.

'Is everything OK?' He said as he started to walk towards the official. 'Can I go now?'

'I'm sorry, sir,' said the man in uniform, flatly. 'You need to come wiz me.'

* * *

Unimpeded by the need to collect any luggage, the Aryan Defence Order/League/Front soon found themselves outside the airport, queuing for a taxi.

The small queue in front of them soon cleared. A silver Mercedes estate with a yellow taxi sign on the roof pulled forward. The passenger window opened, and the driver leant across. 'Où allez-vous, messieurs?' he asked. 'Where are you going?'

Maximilian Dumars reached inside his jacket pocket and pulled out the slip of paper bearing the address of their safe-house contact. 'OK,' the taxi driver started the meter. 'Get in.'

Maximilian Dumars opened the passenger door and sat down in the front of the taxi, leaving the back seats to Nick and Eugene. As Eugene lowered his giant frame into the cab, it listed heavily to one side. The taxi driver winced.

When they were all in, driver slipped the car into gear and pulled gingerly away from the kerb. To get onto the main road, they had to pass through an area of road-works where fresh tarmac was being laid. The taxi slowed to an almost glacial languor as the driver inched down onto the temporary road-surface, clearly fearing for his vehicle's suspension. They crossed the uneven patch at less than walking pace and inched up onto the finished road beyond. Only then did the driver open up the throttle and ease the car up to something approaching normal driving speed.

In the front Maximilian Dumars was quietly admiring the comfort of the leather seats and the masterful Teutonic engineering of the Mercedes. He was not accustomed to travel by means other than public transport, which he hated, but his mind was already conjuring up the fleets of staff-cars that their impending world domination would, no doubt, require.

As they swept along the tree-lined road, Maximilian Dumars continued to envisage the greatness and the trappings of greatness that would so soon be his. The road began to open out. To their left were a few large buildings. The driver turned the taxi left past a large square dotted with fountains. In front of them was an avenue lined with a multitude of national flags. It didn't feel to Maximilian Dumars that they were heading towards the safe-house.

'What is this place, driver?' he asked.

'It iz ze United Nations building,' replied the driver, with a shrug. 'All ze tourists want to see it. I sought you might like it also. It iz practically on our way.'

'Well! I did not ask to see it!' Maximilian Dumars replied indignantly. 'I expect you to take us by the shortest route to our destination – not lead us on unrequested diversions. Do not expect that I shall be paying for your little detour!'

'As you wish, sir,' the driver shrugged again. 'Most people want to see it, is all.'

'We are not most people!' retorted Maximilian Dumars, imperiously.

''Ere, Eugene, someone's been nicking your furniture!' Nick had seen something that clearly amused him. At the edge of the square was a giant chair, over ten metres high, which dwarfed the people on the pavement below. 'Only I'd be a bit cross with them if I were you, because it looks like they've broken one of the legs!'

Eugene leant across to look out of the window, causing the taxi to tilt violently.

'I see what you mean, sir,' said the taxi driver to Maximilian Dumars.

'Just take us to our destination, and no more diversions!' Maximilian Dumars snapped.

They drove on in silence. They continued to pass elegant and important-looking buildings for a while, but these were soon replaced by more and more mundane structures as they headed into the suburbs. Maximilian Dumars was still fuming that they had so literally been taken for a ride. Had he not had his wits about him, they would almost certainly have been ripped off! His mind settled into a more self-congratulatory frame as he considered how his worldliness had saved them from robbery at the hands of the unscrupulous foreigner behind the steering wheel. Then another thought struck him. Had not Mr John suggested that they needed a secondary target, one with which they could get the world's attention. Well, what represented the world better than the United Nations? And there were a couple of smart tower blocks directly in front of the UN building. Supposing the Aryan Defence Order/League/Front's first mission was to be to vaporise one of them? Or even the United Nations building itself? That would surely get the attention they needed for phase two of the plan…

His mind was racing with possibilities when the taxi pulled up to the kerb outside a modest detached house in a fairly nondescript neighbourhood.

'We are 'ere, sir,' said the taxi driver. 'Zis is it.'

Maximilian Dumars looked around. He couldn't make out much in the late evening gloom. The houses were neat and widely spaced.

It was a quiet residential road; perfect for going about your business unnoticed.

'About time,' he said. 'How much?'

The taxi driver pointed to his meter. Maximilian Dumars pulled the thick bundle of notes that he had been given by Mr John from an inside pocket and counted out ten Swiss francs less than the meter displayed.

'I think you'll find that is enough...' he said coldly.

'But, sir,' began the taxi driver.

'...Unless you want to take matters up with my colleague? Eugene?'

From the back seat Eugene growled. The taxi rocked gently.

'Zis is fine,' said the taxi driver, wisely.

The Aryan Defence Order/League/Front extricated themselves from the Mercedes with various degrees of ease. No sooner had they all closed their doors then the taxi sped off in a screech of tyre smoke. They stood together on the pavement for a moment, looking at the house.

'Well, Gentlemen,' said Maximilian Dumars, starting up the path towards the front door, 'onwards to our destiny.'

* * *

'What a complete and utter bastard!' Legion thought to himself with a smile from behind the wheel of the cab as it sped off down the road. Maximilian Dumars had excelled himself with a performance that combined xenophobic superiority and incredible meanness. Legion's faith in him as a total jerk had been confirmed. Legion had always been a very good judge of bad character.

Legion was also pleased with his own performance as a Geneva cabbie. So far this evening he had done Interpol and cabbie. Just one more part to play, he thought, as he rounded a bend, rode up onto the pavement and slammed the Mercedes squarely into some bins that had been left by the kerbside. He was out of the front seat and hopping over fences of the back gardens of the houses in the street he had just left before the airbags could deploy. He was headed back to the safe house.

If nothing travels faster than the speed of light, he mused to himself, how come Darkness always gets there first?

* * *

Maximilian Dumars rang the doorbell. The Aryan Defence Order/ League/Front stood together on the porch, stamping their feet and blowing in their hands against the evening chill. The house remained silent.

'You sure we got the right address, Boss?' asked Nick. 'I mean, you were a bit short with that cabbie. Maybe he dropped us in the wrong place.'

Maximilian Dumars shot Nick a black look. He said nothing, but stepped forward and pushed the doorbell again. He kept his finger hard down on the button for a full twenty seconds, and then gave it two more sharp rings for good measure.

A hall light went on, and they could hear the sound of shuffling footsteps. 'OK! OK! *J'arrive!*' said a voice.

The shuffling footsteps slowly neared the door. There was a brief pause, followed by the sound of large numbers of bolts being drawn back and latches being turned. Eventually, after a final click and a metallic rattle, the door opened a few inches before stopping abruptly as a security chain halted its progress. From the narrow gap, the eyes of an elderly man regarded the three men on the doorstep with suspicion.

'*Qu'est-ce que vous voulez?*' he asked, tersely.

The Aryan Defence Order/League/Front stared blankly back at him.

'What do you want?'

Maximilian Dumars produced the address from his inside jacket pocket. 'Mr, er, Boo – coop – dee – ables?' he read slowly from the slip of paper.

'Yes,' said the old man. 'I am Monsieur Beaucoupdiables. What do you want?'

'Mr John sent us.'

The old man's eyes narrowed. *Mot de passe?* he demanded. 'Password?'

'Oh for heaven's sake!' Mr Dumars almost exploded. 'He didn't give us a password! Just how many groups of three English visitors were you expecting this evening?'

The door closed, there was a rattle of chain, and then it opened fully.

'Very good,' said the old man. 'Of course there is no password – but I have found it best not to take any chances when it comes to the security of the Organisation. Quickly! You 'ad better come in.'

He stepped aside and ushered them into the hall. Then he closed the door and began the task of replacing all the various bolts and latches which secured it.

After a not inconsiderable while, the old man slid the last dead-bolt into place and straightened up, accompanied by a good deal of joint-cracking.

'You can never be too careful,' he said, with a half-smile to his guests. 'So,' he continued, 'you are the Order for the League of the Aryan Defence Front: Welcome.'

'We are the Aryan Defence Order/League/Front,' said Maximilian Dumars frostily.

'Forgive me,' said the old man, humbly. 'My old brain gets confused so easily these days. Anyway, the name is not important. It is what you stand for that counts.' This last sentence was delivered with such a steely ferocity that it was quite unexpected. Behind the old man's eyes, fires blazed.

Maximilian Dumars was unfazed. Whatever ardent fervour burned in this old man, he could match – with ice. 'Our name *is* what we stand for -' he said, glacially. 'Defence of the purity of the Aryan race, its homeland and peoples; Order on the streets; a League of the brotherhood of the right.'

The two men stared at one another, each defiantly facing the other down; locked in mutual loathing.

'Well, you certainly have some front,' said the old man, breaking the deadlock. 'You speak well, Mr Dumars, but can you match your fine words with actions?'

'That,' said Maximilian Dumars softly, 'is what we are here for.'

'Very good!' said the old man, clicking his heels together. 'Gentlemen, follow me.'

He led them down the hall and into the kitchen, where, on the table, sat a case that they had last seen at the Broadfields Estate community hall. Alongside was laid out a neat array of semi-automatic weapons and ammunition clips.

Nick rushed over to the table.

'Wow! Look at these, Eugene! Uzi 9mm. Capable of firing six hundred rounds a minute.' He was practically salivating as he longingly eyed the guns. From somewhere, he remembered some manners. 'May I?' he asked to their host.

'Of course,' said Monsieur Beaucoupdiables. 'You 'ave handled a gun before, I take it?'

'What do you think?' Nick's response was indignant. He picked up one of the weapons and began caressing it lovingly. He pointed it around the room, sighting imaginary enemies. Then he pointed it at Eugene.

'Hey!' complained Eugene. 'Cut it out, Nick. Someone could get hurt.'

'Nonsense, you big fool; there's not even any bullets in it!' Nick grabbed an ammunition clip from the table and slotted it home in the base of the gun. He smiled mischievously and pointed the weapon at his friend once again. 'Not like now! Don't move, Eugene, or I'll blow you away!'

'I don't think that will 'appen,' said Monsieur Beaucoupdiables, breezily.

Nick levelled the gun at him. 'Oh yeah? Why not, old man?'

'You 'ave still got the safety catch on,' said the old man calmly.

Nick looked at the gun, while keeping it pointed at Monsieur Beaucoupdiables. Suddenly he didn't seem so sure of himself. He fumbled around the side of the gun, his fingers scrabbling for the catch. They found something they could press. The magazine slid from the bottom of the gun and clattered to the floor.

'It appears you are a little rusty,' the old man took the Uzi out of Nick's hands and grunted as he bent to pick up the ammunition clip from the floor. 'Not to worry. I very much doubt you will actually need to fire one of these guns,' as he was talking he slotted the clip back into place and cocked the weapon. He levelled the weapon at Nick, who realised he could see the brass of a bullet glinting in the barrel. Nick began to sweat. 'Just pointing them in the right direction is usually enough to achieve the desired effect.' The old man raised the barrel to the ceiling, released the clip and ejected the bullet from the breach. 'But there is time for me to give you a quick refresher course, so you at least *look* like you know what you are doing.'

'I don't think that'll make a lot of difference for me.' Eugene had picked up one of the guns from the table. In his giant hands it looked like a child's toy. He tried to put his finger on the trigger, but couldn't squeeze it past the trigger guard.

The old man looked at him. 'It's Eugene, isn't it?'

'That's right,' said Eugene.

'We were prepared for this. It could be argued that your presence alone would be intimidating enough, Eugene.' He had crossed the kitchen to a door. 'But just in case,' he opened the door, 'we thought you might like this.'

He stood to one side to reveal a shelf-lined larder. The small amount of food that it contained was not what drew the eye. Taking up most of the space was a large, belt-fed machine gun; the sort of gun that was usually seen fixed to a tank. The shelves were stacked with a variety of grenades. Also in the cupboard, on hangers hooked on one of the top shelves, were a number of suit carriers.

'It's not the subtlest of weapons,' said the old man. 'But then I'm not expecting that you will be employing too much subtlety.'

Eugene's face lit up with delight. But it wasn't the gun he was looking at. He pointed to the suit carriers. 'Are those what I think they are?' he asked. 'Can I have a look?'

Monsieur Beaucoupdiables smiled at him. 'I think you will be impressed,' he said.

Eugene reached for the largest of the suit carriers. He hooked it over the back of the open door and began to unzip it. Maximilian Dumars and Nick crowded round him, while the old man looked on with an amused smile on his face. The suit carrier opened to reveal a black military uniform, with shiny silver buttons. It was clearly very well-tailored. Stitched onto the arm was a circular patch, which featured a sort of red cross on a white background. The end of each cross split into three, with each of the three branches terminating in an arrow. Above the patch, the initials of the Aryan Defence Order/League/Front were embroidered.

'An interesting symbol,' said Maximilian Dumars. 'What is it supposed to mean?'

'The cross represents the righteousness of our mission,' explained the old man. 'White is the nobility of our race. The red is the blood that we are willing to sacrifice to achieve the New World Order, and the four directional arrows represent the corners of the earth to which we will spread our message.'

Maximilian Dumars was impressed. He knew the value of symbolism.

'I dunno, Boss,' said Eugene. 'Them arrows look a bit pitchforky to me.'

Maximilian Dumars wasn't really listening. He had pulled his own suit from the larder and had opened the carrier. He was even more impressed. His suit had extra braiding. And a matching peaked officer's cap.

'The Organization has clearly gone to a lot of trouble,' he said. 'We shall endeavour to prove ourselves worthy of the trust that has been placed in us.'

'I'm sure you will,' said Monsieur Beaucoupdiables.

Two more suit carriers remained hanging in the larder cupboard. Nick, still smarting from his embarrassment with the gun, unzipped the outermost one. His already glum face fell further. Instead of a well-tailored, smart black military styled uniform, the suit carrier contained a FedEx uniform. The disconsolate Nick could tell without taking the suit out that it was in his size.

'How come the others get fancy uniforms and I get -' he wrinkled his nose and pointed at the cheap synthetic suit, '- *this?*'

'There is another uniform there, Nick, which matches those of your comrades,' Monsieur Beaucoupdiables reassured him, 'but there are two missions to fulfil tomorrow, don't forget. There needs to be a diversionary attack to draw the world's attention and focus the minds of the international community. The leaders of the Organization thought that you might want to launch the diversionary attack by means of a "special delivery". I think that you will agree that were Eugene to be given this task, he might attract an undue amount of attention. So the honour 'as fallen to you.'

Nick brightened up a bit. He was rarely trusted to do anything. Now he would be striking the first blow for the cause.

Monsieur Beaucoupdiables turned to Maximilian Dumars. 'You 'ave selected a suitable target for the diversionary attack?' he asked.

'I've got one or two ideas.'

'Excellent!' Monsieur Beaucoupdiables clapped his hands together. On his aging frame the sudden movement of his long arms gave him the look of a grounded albatross preparing for take-off. 'We can discuss the details over dinner. You must be hungry after your travels. There is time enough to make the final preparations for tomorrow later. In the meantime, let's eat.'

* * *

Asif wheeled his little case across the shiny stone of the main concourse of Cairo's Rameses Station. The station clocks showed that the time was approaching midnight. The peak busy hours may have passed, but there were still a fair number of people milling about – a mixture of travellers and vendors, with smartly uniformed police and soldiers patrolling casually among them.

Asif had a pre-booked ticket on the overnight train to Aswan. Truly he must be under the wings of angels. His flight to Cairo had passed uneventfully. He had breezed through customs. He had even had a chance to stop at the airport toilets to check on the welfare of his birds. They seemed untroubled at having spent the last eight hours tucked into the pockets of his special vest. Leaving the airport, he had not only found a taxi-driver who was genuinely uninterested in ripping him off, but the man had also taken him to a late-opening general store, where he had purchased a travel-cage, some small dishes and some seed. If the taxi-driver was surprised when Asif conjured two pigeons from his robes and transferred them to the cage, he did not show it. Asif had also bought a towel from the store. He covered the cage with the towel to keep the birds inside calm.

The train was already waiting at the platform. Asif had booked an entire first-class sleeper compartment for himself. It was a bit of an extravagance, he knew, but he didn't want to be disturbed unnecessarily.

He found his compartment, slid the door open, carefully placed the cage on the floor in corner with the case next to it, and then slid the door closed behind him. He sat down on one of the bench seats. The seat opposite had already been made up into a bed.

Asif sat back and closed his eyes. Even though the train had not yet left the platform, his tired body still carried the feeling of motion from the day's travel. At least now he could relax a little bit. He had a long night's journey ahead, but for this part of his mission he would rest while the train ate up the miles.

He was almost dozing off when the door to the compartment slid open. Asif sat up with a start. It was a ticket inspector. He glanced around the compartment, took in Asif, his case and the towel covered cage.

'Ticket, please,' he said.

Asif produced his ticket from his jacket pocket.

'Is it just you travelling, sir?' the inspector enquired.

Asif nodded.

The inspector scanned the ticket, nodded in satisfaction, and handed it back to Asif. 'Good night, sir,' he said. 'Have a pleasant journey.' And with that he left the compartment, sliding the door to a close behind him.

Asif locked the door. He lifted the towel off the cage and filled one of the dishes he had bought with some of the seed, the other with some water from a bottle, and placed them in the cage. He watched the pigeons for a while as they drank and fed. After a while there was a gentle shunt, and the train slowly began to pull out of the station. Asif slipped the towel back over his bird's cage, kicked off his shoes and climbed onto the bed. He flicked off the light-switch and lay back on the bed, watching the dance on the ceiling of the shadows cast by the passing city lights.

He smiled.

This was all just too easy.

Nine

THE EARLY MORNING SUN greeted the green lands of the Nile valley, glinting off the metal and glass of the Aswan Express as it continued its journey south. Asif had risen before dawn to pray. After prayers, he had checked on his pigeons. They cooed contentedly when he lifted the towel from their cage, showing no ill effects from their confinement.

'Only one more day, special ones,' he murmured. 'Then you can spread your wings and fly into history. We have greatness ahead, and the blessings of angels to protect us.'

He made sure that the birds had enough water and seed and then sat down on the bench seat. As the train rattled onwards, he watched the scenery slip by. Asif found the contrast between the greenery of the narrow strip of land on either bank of the river and the buff yellows and greys of the desert sand beyond hypnotic. As he stared through the window, captivated by this living metaphor for the fragile boundary between existence and oblivion, his mind turned to his parents. For a brief moment he found himself wondering if they had suffered.

* * *

Hercules lay on the thinly cushioned bench in the small, window-less cell, staring into the darkness. His watch told him it was early morning, but there was no light from outside to confirm this.

He still wasn't sure why he was being detained. He had been led from the border control post to this room, ordered in, given a bottle of water and a sandwich and the door was locked behind him. The guards had proved quite uncommunicative, despite his best efforts to elicit a response. He had banged the door for a while, demanding to be let out, or at least an explanation, but when no reply had been forthcoming he eventually grew bored and resigned himself to a waiting game.

He took the M.O.R.A.L compass from his pocket. The angel feather emitted its own soft light, making it visible even in the darkness of the cell. Hercules was reassured to find that it still held the same bearing as it had done when he had last checked it at about midnight. He had slept fitfully on the hard bench since then, dreaming disturbed images of everlasting tortures and exploding galaxies. At least it seemed that if he was not moving, neither was his quarry. When he had first been taken into custody he had sat on the bed watching the twitching feather with a rising sense of panic. But the feather had not been active for long. It was unlikely that the men he had been following had moved too far from the centre of Geneva, given the relatively short amount of time the feather was in motion. It had stopped moving about half an hour after he had been locked in the cell and had held the same bearing ever since.

* * *

There was a gentle knocking at the cabin door. Captain Higgs rolled over in his bunk and rubbed his eyes. He looked at his watch. For a moment he thought he must still be asleep, that he was dreaming one of those hyper-real dreams, brought about by the stress of the day before, where the day ahead presents itself to the subconscious in a number of practice sessions as a preparation against the untoward. He sighed with relief and relaxed to the hypnotic throbbing of the ships engines, pulling the bed-sheets over his head and turning away from the door.

The knocking repeated itself, this time with a little more insistence. The captain rubbed his eyes again and had another look at his watch. He sat up with a start. It was ten o'clock! He should have been back on the bridge hours ago.

'Who is it?' he barked.

'Jenkins, sir,' came the voice from the other side of the door.

'Come in,' called the captain, gruffly.

The door opened. Before the Chief Officer had had a chance to put a foot into the cabin, the captain launched into a rapid interrogation.

'What's going on out there, Jenkins? Is there another mutiny in the offing? Why didn't someone wake me earlier?

'I've brought you some breakfast, sir,' said the Chief Officer cheerfully, setting a tray on the small table in the cabin.

'Breakfast?' said the captain, 'Oh.'

'The only thing to report is how well everything's running, really,' continued the Chief Officer. 'I don't know where that new bosun has come from, but he's a bloody godsend, I don't mind saying. He's hardly been on the ship a day and it's spotless. And whatever it is that he's said to the deckhands – well they've all been working like I've never seen. And to think that it's pretty much the same bunch we had all those problems with crossing the Med. Anyway, seeing as how smoothly things have been going, and considering the hours you've had to put in over the last couple of days coming through the canal and then with all that nonsense at Suez, well, I figured you could do with a bit of extra kip to catch up.'

The captain was almost at a loss for words. 'Oh, er, thank you,' he said.

'So have your breakfast and come up to the bridge when you're ready,' said Jenkins, as he crossed back to the door. 'No rush, sir – honestly. I think it's fair to say that everything is totally under control.'

The captain sat on his bed and stared at the door for a few seconds while he gathered his thoughts. Then he pinched himself, hard. 'Ow!' he yelped. So this was not a dream.

He swung his legs out of the bunk and padded across to where his breakfast tray sat on the table: a full fry-up, with fresh coffee and orange juice. Well, he thought to himself as he sat down and picked up his knife and fork. If what Jenkins had told him wasn't true, at least he would find out well rested and with a full stomach.

*　*　*

A light went on in the cell. Hercules swung his legs to the edge of the narrow bench and sat up. There was a rattling of keys and some muttering from the other side of the door, followed by the sound of a key being put into the lock. This was followed by the sound of someone trying to turn the key in the lock, unsuccessfully, which in turn was followed by more jangling of keys and muttering. Another key was slid into the lock. This time the key turned. The door opened a few inches and a slim figure with piercing hazel eyes slipped into the room, pulling the door to a near close behind. She was dressed in the uniform of the border guards, and very nearly looked like a border guard.

'You're not a border guard, are you?' said Hercules.

The stranger glanced down at her uniform and then looked quizzically at Hercules.

''ow can you tell?' she asked.

'It's the tin foil under your hat.' Sure enough, underneath the stranger's peaked cap, she was wearing a helmet of what looked like aluminium foil. 'Oh – and the rucksack.'

'Ah,' the stranger shrugged, '– well spotted,' it was hardly difficult to miss. 'Listen, if you want to get out of 'ere, we'd better get going.' The stranger opened the door a fraction and peered into the corridor beyond to check that the coast was clear.

'What about my passport? I'm sure I'm only being held here by mistake…Why don't I just wait for them to let me out?'

The stranger turned back into the room and pulled the door to a near close again. 'It's 'ercule, isn't it? 'ercule Lick?'

'Hercules Leek – that's right,' replied Hercules. 'Who are you?'

The stranger looked slightly puzzled. 'At the moment,' she replied, 'I'm… I'm Incognito.'

'How did you know my name?'

'I do not 'ave time to explain that now,' the stranger was becoming frustrated by Hercules' apparent reluctance to escape his confinement, '– but I can tell you that you being 'ere is certainly no mistake. Come on! If you want to get out of 'ere, we really do 'ave to go! Now!'

Hercules shrugged and slid off the bench. If it *was* true that there was a sinister motive behind his detention, it was probably a good idea not to stay. If the stranger turned out to be as odd as her tin-foil hat suggested, Hercules could always lose her when he was clear of the authorities.

And if he couldn't stop the impending End of Days, a lack of a passport was going to be the least of his worries.

He stood at the shoulder of the stranger, who had resumed her post peeking through a narrow opening of the door. The stranger decided it was time to move. 'Follow me,' she whispered urgently.

They stepped into the corridor. The stranger quickly locked the door with the keys that had been left hanging in the lock and pocketed them. She then began the most bizarre walk that Hercules had ever witnessed. It was cross between a casual stroll – as bold as brass with a complete sense of entitlement to be in the place – and tiptoeing. It was so odd that Hercules found himself rooted to the spot, fascinated. The stranger had only gone a few yards when she realised that Hercules wasn't following. She turned.

'Really,' she hissed, beckoning to Hercules. 'You 'ave to keep up! Try to match my movements. It will help us avoid detection.'

Hercules found it almost impossible to believe this. Yet somehow this stranger had managed to get through the airport security, locate Hercules, find the right keys and liberate him from his cell. Hercules tried to look serious, and he began to copy the movements of the stranger as she tip-stroll-toed her way down the corridor. He wasn't quite sure which was more difficult; copying the stranger's gait or not bursting out laughing. At least if they were caught he thought it was unlikely that he would end up back in the cell. Moving the way he was, he thought it more likely that he would be sectioned.

They reached a bend in the corridor. The stranger froze and held up a hand to indicate that Hercules should stop. Hercules had been concentrating so hard on copying the stranger's gait that his brain didn't register the signal immediately and he almost crashed into the back of her. Together they peered around the corner in the time-honoured fashion; two heads, one on top of the other. The corridor was empty.

The stranger led Hercules on, until they came to another turning, where they repeated the process of pausing and peering. This pattern repeated itself as the stranger navigated their passage through the private realms of the airport buildings. Sometimes they heard footsteps, sometimes a door closing, but they managed to make their journey without encountering another soul. Eventually they approached a final corner.

'Come on,' whispered the stranger. 'Nearly 'ome free.'

They sneaked around the corner and then resumed their tip-stroll-toeing. A short distance along the corridor was a door. As she approached it, the stranger removed her uniform jacket and cap. Without them she looked like any normal civilian in a white blouse and blue trousers – with a tin-foil hat on her head. She swung her rucksack off her, unzipped it and pulled out a sheepskin jacket. She looked even less official with the jacket on, and even more like a normal member of the public. Apart from the tin foil hat. She paused by the door.

'Right, zis is it,' she said. 'Deep breath.'

'It might not be the right time to ask,' said Hercules, doubting that there was ever a right time for the question he was about to put to the stranger, 'but why the foil hat?'

'It is to not get noticed.'

Hercules' mind raced. 'What, you mean aliens scanning brain-waves, that sort of thing?'

'Don't be ridiculous! I wear the foil to not get noticed by people. Regardez!' And with that she opened the door and strode through it into the public part of the airport terminal that lay the other side.

Hercules followed. They had reached the main concourse at the front of the terminal. They only had to cross this large hall and they would be clear of the airport building. Since he had left the cell, it was the first time that Hercules had seen people other than his rescuer. He watched as the figure in the tin-foil helmet made her way towards the revolving doors. Sure enough, everyone ignored her. It wasn't so much that people didn't see her. It was clear that for the most part, they did, but once they had their reaction was simply to pretend that they hadn't. Only small children stared and pointed – that is until the adult hand they were holding dragged them away, in embarrassment.

It was a peculiar tactic, but then nothing about Hercules' en-counter with the stranger so far had been exactly normal. Strange clearly seemed to be her modus operandi. Certainly, no one paid Hercules the slightest bit of attention as he followed in the stranger's wake towards the nearest exit. Within seconds they were both on the pavement at the front of the terminal building.

'Is the tin-foil still necessary?' asked Hercules.

The stranger patted her head. 'No,' she said, pulling it off and shaking out her shoulder-length hair that had been tucked up inside it. She crumpled the foil into a ball and looked around for a bin. 'I sink it has done its job, for now. But we're still not really safe until zere is some distance between us and ze airport. Come on, ze buses are zis way.'

She started walking towards the bus stop at the end of the road. They arrived just as a bus was pulling up.

'Where are we going?'

'Anywhere, for now – put some distance between us and ze airport. 'ave you eaten?'

'They gave me a sandwich when they locked me up, that was last night.'

'Zat settles it, zen; breakfast it is.'

'Er, I don't mean to be rude,' said Hercules, 'but who exactly are you?'

'But of course – please excuse me. I sink we are safe enough now. Allow me to introduce myself. My name is Albertine. Albertine Whodini.'

* * *

Nick peered through the windscreen at the large building opposite. He turned to Maximilian Dumars.

'Well, I guess this is it, Boss.'

'Indeed. Do hurry up, Nick. We have got other things to do today, you know.'

Nick was dressed in his courier uniform. Beside him, Maximilian Dumars was dressed in black trousers and a smart white shirt, but his jacket was still in its carrier, which was hanging in the back of the van.

'And we're all agreed on the target?' There was a note of uncertainty in Nick's voice.

'We went through this a hundred times last night, Nick,' snapped Mr Dumars. 'We need a building opposite the United Nations office – so they will notice. We need a building that is big – so they will see how powerful we are. And we need something that makes a statement. We agreed last night that this building fits the bill.'

Together they peered up at the curving façade of the home of the World Intellectual Property Organization. The Geneva skyline is not a high-rise cityscape, but this large steel and mirrored glass construction was imposing enough for their purposes. And it was directly across the road from the United Nations Offices. It was one of the largest buildings in the neighbourhood. Its disappearance could hardly go unnoticed.

Maximilian Dumars handed Nick a box. It was covered in labels and a branded packing tape that matched the livery of Nick's uniform. Nick took the box and Maximilian Dumars passed him a small handheld barcode reader.

'It's quite straightforward – even you can't mess this up. Tell me one last time what you are going to do.'

'Go to the front desk. Tell 'em I've got a special delivery. It's gotta be signed for in person.'

'Good. And then?'

'They'll let me through to the offices. On my way to make the delivery I duck into the gents and drop off the special delivery.' He grinned. Maximilian Dumars stared at him coldly. 'Then I go to the office, deliver the box, get it signed for and get out.'

It had been quite a revelation, the evening before, when they had been discussing possible targets with Monsieur Beaucoupdiables. The old man had been extremely well informed about the layout and occupancy of all the important buildings in Geneva. The Organization clearly had tentacles everywhere.

After they had finished their dinner Monsieur Beaucoupdiables had cleared the dishes away. He had returned to the table with a large-scale street map of the district surrounding the United Nations, which he had spread across the table. Together they had pored over the chart in the hunt for a suitable target on which to demonstrate their powers.

'It just so happens,' he said, 'that we have been diverting a few deliveries of late in preparation for your little adventure. By happy coincidence, I have one here that is due tomorrow at the home to the Organisation Mondiale de la Propriété Intelectuelle – the World Intellectual Property Organization. It is perhaps a touch ironic that there is no patent yet on the material that will destroy their Headquarters, non?'

He laid the parcel on the table, roughly folding the map and pushing it to one side. He unfolded the paper he was carrying and laid it in the space just cleared. It was an architectural blue-print.

'Here,' he said, pointing to a point in the centre of the curved plan 'is the main reception on the ground floor. The recipient of this parcel has an office,' he paused and traced the paper with his finger as he searched for the right location, 'here: on the sixth floor.' He pointed triumphantly at a spot on the paper. 'There are some toilets on the floor - here. Hide the Dark Anti-Matter in the toilets. It's not something that will be picked up by scanners or sniffer dogs, so even if they sweep the building when we call in the attack they'll never find it.'

'I still don't see why we have to give them a warning,' said Maximilian Dumars, relishing the memory of the liquefaction of

Schrödinger the kitten, and thinking how inflicting the same fate on some actual people might be a most effective demonstration of the power of the Aryan Defence Order/League/Front; as long as he was well outside splashing distance this time.

'It is not good politics,' said Monsieur Beaucoupdiables patiently, 'to start killing indiscriminately.' He paused before adding coldly, 'At least, not yet. Non, we must display our power *and* our reason. When they see that we are not monsters, the governments will come round to our way of thinking all the more quickly. Besides, the warning will occupy the attention of the authorities, while you direct yours towards your real target.'

And so here they were, about to put phase one of Operation New World Order into action.

'You're a lucky so-and-so, Nick.' Eugene's voice came from the back of the van. There was some movement and the vehicle rocked on its axles. 'I wish it was me doing this.'

'Don't worry, Eugene, you'll get your chance.' Maximilian Dumars turned to Nick. 'Well, go on Nick. You know what to do. Off you go.'

'Right,' said Nick. 'Wish me luck.'

'Good luck, mate.' The voice from the back of the van called out.

'Oh, do get on with it,' said Mr Dumars.

Nick got out. Maximilian Dumars watched him turn into the building and then he was lost from view.

'Do you think he'll be alright, Boss?' There was a touch of concern in Eugene's voice.

'Oh, for heaven's sake! He's only dropping off a box. How hard can that be?'

As soon as the words had left his mouth, Maximilian Dumars realised that he hadn't entrusted any kind of responsibility to either of his colleagues before this. In fact, all they had ever really done was argue about suitable names for their organisation and moan about the state of the country. He suddenly became acutely aware of the ticking of his wristwatch. As he and Eugene waited, the ticking of the watch began to fill the silence like an omen of menace. Each tick was like the drip of a Chinese water torture, stripping away his sanity.

A minute passed. It seemed like an hour.

Five minutes passed. It felt like they had been waiting all day.

Ten minutes. How could it possibly take so long to deliver a simple parcel? They must have been here a week.

Fifteen minutes. The panic was beginning to rise in Maximilian Dumars. He told himself to calm down. Even if Nick had been caught, there was nothing that linked them as long as Nick kept his mouth shut. Nick could never keep his mouth shut. Maximilian Dumars felt the panic surging up inside him like a wave, pressure building with each echoing tick of the watch on his wrist.

The van door opened, and Nick slipped into his seat. Maximilian Dumars nearly leapt out of his skin.

'What the devil…?' he almost shrieked.

'Nick! How'd it go?'

'Piece of cake, Eugene,' said Nick with deep satisfaction. 'Breezed through the front desk, hid the stuff in the bogs and dropped off the parcel like a regular courier. You know, I think if we weren't taking over the world I could be quite good at that job… Anyway – I took the long route back, just in case I'd picked up a tail.' Nick was acting as though he was now a seasoned practitioner of the arts of surveillance, counter-surveillance and anything that came in between.

'Yes, well I don't think that was completely necessary!' snapped Maximilian Dumars, bursting Nick's bubble. He had recovered enough to regain his habitual unpleasantness. 'Let's get out of here. It's high time we moved on to Phase Two.'

* * *

Since time immemorial, the triangular lateen sails and double-ended hull of the dhow has been a familiar sight in the waters between the East of Africa and India.

On this particular morning a large twin-masted dhow is sailing up the Red sea, on the Sudanese side but just outside Sudanese territorial waters. It's a sight that is no more unusual in these parts than the white sand of the beaches that line the coast, or the grey mountains that rise in the desert behind the beaches. It's a sight that is as familiar to the seas of the region as the passage of camels – the ships of the desert – is to the lands that surround them.

* * *

As soon as the Maximilian Dumars and his colleagues had left the house that morning, Legion had slipped out of the guise of Monsieur Beaucoupdiables and into a more comfortable form, but he had stayed in the house. He had decided against going back to Hell. He wasn't leaving Geneva. After all his hard work, when Armageddon began, he wanted a ringside seat.

Legion pottered around the house for a while, killing time until there was something more exciting to do. Human habitations always fascinated him: the meaningless detritus that accumulated around people's lives was a constant source of amazement. Take the owner of this house, for example. In his life he had a managed to amass a fine collection of jugs. Jugs of all sorts were everywhere: in cupboards, on windowsills and shelves. Legion had no idea why anyone should ever need more than perhaps one jug. And yet here the evidence before him was that the owner of this house would rather have spent money on his collection of jugs than doing any-thing to improve the well-being of his immortal soul. What use were all these jugs to the cold corpse in the cellar now? As Legion had choked the life out of the old man the evening before, he had been hoping that the soul of the miserly wretch was irrevocably tarnished, and he would be notching up one more minor triumph in the everlasting struggle of evil over good. But just before the death rattle rasped in the old man's throat, Legion saw a look of resignation in his eyes and positively *felt* the divine forgiveness of the Creator. He watched in dismay as the soul left the limp body and shot *upwards*. Never mind, he had told himself. He hated to lose a single soul, but his ultimate purpose here was going to prove rather more – terminal. For everything.

Legion's iPhone rang. All demons had an iPhone. It wasn't for the slick styling – however important style is to any self-disrespecting demon –or the apps. There was just something about the manufacturer's logo that struck a chord with them.

'Yes,' he answered. Legion found a simple answer best when he was juggling personalities and, as was the case now, he didn't recognise the number calling.

'Monsieur Jean?' Legion recognized the voice of Bartholème, the young border guard.

'Speaking,' replied Legion, slipping into character as the Interpol officer.

'Monsieur Jean, sir, it is Bartholème… calling from Cointrin airport,' the caller added. 'Sir, we 'ave a bit of a problem.'

'Go on,' said Legion.

'I 'ave just come back on shift, sir, and I went to check the 'olding cell. The terrorist we detained yesterday – he 'as gone.'

'Gone?' said Legion. 'What do you mean, gone?'

'He was not in ze cell, sir,' came the reply. 'He 'as escaped.'

'I don't believe it!' exclaimed Legion. 'Do you know how long we have had this operation running? Do you have any idea how many hours of police work it has taken to isolate this individual? How close we were to breaking open the whole ring? All you had to do was keep him in custody for twenty-four hours!'

''E appears to 'ave 'ad 'elp, sir,' Bartholème was sounding nervous now.

'Help? Who did he have help from?'

'I am afraid we do not know zat, sir. We 'ave been checking ze CCTV footage, but we 'ave not been able to find anything yet. Even when 'e left ze cell we 'ave nothing. It is like one minute 'e was zere and zen 'e 'as gone. 'Ooever was 'elping 'im must 'ave 'acked into our camera system. It is ze only possible explanation.'

'Your utter incompetence could be another,' said Legion, crossly. 'Last night I was congratulating you for saving your city from a potentially devastating terrorist attack and how do you repay me? By letting the perpetrator slip through your fingers, that's how! I shall be letting your inferiors know about this.'

There was a puzzled silence. 'Don't you mean superiors, sir?'

'That's what I said,' Legion fumed. 'I shall be letting your superiors know about this.'

'We still 'ave 'is passport, sir. We 'ave alerted the police in the city. Should we alert the media too?'

Legion paused in his anger and smiled to himself. He looked at the clock on his phone. By his reckoning, his friends from the Aryan Defence Order/League/Front should have made their first delivery by now. This was actually a stroke of luck. While the city searched for Hercules Leek, his three bona fide terrorists could go about their business unhindered.

'Normally we would err on the side of caution,' he said slowly. 'But I think in this instance, with the threat as it is, I think it is wise to enlist the help of the civilian population, yes. But make sure the bulletins carry the usual riders that this man is *extremely* dangerous and not to be approached by any member of the public.'

'Yes, sir, I shall see to it, toute de suite.'

'You may well yet have a chance to redeem yourself, Bartholème. Keep me informed of any developments.'

'Of course, sir.'

Legion ended the call and smiled. What had, at first, seemed like a bit of a disaster had actually turned out to be something that could be used to his advantage.

Legion dialled a new number. It was the emergency services. The call was quickly answered.

'Quelle service voulez-vous?'

'Police,' replied Legion. He was connected to a police operator.

'I'm afraid I have to inform you there is a bomb in one of the buildings in the vicinity of the United Nations,' Legion drawled. He really couldn't remember the last time he'd had so much fun.

* * *

Under the fierce Egyptian midday sun, the overnight train from Cairo pulled into the platform at Aswan. Asif stepped from the comfort of the air-conditioned interior into the scorching desert heat. In one hand he carried the cage with his two birds. In the other he held his small suitcase.

Placing the cage and suitcase on the platform, he took a handkerchief from his pocket and mopped his brow. With the sudden change of temperature beads of sweat had erupted from his forehead.

He returned the damp cloth to his pocket, extended the handle of his suitcase, picked up his birdcage and set off along the platform, wheeling his luggage behind him. The station building was mercifully shaded and cooler than the air outside. Asif crossed the concourse towards the exit. He had pre-hired a four-wheel drive truck from the UK and made arrangements with the hire company to be met by one of their agents at the station.

Sure enough, as he approached the station exit, there was a waiting man holding a piece of cardboard with his name written on it. Asif approached him.

'Salaam aleikum,' he said.

'W'aleikum salaam,' the man replied.

'You have my car?'

'A beauty,' the man flashed him a smile that revealed a mouthful of tobacco-stained teeth underneath his full moustache. 'Toyota Landcruiser. Come – let me show you.'

* * *

Until the breakfast had been laid out in front of him, Hercules hadn't realised just how hungry he was; but at the appearance of a plate piled high with croissants and pains au chocolat and a large cup of good coffee his body had begun firmly to insist on refuelling before it would agree to take him any further.

Compared to the spartan surroundings of the cell in which Hercules had spent the night, the café was warm and comforting. It wasn't large, but it was doing a brisk trade. Most of the tables were occupied, and there was a steady stream of customers popping in for items to go. In the corner, a large flat screen television was tuned to a sports highlights show.

Hercules took a break from shoving croissants into his mouth.

'So how did you know I was here?' he asked.

'Internet,' replied Albertine, vaguely.

'I'm not sure I follow you,' said Hercules.

'I am a...' Albertine paused, searching for the right word, '...a Monitor.'

'I'm not sure I know what one of those is.'

'A Monitor?' said Albertine. 'I monitor things – the sorts of things that people should be interested in, but often don't get told about by the authorities. There is a sort of network of us, I suppose, but it is all very unofficial. We are incognito. No real structure, just a few like-minded individuals dotted around the place. We eavesdrop on official communications, 'ack the odd gouvernment network, that sort of thing. And when we find something out, we make sure it finds its way to the right channels.'

'Which are?'

'Protest groups, social media sites – there are a lot of ways to shine a torch onto the wrongdoings of those in positions of power.'

'What does all this have to do with me?'

'Well - there was a post on one of our forums last night. One of our – I 'ate to use the word because it makes us sound like a club, but it is probably the easiest way to explain it – one of our "members" in England was eavesdropping police radio last night and 'e over'eard a strange conversation. Apparently a drunk 'ad just been taken into custody raving about a chap called 'ercule Lick 'oo had come back from the dead and was 'unting down a demon 'oo was going to end the Universe. We all 'ad a bit of a laugh about it at the time, to be 'onest. But later there is a detention at Cointrin – I 'ave a back-door into the airport systems that sends me alerts on this sort of thing – and your name crops up. I guess I 'ad to see it for myself. May I?'

'See it?' asked Hercules, puzzled. 'See what?'

'Well, apparently the old drunk said you 'ad an angel feather. Do you?'

Hercules paused. Obviously it turned out that the last time he had trusted his story to someone, his trust had been betrayed almost immediately. In fairness to the homeless man, though, he hadn't hidden from Hercules what he was going to do with the information, and Hercules certainly didn't envy him having to sleep rough, even at this time of year. As it had turned out, the tramp's indiscretion had actually served to Hercules' advantage. Without it, he would still be in that cell.

Carefully, and guarding it from the other diners by cupping his hands around it, Hercules took the M.O.R.A.L compass out of his pocket. He held his hands across the table and parted them slightly. The light from the angel feather glowed out of the gap. Albertine leant forward and looked into Hercules' cupped hands. Her brown eyes widened.

'Wow,' she said. 'If you are making this up, that is an absolutely incroyable trick. No apparent power source, but it is emitting light. No obvious method of suspension, and yet it is 'olding dead centre of your little globe. It certainly does not look like ze feather of any bird I recognise. So what about the rest of it, eh? Demons? The End of Days? Is zat all true as well?'

Hercules explained, as best he could, in between sips of coffee and the odd bite of pastry, the events that had followed his first encounter with the wheels of Moses Malone's truck, up to his incarceration in the holding cell at the airport.

'Which is where you come in – so you know the rest,' he finished. He swirled the last of his coffee in his cup, lifted the cup to his lips and drained it. 'You don't mind if I get another one of these, do you? It really is very good.' He waved at a waitress who came over and took his order. From outside, there was the wail of a police siren crossing the city at speed.

'So what now?' asked Albertine. 'What do you think those guys you were following are up to?'

'I've really no idea,' said Hercules. He had noticed when Albertine had asked to see the M.O.R.A.L compass that the feather had started to become agitated again. He was beginning to feel that they would have to start trying to track down the men he had been following, but he really did need to stock up on coffee and carbohydrates after the night he had had, if he was going to be able to do anything. The waitress returned, bringing him his fresh cup of coffee.

'What would you attack, if you were them?' asked Hercules. 'You know Geneva.'

'Tell me about the un-fundamental material your friends say they 'ad,' said Albertine.

'Well, I don't really know much about it,' answered Hercules, honestly. 'It's obviously very powerful. From what I gathered it's part of the fabric of Hell, but how they would use it on the mortal plain, I've no idea. I guess anything could be the target.'

'Hmm,' said Albertine, 'if what you say is right, I guess anything *could* be the target, but then why Genève? Why bother leaving England. It must be something that is *'ere.*'

'Do you have any ideas?'

'Well I don't know about un-fundamental material, but Genève is home to the biggest study of *fundamental* particles in the world. And that 'as just got bigger.'

Hercules looked blank.

'CERN? The Even Bigger Hadron Collider? It is the main reason that I am 'ere, really.'

Hercules kicked himself. He had followed the story of the expansion of the tunnels at the CERN facility with some interest before his death. As an armchair scientist, he was always hopeful that physics would achieve some unifying theory that would put an end to the need for the agnostic element of his atheism. As it transpired, his death had actually managed that, but for a completely different reason. Another siren wailed in the distance.

'The upgrade of the old Large Hadron Collider is causing quite a stir in certain circles. When the LHC found the 'iggs boson CERN set out to create an even bigger accelerator. Some people think it is a total waste of money, others that it is going to create the black 'ole that the LHC never did and that will swallow us all.'

'And you?'

'Moi…I am a Monitor – I just report on anything they try to 'ide.'

'And are they hiding anything?'

Albertine shrugged. 'They are scientists. They live to publish data – they are pretty good at that. But they do not tend to be that open about the possibility of things going wrong: particularly at the energy levels that this new collider will generate. That is why I am interested. And if you ask me, if I 'ad a dangerous particulate matériel that could cause a massive explosion, I know where I would be 'eading if I wanted to make an even bigger bang.'

'So you think we should head over to the CERN laboratory then?' asked Hercules.

'If I were a gambling woman,' replied Albertine, 'I would put money on the EBHC being the target.'

The sports program on the television in the corner of the café was suddenly interrupted by a news bulletin. As the anchor delivered his stern synopsis of the breaking headline, the café owner grabbed the remote off the counter and turned up the volume.

Hercules and Albertine turned to look at the screen.

'What's he saying?' asked Hercules, as the shot cut to a roving reporter doing his piece to camera. He was speaking French. In the background of the shot, police had set up a barrier and an array of emergency vehicles was parked with their blue lights flashing. Beyond the police cordon, a stream of people could be seen leaving buildings and directed away from the hazard zone.

Albertine held up a hand for silence as she listened to the conclusion of the report. The cameras cut back to the studio.

'If I were a gambling woman,' she said, 'I think I would just 'ave lost a lot of money. They're clearing buildings around the United Nations offices. It seems that someone 'as called in a warning that there is a bomb there.'

Hercules swigged his coffee. There were a couple of croissants left on the plate in front of them. He shoved them in his pocket.

'You think we should get over there?' asked Albertine.

'I'm pretty sure it's not a coincidence,' said Hercules as he pushed his chair back and stood up.

'Uh oh,' said Albertine.

'What is it?' Hercules followed Albertine's gaze back to the television screen.

Staring back at him, was his passport photo.

'Don't panic,' said Albertine calmly, pulling a 20 franc note from a pocket in her jacket as she stood up. 'No one looks like their passport photo. Do not do anything to draw attention to yourself.'

'But you recognised me,' pointed out Hercules, uncomfortably aware that the other patrons of the café were all beginning to look in his direction.

'Hmm. Good point,' said Albertine, laying the money on the table and carefully pinning it under one of the coffee cups. 'Run!'

Together, they rushed from the café and into the street.

* * *

Hercules hurtled after Albertine as she raced across the square and disappeared down a side street.

They sprinted along for a few hundred yards. Hercules could hear his heart pounding in his ears as the air rasped into his heaving lungs. The distant wail of sirens now carried a new significance. Hercules began to imagine a net closing around him.

Suddenly, Albertine swerved and ducked into a narrow alley. The rapid change of direction caught Hercules by surprise, and as he struggled to adjust his direction of movement, while still travelling at full tilt, his foot hit something slippery on the pavement and his legs shot from beneath him. His body was thrown up into the air and he came down hard on his side, knocking the wind from himself.

For a moment all he could feel was the grey thump of the sudden impact. Adrenalin quickly forced his brain back to the urgency of his situation.

'Albertine, wait!' he called out, pushing himself up and gingerly examining his side with his fingers. He was badly bruised, but he didn't think he had broken anything. Instinctively his hand went to pat the pocket in which he had been carrying the M.O.R.A.L compass. It was flat. The familiar bulge of the celestial sphere was no longer there.

A cold wave of nausea swept over him.

'Are you alright?' Albertine was standing over him. 'Come on, this is not the time for a lie-down. You are Switzerland's Most Wanted, do not forget.' Albertine saw the look on Hercules' face.

'What is it?' she asked. 'What is wrong?'

Hercules carefully turned his pocket inside out. There was a tinkle as shards of glass fell to the pavement. Left clinging to the out-turned material of his pocket lining was the angel feather, which was glowing faintly. As the pair of them watched, open mouthed, the light emitted by the feather began to intensify. Spears of luminescence emanated from each delicate barb. The gentle glow of the feather became stronger and stronger until its incandescent brilliance illuminated the street. The brighter the feather shone, the more its substance faded, until, with a final blinding flash of dazzling luminosity the feather vanished, and the street was returned to the grey light of day.

It took precious time for Hercules' and Albertine's eyes to readjust to normal daylight. They were still half-blind when Albertine dragged Hercules to his feet and together they stumbled down the alley into which she had turned. Albertine was running her hands along the wall to guide them.

'I bet that attracted a fair bit of attention,' she grimaced, leaning against the wall and rubbing her eyes. 'How is your vision?'

'Still very bleached,' replied Hercules, leaning forward with his hands on his knees and breathing hard. With each draw on his lungs, his side shot through with stabs of pain.

Hercules looked up at Albertine. She was standing with her back to a boarded-up door, staring back down the alley in the direction from which they had come.

'Can you see anyone the other way?' Albertine asked.

Hercules scanned the alley in the direction they had been going.

'No,' he answered. 'There's no one there.'

'Good,' replied Albertine. She pulled on a brick at the corner of the door frame. There was a *click*, and the whole boarded up door, frame and all, swung open a couple of inches.

'Vite! Quickly! In 'ere!' Albertine urged, pulling the door wide enough for him to slip through. Hercules didn't need a second prompt. He ducked through the opening and Albertine followed, pulling the door shut behind her.

The darkness inside was a blessed relief. As they sat with their backs to the door, their breathing became shallower, and the burning impression of the incandescent feather faded from their retinas. After a few minutes their eyes had adjusted to the gloom. Hercules realised that they were at the end of a corridor. There were no windows, but a faint glow dimly lit the far end.

'What is this place?' asked Hercules.

'This,' said Albertine, pushing herself to her feet and extending a hand to help Hercules up, 'is my base. Welcome to Incognito: headquarters of the Geneva Monitors.'

'Headquarters? Monitors?' questioned Hercules. 'How many monitors are there?'

'Well, it *was* just me,' said Albertine, breezily. 'But you are 'ere now, so I guess there are two of us. Come on,' she continued as she started to make her way down the corridor in the direction of the glow, 'I will give you the grand tour.'

Ten

AS THEY APPROACHED the faint glow at the end of the corridor, Hercules realised that its source was light spilling under a closed door. They got closer and he became aware of a dull humming noise combined with the ultrasonic whine of electrical devices consuming power. Albertine paused with her hand on the door-handle.

'Behold,' she said with a grand sweeping gesture as she pushed the door open, 'the base.'

It wasn't on the same scale as the Information Wall, but Hercules had to concede that it wasn't a bad attempt for a single mortal. One wall of the room was completely covered with an array of flat-screen monitors, each streaming different images. A second wall was given up to a number of server racks, each stacked with boxes of flashing, winking lights. One of the remaining two walls was stacked high with books and magazines. The other wall was bare, but for a large poster of a familiar-faced old man with a shock of white hair and a twinkle in his eye, sticking his tongue out. Facing the bank of screens was a large leather sofa, in front of which stood a long coffee table. The coffee table and sofa were buried under even more books, magazines and computer peripherals, along with the remains of a number of take-away meals and the odd item of clothing.

The humming that Hercules had heard was coming from two powerful-looking air conditioners, which were battling with the heat output of all the electrical equipment to keep the room at a pleasantly cool temperature.

'Wow!' said Hercules, taking it all in. 'Not bad, for a ....'

'Girl?' Albertine flashed a fierce look of defiance with her impenetrable brown eyes.

'...Er, no. I was going to say "mortal". I mean, it's not quite on the scale of my last post,' Hercules grinned at her and her glare softened, 'but it's pretty insane all the same. Your electricity bill must be massive.'

'It probably would be,' shrugged Albertine, 'if I paid one.' She pointed to a thick cable that disappeared into a corner of the room. 'It sort of goes directly into the mains supply for the street.' This partial explanation was delivered with a mischievous grin of her own. 'A bit – 'ow do you say – makeshift, but the thing about Monitoring is that you never know 'ow long you're going to be in one place.'

Hercules looked at the racks and screens. It didn't look *that* makeshift.

'What is this place?' he asked.

'It is an old industrial unit. There are a few rooms back 'ere that used to be the back offices. On the other side there is some ware'ouse storage. It is piled 'igh with junk by the doors. I find that dissuades intruders.'

'What about the owners? Haven't they tried and to get new tenants?'

'Oh, I think they 'ave pretty much given up,' answered Albertine as she went over to the coffee table and started piling up takeaway cartons. 'They were trying to lease it when I first – er – moved in. That's how I found the place, actually, through one of their adverts.' She motioned to Hercules to hold open a bin bag, into which she dropped the rubbish. 'But after I took up residence, their adverts started mysteriously disappearing from the letting agencies' computers. I can't begin to think 'ow that might have 'appened.' She smiled innocently at Hercules, took the bin bag from him, and slung it unceremoniously past him through the open door and into the hall.

'Ah,' was about all Hercules could find to say. He turned his attention to the bank of screens on the wall. It looked like most of the screens were linked to CCTV feeds, except the one in the middle of the array, which was showing an old Tom and Jerry cartoon. 'So where are all these pictures coming from?' he asked.

'Places of interest,' Albertine replied vaguely, as she continued to clear a space towards the usable surfaces of her furniture.

On closer examination of the pictures, Hercules recognised a couple of views of the airport where he had spent the last night as a captive. As he watched, he realised he could track the passage of some of the people on view across a number of the screens as they moved around the fields of view of different cameras.

'Hey,' he said, 'isn't that the airport?'

'Mostly,' replied Albertine, rummaging down the side of the sofa. 'Sort of,' she added.

'"Sort of"?' asked Hercules. 'What do you mean – "sort of"?'

For a moment, Albertine did not reply, as she stretched her arm deep between the sofa cushions. Her fingers found what she was looking for. With a triumphant 'Voilà!' she pulled her arm back out. She was holding a remote control. She pointed it at the screen in the centre of the array. The cartoon disappeared and was replaced by a computer operating system. Albertine tossed the remote back onto the sofa.

'Some of it is actual live feeds from the airport,' she replied at last. She began waving her hands around, pointing to screens and flicking her hands. The pictures began to change. 'And some of it,' she continued, 'is what I've been playing into their system so they wouldn't see me come and rescue you.' Behind her on the sofa, unwatched, the remote control began its slow osmosis back into the hidden depths of the sofa.

Hercules stared in amazement. By rights, he felt that he shouldn't have been as impressed as he was. He had, after all, spent time in the I.T. department of Heaven. But Albertine was controlling her bank of screens with nothing more than gestures, and she seemed to have access to cameras all across Geneva.

'How are you doing that?' he asked.

'Which bit?' retorted Albertine casually. 'The gesture control is something I built after jail-breaking the motion sensors of a games console. It is not quite the Minority Report, but I'm quite proud of it.'

'It is pretty impressive,' agreed Hercules. 'How come you've got access to all those cameras?'

'Well, a lot of it is good old-fashioned 'acking,' said Albertine. 'But the airport, well it is almost like they invite you in.'

'How do you mean?' asked Hercules.

'Self-service boarding passes,' replied Albertine.

Hercules was getting used to the need to be persistent. 'How does self-service boarding give you access to their cameras?'

Albertine took a break from waving her hands around and looked at Hercules.

'What's on a self-service boarding pass?' he asked.

'I don't know,' replied Hercules, 'flight details, your name and passport number...'

'And...'

'I don't know what you're getting at.'

'How is the boarding pass processed?'

'Er – they scan a barcode?'

'Exactly! A barcode that contains a computer readable version of the details printed on the boarding pass. Well, actually it's a database reference to the record of your reservation details…Unless you know how to make it into something else.'

'Something else?'

'Well, obviously you need to keep the reference to your flight reservation. Otherwise you'd never get on the plane. But I've found it can be useful to bury a few additional instructions in the barcode that can sit on the airport network and provide me a useful back door. I think that last night it more than paid off the efforts it required to devise.'

Hercules thought about it. It hadn't seemed strange at the time that the alarm had not been raised, but then the adrenalin had been coursing through his body. As he watched the images of empty corridors be replaced with pictures of the same locations showing people moving about, Hercules realised that in part their escape was due to the fact that Albertine had hijacked the airport security system and that while they had been tip-stroll-toeing to freedom, the CCTV had been relaying images of empty corridors. They had been invisible to any watching cameras.

'Hold on,' said Hercules slowly, 'you made me do that ridiculous walk.'

Albertine burst out laughing. 'You were actually not bad at it, for a first attempt!'

'What about the tin-foil hat?' he said.

Albertine stopped laughing and looked at him seriously. 'Tell me,' she said, 'when we crossed the airport concourse, 'ow many people were looking at *you*?'

'Ah.'

'Exactly. Now, I think it is time we started doing something useful. The men you were following were on the same flight, you say?'

Hercules nodded. Albertine turned back to the screens and began gesturing again.

'Well, while we are connected to the airport system,' she began spinning her left index finger in an anti-clockwise circle in the air, 'let's 'ave a little rewind to when the rest of the passengers from your flight cleared customs, and if we can find some decent pictures of them, we will see if there is any background information we can dig up that might 'elp us.'

* * *

A van pulled into the petrol station across the road from the CERN visitor centre. Maximilian Dumars looked at the large wooden Globe building in front of them and tutted. Maximilian Dumars' psyche did not contain the space for people to construct large spherical wooden buildings; at least, not *right*-minded people. Such frivolous architecture was obviously the product of tree-hugging communists. It was not the sort of thing he would condone. Not that this mattered. Very soon, *he* would be in charge. Maximilian Dumars made a mental note that the first edict of his reign would see the building before him reduced to something more practical – matchsticks, perhaps. Or, better still, just burn it where it stood – a symbol to the world of the New Order that was taking place and a warning to those who stood in its path.

'Right,' he said. 'You both know the plan. Are we all ready?'

* * *

Abdul sat at the back of the dhow, watching the fishing lines that trailed in the foaming waters of the ship's wake. He had been a part of the crew of this boat for a couple of years now, and had experienced more than his share of adventures. As the boat made its stately progress northwards, though, adventure seemed a million miles away.

To Abdul, nothing felt better than the sea breeze on his face and the promise of freshly baited fishing lines. Like his father before him, and his father's father before that, and the crewmates that he worked alongside, Abdul was a fisherman.

A movement on the horizon caught his eye. He cupped a hand across his brow to shield his eyes from the bright sunshine that washed all colour from the distance and made an endless whole of the place where sea met sky. A boat was approaching at speed, making a bee-line through the gentle swell straight towards them.

Abdul stiffened. A sharp whistle through his teeth alerted his crewmates. They abandoned the various tasks they had been engaged in and crowded around the stern, following Abdul's gaze towards the vessel that was fast approaching them. Only the ship's captain had kept his post. He was already at the stern, trimming the large tiller that kept the dhow on its course. He had spotted the approaching launch at almost the same moment as Abdul.

'Back to your posts, men,' he barked. 'Lower the sails.'

'But we will be sitting ducks, Captain!'

'They are much too fast for us – we cannot outrun them... It would be pointless to try. Let us see what they want – when they see we are just poor fishermen they will probably leave us alone, Inshallah.'

His men could see the sense in the old tar's words. They set about the task he had given them. Ropes were unhitched, the large triangular sails furled towards deck and their vessel slowed in the water.

The boat that was closing towards them altered its course to account for the loss of speed of the dhow which was no longer being pushed forward by the breeze. The approaching launch was close now – the figures of its crew could be made out. One man standing on the prow was clearly armed with a machine gun. The crew of the dhow watched with a shared look of grim anticipation as it neared.

The motor launch came in close, cut the throttle on its powerful engines to idle, and slowed till the two boats were rolling gently side by side, separated by about thirty feet of water.

'Salaam,' called out the man on the prow of the launch.

'W'aleikum Salaam,' the captain of the dhow called back.

'What is your business here?' the figure on the launch called back. He was wearing a tan military uniform, as were the two colleagues who joined him from the small wheel house. They were also armed; all three men carrying their weapons casually, but with their fingers close to the triggers and ready for confrontation. A fourth figure remained at the boat's controls.

'We are fishermen,' replied the captain, pointing to the lines trailing from the back of the dhow. 'Our village is half a day's sailing down the coast. The winds have blown us this way and, Inshallah, it has lead us to a spot where we will catch food for our families and for market.'

The armed men conferred amongst themselves.

'We would like to come aboard and check your vessel.'

'Be our guests, but all we have is nets and fishing lines.'

Despite the captain's offer of hospitality, it was clear that the crew of the dhow did not like the sound of being boarded. The men on the launch sensed their unease, and their grips tightened on their weapons. Although it was the men on the launch that were armed, they were outnumbered by the crew of the dhow. As the small waves slapped against the sides of the two vessels, the tension in the air was palpable. The flag on the motor launch fluttered gently in the breeze.

One of the lines trailing from the back of the dhow suddenly twanged taught. The attention of the men on both boats turned to the straining cord. Abdul looked at the captain, who nodded slightly at him. Abdul leapt forward, freed the line and began to play the fish on the end. Whatever had taken the baited hook was obviously not small.

The line zipped back and forth through the water. The men watching Abdul's battle with the big fish, from both crews, called out encouragement and advice.

'Let it run, let it tire!'

'Bring it up slowly!'

'Don't lose it!'

But this was an art that Abdul was well practiced in. He ignored the comments and played the fish with expert skill. Even so, it was strong and heavy. After what felt like an age to his aching arms, some of the men who had started leaning over the side of the boat to see if they could catch a glimpse of Abdul's adversary through the clear blue waters called out.

'There it is!'

Flickers of sliver shone from the depths as the fish continued to fight the line.

'It's a monster!'

Slowly Abdul brought the tiring fish to the surface. A huge silvery trevally, with its bluntly domed head, broke the surface and rolled on its side, worn from exhaustion. It was quickly gaffed in the gills and two men struggled to bring the enormous weight of the fish on to deck.

The men on the boat clapped their delight, and the crew of the motor launch joined in the round of applause.

'You see,' called out the captain of the dhow. 'We are just simple fishermen. If you would like to share in our catch...'

The men on the motor launch exchanged a few quick words among themselves.

'No, we do not wish to disturb your work. We just have to keep these waters safe for honest seafarers like yourselves. May you enjoy good fishing!'

'Thank you,' replied the captain. 'Inshallah, we will. But there is little to trouble us here, it is too far north for the pirates that plague the south of this sea.'

'And may it stay that way.' The man in the wheelhouse pushed forward on the throttle easing the launch forward through the water. His crew mates waved as they passed alongside the dhow.

As the crew of the dhow watched the motor launch shrink into the distance, the captain stepped forward and gently closed the lid over a locker that had been opened, unseen by the men on the motor launch, when they had prepared to board to dhow. As the wooden lid came down, an arsenal of machine guns and rocket launchers, far superior in number to the armaments of the coast guard patrol, was hidden once more from daylight.

Yes, Abdul and his crewmates were fishermen. At least, that was the trade that they had learned from their fathers, who had learned it from their fathers before, whom in turn each came from a long lineage of fishermen. Generations of men from the villages on the Somali coast from where they came had supported their families by harvesting the riches of the sea. And so, as a young man, Abdul had believed he would one day pass his skills to his own sons and the traditions would continue.

But then the strawlers had come.

Big ships, dragging huge nets and powered by engines and not the wind came and plundered the waters on which Abdul and his countrymen relied. The captains of these foreign vessels were unconcerned with the destruction they wrought on the reefs with their dragnets, or the poverty they inflicted on the villages of the coast. Unsupported by a government that itself was in chaos, the villagers continued to suffer until they realised that if a lawless government would not help them, it was also unlikely to stand in their way if they took the law into their own hands.

The first pirate raids had succeeded as much thanks to the element of surprise as any detailed planning. The ransoms they demanded had been modest. But it soon became clear that international shipping included some very valuable commodities that insurers were happy to pay handsomely to retrieve. In next to no time piracy had replaced fishing as the prime source of local employment.

But even as the rewards of the early raids were reaped, and re-invested into weapons and better engines to carry out more daring raids, so the response of the international community made the whole enterprise more challenging.

Now naval vessels from several countries patrolled the old hunting grounds. Ships travelled in convoy for mutual protection, and merchant crews were better trained in repelling attacks. Some were even armed.

So the captain of the dhow on which Abdul sailed had taken the decision to head north and seek victims among those who thought they were safe. It seemed that fortune favoured the bold – their recent run-in had shown that even the coastguard did not expect pirates at these latitudes.

Once more the element of surprise would be theirs.

* * *

Nick watched Eugene and Maximilian Dumars cross the road and head into the Visitor Centre. It was his turn to take a back seat in the operation, but, flushed with success of his role in the guise of a courier, he was happy for the others to take centre stage for a while. He wasn't going to be idle: he had a vital job to do in providing support to the next, pivotal, part of the mission. And besides, it gave him a chance to get out of the cheap synthetic fibres of the delivery uniform and into the more refined tailoring of his new Aryan Defence Order/League/Front apparel.

The previous evening, Monsieur Beaucoupdiables had informed Maximilian Dumars that he and Eugene were booked onto a guided visitor tour of the CERN facility. The guided visitor tour, Monsieur Beaucoupdiables explained, not only provided a straight-forward means of access to the EBHC, but came with the added merits of a perfect opportunity for hostage–taking, which should provide the means not only to keep security services at bay for the requisite time period while the details of the plan were executed, but also a means to coerce the scientists into doing as they were told. Monsieur Beaucoupdiables was quite matter-of-fact. If they needed to kill a hostage or two to get the right level of co-operation from the scientists, they should not hesitate.

Not only was the guided tour perfect access to the CERN facility in its own right, but the day of their visit had been carefully selected for other reasons. It just so happened that on this particular day the Director-General of CERN was due to be conducting his own VIP tour of the ATLAS experiment, conveniently located just across the road from the Visitor Centre. The Director-General's tour was arranged to coincide with the public tour.

The Director-General was particularly proud of the educational aspects of CERN's work. With the trillion-euro investment in the extension of the LHC complete, he was engaged in a relentless pro-gramme of hospitality events where eager sponsors were given the opportunity to see for themselves the output of their philanthropic investments. The fact that the facility was open to the public, and as such meant that the story of particle physics could be told to anyone who turned up with an interest, was something that, the Director-General felt, exemplified just how much the work at CERN was carried out for the good of all mankind.

Nick slipped into the back of the van and started to get changed. As he was changing, he sat on a large box which contained some of the more extravagant weaponry that Monsieur Beaucoupdiables had furnished them with, including Eugene's belt-fed machine-gun. He had shown them all how to handle the various weapons after dinner the night before, and Nick had managed to regain some of his pride when he showed a natural talent for stripping down and reassembling the Uzi with which he had been presented.

He bundled his cheap courier jacket and trousers into a corner and slipped on the black uniform. The insignias on the jacket were covered with black patches for the time being. They would see the light of day soon enough.

Nick's job at the moment was to wait until the tour group had made its way into the ATLAS building, and then turn up with the weaponry to ensure that they had enough hostages. He slipped back into the driver's seat of the van and began to watch the doors of the Visitor Centre, wondering how long it would take before the tour group came out.

A tram rolled down the rails in the middle of the road and pulled to a halt. A few passengers stepped off and crossed the road away from him. If people were still arriving for the tour, thought Nick, it would be a while before he was called for.

Then, as the tram pulled away, the sight of a familiar figure made him sit up. Standing at the tram stop was an immaculately dressed gentleman with slick blond hair and a goatee beard, carrying a silver-topped walking cane. Nick's simple mind began to race as he watched Mr John cross the road and head off towards a different part of the complex of buildings.

* * *

'Wow! Look at this, Boss!'

Eugene had his hands on the surface of a large glass ball. Blue and pink lightning danced from a small sphere at the centre of the globe to the surfaces where Eugene's fingers touched the outer shell.

'It's bloody magic, Boss, this is.' Eugene's face was lit up in childish wonder.

'It's not magic,' said Maximilian Dumars coldly. 'It's a plasma sphere. Invented by Nikola Tesla,' he continued, passing off the knowledge that he was gaining from reading the plaque by the sphere as his own. 'And I've told you not to call me "Boss",' he hissed. 'Max will do, for now.'

Maximilian Dumars and Eugene were milling around in Microcosm, an exhibition set up to explain to visitors some of the background of the world of particle physics. Many of the intended audience of the displays were children, and it was perhaps for this reason that the level resonated so well with Eugene's uncomplicated brain. Maximilian Dumars, on the other hand, was much less engaged. It might not have been magic, but as far as he was concerned it was all fairly close to witchcraft: those elements that were not just plain mumbo-jumbo, that is.

'Hey, it says here, Max,' Eugene's lips moved as he read the notice in his head, 'that if you travel very, very fast time goes slower and distances get smaller. That's *amazing!*'

'Sounds more like total nonsense to me. Time doesn't change depending on how fast you're going! They've just made that up to fool gullible idiots like yourself.'

Eugene's brow furrowed. 'Yeah, I suppose you're right. I mean, when I'm waiting for a bus, five minutes can seem like ages, and then I'm not even moving. Huh, funny to think all these boffins have got that wrong. That's what I like about you, Bo... I mean Max. You can see straight through all the nonsense. Me and Nick are lucky to have you as a lead... I mean lucky to know you.'

Maximilian Dumars swelled at the compliment. For a brief instance his habitual meanness slipped.

'Thank you, Eugene,' he said. The thought crossed his mind that maybe he would not have to see to Eugene and Nick's "retirement" after all. It was quickly followed by another thought that said that however useful Nick and Eugene had been up to now, they were simple souls and would probably struggle to adapt to the New World Order. "Retiring" them would be doing them a favour.

Maximilian Dumars looked at his watch. The tour was due to commence in a matter of minutes. Other visitors were beginning to make their way towards the entrance of the exhibition hall and back to reception.

'You see,' said Maximilian Dumars. 'Time is passing at exactly its correctly allotted pace. We'd better get back to reception. Destiny awaits us.'

* * *

The Land-cruiser sped east from Aswan along the Halayeb road through the desert towards the coast.

The Toyota had been kitted out with a couple of tarpaulins, a sleeping bag and a selection of cooking and other camping utensils, including a shovel and some sand-ladders in case he ventured off-track. At Asif's request, the rental company had also provided a selection of food that would not spoil in the desert heat – mostly tinned food and rice, but also some flat-breads wrapped in a cloth. There was a small cool box, powered from the cigarette lighter, which was packed with a few perishables, and two large jerry-cans of water. On the back of the vehicle another jerry-can, carrying spare fuel, was fixed.

The road was flat and well-made, a dark tarmac strip that stood out from the sand of the surrounding desert. Mirages danced in the scorching heat of the early afternoon, but inside the air-conditioned comfort Asif was insulated from the extreme temperatures. Apart from his Land-cruiser, the road was deserted. The white lines in the centre of the road flashed past hypnotically, carrying Asif toward his destiny.

***

'That's it – that's them! Oh – you've gone past. Go forward a bit.'

Albertine stopped the tape rewinding and set it forward at half speed.

'There!' Hercules pointed.

Albertine paused the frame. There on the previous evening's footage from the immigration desk at the airport were the distinctive figures of the Aryan Defence Order/League/Front.

'Woah! That guy is massive!'

'The one in the middle is the leader. The other two kept calling him "Boss".'

Albertine stepped forward and spent a few moments examining the faces of the three men in close up. Then she stepped back and began waving her hand in the air as though she was rubbing writing from an imaginary whiteboard. As her arm arced to and fro, the screens went blank – except for the one containing the freeze-framed image of their adversaries and the screens at each corner of the array which appeared to contain feeds of CCTV cameras from the streets surrounding Monitor HQ.

Albertine gestured at the frozen image of the Aryan Defence Order/League/Front. The image zoomed into close-up on Maximilian Dumars. She then made a circular motion around Mr Dumars' face opening and closing her first two fingers as she did so. Her actions created a cut-out image of Maximilian Dumars' face, which she threw at another screen. She repeated the process for Eugene and Nick.

'Right,' Albertine said, turning to the screens that held the images of the three faces. 'Let's drop these faces into your British police force's face recognition system and see what turns up. I'm afraid this might take a bit of time...'

'You can do that from here?'

Albertine looked at Hercules. The look was obviously all the answer she thought the question deserved.

'And since it will take some time,' Albertine continued, as her gestures brought screens back into life with new connections, 'we should probably also be checking the local CCTV feeds from around the United Nations buildings to see if any of these gentlemen 'ave been in the neighbourhood today.'

****

'Hello, Everybody. My name is-a Gian-Carlo and I will be a-one-of-your tour guides today. Welcome to CERN.'

His announcement was met with some mumbled greetings from the assembled crowd by way of a response. Gian-Carlo smiled broadly.

'It's-a quite-a large-a group-a today. When-a we go over the road, to the ATLAS experiment, we will split into two groups. I will lead-a one group and my colleague Karl will lead-a the other. But now we watch a short film.'

He hit a key on a laptop at the front of the room that was connected to a projector, while Karl dimmed the lights. Fireworks lit up the screen at the front of the auditorium, accompanied by a musical score. A voice-over began.

'It is a time of celebration, here at CERN...' The camera closed in on a single spark from a firework, which morphed into a particle which the shot followed accelerating through a tunnel at incredible speed. 'And a time of great breakthroughs...' The particle suddenly met others coming from the opposite direction, and there was a spectacular on-screen explosion.

The computer graphics were replaced by images of the buildings of the CERN complex. 'What is the nature of matter? What gives matter mass?' the voice-over asked. Images of the buildings above ground gave way to pictures of tunnels and massive and complicated looking bits of machinery. 'These are some of the questions that the scientists here at CERN hope to answer, aided by their new Even Bigger Hadron Collider.

'Spanning the Franco-Swiss border around Geneva, this marvel of scientific and engineering achievement is truly one of the seven wonders of the modern world. The Even Bigger Hadron Collider, or EBHC as it is commonly known, extends the circuit of the earlier Large Hadron Collider – the LHC. If the scale of the LHC was amazing, the facts behind the EBHC almost defy imagining.

'The EBHC extends the original circular orbit of twenty-seven kilometres of the LHC into a new elliptical circuit which extends to the west under the Jura Mountains. The new circuit is a full forty-two kilometres in circumference.

'Some of the old experimental sites have been retained, and some new ones added. The largest particle detectors, operating at some of the coldest temperatures, the list of superlatives is almost endless.'

The voice-over began to reel off lists of figures about the size and weight and power-consumption of various aspects of the installation. Footage of the excavation work and construction phase of both the EBHC and the LHC, and even earlier black and white footage of the founding days of CERN were woven into the story the film presented.

Maximilian Dumars yawned behind his hand. Fascinating as this drivel might be to the gawping idiots that surrounded him, it was all nonsense. The EBHC had only really built for one purpose: to see him, Maximilian Dumars, take his rightful place in history.

'So what is the purpose of all this effort?' The voice-over posed a different version of the questions it had asked at the start of the film. 'Well, while it was operational, the LHC confirmed the existence of the Higgs Boson, the so-called "God Particle". It is this fundamental particle that some scientists believe lies at the very heart of understanding how matter attains mass. It is hoped that the increased energy levels available in collisions within the EBHC will throw more light on this mysterious particle, paving the way for increased understanding into the Universe around us.

'Sub-atomic physics has already given the world so much – MRI scanners in hospitals, the internet...' The footage was now of people in everyday life using items that had been invented as a bi-product of the scientific work at CERN. The shot turned to time-lapse of a city day running through into night in a matter of a few seconds. The cameras panned back to focus on the stars in the night sky. The camera shot began to accelerate upwards towards the sky, like a rocket, as the computer graphics took over, and once again the audience had the perspective of an accelerating particle. 'It is hoped that with this new experiment,' the voice concluded grandly, 'physics will provide us the very key to unlock the secrets of Creation.' Once more the particle met others travelling the other way and the film finished with a final, spectacular explosion.

There was a smattering of applause and the lights went up. Gian-Carlo addressed the audience.

'Right, Ladies anna Genlemen. Now we go across to look ata the ATLAS building; if you would kindly follow me.'

* * *

The group of visitors convened in the foyer of the building.

When the old circuit of the LHC had been extended to the new larger orbit of the EBHC, the monstrous feat of engineering that was ATLAS was one of the experiments that had been retained.

The building was readily identifiable beyond the spherical wooden dome of the Globe; its exterior had been decorated with a stylised graphic of the huge detector that was housed deep underground below the surface structure.

The tour group had split into two parties. Eugene and Maximilian Dumars had joined the group being led by Karl, who, he told the group, was originally from Austria. After graduating university he had been a research physicist at CERN for most of his working life. Now that he was retired, he kept involved by volunteering to take these tours.

'Please, if you have any qvestions, do not hesitate to ask. It is only by asking qvestions, after all,' he concluded, 'that we learn anything.'

The group was a broadly mixed collection of individuals. At Karl's invitation a rather intense looking young man stepped forward.

'E-excuse me, yes, I have a question,' he blurted, as though he had been waiting for this opportunity. There was something about his slightly sweaty fervour and bible-belt American accent that suggested he had not come on this tour to expand his understanding of sub-atomic physics. 'All this,' he waved his hands vaguely around at the buildings that surrounded them, 'all this,' he went on, 'has been built at huge cost to prove the theory of the Big Bang. It cost billions of Euros to build the LHC and it has cost billions more to build the new accelerator. What happens if the experiment shows that Big Bang is wrong?'

The young man looked around at his fellow tour members and smiled triumphantly. In his own eyes, he had played his ace card. He had trumped the sacrilegious Satan of science.

Karl was unphased. 'What is your name?' he asked the young man in a kindly manner.

'Luke,' he replied.

'Well, Luke, the EBHC, like the LHC before it, has been built to study physics. The Big Bang is not physics,' he explained evenly and patiently. 'Big Bang requires a set of circumstances that are not physically possible: infinite pressure, infinite temperature, so forth. These are not things that exist in nature, so they cannot be physics. Physics is the study of what happened *after* Big Bang. And as scientists, we hold a theory and test it against evidence. If a theory is not supported by the evidence, it is abandoned. That is the scientific way.'

There was another young man in the group, with a similar fervour to Luke, but his question suggested a diametric opposition of views.

'If God created the Universe and everything in it,' he stared pointedly at Luke, 'how come there were no anti-matter atoms until anti-hydrogen was produced at CERN?'

'That is also not a problem,' replied the retired physicist with a smile. 'If you believe in God, then it was He who created anti-atoms, at CERN, in 1995…and before anyone asks, if you so choose to believe, it was also He who decided that we should discover the Higgs Boson here in 2012.'

Karl looked around at the group. No-one else wanted to try and best the old man in a philosophical debate. Maximilian Dumars took the opportunity to take matters in a more practical direction.

'Will we be able to go down and see the accelerator?' he asked.

'No, this is not possible now,' replied Karl. 'The accelerator is operational. It is not a safe environment.'

The group accepted this statement at face value. Maximilian Dumars wondered what the danger might be, but nonetheless nodded sagely. 'And the material that is injected into the accelerator, where does that take place?'

'In a building about a kilometre that way,' replied Karl, waving a hand vaguely in the direction back past the Visitor Centre. Clearly these mundane matters did not register highly in a mind that had spent a lifetime in the dedicated pursuit of furthering man's understanding the Universe. 'Now, if there are no more qvestions, we go and look at the ATLAS, ya?'

He led the group along a path towards the colourful ATLAS building.

Access to the building approach was restricted by a heavy security gate that was controlled by a card swipe device. Karl used a security pass he had dangling from a lanyard around his neck to open the gate. Maximilian Dumars nudged Eugene in the ribs. Eugene stepped towards the tour guide while Maximilian Dumars held the gate open as the rest of the tour group passed through.

'So,' said Eugene to Karl, screwing up his face in an effort to remember his lines, 'do you think this co-llider will live up to the hype? Do you think that it will successfully further the study of the H-i-g-g-s Bo-son?'

This was clearly a subject closer to Karl's heart.

'The Higgs Boson is publicity,' he said. 'It gets the newspapers interested in what we do here, so in that way it is a good thing. They have to have a story. But a story is not physics. Now the collider is up and running, we can do physics.'

The last of the tour group had passed through the gate. Eugene stepped aside and Maximilian Dumars let the gate swing shut. Some people had paused to take photos of the artwork decorating the exterior walls of the ATLAS experiment. Karl waited a few moments and then continued to lead his charges towards the front doors of the building.

Karl hadn't noticed that while he had been engaged in conversation, behind Eugene and masked from sight by his colleague's massive frame. Maximilian Dumars had deftly removed a small tube of superglue from his pocket. He quickly unscrewed the cap and emptied the entire contents into the lock mechanism of the gate. The gate had swung shut, but the bolt of the seized-up locking mechanism no longer slid into place…

* * *

The screens on the wall in Albertine's hideout flicked from image to image as the databases of the British police and Geneva CCTV were searched for matches of the likenesses of the three men that Hercules had followed to the city. As the computers did their thing, Albertine quizzed Hercules in more detail about the events that had occurred since his death.

'It all seems a bit far-fetched now,' said Hercules. 'I mean, it's like a dream or a memory of a night when you've had too much to drink. I'm not really sure what to make of it myself now. Hey, why has that screen stopped changing picture?'

Albertine's eyes followed his pointing finger. Sure enough one of the screens had frozen on a picture. It was a police mug-shot of Nick.

'It is the police database,' said Albertine. She pushed herself up from the sofa and took up her control position.

'Have we found something?'

'Let's see,' replied Albertine. She pinched her fingers together and waved her hand to one side. The flicking images all shrunk to thumbnails. She pointed at the static image and spread her fingers. The mug-shot spread across the entire monitor array.

'So,' said Albertine, 'one of them has a name now; Nicholas Turpin, known as Nick. Let's see what he got in trouble for.' She pointed to an icon indicating more information and the screens re-adjusted so that a couple were given over to the details of Nick's criminal record.

Together they read through the list of Nick's encounters with the powers of justice.

'I don't get it,' said Hercules. 'A couple of charges of drunk and disorderly – it doesn't really add up to "member of master criminal organisation bent on world destruction", does it?'

'Maybe they have been chosen for this mission because they don't have too much – baggage.' Albertine waved and Nick's image shrunk down to a single screen. The other pictures resumed their previous positions and continued their flickering searches.

'I guess we'll just have to wait and see if anything crops up from the local footage.'

* * *

Captain Higgs paused at the foot of the ladder leading up to the bridge. In contrast to the stress of the previous couple of weeks, and the last couple of days in particular, today he felt enveloped by a blissful calm. What his Chief Officer had told him was true. The ship was almost unrecognizable from the vessel that had docked in Port Suez a day and a half before. The crew who were currently on shift were all happily engaged in their work, officers and deck-crew labouring with a common sense of good humour and a shared purpose. Captain Higgs had never witnessed such a dramatic turn-around in the fortunes of one of his charges. He had certainly never seen the *Good Ship* looking more, well, *ship-shape*.

* * *

There was another film to watch in the ATLAS building. It was a 3-D presentation of how the enormous detector had been lowered into place in its subterranean home when the original tunnels for the LHC had been excavated. Eugene was captivated by the 3-D imagery, even ducking and swaying when the crane swung the giant metal construction into place. This had something of a domino effect as the people around swayed out the way of Eugene's reactions to the film. As usual, Maximilian Dumars was less enamoured.

'How much longer are we going to have to wait?' he muttered to himself.

Eugene cast him a disapproving look. 'We've got to wait for the VIP guests, remember,' he hissed in a whisper. 'Can't you just try and enjoy yourself, Bo - Max. You might even learn something.'

Maximilian Dumars stared at Eugene. For an instant he was so shocked at the way he had been addressed that he didn't know how to respond. Then the poison bubbled up inside him. He seethed. He would not forget this slight. Eugene would pay.

* * *

It was approaching midday in Geneva, and the visit to the ATLAS building was drawing to a close. The two tour groups had reunited on the ground floor of the building, while their respective guides talked them through some of the activities of the half dozen physicists manning workstations the other side of a glass wall.

Maximilian Dumars was standing at the back of his group. He was not really paying attention to Karl's words. Instead, he was watching the small group of smartly dressed individuals approaching the building along the path outside. He hoped Nick was paying attention. He would be needed soon. Maximilian Dumars started. At the back of the group, strolling nonchalantly and twirling a silver topped can was a familiar figure.

Maximilian edged forward into the group and nudged Eugene. Eugene had been paying rapt attention to every word the old physicist had uttered. It was disconcerting to Maximilian Dumars, who had known Eugene for long enough as to be sure that he didn't understand a word of what he was being told. But Eugene was displaying the attentive demeanour of a young puppy and this troubled Mr Dumars. He nudged his large colleague hard in the ribs – harder than was necessary. Eugene barely noticed.

'Eugene!' he hissed.

Eugene turned and looked down at him.

Maximilian Dumars nodded towards the door. 'It's time.'

Like a sunrise, a look of realisation slowly crossed Eugene's face. He nodded and the pair of them backed out of the group towards the door.

Maximilian Dumars glanced back through the glass. The VIP party was almost at the threshold of the building. He looked anxiously back down the path towards the security gate, and breathed a sigh of relief. Nick had just pushed the gate open. He was struggling under the weight of a large canvas hold-all.

The door clicked open and one by one the VIP party filed in. Karl and Gian-Carlo exchanged glances. Karl stopped talking and deferred to his colleague.

'Ladies and-a Gentlemen,' Gian-Carlo addressed the members of the two tour parties, 'today we are honoured to be joined for the close of our tour by no less than the Director-General of CERN himself, and a group of his guests.'

The visitors turned towards the new arrivals in the building. There was some polite applause. Maximilian Dumars was staring past the Director-General at Mr John. Mr John winked at him. Behind, Nick slipped into the back of the room. He handed Eugene the hold-all, skirted the edge of the room and slipped through a side door towards the interior of the building. Amongst all the smart suits that had entered with the VIP guests, Nick's military styled uniform did not attract any attention; nor did the bulge in the back of his jacket, just above the waist.

The Director-General beamed at the applause. He held up his hands in gesture of modesty.

'Thank you, Gian-Carlo. I hope you are enjoying your visit, Ladies and Gentlemen.'

There were general murmurings of agreement.

'We are not here to interrupt your visit. Please continue as if we were not here.'

Gian-Carlo cleared his throat to resume speaking, but before he could continue, a voice piped up from the back of the room.

'I'm afraid that won't be possible, Mr Director.' It was Maximilian Dumars who was speaking. He was waving an Uzi casually in the air. It had the desired effect of focussing the attention of everyone in the room. Eugene had taken up position covering the doors. He slipped his huge machine-gun out of the canvas hold-all, draping a belt of ammunition over his arm as he did so. This focussed the attention of everyone in the room some more.

A brave soul closest to the side door leading into the rest of the building made a sudden start towards the opening. Maximilian Dumars had anticipated such a move and fired a short burst from his weapon into the air above the door.

The burst of gunfire was the first notice the scientists behind the glass wall had of the drama unfolding in the viewing gallery. They all turned from their screens toward the public area, just as Nick burst through the door into their lab and started waving his own Uzi at them.

'Reach for the sky!' he yelled. The half dozen scientists looked at one another, some with puzzled looks on their faces. There are seventeen languages spoken amongst the twenty member nations of CERN. Many of the scientists can communicate in English. Not all of them, however, are familiar with the vernacular of the Western movie.

'Hands…Up…!' tried Nick. 'And lie down on the floor with your hands behind your back!'

This was met with more puzzled looks, mixed with a healthy amount of fearful apprehension at the gun wielding lunatic who was shouting at them. Habituated by a lifetime in classrooms, one of the bolder scientists raised a single hand into the air.

'What!?' yelled Nick.

'Which is it you would like us to do?' asked the trembling physicist. 'Would you like us to put our hands up, or lie down on the floor with our hands behind our backs?'

Under the influence of adrenalin and the effects of being in possession a lethal fire-arm, Nick was not in the mood to be trifled with. He eyeballed the physicist that had spoken and then stared round, wild-eyed at the others.

'First you put your hands up in the air...' he said, as though addressing a roomful of particularly dim-witted children. He raised his own arms slowly while keeping the barrel of the Uzi pointing towards the scientists. They cautiously followed suit in raising their arms. 'AND NOW YOU ALL LIE DOWN ON THE FLOOR WITH YOUR EFFING HANDS BEHIND YOUR BACKS!'

The scientists hurriedly dropped to the floor and did as they were told. Nick made his way among them, securing their hands with cable ties as he went. When the last scientist had been secured, he turned to the glass wall and made a thumbs up gesture towards Maximilian Dumars.

Everyone in the public gallery had been transfixed by the action in the lab. The potential escapee opted for discretion over valour and melted back into the crowd.

Maximilian Dumars gave a little cough.

'As I was saying,' he said, 'I am pleased to announce that, although it might be something of a deviation from whatever plans you had made for the rest of today, you are all about to become a part of history.'

'Who are you? What do you want?' The Director-General could barely control his own outrage at having his facility, his tour, and his own person, hijacked.

'We...' said Maximilian Dumars as he slipped his jumper over his head in a swift movement while keeping the gun pointed deliberately at the Director-General, 'We are the *future*.'

He reached inside the canvas hold-all and pulled out his uniform jacket, which he put on, deftly switching hands with his gun as he pushed his arms into the sleeves.

'That is all you need to know for now. You will find out more about who we are and what we want in good time... As long as you do nothing to jeopardise your, ahem, existence. And the first thing you can do to ensure your continued well-being is to follow the example of your research colleagues next door and kindly lie on the floor with your hands behind your backs.'

For a moment, there was no movement. Never a very patient man at the best of times, on the brink of history, Maximilian Dumars was not in the mood to entertain dithering. He fired another rapid burst of bullets into the ceiling.

The response was instant. The members of the public tour, their guides, the Director-General and his VIP guests all dropped to the floor, with their hands held behind their backs. All except one. In the middle of the room, a tall, elegant, impeccably dressed man with immaculately swept back blond hair and a precisely groomed goatee beard leant casually on his silver-topped cane.

Maximilian Dumars' eyes bulged. The vein in his temple began to throb.

'I said everyone,' he said in tones of pure ice.

Mr John examined his perfectly manicured finger-nails and looked disdainfully at the floor. 'Me? Lie down on this floor? In these clothes?... This is Armani. So – lie down? No, I don't think so.'

Maximilian Dumars was apoplectic. He stared at Mr John, outraged. But another thought was also vying for space in his brain. *He* had the Dark Anti-Matter. *He* had the power. Mr John might have been the agent that brought him these things, but was he, Maximilian Dumars, going to rule the world in the name of another – be a mere puppet? He rather thought not.

'I've asked you politely,' he said aloud. 'Do not try my patience.' Little flecks of spittle were gathering at the corner of his mouth as he sought to control his emotions. 'Lie – down –' he spoke very slowly and deliberately, 'on – the – floor – with – your – hands – behind – your – back.'

Mr John grinned broadly. 'Or else?' he asked, innocently; or at least as innocently as a demon could muster. He had witnessed the thoughts in Maximilian Dumars' head. He was lost in admiration at the duplicity of the man.

'Or else Eugene here will shoot you in the head.'

Eugene was visibly shocked. He had thought he might need to hit a few people to get what they wanted. After all, Eugene reasoned that if you couldn't make an omelette without breaking eggs, he thought it quite unlikely that you could make history without breaking legs. But he hadn't expected there would be a need for any greater levels of violence. Besides, Eugene had never fully trusted Mr John and for some reason he felt sure that any violence against him would ultimately end up coming back to haunt its perpetrator. Nick, too, was watching the exchange and particularly his leader's reactions from behind the glass partition with concern.

Some of the hostages on the floor were craning their necks to see what was going on. This was the last straw for Mr Dumars. He was losing face.

'Eugene!' he ordered. 'Shoot him!'

'Um... I'm not sure I want to do that, Boss.'

'Eugene, I just gave you a direct order!'

'I know, Boss, it's just that…'

Maximilian Dumars had no time for excuses. 'If you want anything doing…' he muttered, as he strode forward towards Mr John and levelled the barrel of his Uzi at Mr John's forehead from point blank range. 'This is your last chance. Lie down on the floor - now!'

The atmosphere in the room was electric as Maximilian Dumars faced down his un-compliant hostage. Some of those lying on the floor continued to try and crane their necks to see what was happening. A few others began to sob.

'For God's sake, man!' said the Director-General from his position prostrated on the carpet. 'Do as he says, before you get hurt.'

Mr John stared deep into Maximilian Dumars' eyes. Behind his coal black pupils, flames flickered. Maximilian Dumars felt light-headed; his skin was clammy and damp. A single bead of sweat welled in his temple and began to trickle down the side of his face. It reached the edge of his jawbone, the bead growing as moisture continued to rise from his pores. The bead became a drop, pregnant on the side of his face, poised, ready to fall.

Mr John smiled wickedly, and said, simply, 'No.'

Gravity dragged the drop of sweat from Maximilian Dumars' face and it tumbled towards the floor.

'Very well,' he said.

He squeezed the trigger of his gun.

The staccato rattle of the Uzi was almost instantaneously followed by a crimson explosion from the back of Mr John's skull as it splattered across the glass partition wall.

* * *

The visitor room at the ATLAS building was filled with screaming.

Pale faced and numb, Eugene and Nick stared at their boss in disbelief.

Maximilian Dumars, however, was elated. He was *flying*. The shots from his Uzi were still ringing in his ears, but he felt the *power* coursing through his veins.

The screaming and the sobbing began to penetrate his ears, making him annoyed. It was distracting his focus away from the immense sense of fulfilment that he was currently feeling. In that one moment when he had squeezed the trigger he felt he had stepped into the shoes of his destiny. He called for silence.

Amongst the sobbing and the muttered prayers for deliverance, the prostrate figures of his hostages failed to hear him.

'Silence!' he yelled again, but this only had the effect of re-doubling the wailings of the more fearful of his victims. One of the prone figures vomited and the acrid stench of puke filled Maximilian Dumars' nostrils with disgust at the weakness of his fellow man. He raised his gun emptied the remnants of his ammunition into the air, released the spent clip and reloaded. In the second of silence that followed the gun-burst, he announced in a voice all the more chilling for the calmness of its tone.

'The next person to make a sound will be the next one to die!'

The hostages did their best to stifle their noise.

'That's *better*. And now that I have your full attention...'

* * *

Hercules was getting restless. 'This is taking too long,' he said.

Albertine was unmoved. 'What did you expect?' she asked. 'We 'ave to trawl through all the footage from the cameras around the UN buildings and we can only run the footage in real time because the face recognition software cannot cope with anything faster. Our time window is anything from about 'alf an hour after your plane landed last night. I've managed to partition the footage into three hour periods. Even so, there are enough feeds that it is using all the processing power that I've got 'ere and most of my botnet as well.'

'Isn't there anything you can do to make it go any faster?'

'I've already told you. I know time is not on our side, but really, we do just 'ave to be patient.'

'But we've been sat here waiting for over two hours now.'

'...Which means that with each passing second the chances of us finding something soon, if indeed your friends did visit the area, must be increasing.'

Almost exactly on cue to Albertine's last statement, one of the screens froze. They both leapt to their feet and stepped forward to examine the picture. They could both clearly recognize the face of Nick – but his courier's uniform was not something they had expected.

'What did I tell you?' Albertine asked, triumphantly stepping back into her command position. Already she was gesturing at the screens, and the images surrounding the frozen picture began to be replaced. 'That feed is from the cameras covering the car park of the International Telecommunications Union. It's just down the road from the UN 'eadquarters. Now that we 'ave our fix we can realign our search to other cameras near this one and see what Monsieur Turpin 'as been up to.'

The images on the other cameras began to build up different aspects of the same district, and sure enough across a number of them, Nick's movements were tracked until he turned into the entrance of a large mirror-windowed building.

'What's that building?' asked Hercules.

'It's the O.M.P.I. – the building of the World Intellectual Property Organisation.' Albertine was gesturing madly at her screens and some of them began showing footage from inside the building itself. They watched as Nick walked up to the main reception desk, placed a box down on the counter, signed himself in and was given a temporary pass by the reception staff. He picked up his box and was directed by the desk staff towards the lift.

Another screen had footage of him standing casually in the lift until it reached the sixth floor. Nick stepped out of view of the lift camera. Albertine shrugged.

'I have no other feeds from that building,' she said, 'just the reception and the lifts.'

'Let's wait a minute,' said Hercules.

Sure enough, a couple of minutes later, Nick reappeared on screen in the lift grinning broadly as he came into the picture. He pressed the button for the ground floor. He was no longer carrying a parcel.

'Well, that settles it,' said Hercules, 'I think we can safely say that we know what their target is now.' He started towards the door. Albertine didn't move.

'I do not think it is quite that simple,' she said.

Hercules stopped in his tracks. 'What do you mean?'

'What exactly do we know about this "dark material"?' she asked. 'I mean, sure, we know your Mr Turpin walked out of the lift on the sixth floor of the OMPI carrying a box, and a few minutes later 'e got back into the lift without it, but what was *in* the box? What does this stuff look like? 'Ow are they controlling it? Most of all, even if we find it, 'ow do we even know if we can stop it from detonating?'

The determination with which he had headed towards the door a few seconds before drained from Hercules as he realised the truth in the words that his new friend spoke.

'You're right,' he said at last. 'So what *are* we going to do?'

Albertine looked just as lost. She shook her head. 'I do not know.'

The pair of them slumped back onto the sofa. The screens on the wall in front of them continued to relay images from the various

CCTV feeds that Albertine had hacked into, but they weren't really paying attention. It was one thing to be a Monitor. It was quite another to know what to do if you actually saw something.

Eventually Hercules stirred.

'What's the flashing box on that screen on the bottom row for?' he asked. Sure enough there was a flashing red box on one of the screens on the bottom row of the wall in front of them.

Albertine sat up. 'News feed,' she said simply. 'I 'ave a program that takes the search criteria from whatever I am working on and runs checks for related items through the rest of the web – trends on Twitter… Facebook…that sort of thing. Sometimes it is even good old fashioned television news that is first with the story – although I must say that 'appens less and less these days.'

She reached her hand up and pointed at the flashing red box. It stopped flashing. She swung her arm in a wide arc that passed across all the screens in front of them. An image expanded to fill the entire wall in front of them.

Hercules and Albertine stared at one another in disbelief. Looking back at them, his image split across the many screens of the wall, was the unmistakable face of Mr Maximilian Dumars. He was in some kind of control room. There were desks with computers visible behind him, along with some larger screens mounted to the wall. Dressed in a smart, black military style uniform, he nonetheless looked slightly uncomfortable in front of the camera. With a look of annoyance, he addressed a person that they took to be that camera operator.

'Is this it?' he asked. 'Are we live?'

There was a slight nodding from the camera.

Maximilian Dumars stiffened momentarily, and then relaxed. He smiled ingratiatingly at the camera. It was a disturbing sight.

'Citizens of Europe,' he began, his face taking on a more serious demeanour, 'a tide of change is lapping at our shores. I am humbled that history has called on me to announce to you the dawning of a New Age...'

* * *

It was amazing the respect people gave you, Maximilian Dumars reflected, when they had just watched you stand up to insolence. He had ordered Eugene to drag Mr John's body into the corridor and out of sight. Then he had forced the Director General to contact the press office and get a television crew from a local station over to the ATLAS building. It was easy enough, with the world's press always eager for breaking news from the home of particle physics. When the crew had arrived, the reporter was tied up with the other hostages. The cameraman had been left free to carry out the work for which Maximilian Dumars required him.

Maximilian Dumars looked back through the glass partition to the public area of the ATLAS building. He had moved into the physicists' lab to deliver his speech. He felt that the ordered and technologically sophisticated environs of the lab would lend more gravitas to his announcement than the relative chaos the other side of the glass.

From where he stood, Mr Dumars had a clear view of the red smear decorating the viewing window that was the remnants of Mr John's brains. He didn't want his moment of destiny diverted by the sordid details of the hostage taking.

On the other side of the glass, in the public gallery, Eugene was standing guard over the hostages. They had been bound in pairs, back to back. The scientists from the lab had been taken to join them. A large TV screen on the wall had been tuned to the news channel, and on it the feed from the television camera in the adjacent room was being displayed. Eugene glanced at the framed head-shot of Maximilian Dumars in eighty-five-inch-high definition. He gave his boss a thumbs up.

Maximilian Dumars re-focused on the camera in front of him.

'For too many years now,' he continued, 'the nations of this great continent of ours have been in decline. Brought to their knees by the corrupt politicians who steal when they are supposed to serve; the greedy bankers who rewarded themselves for gambling with *our* money – and who have continued to reward themselves even when they have brought the world to the brink of bankruptcy; media empires that know no bounds of privacy – that act without morals.

'These are some of the symptoms of the decline, but they are not the cause. Do not be mistaken, I share your disgust with the parasites that have brought us to this – *nadir,*' Maximilian Dumars paused. He had been working on this speech in his head for longer than he could remember. He had come across the word nadir in an article in a magazine and had gone to the uncharacteristic bother of looking up its meaning. From that point on he had known that he would one day use the word in the speech that he would give as he wrested control from the idiots in government. On that day, which was now *today,* he would create an order that he, and people like him, could admire. '- to this lowest point,' he continued, remembering himself and translating his intellectual prowess into language his everyman audience might understand.

'But I am blessed by destiny, and you are blessed by the happy accident of circumstance that sees you alive today to share in this moment. For we, my colleagues and I, the forces of the Aryan De-fence Order/League/Front have been gifted a power that bestows on us the ability to truly make a difference. It falls on me now to draw the attention of the world to the power of which I speak.

'Earlier today a warning was issued concerning an explosive device in the United Nations district here in Geneva. Instructions were given to clear the area. As long as our instructions have been followed precisely, no one is going to be hurt. But trust me when

I say this: our power is unlike anything the world has witnessed to date. To show that I am here in good faith driven purely by values of humanity, I will give you a further five minutes to ensure that the area around the World Intellectual Property Building opposite the UN offices is clear. I would suggest that anyone still within, say, two hundred metres of this building in five minutes will seriously regret it: but only for a very short time indeed.'

He looked at his watch. 'By my reckoning, it is coming up to five past twelve...now. The device explodes at exactly ten past. Please don't waste any time wrongly assuming I am not serious, or believing that you have any chance of finding our weapon.

'Just move your people.'

Eleven

ALBERTINE AND HERCULES watched as the frame froze on Maximilian Dumars' face which became the backdrop image in the newsroom. The anchor announced that they were cutting live to their cameras in the United Nations district.

It soon became pretty clear that the police had taken the earlier warnings seriously, and that there were only limited security personnel and emergency services still in the area. All the same, the cameras at the perimeter of the police cordon witnessed the few remaining people rushing from buildings, followed by flashing lights and sirens as numerous police cars, fire engines and army bomb disposal units withdrew at speed from the target zone.

'Right now I'm feeling pretty glad you talked me out of going over there,' said Hercules.

The danger zone had been fully cleared within four minutes.

Albertine gestured at her screens. In response to her motions, the image flicked from one news channel to another. All showed the same images, filmed from slightly different angles: pictures of the crowds gathered at the edge of the police cordon, all staring towards the modest mirrored skyscraper.

Hercules was used to seeing the time displayed on news channels, but now the clocks displayed had all gained an extra feature. As well as hours and minutes, they were showing seconds. The watching world held its breath as the time ticked relentlessly forward:

12:09:51…52…53… Many people were holding up mobile phones to capture their own footage of the events they were witnessing.

54…55…56… The gathered mass of people was making next to no noise. It was like watching television with the sound turned off.

57…58…59… The occasional background noise that carried to the microphones of the news crews imbued the scene with a surreal quality.

The minute count ticked over.

12:10:00.

For a moment, nothing happened.

And then it did.

The building splintered into fragments. The mirrored external windows shattered into billions of pieces, each a shining jewelled particle. But the atomisation of the outer layers only served to reveal a similar process unravelling within the inner structures of the building as well. Starting from the epicentre on the sixth floor, layer by layer, room by room, desk by desk and filing cabinet by filing cabinet, the entire edifice fractured into a trillion separate bodies which sort of hung together in space for a moment, like the ghost of the building they had recently formed.

As if the spontaneous disassociation of the fabric of the construction was not strange enough, it revealed an even odder phenomenon. Since each floor of the building was no longer, in its truest sense, actually a floor, it would be wrong to say, "on every floor". Nevertheless, on every level that had previously *been* a floor, the various pot plants that had enlivened and oxygenated the working environment of the members of the World Organisation for Intellectual Property hovered in space – apparently unaffected by whatever had caused the disintegration of their surroundings.

There were initial gasps from the watching crowd. But as the number of seconds grew that the ghost building and office greenery hung in space, a feeling began to spread through the throng that the overall danger levels had been vastly overstated. A policeman crossed the cordon and started to walk towards the fragmented building...

...Which promptly exploded. The countless millions of pieces of what had, until recently, been the home of the World Intellectual Property Organisation shot outwards in an omni-directional cloud. The shock wave that preceded the expanding nebula knocked the policeman off his feet and sent him sliding back along the road towards the cordon. The cloud itself came within metres of the watching crowds before seemingly hitting an invisible barrier that brought a sudden halt to the second stage in the process of the building's destruction.

For a few more seconds the bits of the building simply hung where they were. There were more gasps from those watching. The potted office shrubbery remained suspended in space by who-knew-what strange force. This time no one ventured forward. This was probably for the best. Before the sight of gravity-defying mini-ature palms had too much opportunity to stretch the incredulity of the on-lookers, the plants exploded, too.

As a huge surprise to those within the splash zone, but not entirely unexpected to the members of the Aryan Defence Order/League/Front, the sudden decomposition of the plants generated a miniature tsunami of green liquid which rapidly decorated those who had mistakenly felt that, beyond the outer reaches of the exploding particles of building, they were out of harm's way.

In contrast to the abruptness of the two explosions, the next movement of the tiny pieces started in a gentler fashion. The cloud began to rotate around the epicentre of the explosion. The movement was slow at first, barely discernible in fact, but the mass of moving pieces gradually built-up speed until visibility back to where the building had once stood was impeded by the swirling cloud. As it spun and spun, the inner edges began to get drawn back towards the source, like candy-floss being wound onto a stick. The organic paint that had coloured the crowd was also caught up in the pull, and drop by drop the onlookers were stripped of their liquid redecoration and returned to their pre-explosion hues. As the cloud of dust and droplets was drawn inwards the view back down the road became clearer.

It was apparent that the whole building had been drawn into a tightly circling orbit occupying about a cubic meter of space. Its full mass had been condensed into this small volume floating at an approximate location that had once housed the sixth-floor toilets. The denseness of this small cloud was plain from its opacity. This small inner cloud continued to spin until the last motes of its former construction and the last drops of the liquefied plants had been drawn into its bosom.

Then the small cloud collapsed on itself, and disappeared entirely.

* * *

'Huh! You are probably no longer at the top of Geneva's most wanted list now,' Albertine joked. But her face was deadly serious.

The newsroom on the screens in front of them once more gave way to the image of Maximilian Dumars.

* * *

'Perhaps, on reflection, I should have advised a safe distance of two hundred *and fifty* metres,' Mr Dumars grinned mischievously. 'But then a little gentle soaking never harmed anyone.' His face hardened.

'You were wise to listen to our warning and take it seriously. I thank you for that. As there can now be no doubt, my men and I wield an *extraordinary* power. But we are not monsters. We have shown this by giving ample opportunity to avoid any *unnecessary* loss of life. A few people might have been temporarily wetted, but please think what might have been the consequences were we not *reasonable* men.

'So now, Citizens of Europe, I come to our true purpose here today. Earlier I referred to the symptoms of degeneration that have inflicted our society. The corruption of politicians and the press, the greed of bankers – these are merely the indicators of a greater ill that afflicts us all. That ill has a name. It is immigration.

'It is the influx of undesirable elements to our lands that has diluted our morals, broken society and riddled us with debt to the point of bankruptcy. Were it not for the relentless waves of parasites and scroungers that come to our lands, seeking the benefits of our more advanced society, but bringing nothing in return, we would still be *pure* - still be *strong*. They use our healthcare and our schools, and then *we* have to pay for interpreters in hospitals. Our children have their learning hijacked by cultures that are not their own. They take *our* jobs; they force us out of *our* housing. And how do they thank us? I'll tell you how they thank us: by sending their sons to terrorist training camps so they can commit atrocities against the peoples that have nurtured them, on the soil we allowed them to call home.

'Well, I say – ENOUGH!' Mr Dumars had worked himself into quite a state. He took a second to calm himself before turning to the camera and fixing the lens with a look of steely intent. To almost all of those around the world watching, now locked into the unfolding events, it was chilling.

'I say they *cannot* take our jobs any longer. I say we *will not* have the futures of our children compromised by making allowances for those who cannot speak our language. I say we *will not* be attacked on our own streets. I say – No more free rides! I say – GO HOME!'

In his imagination, the foot-soldiers of the cause were uniting behind him and cheering their support. In his imagination, he could see the stadiums filled with ecstatic followers, drunk on the power of his rhetoric. In his imagination, the world applauded. He inhaled deeply, breathing in a vision of events that existed nowhere but in his mind.

'So, to the governments of Europe, I say this:' he continued, his voice returning to level tones, 'You have twenty-four hours to begin the repatriation of all non-European peoples from the countries of Europe. And I'm not talking about matters of birth here. I mean by race. We need to clear our borders of all the blacks, Arabs, Asians and Jews that have brought nothing but demeaning ways to our communities and have unpicked the fabric of our society to create the rats' nest we have today.

'I am a reasonable man. I do not expect this repatriation to be completed in a day. I know this epic and righteous crusade is not the work of a day, or even days. We have many months, years even, of struggle ahead to cleanse our shores. What I need to see is the *evidence* that it has begun. Take television crews to airports. Show me planes beginning to be filled. Give me a sign that we can move forward together...'

Maximilian Dumars was discussing his plans for his mass human relocation program as though he saw nothing unreasonable in his requests. But never far below the surface of his casual tones lurked a very real sense of threat. That threat now surfaced.

'...Because should I fail to be satisfied that you are sufficiently committed to complying with my proposal – a proposal that will benefit *us all* – I shall be forced into... alternative arrangements.'

The camera shot panned out. Maximilian Dumars walked across to one of the lab desks, upon which sat a large case. He put his hands on the clasps and clicked them open.

'You have already witnessed the power at my disposal. You have witnessed not just the destruction, but the complete disappearance, of a sizeable building. The recent events at the Intellectual Property Building were the product of a mere fraction of the power I have at my disposal.

'I have chosen CERN as the venue for my announcement for a couple of reasons. The first is so that it is clear that I am not acting alone. This establishment represents the finest endeavours of science from a corrupt world. I, on the other hand, am backed by an organisation that is aligned to principles of rigorous purity, and it is the endeavours of *our superior* scientists that have isolated the powerful material that you have all just observed in action.

'This brings me to the second reason for being here. Although the scientists here are ineffective in comparison to those from our organisation, they nevertheless have enough credibility with existing governments to be able to provide verification of some simple facts.'

He reached inside the case and drew out a cylindrical container, about the size of a thermos flask. The resemblance to a thermos flask began and ended with its dimensions: It was made of a dark metallic material that was etched and inscribed with strange glyphs and symbols.

'Our earlier demonstration involved a thousand particles of the same substance that is held in this container. *This* one holds one million particles of the same material. Or rather, it contains a million anti-particles. The contents of this flask are a material called Dark Anti-Matter. It is to dark matter what anti-matter is to normal matter, or so our scientists tell me. *Your scientists* don't even know what dark matter is, beyond a vague calculation required to fill the gaps in their understanding of the universe.

'Dark Anti-matter has, it turns out, some interesting properties.' He was casually passing the tube from one hand to another. 'For example, it exerts an anti-gravitational force. In fact, the makers of this flask have perfectly balanced its mass with the anti-mass of the material it contains so that I can do this.' Maximilian Dumars made as if to pass the tube between his hands, but instead released it from one hand and did not grasp it with the other. The tube floated in mid-air. Maximilian Dumars walked to one side to show that there was no trickery. He nudged the container, which floated gently through the air.

'Although I am not here to show you parlour tricks,' he plucked the cylinder from its flight-path. 'No. We are more concerned *here* with the other salient property of this Dark Anti-Matter, namely its somewhat excitable reaction in the presence of the more mundane, common-or-garden, good old-fashioned, normal matter.

'So how dangerous is this one little container. Don't worry – it's perfectly safe in this canister. Extremely strong magnets hold it in suspension in a total vacuum. But supposing it got out? Well, let's not take my word for it. Maths never was my strong suite. I'm more of a man of action. So, let's ask a scientist. Now, where can I find one of *those?*' Maximilian Dumars stroked his chin in mock contemplation.

'Ah, yes!' He had his Eureka moment. 'As luck would have it I have some keeping me company now. In fact, I've brought one along to help me with just this problem.'

The camera swung to the side. A very worried-looking man in his early thirties was sitting on one of the lab's chairs. His hands were cable-tied behind his back and had been further secured to the post supporting the back-rest of the chair.

Maximilian Dumars smiled his best ingratiating smile at his captive. 'What is your name?' he asked.

'Mikael,' replied the man.

'Very good, Mikael. And what is your job?'

'I am a physicist here at CERN, working on the EBHC.'

'Excellent!' Maximilian Dumars clapped his hands together in glee. 'Perhaps you would be so good as to help me with a little problem, Mikael.' The scientist nodded nervously. 'If I have a thousand particles of Dark Anti-Matter and it causes an explosion which extends to two hundred – I'm sorry, I mean two hundred and fifty metres – what would be the expected radius affected by a *million particles* of the same material?'

The distraction of a simple mathematical problem seemed temporarily to take Mikael's mind off the fact that he was in the presence of a man who he had recently seen commit murder simply because his victim had refused to lie down. 'Well,' he began, eyeing the flask with a mixture of trepidation and marvel, 'it depends what we know about the material in question. For example – can we assume a linear increase in destructive power?'

Maximilian Dumars was slightly taken aback. He hadn't expected to be derailed by a detailed analysis. 'Yes, yes,' he said curtly. 'Just scale it up for me.'

Mikael quickly remembered the nature of his interrogator.

'Well, assuming a linear increase in power, it would affect a thousand times the radius – so that would be two hundred and fifty metres times by a thousand – which would give you two hundred and fifty kilometres.'

'Two hundred and fifty kilometres! From this one small flask? Well, well – that is something.' Maximilian Dumars dropped the mock humour. 'I don't need to paint a picture of the destruction that could be caused with this one small device. You might be tempted to call my bluff – to think that Europe can survive with a large hole in the middle. Please do not think that an organisation that can engineer this situation, that can synthesise *this* material, would operate through a single cell.'

Maximilian Dumars drew himself up and stood rigid and proud, and held his right fist clenched in front of his heart. 'We are *many!*' He declared.

He *was* bluffing now, but it was a calculated gamble. For some reason it felt like the right thing to say. Everything so far had been so spectacular that Maximilian Dumars was sure no one would question this one lie.

'This is *not* a suicide mission. We have come here to *negotiate*: to negotiate a brighter future for our continent. But if things go wrong, we have enough allies strategically placed around Europe that it will cease to exist. You see – I said I am a reasonable man. All we wish to do is reclaim the lands that our rightfully ours. I said that my proposal was one that would benefit everyone concerned. I am offering our *visitors* the chance to leave and continue their lives elsewhere: it cannot be said that offering them continued existence is not to their benefit. I am offering the *true* people of Europe what they deserve: a better tomorrow.'

Maximilian Dumars looked imploringly into the camera, willing the belief that he was, indeed a reasonable man. Out of the corner of his eyes the red smear on the glass wall caught his eye. Anger erupted across his face.

'You have witnessed the extent of our power. I personally have already had to kill a hostage to show the fools here that we mean business. Do not cost more lives by trying to test our terms or assuming that we are not deadly serious. It would be tremendously stupid and dangerous for everyone if you try and stage a raid on this facility. Remember, we are not alone.'

His anger faded and he almost pleaded. 'Show me that you are trying. Get cameras to the airports. You have twenty-four hours.'

* * *

The picture froze as the live broadcast stopped, and the screen switched back to the anchor in the newsroom.

Albertine turned to Hercules. 'Do you think there are really more of them, like 'e said?'

'He's bluffing,' replied Hercules. 'There was only one way that feather was pointing. I'm sure that if there was more of that Dark Anti-Matter, the M.O.R.A.L compass would have been so confused that that I'd never have been able to track them down.'

'So what do you think we should do?'

'I don't know about you, but I have to do what I came back from Heaven to do. I have to try and stop them.'

'Well, at least we know where to find them now.'

* * *

Asif had been driving for nearly five hours. The golden sand of the desert outside Aswan had given way to a pale grey dust. The basalt rocks that formed this lighter sand were harder wearing than the yellow sandstones further west, and as Asif had progressed eastwards the landscape had become increasingly mountainous and contoured.

He knew from the size of the ridges that surrounded him and the time that he had been driving that he was close to the coast. It was late afternoon. He started to look for a suitable place to pull off the road where he could head into one of the gullies that cut through the hills and make camp.

* * *

The CERN bus had not gone far past the airport when the driver pulled to a stop and made an announcement to his passengers.

'What did he just say?' asked Hercules, who had only caught a few words of the rapidly-spoken French.

''E says 'e cannot go any further and is turning the bus at the next roundabout. If we do not want to go back into town, we 'ave to get off here.'

Hercules and Albertine stepped off the bus. A few hundred yards ahead the road was blockaded by a host of emergency vehicles. The skyline sparkled with flashing blue lights. Overhead, three military helicopters hovered over the CERN complex. Outside the cordon, more helicopters from the world's press buzzed back and forth like midges over a summer hedgerow. Between the bus stop and the police cordon rows of press vehicles were parked alongside the road. Reporters were filing constant updates to their twenty-four-hour rolling news stations.

Albertine and Hercules assessed the situation from the pavement. There was no way they were going to get close to the ATLAS building.

A moped stacked high with pizza boxes puttered up the road like a drowsy fly. Albertine and Hercules watched as it droned past the press vehicles and pulled up to the roadblock. A police car was reversed from its position across the road and the pizza delivery was waved through.

The police car pulled forward, closing the road once more.

'We should have thought of that,' said Hercules glumly. 'Everyone knows that hostage takers always end up ordering pizza. If only we'd been a bit more on the ball…'

'Not to worry,' said Albertine, cheerily. 'I've been monitoring this place since before they drew up the plans for the extension. I know of another way in.' She paused. 'I hope your shoes are comfortable, though,' she added as a bit of an afterthought.

'Why?'

'I'm afraid it is a bit of a walk.'

* * *

Asif gazed into the glowing coals of his fire. A short drive from the road had brought him to a secluded wadi that was an ideal spot for his campsite.

Night had fallen quickly. It came as something of a shock to Asif, how quickly darkness took over the world away from the lights of civilization. Almost as soon as he had set up his basic camp and gathered some firewood from around the bases of the scrubby bushes that sprouted here and there in the gully, the huge golden orb of the sun had kissed the horizon and sunk from view.

By the light of a kerosene lamp that had been included amongst his camping equipment, Asif had laid a fire and set a pan of water to boil. Then he busied himself tending to his birds, checking that they were still healthy and replenishing their seed and water bowls. When his pot began to boil, he made himself some sweet mint tea, which he drank with a simple meal of bread and some cold falafel.

After his meal, Asif laid out his mat and saluted Mecca. He was now only a few hundred miles to the west of the holiest of cities. He finished praying and a moment of doubt crept into his mind. Did he really need to destroy all those lives? His thoughts turned to his parents.

* * *

'You weren't lying when you said it was a bit of a walk.'

They had skirted round the cordoned off area to the north of the CERN facility and headed in a north westerly direction. Mostly they had progressed through fields, but sometimes they followed roads and they had passed through the occasional small village and hamlet. Hercules had barely noticed that they had crossed the border and were now in France. As the afternoon wore on, they trudged onwards towards the Jura Mountains.

'Of course this is only 'alf of it,' said Albertine brightly. 'When we get in, we 'ave to follow the tunnel all the way back.'

***

Asif had arrived back from his trip to Wiltshire in a state of elation. For the whole drive home his heart had been racing. Every police car he had seen had set it into overdrive. He was in a constant state of expectation that he would be pulled over and arrested for his audacious theft. Every car on the motorway was potentially full of government agents, waiting for the order to close the net...

Only when he had returned the hire car, and was back in his battered old van, did Asif began to realise that he had got away with it. He hadn't been stopped. No one suspected a thing. And now the wolf had his teeth.

'Is that you, son?' his father's voice called from the front room.

Asif didn't answer. He bounded up the stairs and into his room, closing the door behind him. He sat on the bed, hitched up his trouser leg and fished the three little canisters from their holster in his sock. He laid them on the bed and stared at them with quiet satisfaction.

He barely registered the sound of footsteps on the stairs, and it was only when his door began to open that he broke from his reverie with a start. His mother's face appeared around the opening door.

Asif leapt to his feet. He was furious.

'Get out, Mum! What have I told you about coming into my room?'

His mother appeared saddened by the sudden rage of her son, but was not taken aback. His temper was something she was all too used to having to deal with.

'You look nice, son,' she said with a weak smile, taking in the suit. 'Have you been for a job interview?'

'It's none of your business! I said get out!'

Asif pushed her out of the room. He leant on the closed door and buried his face in his hands. How dare she invade his privacy!

From outside the room he heard her voice. 'It's just that me and your father worry about you so, Asif,' she said. 'We both love you, you know that.'

'Go away, Mum,' was all Asif could reply.

He remained leaning against the door, listening. It was only when he heard the sound of footsteps retreating down the stairs that he moved away from his sentry post and returned to his bed. He picked his laptop from the floor, opened the lid and logged on. A few minutes later and he was in conversation with his mysterious mentor.

Sheik> You were successful?

Al Thi'b > It all went just as you said it would. No problems

Sheik> And you can test the virus is still viable?

Al Thi'b > It will be done...

After he had finished his report, Asif closed the laptop and retrieved a box that the Sheik had sent him from its hiding place under the floorboards beneath his bed. Inside were three little caps, which could be fitted on to the canisters – one cap for each. He took one out. On its top was a tiny digital clock display, which was so small that it was barely readable to the naked eye. Asif opened the drawer of his bedside table and rummaged around until he had found the things he needed – a magnifying glass and a pin.

He checked his watch. It was eight o'clock now. His parents were usually in bed by ten. In six hours' time they would be deep in sleep. He carefully set the cap on his bedside table and, using the magnifying glass, brought the tiny digits of the clock display into focus. Next to the display were two small pits. Asif guided the pin into one of the pits and pressed. The digits set to 00:00. Asif moved the pin to the other pit and pressed six times. With each press, an hour was added to the timer. Then he pressed the pin into the first pit again and the time returned to the display. The dots between the digits began to flash at steady one second intervals. The timer was set.

Asif carefully screwed the cap onto the top of one of the virus laden containers. He went to the door of his room and listened for a few seconds. The hall sounded quiet. He cautiously opened the door a crack. He could hear the sound of the television down-stairs and his parents' voices. He slipped across the hall into their room.

He was only in their room for a few seconds: just long enough to secrete his little canister behind the headboard of their bed. He quickly checked that the windows were closed – knowing that this late in the year they almost certainly would be, and his parents never opened them at night. Then he slipped back across the hall and into his own room.

The hours that passed before his parents went to bed dragged by at a glacial pace. Asif tried to busy himself with other distractions, but every time he checked his watch, only a few minutes had ticked by. He prayed. He tidied. He took a reel of gaffer tape from his beside cabinet and laid it on the bed. Time crept slowly on.

Finally, to his blessed relief, he heard the sounds of movement coming up the stairs. He sat and listened as his parents took turns in the bathroom, and, after another dragging eternity, went into their room and closed the door for the night.

Asif sat in silence for an hour, just watching the door. The house was silent. Asif picked up the reel of tape. Moving stealthily, he inched his door open and crossed the hall. He didn't need to press an ear to the door to hear his father's heavy-breathed half snore.

Taking the roll of gaffer tape, he began to peel the end free. He unrolled the tape with painstaking care, making sure not to make a noise. When he had a decent length strip, he taped across the door frame onto the door, making the beginnings of an air-tight seal. He repeated this activity until all the gaps between the door and the frame were blocked.

The room next door to his parents' bedroom was the bathroom. Asif closed the bathroom door and crept back into his room. He returned with a length of strong thin cord. He made a loop in the end of the cord which he slipped over the handle of the closed bathroom door. He then passed the free end over the handle of the door to his parents' room and pulled it tight. He continued to wind the cord back and forth between the two door handles, making sure it was tight at each pass, until the length remaining would not complete another circuit. He securely knotted the free end. He tested his barricade by trying to open the door into the bathroom; the cord pulled tight on the handle of his parents' door and the bathroom door wouldn't budge. He was sure the other door would be just as immovable. But he doubted his parents would have the strength even to try and open it.

Asif returned to his bedroom to wait. This time he sat on the floor, with the door open, staring across the hall.

The night wore on. After hours of sitting motionless, Asif had passed into a trance-like state when the coughing started. He tensed – suddenly fully alert – watching the door across the hall intently. The coughing was soon accompanied by low moans. Shortly afterwards there was a loud bump that made Asif start.

There were weak cries, but Asif blocked his ears to them. A series of scraping noises followed; something or someone being dragged across the floor. There was another bump, this time right against the door. Asif held his breath. The handle began to turn. But whoever was turning it lacked the strength to push far enough even to begin to try and open the door – let alone to overcome Asif's barricade. There was another violent bout of coughing and the sound of someone slumping to the floor.

The coughing and moaning continued for about half an hour. Asif thought it would never end, but eventually the house fell quiet.

* * *

Asif spent a sleepless night staring at the door across the hallway. He didn't move for most of the next day – even forgoing his habitual prayers. Eventually, as night began to fall, he summoned up all his courage and forced himself to his feet.

He untied the cord that had bound the door handles shut. He ripped the gaffer tape from the door surround. He pressed down the handle and pushed. It opened a couple of inches and then stuck fast. Something heavy was blocking it. Putting all his weight behind it, he gave the door a hefty shove, managing to open it about eighteen inches – enough to poke his head round.

The sight that greeted him sent him dashing for the bathroom, where his empty stomach complained bitterly as he dry-retched into the toilet bowl. When he had finished throwing up, he wiped his mouth and splashed water onto his face. He had regained enough of his composure to make a dash past the bedroom doors and down the stairs.

He headed straight out of the house and into his little van. As he passed under the cold orange glow of the streetlamps, visions of the blood splattered walls of his parents' room flashed before his eyes. It had been his father's body lying by the door. His face, contorted with pain and smeared with his own blood and snot, had been almost unrecognisable under the rash of blisters that covered it.

Asif was sweating heavily as he passed the bolt and padlock to the youth at the checkout at the DIY store. The teller looked at his perspiring customer. 'You OK, mate?' he asked.

Asif was too dry-mouthed to answer. He nodded weakly as he handed over his money, grabbing his purchases from the counter and hurrying from the shop without waiting for his change.

Back home he fetched some of his fathers' tools from the small shed in the yard and then sat at the bottom of the stairs, gathering his courage. He steeled himself and made his way upstairs. Careful not to look inside, he pulled the door to his parents' room shut and set to fitting the sliding bolt in place, before locking the bolt closed with the padlock. He took the keys downstairs and dropped them into the kitchen bin. He wouldn't be needing them again.

* * *

Albertine and Hercules had been walking for hours. It was dark and Hercules was tired, and his feet ached. For the most part they had trudged on in silence. Hercules was beginning to doubt his companion, when Albertine suddenly stopped.

'It is definitely around 'ere somewhere,' she said.

'What are we looking for?' asked Hercules.

'Our way in. Of course, the last time I was 'ere was quite a while ago: when they were still building the extension for the EBHC, to be honest. And it was daylight.'

As Albertine cast around, Hercules stepped back to get out of her way. As he did so, his leg struck something hard.

'Ouch!' he cried.

Albertine turned. 'Well done!' she beamed. 'I knew it could not be that 'ard to find.'

Hercules watched, massaging his sore ankle, as Albertine pushed past him and began to clear the vegetation which had started to grow over the hatch that Hercules had, quite literally, stumbled upon. She swept debris away from the handle, and together they swung open the heavy steel door. They peered into the shaft. A metal ladder led down, towards the distant bottom which was lit by a faint glow.

Albertine gestured towards the ladder. 'After you,' she grinned.

* * *

Under the cloudless sky Asif gazed up at the countless stars. From the unpolluted dark of the desert night they were so much more vivid than he could ever remember having seen them before. The infinity of space made him giddy with anticipation. His parents' sacrifice was about to be vindicated.

Tomorrow was going to be a special day.

* * *

Night had long since fallen over CERN.

After the initial outburst of violence that had marked the take-over of the lab by the Aryan Defence Order/League/Front, the processes of both hostage taking, and being a hostage, had descended into a boring waiting game.

Maximilian Dumars had calmed down to the point where he had addressed his assembled captives and explained to them, in almost convincingly reasonable tones, that as long as no one tried anything stupid, all they had to do was wait patiently until the following day. As soon as he had evidence his demands were being met, the hostages would be released unharmed. None of his captives dared to question how he so sure that his demands *would* be met: the stains of Mr John's brains were still too fresh in their minds and on the partition window for that.

When it had become dark, the security forces had briefly tried shining searchlights onto the building. Maximilian Dumars' outraged phone-call to the hostage negotiator had soon put a stop to such nonsense. Maximilian Dumars had been angered enough that a hostage negotiator had been called at all. He saw no reason to be involved in any negotiations. He felt that he had stated his demands perfectly clearly in his television broadcast. And yet, as it turned out, the man *had* proved useful – if only for arranging pizzas and maintaining comfortable levels of luminescence. At least, from Maximilian Dumars' point of view, when he made demands of the security forces via the negotiator, they were swiftly fulfilled. Many in the police cordon surrounding the building had witnessed at first hand the disappearance of the OMPI. None of them was overly keen on being splashed across Europe.

In the public gallery of the ATLAS building, the hostages were doing their best to make themselves comfortable and bed down for the night. They still had their hands bound, but at least they had been fed.

Maximilian Dumars had no intention of sleeping. He was alone in the lab, while Eugene and Nick stood guard over the hostages in the public gallery, and he had been watching the news, as he had been doing almost non-stop since his first broadcast. Much of the coverage involved footage of the police vehicles in their barricade outside - interspersed with clips of the helicopters buzzing back and forth overhead. He could have seen pretty much the same thing by looking out of one of the windows, but he wasn't taking any chances with the snipers that he knew to be sighting their scopes on the building. He could trust the negotiator to meet such demands as he could witness being fulfilled. He trusted less what he couldn't see. What he definitely hadn't seen so far was any evidence that the governments of Europe were complying with his demands.

He had expected to see at least one report that indicated they were taking the threat he and his men posed seriously. So far the only interruptions to the rolling news footage being broadcast from the road outside showed traffic jams and travel chaos as everyone within a two-hundred-and-fifty-kilometre radius of Geneva sought to get to a safe distance beyond that.

It would be an understatement to say that Maximilian Dumars was not happy. This was not how it was supposed to go. He had believed that the weak and corrupt leaders of the countries under threat would crumble once they had witnessed the power of the Dark Anti-Matter. Certainly, the soldiers that surrounded the building knew better than to openly defy him. But the government leaders – in Paris, Berlin, London, Rome and beyond – they believed they were safely out of his range.

Maximilian Dumars fingered the USB memory stick in his pocket. It was time to escalate matters. He stood and picked up the Dark Anti-Matter from the desk in front of him. There was a specially designed pouch on his belt into which he fastened the container. He grabbed his Uzi and headed from the lab back to where the hostages were being held.

Eugene stiffened visibly as Maximilian Dumars came into the room, keen to show that he was alert even after the long hours of listless waiting. Maximilian Dumars ignored him and strode over to where the Director General was doing his best to make himself comfortable amongst the prone figures on the floor trying to get some rest.

If the Director General was hoping that he was not the focus of Maximilian Dumars' current attention, he was soon disappointed.

'I trust you are comfortable, Mr Director,' said Maximilian Dumars.

'Not really,' replied the Director General, as tersely as he dared, given his appreciation for Maximilian Dumars' limited ability to deal rationally with defiance.

Maximilian Dumars barely seemed to notice. 'It's not as if you can expect history to be made without a *modicum* of suffering,' he said grandly, totally ignoring the fact that any of the suffering that might be occurring was not his own. 'Anyway,' he continued, 'I didn't come here to discuss our positions in posterity.'

'Oh?' answered the Director General, quite unsure that that was what they *were* discussing.

'No.' Maximilian Dumars paused. 'This Even Bigger Hadron Collider of yours…'

'Yes?' With a slight grunt, Director General pushed himself up into a sitting position.

'…Well, is it actually *doing* anything right now? I mean, we've probably come in here and disrupted a load of science that your people have been doing, haven't we? We must have totally ruined a day's worth of experiments…All those particles whizzing round, not getting observed.'

The Director General looked at Maximilian Dumars suspiciously. The very last thing that he had expected was this sudden concern for the well-being of scientific progress.

'Anyway…I was thinking. Tomorrow – when our demands have been met, of course – we'll be out of your hair. I would have thought that you'd want to get back to doing your experiments as soon as possible. I'm sure there is a place for what you do in the New World Order, after all… The point is this… I don't want to cause you any more inconvenience than is absolutely necessary. So if there was some kind of routine that you need to run to clear the collider, to set it up for new experiments tomorrow – well, I'd be happy if you wanted to run the programme now.'

The Director General looked at him blankly, lost for words.

'Look, Mr Director. I'm not a barbarian. Your work is important to you. But more important are the resources of this planet – it's the only one we've got. It makes no sense for you to be wasting the huge amounts of energy it must take to keep your machine going if it's not doing any experiments. I know you can't simply switch it off and switch it back on again. But at least you can be ready to get on with your work as soon as we're gone. Minimise the impact of our visit, so to speak...'

'As a matter of fact,' began the Director General, hesitantly, 'there is a routine we run from time to time: all that bashing particles together eventually means we need to purge the collider and refresh the material inside.'

'Excellent,' Maximilian Dumars clasped his hands together. 'I knew you would understand that I am, in reality, a reasonable man. Are you personally familiar with the procedure involved?'

'Me? Heavens no! I haven't had hands on experience with the experimental workings here since the very early days of the LHC. You'll need one of the current lab physicists.'

'Well, could you suggest one? Better still, I would like you to tell them to run the procedure. It would be better coming from you. At the end of the day, they are *your* employees.'

The Director General pointed to the young scientist that Maximilian Dumars had used in his television broadcast. 'Mikael knows the systems here as well as anyone,' he said.

Maximilian Dumars fetched the scientist in front of his boss, and the Director General explained that Maximilian Dumars had agreed to let them purge the collider so they could recommence experiments at the earliest possible opportunity. Mikael looked sceptical, but he also knew that however rational Maximilian Dumars appeared, this was the same individual who had murdered a man for refusing to lie down. Though he was naturally mistrusting of his captor, he failed to see what additional danger purging the collider could expose them to. 'As you wish, sir,' he said to his boss.

Maximilian Dumars levelled his gun at the young scientist. 'Just remember,' he said, 'no funny business.' He ushered him into the lab.

Mikael set to work at one of the computer terminals.

'So you can control everything from here?' Maximilian Dumars asked with idle interest.

'We have one of the most sophisticated computer networks in the world,' replied Mikael proudly.

'Yes, I suppose you must. So how long does this purge process take?'

'Well, usually we leave between four and six hours from a purge to starting up a new set of experiments.'

'Really?' said Maximilian Dumars. But he was not conveying a great deal of interest. Mikael watched him for a second. He was staring at the large control screens on the lab wall, but he looked decidedly bored. Mikael decided that Maximilian Dumars was only asking questions out of the British fear of silence. He returned to his work.

The large control screen had a clock display in the bottom corner. It was eight o'clock in the evening. Maximilian Dumars had not really been paying much attention to the rest of the information on the screens. But he had made a note of the time.

* * *

Hercules and Albertine trudged along the tunnel beside the metal tube of the particle accelerator. Although Hercules knew that, while over its full forty-kilometre distance the tunnel completed a loop, its size was such that the gradual bend to the left – as they travelled anti-clockwise – was barely perceptible. The tunnel seemed to stretch on, unchanging, for an eternity. Each step was a déjà déjà vu.

Although Hercules was prepared to bet that they were the only humans present in its entire length, the tunnel was, nevertheless, brightly lit. He supposed that in comparison to the energy consumption of the gently humming accelerator, the drain on resources of the lighting was almost insignificant.

The other significant feature of the tunnel was that it was cold: very, very cold. Hercules shivered involuntarily.

'It takes a good part of the world's 'elium reserves to keep these magnets super-cooled,' remarked Albertine. 'And it is difficult stuff to keep hold of – 'elium. It is so light that not even the earth's gravity is enough to keep it on the planet. Left to its own devices, it would all just drift off into space.'

Hercules was in no mood for a lecture.

'Albertine,' he said wearily, 'we have to take a break; even if it is only for a couple of hours. We've been walking for ages now, both above and below the ground. We've hardly drunk anything since we left your place, and we've barely eaten since breakfast. If we were to come across our adversaries now, I'm not sure I'd have the strength to do anything at all. Is there nowhere that we can rest for a bit? Preferably somewhere that isn't so damned cold?'

Albertine looked at Hercules. Hercules could see that although Albertine was doing her best to maintain her habitual cheerfulness, she, too, was exhausted.

'I guess you are right,' said Albertine. 'I am sure it will not be the end of the world if we take a break for a bit.' She grinned. Tired as he was, Hercules managed a half smile of his own in response to his friend's feeble joke. 'There should be the entrance to a service tunnel coming up. I'm not promising the 'ilton, but at least it should be a bit warmer.'

* * *

'I say we do somesing. Fill ze airports with coloured faces – send zem on holiday or whatever – while we sort out zis mess. We cannot stand idly by and watch zis maniac destroy 'alf of France.'

'Herr President, we cannot give in to this madman. I suggest we continue with the only course of action that has been left open to us – a course of action many of our citizens have begun to enact for themselves. We must simply get as many people as possible clear from the danger area.'

'Zat is all very well for you to say, Madame Chancellor,' replied the President de la Republique coldly. 'Zere is only one German town of any size in ze red zone. France faces ze loss of her second biggest city. Movement of civilians on zat scale is no small matter.'

'A far greater portion of Switzerland will suffer,' the Swiss President added. 'Almost our entire country faces annihilation. But I echo the sentiments of Monsieur le President. Evacuating such large numbers of people in the time allowed is simply not possible.'

The heads of states of those European countries being directly threatened by the Aryan Defence Order/League/Front's ultimatum were meeting via video link. The British Prime Minister had also been invited, for no less reason than the other leaders felt it might be good to have someone there on whom they could pin some of the blame. Whoever was providing backing for the terrorists, one thing was clear: Mr Maximilian Dumars, their leader, was British.

As events had unfolded during the afternoon, the Prime Minister had convened a meeting of the Cabinet Office Briefing Rooms, COBRA. The leaders of the other countries had engaged with their own emergency planning departments, but in the face of the totally new kind of weapon that was threatening the continent, the way forward to all of them was equally unclear. The leaders of Germany, Switzerland and France turned to their Italian counterpart.

'What about you, Signor Presidente? Do you have any ideas?'

The Italian Prime Minister did not really appear to be paying very much attention. He had a laptop open on the desk in front of him and was clearly more focussed on what was on that screen than on the screens linking him to his fellow heads of government. The microphones on the video conferencing equipment were sensitive enough to relay to the other leaders the rather disturbing moans that were coming from the laptop.

'Signor Presidente?'

The Italian Prime Minister looked up. 'Scusi,' he said, adopting a more serious demeanour.

'The terrorist threat, Signor Presidente; do you have any ideas?'

'Si! Si!'

'Well…'

'It eez Milano that is under threat – si?'

'In Italy, yes – that is correct.'

'Well, it is obvious.'

'Go on.'

'We will have to cancel the fashion week and I will have to buy another football team.'

'Is that it?'

'Si – what more do we need to do? It is a shame for the fashion week though… All those bella gnocca…' The Italian leader's eyes glazed over with happy memories, and he returned to staring salaciously at whatever it was that was on his laptop screen.

The French President had been hoping for some support from his Italian counterpart. He was fighting a losing battle for re-election, and it had not been lost on him that the current crisis presented a potential political opportunity. In seeming to follow the demands of the terrorists, he could appeal to the nationalist vote by appearing tough on immigrants while at the same time, in the name of national security, removing a large portion of the population who were likely to vote against him anyway. Unfortunately, his preferred course of action did not look like it was gaining much support.

The British PM cleared his throat. 'Err, If I may perhaps … Um, that is to say, if I may add something?'

The other leaders fell silent. 'Listen,' continued the PM. 'Don't get me wrong…Make no mistake…We're all in this together…'

Like many career politicians, the leader of Her Majesty's Government was now almost incapable of speech that was not, to a greater or lesser extent, an arrangement of meaningless sound-bites. As the leader of a country, when you said 'We're all in this together…' the "this" to which you were referring tended not to be your chauffeur-driven limo or privately chartered jet. It certainly didn't refer to your underground security bunker.

'… but the point is this; the British Government *does not* and *will not* give in to the demands of terrorists.'

'Zat is alright for you to say,' fumed le President. 'It is not your people in danger.'

The PM stared impassively from the screen. His outwardly calm exterior served to highlight the fact that, as far as he was concerned, this was, indeed, the case.

That was about to change.

* * *

Maximilian Dumars watched the clock on the large control screen tick over to show 03:00. Once more he was alone in the lab. He stood up and returned to the public gallery.

The heat and stale air generated by nearly forty slumbering bodies struck him as he slipped through the door. Eugene was snoring gently on a chair. Maximilian Dumars kicked him viciously in the ankle.

'Huh! Wassa!' Eugene sat bolt upright and scanned the sleeping hostages in a moment of pure panic. Then he noticed Maximilian Dumars. 'Oh – hi, there, Boss. I wasn't sleeping – you know. Just resting my eyes for a bit...But not sleeping. No, sir. You can trust me.'

Maximilian Dumars looked at him contemptuously. 'All it would take, Eugene, is one have-a-go hero and all our work would be undone!' His words came out in a hiss; he deliberately kept his voice low. He did not want to disturb the hostages and alert them to his activities, but his anger was nonetheless obvious. 'You can't afford to drop your guard! Not for one second. Do you understand me?'

'Yes, Boss.'

'Well, it's lucky for you that Nick has managed to stay alert,' he said.

Nick wasn't just alert. He was wired. Worried that he might tire, he had been popping caffeine pills like sweets since nightfall. These he had been washing down with energy drinks. He looked awake – but he did not look well. He was sitting in a chair, watching over the sleeping hostages, his gun at the ready and his head jerking back and forth like a hyper-vigilant meerkat. Every now and then his whole body would succumb to a massive involuntary twitch.

'Nick!' Maximilian Dumars addressed his other lieutenant in a loud whisper. At the sound of his name, Nick almost jumped out of his skin. He calmed slightly when he realised who it was that was addressing him, but he still did not look altogether composed. There was a strange far-away look in his eyes.

'Nick?'

'Yes, Boss?'

'Nick – it's time to move things up a gear. So far, the authorities do not appear to have been listening to us. I'll take the physicist that purged the accelerator earlier on. He seems to know what he's doing. I need you to make sure that there are no dramas while I'm gone. And for God's sake stop taking whatever it is that you've been taking – but maybe give some to Eugene. Both of you – stay alert! Can I trust you to do this one thing right?'

'Yes, Boss.'

Maximilian Dumars looked at the pair of them. It was not a promising sight, but then he didn't really have any choice. He went over to where Mikael was sleeping and gently shook him awake.

'Mikael!' the scientist looked up bleary eyed. 'Come with me – I need your help with something.'

Mikael regarded the Uzi that was pointed in his direction.

'I suppose I don't have a choice about this.'

'Of course not! Now get up.'

Mikael was ushered back into the lab.

'What is this all about? What do you want me for?'

'I'm interested to see how you start an experiment running.'

'We can't do that from here. Particles are injected into the accelerator complex from a building about a kilometre to the south of here. It's the other side of the police road-block. With all due respect, there's no way that they would let you cross their cordon now, I think.'

'I suppose you are right. Of course we don't have to go across the road-block. We can travel as the particles do.'

'I'm sorry, I'm not sure I understand.'

'We can go through the accelerator tunnel!'

'Oh it's not safe when the accelerator is operational. We don't go down there when experiments are running.'

Maximilian Dumars looked at the young scientist. Then he looked at the muzzle of his small machine pistol. Then he looked back at the young scientist. 'Oh?' he said. 'I think you'll find these are very *special* circumstances.'

Twenty-five minutes later, Maximilian Dumars and Mikael were standing in front of a complex looking set of apparatus that made up the start of the linear accelerator – LINAC – that prepared heavy particles for injection into the collider ring. As Mr Dumars had predicted, the route that they had followed through the collider tunnel had been, quite literally, completely overlooked by the security forces.

The particle generator had been built with functional rather than aesthetic considerations in mind. Nonetheless the symmetry of its complexity conferred on it a strange beauty. Rows of pipes and tubing snaked back and forth amongst a myriad of different sized cylindrical components largely composed of finely machined metals of different sorts. The whole assemblage was held together with yet more shiny nuts and bolts and liberally decorated with warnings and hazard labels. At the very rear of the machine, a long rod protruded, attached to a red rubber hose.

'I'm not sure why you made me bring you here,' said Mikael. 'I'm not expert in how this equipment works. My own research is confined to processing observations at the ATLAS experiment.'

'Your job was simply to bring me here,' replied Maximilian Dumars dismissively. He began to unscrew the long metal rod that was sticking out of the back of the apparatus. 'I suspect if I keep unscrewing this it will come out,' he said. The rod did indeed come free. 'Ah,' he said, feigning surprise, 'you see, I did not need to be a rocket scientist – or even a nuclear physicist – to work that one out.'

He took the Dark Anti-Matter canister from its pouch on his belt and offered it up to the fixture from which he had just removed the rod. The end of the canister was machined to a perfect fit for the hole. He screwed it into place.

Maximilian Dumars looked at Mikael. 'At this point, it would have been useful to have someone here who actually knows how to make this equipment do what I want it to. But, as you say, you do not know how to operate it. So really, I have no further use for you.'

He calmly levelled his gun at the young scientist's head.

'B – b – but… you said… None of us would be harmed.'

Maximilian Dumars paused. 'Oh yes, I did, didn't I? How very forgetful of me.' His tone of voice suggested that he had not, in fact, forgotten at all; he just rather enjoyed milking every last little bit of suffering out of others that his current position of power allowed. Maximilian Dumars had been given the chance to pay the world back for all the wrongs he had suffered in his miserable life – and he wasn't going to waste a single opportunity.

'Anyway, luckily for you,' he continued, 'I have no need of experts. I have this!' with a flourish he produced the USB memory stick from his pocket.

He inserted the drive into a vacant port on a computer terminal that was conveniently positioned by the generator. A box popped up on the screen displaying the contents of the device. It contained a single file: execute.exe.

Maximilian Dumars clicked on the file icon. Another box popped up. Underneath a heading was an inner box that was crammed with tiny text and scroll bars that indicated that the text continued not only down, but across the page as well. The title read:

"By running the following program, you are agreeing to abide by the following terms and conditions:"

The inner text box was labelled "Terms and Conditions". Below it was two buttons. One read "I accept the terms and conditions". The other button was the bigger of the two. The text in the second button read as follows: "Really? Who's got time for all this terms and conditions nonsense? Of course I haven't read the terms and conditions – but you can't hold that against me. What the hell. Just run the damned program anyway."

Maximilian Dumars was momentarily nonplussed. He started dragging the scrollbars on the inner text box. There were clearly a *lot* of terms and conditions; all neatly laid out in fully justified six-point font. Just looking at it made his eyes swim.

'What are you doing?' asked Mikael.

'Why, I would have thought that was pretty obvious,' answered Maximilian Dumars. 'I am about to inject the Dark Anti-Matter into your Collider.'

'But that will destroy us all! I thought you said we'd be released unharmed.'

Mr Dumars fixed the young scientist with a hard stare. 'I'm told,' he began, 'that the program I am about to execute performs the injection of the Dark Anti-Matter as a two-stage process. I have been told that the EBHC maintains a vacuum that makes the atmosphere on the moon seem positively crowded with matter. Nevertheless, there is still *some* matter in the collider, and as you have seen, Dark Anti-Matter can be quite – volatile in the presence of matter.

'In the first stage of the injection process a single Dark Anti-Matter particle is fired into the collider at high speed. It passes round the tubes of the accelerators in next to no time, mopping up any stray atoms that exist in the current near vacuum of the apparatus.

'As soon as a *perfect* vacuum has been created, the remaining Dark Anti-Matter is released into the collider in rapidly pulsed bursts. An absolute vacuum should cause the collider to collapse in on itself; but the repulsive force of the Dark Anti-Matter will prevent that from happening. The magnets in the collider will prevent the Dark Anti-Matter from touching the sides of the collider and blowing us all to kingdom come. At least that's what I've been told. I wouldn't *really* know of course...' there was only one word to describe the smile that played across his lips as he revelled in the anxiety of his hostage – it was pure evil '…I'm not, after all, a *scientist.*'

And with that he clicked on the larger of the two buttons on the screen in front of him.

* * *

For a fraction of a fraction of a fraction of a second the Universe stood still.

Even after this briefest of moments of stasis, space-time had quite some distance to travel to catch up with itself.

The earth jarred.

* * *

'W – What was that?' Hercules sat bolt upright.

Albertine had also been shocked from slumber. 'Maybe I was wrong that us stopping for a rest would not be the end of the world.' She looked worried.

Hercules realised that it was his turn to reassure his new friend. 'It's not over yet,' he said. 'Besides, that Mr Dumars gave noon to-morrow…' he looked at his watch '…I mean today – as his deadline. I'm sure that – whatever happened just now – we still have some time on our side.'

'Yes, well if we do have time on our side now, it won't be for long,' she said, getting to her feet. 'Come on, it's time we pressed on.'

Twelve

THE DAY WAS LESS than an hour old, but already the desert heat was intense. Asif was eating his breakfast in the shadow of a tarpaulin fixed to the side of his truck. He had scarcely seen another living thing since he began his drive; and yet within minutes of daylight, he had been joined by a pair of flies which buzzed annoyingly back and forth around his head.

He had woken before dawn, while the chill of the desert night still hung in the air. Rubbing the sleep from his eyes, he stood up, stretched, then gathered his prayer mat before scrambling to the top of one of the rocky hills between which the wadi, where he had made his camp, nestled. He had reached the summit just as the first orange sliver appeared above the eastern horizon. From his vantage point the spreading dawn gave him his first glimpse of the Red Sea. Beyond those waters, in almost the exact direction from which the sun was now casting its light, lay the object of his prayers – Mecca!

Mecca. Today it was the target of his weapons.

In the early, kind rays of sunlight that kissed the desert, the place was like a paradise and Asif felt blessed. The rocks were ablaze with colour and the edge had been taken from the chill of the night leaving the air pleasantly cool. In his heart Asif felt with a searing certainty that he *had* been chosen. He was appointed to a higher cause. He was *special* – and today he would prove it.

The sun rose quickly, though, and with it, the temperature. As the fiery orb climbed in the sky, the shadows shortened. The colours that had painted the landscape from a rich palette were bleached from the rocks until the reflected light hurt the eyes. Suddenly Asif began to feel exposed rather than exalted – hunted rather than hunter.

He scooped up his mat and scurried back down the slope to his camp and the small respite from the rising temperature that the diminishing shadows in the wadi still afforded.

Back in his camp, he tended his birds before setting himself to the task of making his own breakfast. He prodded the embers of his fire from the previous night but there was no life left in them. He set a small pot of water to boil on a single ring gas burner.

Asif looked at his birds. People often thought pigeons were grey. How wrong they were! Sure, at first glance to the unobservant eye the plumage was a mixture of greys and white. The only obvious colour came from the bright coral pink of their legs. But if you took time to watch them closely – to study the light playing off the feathers of their breasts – you could see that they were painted with the colours of the rainbow. From vivid pink to lurid green, with sparkling sheens of yellow and gold between, their plumage shone with an ever-changing iridescent splendour.

'Not long now, my beauties. Soon we will write our names in the history of the world.'

* * *

The dawn that broke over the CERN complex brought with it an eerie stillness. Beyond the police cordon that surrounded the ATLAS building, the city of Geneva had fallen silent.

Those that could had long since fled. Planes were no longer landing at the airport in Cointrin. Only the occasional car passed along what had recently been the city's busiest thoroughfares.

Inside the ATLAS building, Maximilian Dumars did not need to rely on his gut instincts to tell him that all was not going to plan. Rather than bringing him an indication that his demands were being met, the rolling news channels had instead covered the exodus from the danger zone around Geneva and beyond. Despite Maximilian Dumars' threat that the attack on CERN was being made by but one of a number of active cells of the Aryan Defence Order/League/Front, it seemed that the people of Geneva were more concerned with fleeing the threat that they were *sure* existed, rather than worrying about any others that *might*.

All major roads had been packed with the fleeing populace. Some people had hung back in the towns as their fellow citizens took flight. There had been some looting in Lyons and St Etienne until reluctant army units had been sent in to protect the property that was almost certainly destined for destruction. The looters quickly dispersed and left with their bounty. The soldiers soon followed, leaving the streets empty.

Now, with the exception of those few too ill or too old or too stubborn to join the exodus, all that remained of the population of Geneva were the police cordon, the Aryan Defence Order/League/ Front and their hostages, and a few sorry journalists who were seriously beginning to consider whether their futures would not best be served by covering a news story that involved them being perhaps two hundred and sixty kilometres – in any direction – from their current positions. Not, as it turned out, that that would do them any good. Maximilian Dumars was about to tell them why.

He stood up and stretched, trying to squeeze some life into his stiff limbs. He rubbed his eyes, which ached from obsessing over the news channels for most of the night. He had been awake for twenty-four hours, but he was not going to let tiredness stand in the way of success. Not when he was this close. Not when he was about to change the course of history. He was a man with an iron will, he told himself – and destiny beckoned.

He went back into the public gallery. Some of the hostages were beginning to stir. Nick and Eugene had managed to stay awake. Nick was still round eyed, but less twitchy than before. Eugene was sitting across two chairs, munching disconsolately on a cold pizza crust. They both looked up as their leader came into the room.

'Morning, Boss,' they grunted in unison.

'Yes, it is,' said Maximilian Dumars simply. He was scanning the sleeping bodies on the floor, looking for one in particular.

'Boss?' said Eugene. 'Boss?'

Maximilian Dumars ignored him.

'Boss - when are we going to get some more food? I'm starving.'

Maximilian Dumars saw the person he was looking for. 'All in good time, Eugene,' he said without even looking at his lieutenant. He picked his way between the recumbent figures and gave the person he sought a kick. It was the news cameraman. 'Come on,' he ordered. 'Get up, and get your equipment.' He looked around and, locating Mikael, nudged him with his booted foot as well, 'You too, Mikael. There's work to be done.'

* * *

Clear water lapped gently at the white sand between Asif's toes.

He had pulled off the road just to the north of the trading post at Halayeb and found a secluded beach. As he had approached the Sudanese border there had been a noticeable increase in the amount of traffic on the road, mostly large trucks carrying goods to trade. There was also more traditional transportation in the form of camel trains – some beasts laden with merchandise, some to be sold for meat. The presence of extra people had made Asif nervous and at the first opportunity to move unobserved, he had deserted the road and cut across the short strip of desert to the coast.

At least here by the sea the softest of breezes coming in off the water took the edge off the heat. He moved the cage into the small shadow cast by the Toyota, took his shoes and socks off and hurried down to the water's edge. The roasting sand burnt the soles of his unaccustomed feet, and the coolness of the water was a blessing.

Asif had never seen a sea as clear as this. He could see the sands beneath the still waters and a short distance offshore the mounds of corals that further out merged into a large reef. Even from the shore, colourful fish were visible beneath the surface.

He shielded his eyes from the glare of the sun and gazed out to the east. Out there, across *those* waters, his pigeons were about to change the world!

He snapped from his reverie. It was time for action. Asif trotted back up the beach and opened the boot of the truck, reaching inside for his small suitcase, which he opened to retrieve the bundle containing the homing hoods and harnesses. Placing these to one side, he closed the case and extended the handle. The handle consisted of two metal struts which were hidden within the body of the case when retracted, joined by a plastic hand grip, which was attached to the struts by a small screw on each side.

With a small screwdriver, he removed the screws, put them to one side and gently slid the hand grip from the struts. Inside each was a small, cloth wrapped, package containing a small canister, identical to the one he had left in his parents' bedroom.

Asif had brought with him the other items he needed to prime the weapons – the same magnifying glass and pin that he had used to set the detonating cap on the test vial. He checked a map and measured the distance from his current position to Mecca. It was about two hundred and twenty miles as the crow – or more appropriately, pigeon – flew. He looked around himself at the cloudless sky. There was no wind. His birds would probably manage a good fifty miles an hour in the conditions. To allow a bit of leeway, he set the first timer for six hours.

He repeated the action on the second cap, carefully fitted them both onto their respective canisters and then set about preparing his pigeons for their journey.

Speaking softly in reassuring tones, he unlatched the cage door to and reached inside to take out the first bird. Holding it firmly but gently across the back he took it out and began the by now well-practiced process of strapping the creature into its harness and hood. Then he slotted one of the little canisters into a tiny holster on the harness. He returned the bird and repeated the process with its companion.

When he had finished preparing the second bird, he reached back into the cage so that he had both pigeons together. He kissed them each gently on the head.

'This is it, this is our moment,' he murmured. The pigeons cooed. 'Go now, with the blessings of Allah. Together we shall unite Islam against the world.'

He threw his arms open, one bird flapping from each hand as they climbed rapidly into the sky. Together the birds circled the beach once. Then, in unison, guided by the magnetic adjustments in their special hoods, they struck out like arrows across the expanse of sea before them.

* * *

Captain Higgs stood on the bridge and surveyed the scene ahead. Above, the sun shone down from another blameless sky. Ahead, the clear blue waters of the Red Sea stretched as calm as a boating lake in a park.

After his long lie in the day before, the captain was feeling slightly guilty. Accordingly, he had rostered himself onto the early morning shift, although in truth it didn't make much difference. There was little to do while they were at sea besides sleep and work and the meals in between.

The captain had spent much of the previous day trying to account for the vessel's remarkable rate of progress. There had been calls from *the Good Ship*'s owners – worried that the captain was being profligate with the fuel that they were paying for. He had checked with the chief engineer. The engines were turning at the normal rate, and they were burning no more fuel than they would have at their plotted rate of nine and a half knots. He relayed this information to the freight line. They had computers that monitored pretty much all of the goings-on on the vessel, so they grudgingly accepted that he was telling the truth.

He had looked for other possible causes. They hadn't lost any cargo. There was no wind. Nor were there any unusual currents that had suddenly spring up which might offer an explanation for their accelerated pace. Nevertheless, with each hour that passed, when he checked the GPS, the captain found that they were running further and further ahead of their scheduled itinerary. They had more than caught up the delay dealt to them by the harbourmaster at Suez. At this rate of progress, they would arrive days early at their destination. Since their cargo was aid relief for the East African famine, every hour early that they arrived had the potential to save lives.

The captain looked at the GPS once more. To their east lay the Saudi coast. To their west was the Halayeb triangle – an area of land of disputed sovereignty between Egypt and the Sudan. Once more their progress suggested a speed that was higher than the rate at which the engines were set. But Captain Higgs was getting used to reckoning in terms of the speed that they were actually going, rather than how fast they should have been going. He couldn't explain it, but if it meant that their cargo of aid reached the needy earlier than expected, he was happy to sit back and let it happen.

* * *

To the south of the *Good Ship* – under the same blameless sky – floated a vessel whose silhouette spoke of a different age. Although the dhow hailed from a bygone era, the activity that engaged those on board was a thoroughly modern one – albeit an activity that has roots as deep as man's connection with the sea. Piracy may not be as old as the hills, but it has been a feature of nautical travel since the first-ever seafarer looked enviously on as the second-ever seafarer floated past on a bigger log.

On board the dhow, Abdullah and his shipmates were making ready their equipment. The deceptively spacious hold had been opened and two large fibreglass skiffs were being manoeuvred by the crew onto deck and over the side of the mother ship into the water. Powerful outboard motors were winched overboard and lowered onto the sterns of the launches. A sophisticated marine yachting radar system was brought up from below. The radar antenna was hoisted above the deck attached to a pole and slotted into a hole in the deck. Both pole and hole had been custom made for the purpose. The crew laid out an assortment of modern weapons, from heavy machine guns to rocket propelled grenades, on the deck and began to check them. The spoils of previous raids had afforded them the very best equipment their profession demanded.

The captain had taken his vessel as far north as he dared. They were almost level with the Sudanese border with Egypt and the disputed territory that lay beyond. They were far from waters where the shipping was more habituated to the risks of their activities, so the captain expected they would be able to catch their quarry quite off guard. But they had not ventured so far north as to run the risk of encountering the better prepared patrols of the Egyptian navy. Sudanese waters, by comparison, offered a relatively safe haven – to those from whom others were at risk.

* * *

'Citizens of Europe…' there was a long pause as Maximilian Dumars stared directly into the camera. In his mind's eye he looked statesmanlike. To most of those watching, he looked both disturbed and disturbing. '…You *disappoint* me.'

He dropped his head and shook it slightly as though he was addressing a wayward child. He continued in this vein.

'You disappoint me – but I don't blame *you*. You lack leadership. If the governments of this continent were capable of true leadership, I would not – *we* would not – be in this position. It is only because of the failures of our so-called governments that I and my colleagues felt it necessary to mount our campaign. Had our countries been given the governance they need – they *deserve* – I should never have found myself before you. But we have been failed – failed in the past as our countries have become awash with the tides of immigration. And so in truth I see no reason why today should have been any different.

'With this in mind, it is lucky that I planned for this eventuality. Using the scientists here to confirm the validity of our threat was not the *only* reason for us being here. As it turns out, they also have this rather wonderful toy!'

His grin was not statesmanlike. It had maniac written all over it.

'Those of you who were watching yesterday may remember Mikael. Say "hello" to the good people of Europe, Mikael.' The camera panned onto the young scientist, who was once again cable-tied to a chair.

Mikael stared blankly at Maximilian Dumars for a moment. He caught the look on his captor's face. 'Hello,' he said nervously.

'Excellent. Now, Mikael, perhaps you could tell the good people of our continent something about the Even Bigger Hadron Collider for me?' It wasn't really a request.

'Er, well...where to start...The Even Bigger Hadron Collider is the pinnacle of scientific achievement in the twenty first century -'

'I think I've already proved that it's not quite that,' interrupted Maximilian Dumars. Mikael was taken aback by the sudden interjection. 'Before yesterday you had never even *heard* of Dark Anti-Matter. But never mind, go on.'

'Yes, well, where was I? The collider is *one* of the finest achievements of scientific engineering. One hundred meters below us, carved into the rock is a forty-kilometre tunnel that extends in a circuit that spans the Swiss and French borders. The tunnel houses the biggest, most powerful particle accelerator ever constructed.'

Mikael was getting into his flow reciting tour guide facts about CERN's work. Once again Maximilian Dumars interrupted him. 'And what does this accelerator do?'

'Two beams of particles are accelerated to near light speed around the circuit in opposite directions. At various experimental stations around the tunnel, the beams are smashed into one another. The resulting collisions break matter into its component parts and teach us about the fundamental nature of the Universe.'

'Very good, Mikael. But I'm sure that sort of information could be easily located – on the internet, for example, or one of the fine publications from your excellent visitor centre. Heaven knows, they've been padding the news stories with little else all night. No.

I think you should tell the good people of Europe something that they don't already know.'

Mikael looked blankly at Maximilian Dumars.

'Come now, Mikael, don't be shy,' said Maximilian Dumars, walking behind the scientist and placing a paternal hand on his shoulder in a quasi-amicable manner. 'You know how I detest violence; but I really think you could be making more of an effort.' He gave Mikael's shoulder a squeeze. It obviously wasn't a gentle one. Mikael winced.

'Tell the people something that they couldn't possibly know; something that only you – and perhaps one other person – know. What makes the Even Bigger Hadron Collider so very special, *right at this present moment?*'

Mikael glanced nervously upwards at the figure standing behind him, trying to read his face, looking for an answer. Maximilian Dumars' knuckles whitened once again as his fingers dug into the soft tissue under Mikael's collar bone. He smiled a cold, hard, false smile. 'Come on, Mikael! Don't keep us all on tenterhooks. What can you tell everyone about the Even Bigger Hadron Collider that would be news to them all?'

'Er...,' Mikael paused. Maximilian Dumars squeezed again. Mikael winced, before beginning hesitantly, partly from the pain being inflicted on him and partly from fear of saying the wrong thing, '...you...injected...the...Dark...Anti-Matter...into...it...last...night?'

Maximilian Dumars relaxed his grip. 'Oh, yes!' he exclaimed with exaggerated mock surprise. 'I *did* do that, didn't I?' He fixed a stare directly at the camera, before returning his attention to the scientist. 'And tell me, Mikael, what do you expect the effect of *that* will be?'

'W-w-well – the collider is used to accelerate particles. It gives them more energy. At the higher energy levels, collisions become more extreme – easier to detect. The likelihood of discovering new energy states increases.'

'So what do you think will happen with the Dark Anti-Matter whizzing around in your collider?' prompted Maximilian Dumars.

'We don't really have much experience of the properties of Dark Anti-Matter…' Mikael quickly read the look on Maximilian Dumars' face, '…but I would suppose that it would increase its energy in exactly the same way.'

'By how much?'

Mikael was pale. 'I don't know,' he said, shaking his head. 'A lot.'

Maximilian Dumars had had enough of baiting the scientist. He turned back to the camera.

'It would appear,' he said, 'that I won't be needing to call on the services of our colleagues in other cells around Europe. It would also appear that all the people that I watched on television last night fleeing from the two-hundred-and-fifty-kilometre zone around us have done so in vain. I have been reliably informed by minds far sharper than *his*…' he nodded dismissively towards Mikael, '… that the power of any collision of the Dark Anti-Matter will increase the destructive force of the explosion by *at least* a factor of ten. That is two and a half *thousand* kilometres, Ladies and Gentlemen: the whole of Europe.

'Now I told you I am a reasonable man. But I would rather that Europe ceased to exist than that it continues to be infected by the tainting impurities of races which have contaminated our societies.

'This is my final warning. Start showing willingness to comply with my *simple* demands. Please don't try and interfere with the power supply to the collider. There is already sufficient energy in the Dark Anti-Matter that such a move would simply cause the sort of explosion I am trying to avoid.'

Suddenly Maximilian Dumars' tone shifted. For a brief moment it was as though he had suddenly woken in the middle of a nightmare only to find the hell he was caught up in the process of creating. In the same way as he had ended his first broadcast, for a few short words, a shadow of humanity returned.

'Show me,' he was pleading with the camera lens. 'Show me that you are prepared to take the right steps – please...

'Show me.'

* * *

The skiff rocked gently in the clear, blue waters. Overhead, the fierce tropical sun beat down unrelentingly from a cloudless sky. Abdullah and his crewmates lazed around on the plank seats of the launch, heads swathed in cloth to protect them from the heat. Not far off floated the second skiff, its crew in a similar state of relaxed readiness.

Neither skiff had moved far from the mother ship. When one of the hand-held walkie-talkies crackled into life, the pirates had already been alerted by the commotion on the dhow. Their comrades left aboard the larger vessel were waving and pointing excitedly to the north.

'North-north-west, six miles,' barked the voice of the captain of the dhow, 'heading this way at about fourteen knots. This is it, men, Inshallah. Bring me back a big, fat fish!'

* * *

High above the glistening sea, two small shapes sped across the sky on a bearing that was a little south of east. Despite the unaccustomed heat their infallible senses of direction told them they were homing in on their loft in an old mill town in Yorkshire. Had they been given to too high a degree of rationalisation, they might have questioned the many unfamiliar aspects of their current environment. But the signals in their small brains told them they were on the right course, and the muscles in their breasts responded with the effort that drove them forward through the warm air.

They were doing what they were hatched to do. They weren't simply flying – they were racing.

* * *

Albertine and Hercules had been trudging along the tunnel for hours.

'You know,' said Albertine conversationally, 'that within space-time, the faster you go the slower time goes and the smaller distance gets. When particles are whizzing around the accelerator at near the speed of light – that is about seven and a half thousand times around the circuit each second – they only travel a fraction of the distance that we are.'

Hercules was too exhausted to puzzle at this. He stopped in his tracks. His legs ached from almost a full day of non-stop walking; his head hurt from the endlessly repetitive view of the tunnel stretching before them and the constant background hum of electrical equipment; and he was cold.

'I know you're just trying to keep our spirits up, Albertine, but I'm afraid it's not really helping. I honestly don't care how long it takes a particle to get round the circuit, or how far it has to travel. All I want to know is – how much longer do *we* have to keep going down this damned tunnel?'

Albertine looked ahead. For the first time in an age, the far distance was not an exact replica of the near. There was a hint of an opening ahead. Hercules noticed it too.

'Not very long at all – by the looks of things. That must be the cavern for the ATLAS experiment. I hope you 'ave 'ad a good chance to think about what we do next!'

Buoyed by the prospect of an exit from the tunnel, Hercules and Albertine hurried forward. Sure enough, a little way ahead the tunnel opened into a huge cavern that housed the massive lump of precision engineering that was the ATLAS collider. Hercules stared in awe at the enormous construction. Albertine noticed that her companion had stopped.

'Come on!' she said. 'No time for sightseeing now!'

She grabbed Hercules by the arm and dragged him towards a door of much more human proportions in the corner of the chamber. The door led through to a twisting corridor. Albertine seemed to know where she was going. After a few turns they came face to face with two doors. One was a wire cage lift. Next to it was a door marked 'Stairs'.

'Lift or stairs?' asked Albertine.

* * *

Maximilian Dumars was pacing the lab. Since his second broadcast he had been growing ever more agitated. In the two hours that had passed since his appeal he had watched in increasing frustration as the evidence that his demands were being met singularly failed to be relayed to him through the multiple news channels that were broadcasting the events unfolding across the continent.

The pictures instead told a story of panic. In some places there were demonstrations. In others looting. The exact purpose of stealing consumer items they would have no time to enjoy was not something that Maximilian Dumars could understand however he looked at it. He had begun to mutter to himself as he paced.

'Where is the leadership?' he asked no one in particular. 'Where is the direction?'

He flicked through the channels from one scene of civil chaos to the next.

'Where is the *Order*?'

There was a knock at the door of the lab. Maximilian Dumars spun on his heels. It was Eugene and Nick. Between them they were ushering forward a group of the scientists.

'Er, Boss,' ventured Nick, cautiously. He was used to seeing the nervous tick at the side of his boss's temples when he was roused and in the full flow of one of his speeches, but he had never known it to be a permanent feature of Maximilian Dumars' demeanour. Mr Dumars' mood was making both Nick and even the usually unflappable Eugene decidedly uncomfortable.

'Yes, what is it?' snapped their leader. 'It'd better be important,' he added, eyeing the gaggle of scientists being herded into the room. Then a thought suddenly struck him. 'Hang on a minute. If you two are in here – who's guarding the rest of the hostages?'

'Oh – don't worry about them, boss. They're all still tied up and we locked the door on the way out. Besides, they all pretty much realise that unless your – I mean our – demands are met we're all pretty much doomed anyway. What with you putting that Dark Anti-Matter stuff into the Even Bigger Hadron Collider and everything. If the whole of Europe is going to be destroyed in a little while they all figured that there's not much point in trying to run away.'

Maximilian Dumars glanced through the glass divide. The hostages on the other side had indeed refrained from making any kind of break for a short-lived freedom. They were all attentively watching the goings on in the lab. Nick coughed.

'Which sort of brings us to why we're here. Some of these here science chaps...'

Eugene interrupted. 'Really, Nick,' he said. 'Haven't you learnt anything since we've been here? They're not called "science chaps". They're called...' his face screwed up in concentration.

'...fizzicksists.' Eugene's face beamed with pride at the level of his learning. Travel had certainly broadened his mind.

It was Nick's turn to show annoyance. He scowled at Eugene before continuing. 'These "fizzicksists" have been discussing something which we thought you should hear.'

'Really?' Maximilian Dumars raised an eyebrow inquisitively.

'Yeah,' said Nick, strongly conveying the impression that he was now not so sure that whatever the scientists had been discussing, was really something that need disturb his boss. 'I mean – I know you've got this all planned out – and it's probably something you've already thought of...' He prodded one of the scientists with the barrel of his Uzi. '...Go on... tell him.'

Once more the unfortunate Mikael found himself face to face with the questionably-balanced leader of the Aryan Defence Order/League/Front. He hesitated, and turned to the group of scientists for support. They made encouraging faces at him, while at the same time collectively shuffling backwards. Maximilian Dumars approached like a circling shark that has just noticed a straggling fish separated from the safety of the shoal.

'Well?' Maximilian Dumars was considerably shorter than Mikael, but as he delivered the question he seemed to loom over the physicist.

'W-w-well,' stuttered Mikael, shrinking back. 'It's just this. You managed to get the Dark Anti-Matter *into* the EBHC. But – when your demands are met, of course – how were you planning to *get it out?*'

* * *

Captain Higgs examined the radar screen, his brow furrowed with a look of deep concern. Two ghostly dots had appeared. They flickered and faded, and then reappeared with each sweep of the antenna. One thing was certain. The distance of the dots from their own vessel was rapidly decreasing and their courses were set to cross.

'What do you make of that, Jenkins?' asked the Captain. 'Whoever they are, they are clearly set to intercept us.'

'If we were further south, Sir, I'd suggest we start preparing to repel a pirate attack,' replied the Chief Officer with a half grin. 'But we're far too far north for that sort of thing – wouldn't you say, Captain?'

The captain looked at his Chief Officer. Since they had left Suez, things had been going so well that it appeared that the other officers on the bridge had started to accept the freakishly smooth running of the ship as normal. How quickly they had forgotten the difficulties that had plagued them on their voyage through the Med! Captain Higgs had not grown so complacent. He had been *waiting* for things to start going wrong.

The Chief Officer read his captain's expression. 'You don't really think, Sir...?' he began. 'Not seriously...This far north...?'

Captain Higgs had moved over to the bridge window and picked up a pair of binoculars with which he was scanning the horizon. 'It's been getting more and more difficult for them close to home...' he said without lowering the binoculars. 'The combined efforts of the international naval patrols have seen to that. But if they widen their areas of operation, the bigger the area under threat, the more difficult it's going to be to contain. The patrols can't protect every inch of ocean. It was probably only really a matter of time...'

Suddenly he stopped his scanning sweeps of the horizon and locked his position. His finger reached to adjust the focus of his lenses.

'What?' said Jenkins. 'What have you seen, Sir?'

The boats were still too far off and too small to be clearly seen; but at the very edge of the distance, two white streaks were homing in on an interception course with the *Good Ship*.

'I don't know,' replied the Captain. 'Whoever they are, though, at that speed and on that bearing, I'm not altogether sure that I really want to hang around to find out their intentions.' He lowered the binoculars.

'Sound the alarm, Jenkins. If they are not what I think they are, then this might just be a good practice drill for when we get further south. Either way, I have no great desire to sample Somali hospitality at first hand. It's time to prepare for some evasive manoeuvres.'

* * *

Hercules and Albertine had reached the top of the stairs without incident. They approached the door that led into the laboratory building beyond with caution. Ever so carefully, Albertine eased the door open a crack. They peered through the narrow gap. The corridor beyond was deserted.

Albertine opened the door still further. The corridor was indeed empty. The floor, though, bore a large dark stain that spoke of earlier activity: a large dark stain that suggested that something heavy and bleeding had been dragged into the corridor and dumped. The drag marks ended in a thick puddle that had spread to form the outline of a body.

But of the body that had lain there and bled, there was, however, no sign.

* * *

Under Captain Higgs' orders the engines had been opened up to full throttle. In normal conditions, at full steam the *Good Ship* could manage seventeen knots – not that the owners ever sanctioned such profligate oil-burning speed. But the conditions that they had been sailing under since leaving Suez were anything but normal. The *Good Ship* was forging ahead at well over twenty knots. All the same, the two powerful motor launches were steadily narrowing the gap to them.

As the pirates closed in on the *Good Ship,* Captain Higgs began to steer a meandering course of wide arcing sweeps in the ocean. The zig-zagging container vessel threw up great foaming walls of wake which threatened to capsize the smaller boats of their would-be assailants. Rather than risking being swamped by the churning mass of water, the two fibre-glass skiffs withdrew to a respectful distance to weigh their options. But their retreat was a tactical respite – they had not given up the chase.

From the bridge, Captain Higgs could clearly make out the figures on the two motor launches as they waved signals at one another. Equally clear through the lenses of his binoculars were the masses of weapons that the crews of each of the skiffs were carrying. The captain watched as the boats circled one another in tight formation. They appeared to decide on a strategy and suddenly broke formation. One of the boats sped off in a looping course that looked set to position itself ahead of the *Good Ship.* The other disappeared somewhere to stern.

'Damn it!' muttered the Captain. 'What are they up to now?'

* * *

'What do you mean – "How am I going to get it out?"?' Not only was the tick in Maximilian Dumars' temple now beating double time, but he had gone an alarming shade of red as his blood pressure rocketed. He realised that the question being put to him was not, indeed, something that he had considered. He had been so caught up in his moment of history that the plan had never really extended past the point where his demands had been met.

'Easy there, Boss,' Eugene attempted to sound casual, but his tone barely masked his palpable concern. 'We've got it all in hand, that's what I told 'em. Isn't that right? We know what to do with that stuff when everyone starts doing what they're supposed to – don't we?'

Maximilian Dumars looked up at the trusting face of his man mountain of a lieutenant. Something about the whole-hearted faith of Eugene temporarily restored some hope to his leader.

'Of course we know what to do, Eugene. But it's not something I need to share with anyone *until our demands are being met!* If I were to tell these fools how to make the Dark Anti-Matter safe what would stop them from trying to do so themselves?'

Eugene waved his massive machine gun in the air. Even though it was something that looked like it should be fitted to a tank, it still looked like a toy in his hands. 'Apart from this, you mean?'

'You never know the lengths desperate people will go to, Eugene.' His eyes narrowed as he looked pointedly at the group of scientists. 'Even with all this machinery,' Maximilian Dumars waved vaguely around the lab with his own weapon, 'these fools failed to discover Dark Anti-Matter. And they think they can trick me into revealing how to make it safe. The very idea is an insult!'

* * *

Two small dots sped across the sky with relentless, rapid wing beats. Theirs was not the silhouette of the avian form adapted for a life riding the ocean updrafts – long tapered wings that could keep their owner aloft for miles on a single glide, barely ever a need for flapping. These were utilitarian fliers, no less well adapted to their own method of carving a path through the heavens.

A couple of miles ahead of the pigeons, it was the container vessel and the two small launches that circled it that were mere specks in the birds' vision.

On the deck of the *Good Ship*, bosun Boson was organising the deckhands in preparation for impending attack. The *Good Ship* did not carry any conventional weapons, but as a precautionary measure for their journey through the troubled waters to the south, large beams of wood had been lashed to the sides of the vessel. These were now hoisted into place ready to be dropped onto any boat that attempted to board them from port or starboard. The ship's powerful fire hoses made up the rest of the arsenal at the bosun's disposal. They had been unreeled and were held at the ready on each side of the vessel to unleash a torrent of water on anything that ventured within their not inconsiderable range. Thus armed, bosun Boson and his crewmates readied themselves for a confrontation with adversaries wielding heavy machine guns and rocket propelled grenades.

* * *

When they had reached the end of the corridor, Hercules and Albertine could hear raised voices. It was impossible to tell if the speakers were angry or excited.

They crept on in the direction from which the voices were coming. A wooden door with a small glass window separated them from the main ATLAS lab. The voices were coming from the other side of the door. Hercules and Albertine dropped to the floor and stole forward until they had reached the door. Verrrry slowly they stood up and peered through the window into the room beyond.

Their uniforms made the three men that Hercules had followed from London instantly recognisable. But the members of the Aryan Defence Order/League/Front were not alone in the lab. A group of hostages was cowering in front of Maximilian Dumars, who was pacing back and forth in front of them, waving his arms.

'You think I can be tricked by such a school playground trick?' he asked, almost at a yell, as he turned on the shrinking scientists. White flecks of spittle flew from the corners of his mouth. His temples bulged and throbbed.

'Why…this operation has been the culmination of *years* of planning,' he continued. In fairness to Maximilian Dumars, he *had* been planning his take-over of the world for years; as fanciful scenes that played out in his mind during the duller moments of his employment at the Job Centre. However, the question of how to get Dark Anti-Matter *out* of an Even Bigger Hadron Collider was not something that had *ever* featured in any of his planning. And now he came to think about it, although the enigmatic Mr John had been most precise in his instructions about how to get the Dark Anti-Matter *into* the collider, he had been singularly unforthcoming on the procedures to follow once the demands of the Aryan Defence Order/League/Front had been met. The fact that he had always managed to evade Maximilian Dumars' questions on the matter, or simply change the subject, had led Mr Dumars to assume that it was not something that was a big deal. There was not one of Maximilian Dumars' fantasies for world domination that had played out like this.

* * *

The first skiff launched its attack from the front. Speeding in from the waters ahead, it crashed over the bow wave of the bigger ship into the relative calm between bow and stern. With consummate skill, the helmsman of the skiff slewed his boat into a rapid about turn so that it was now travelling along the port side of the *Good Ship.* The rest of the pirates, who had been desperately clinging on to the sides of the launch as it rocked and turned, now levelled their weapons at the crew on the deck of their target vessel.

As the skiff bounced alongside the larger ship, the pirates unleashed a volley of machine-gun fire. The bullets were not well directed. Some struck the metal sides of the ship, some flew harmlessly overhead, yet others ricocheted dangerously off the containers and between the crew members. Luckily for the deckhands, no bullet found a human target. Unluckily for the pirates, their skiff had strayed into range of the wooden beams that had been readied for this kind of attack.

As the pirates drew alongside the *Good Ship,* the bosun gave a signal and the cables holding the heavy beams were released. Enormous lengths of wood tumbled down onto the launch. There was no time for the helmsman of the skiff to react. There was only time for the quicker witted pirates to fling themselves into the water to avoid the timbers crashing down on them.

A great cheer went up from the deck-hands as, a few seconds later, the broken wreckage of the first skiff disappeared to stern.

* * *

'It's all rather coming to pieces, isn't it?' The voice from the back of the room was a louche as its owner. Leaning against the wall was a figure of almost impeccable grooming, twiddling a silver-topped cane. A few minor details detracted from his otherwise perfectly elegant appearance. For starters, there was a small, perfectly round hole in his forehead. His clothes were soaked in blood. And the back of his skull was almost completely missing.

Maximilian Dumars stopped in his tracks. His knees buckled slightly, and he clutched the back of a chair for support. Behind him, one of the scientists vomited. Instinctively Nick and Eugene both levelled their weapons in the direction of Mr John. Maximilian

Dumars noticed the relative composure of his two lieutenants and regained some of his own, raising his own Uzi in a shaking hand and pointing it towards the figure of the man he had shot dead the day before.

'Y-y-you!? H-h-how?' he stammered.

'Please,' said Mr John in tones of utmost civility. He straightened himself from leaning on the wall. He pointed at the guns, 'and I don't think *those* are really necessary.' He turned to show the empty mess that was the back of his skull. A second scientist vomited. 'It would appear that bullets don't seem to have that much of an effect on me.'

Slack-jawed, Eugene, Nick and Maximilian Dumars lowered their weapons.

'What do you want?' Maximilian Dumars managed to utter through the voices in his head that were screaming how wrong this all was.

Mr John smiled. 'Well, I must say you've handled everything up to now just as my employers expected you would… but it seems that now you've rather hit on something of a stumbling block. It seems I omitted to explain to you how to get the Dark Anti-Matter out of the collider. Very remiss of me. That's probably an important detail – wouldn't you say?'

'B-b-but…your head… You were dead…'

'More a flesh wound, I'd say,' Mr John walked over to one of the workstations and started tapping idly at the keyboard. 'Besides,' he added, 'it turns out I'm something of a fast healer.'

As he spoke, the blood stains in his clothes grew lighter. In front of his aghast spectators, the gaping void at the back of his skull began to close over. Once flesh and bone had completely healed, hair sprouted in the new flesh and grew to an exact and perfectly-groomed and waxed length. Finally, the small wound on Mr John's forehead, the mark of where the bullet had entered his skull, closed over to leave his skin smooth and flawless once more. A third scientist vomited.

'Who the 'ell is that?' whispered Albertine to Hercules.

'I've no idea,' replied Hercules. 'But you don't need me to tell you that that wasn't normal. He must be the agent of the Other Side that the folks in Heaven were talking about.'

'You see,' said Mr John performing a little pirouette to reveal his sartorial elegance restored and no hint of injury, 'all better now. So no hard feelings, eh?' he smiled wickedly at Maximilian Dumars. 'The point is, Maximilian, I am here to help you; remember? You need help in getting the Dark Anti-Matter out of the collider. The answer was in the computer program I gave you. See?'

He turned the monitor of the workstation he had been toying with towards his audience. The screen was blank except for a flashing command prompt alongside which was a simple message. It said: 'End now?'

* * *

The joy of the deckhands was short-lived. The second skiff had found a way past the giant wall of wake thrown up by Captain Higgs' zig-zag course and was closing in. The pirates on the second launch had taken note of the fate that had befallen their colleagues. The helmsman held a respectful distance.

* * *

'How do we know we can trust him, boss?' It was the first time the Eugene had spoken since Mr John had reappeared. 'He's supposed to be dead.'

'Yeah,' echoed Nick in a far-away voice. 'That's not normal.'

Maximilian Dumars didn't appear to hear his colleagues. Almost in a daze, he stepped forwards towards Mr John and the workstation by which he stood. His arms hung loosely by his side. From his right hand still dangled the weapon with which he had committed murder.

'STOP!!!' before Albertine knew what her friend was doing, Hercules had crashed through the door that, up to now, had kept them hidden and had burst into the lab. 'Stop! Don't do it! It's a trick!'

Dazed as he had appeared scant seconds before, Maximilian Dumars reacted to the sudden intrusion with admirable speed. He raised his weapon and fired a controlled burst just above Hercules' head, stopping him dead in his tracks.

'Who the hell are *you?*' Maximilian Dumars demanded. His face was crimson once again. 'And *where* did you come from?'

Hercules threw his hands up in the air in a gesture of surrender. 'Hercules. Hercules Leek. Don't press that button! He doesn't want you to get the Dark Anti-Matter out of the collider. He doesn't want that at all. He's been playing you all this time. He wants you to destroy the Universe! Not just the Universe – the Multiverse!'

One of the scientists nudged a colleague. 'You see,' he said excitedly in a coarse whisper, 'I told you my calculations were correct. The Multiverse model is the only way to explain...'

Maximilian Dumars silenced the scientist with a withering look. He kept his Uzi trained on Hercules but turned to Mr John. Mr John was examining his fingernails. He seemed quite unperturbed by the sudden intrusion.

'Well?' said Maximilian Dumars. 'Is this true? If I press this button will it cause the end of the Multiverse – whatever that is?'

Mr John stopped examining his fingernails. 'Maybe,' he said. 'Maybe it will destroy life in this Universe and all the other possibilities of Universes that have been or will be. But so what? Tell me, Max; what has life ever done for you?

'And think about it…No one has listened to your demands. People don't want purity. They'd rather have chaos.' He snapped his fingers and the large screen on the wall of the lab flicked onto a news channel showing scenes of urban rioting. Under normal circumstances his audience might have been amazed at this unique method of remote control. But they had just watched Mr John grow a new skull in front of their eyes. They let it slide. 'Press that button and it won't just be Europe that you will be cleansing. The world will be free from impurity. Not just the world…the Universe…the Multiverse. You see, I rather think that if you *had* bothered to read the licence agreement, you would have found that the *devil* was very much in the detail.'

The scale of the enormity with which he had been tricked crashed over Maximilian Dumars like a tsunami. Sweating and grey-skinned, his eyes grew distant as the tiredness of his exertions rolled over him in successive waves. Suddenly he just wanted to make it all stop – to make it all go away.

His legs had lost their strength again. His knees buckled slightly, and he leant on the edge of a desk for support. His ears were filled with buzzing, yet he could hear the rapid thump of his own heart. He felt sick and jaded. His breathing was rapid and shallow. His skin was clammy. His eyes itched. He placed his gun on the desk and leant heavily on both arms, lifting his head slowly and looking back across the lab at the small crowd that was watching his movements in fearful anticipation. His throat was dry, his voice cracked.

'I'm sorry,' he said.

He reached out a hand towards the keyboard on the desk in front of him.

'NO!' Eugene's visceral bellow filled the room. Maximilian Dumars' hand halted in mid-air. Everyone in the room turned to look at Eugene, who had raised his enormous machine gun and was aiming it in the direction of his leader. 'I'm sorry, Boss. I can't let you do it. I didn't sign up for no ending of the Multiverse. We woz going to rule the world. That's what I came for. Not...not this.'

His finger tensed around the trigger of his weapon. Tears were welling up in the big man's eyes. It was clear to all the level of inner conflict he was experiencing. Loyalty was everything to Eugene. Maximilian Dumars had given him everything. He had taken him from a run-down estate and brought him to the brink of glory, and yet this was *wrong,* and he couldn't take it. His one true friend came to his aid.

'Yeah, Boss, this is wrong. Step away from the keyboard.' Nick, too, was now pointing his weapon in the direction of the leader of the Aryan Defence Order/League/Front.

'I'm not sure that this really helps anything.' Mr John had stepped forward – blocking the line of fire from both Eugene and Nick to Mr Dumars. He spread his arms, palms toward the two lieutenants of the Aryan Defence Order/League/Front, and began to walk slowly forward.

'I suppose you could try shooting,' he said with a mischievous look on his face, 'but then you've seen for yourselves that bullets don't have much of an effect on me...' he kept walking forward. The further that he moved from Maximilian Dumars, the larger he seem to get, so for both Eugene and Nick the possibility of either one of them taking a clean shot at their boss remained out of the question.

'...Besides...' As Mr John moved slowly forward, Hercules took the opportunity to slip unnoticed around the edge of the room towards Maximilian Dumars. '...I'm not sure that those weapons are really that effective anyway!' Mr John pointed a finger at each of the guns. The barrels drooped towards the floor like something out of a cartoon. Nick and Eugene looked at one another in disbelief.

'Go ahead, Maximilian,' Mr John said over his shoulder. 'Do what you think is right.'

* * *

On the *Good Ship*, bosun Boson noticed with alarm the two pirates at the front of the skiff had shouldered grenade launchers, which they were struggling to aim. But it was only a matter of time before they got their opportunity for a shot.

He grabbed a fire-hose from the deck and signalled to a crew member to open the valve. The powerful hose sprung to life and the bosun had to lean against the recoil with all his weight. Nonetheless the powerful jet of water fell short of the pirate skiff which held its position just out of range. The pirates with the rocket propelled grenades had both been shaping to aim their weapons at the bridge. Facing the stream of disrupting water from bosun Boson's fire hose, one of the pirates adjusted the launcher on his shoulder and began to sight on the bosun himself.

Abdullah watched as the rocket propelled grenade sped from the launcher on his shoulder towards the man aiming the fire hose at them. There was a hiss next to him as his colleague fired his own weapon in the direction of the bridge of the *Good Ship*. Both shots were true, they watched the flight of the grenades in the brief anticipation of the explosions that were destined to follow.

* * *

Maximilian Dumars looked once more at the assembled, expectant faces. 'I'm sorry,' he croaked once more. His hand hovered over the keyboard.

'NO!' yelled Hercules.

He dived forward towards the keyboard, his arms outstretched to knock it from the desktop. With a speed of reflex that made his actions seem to play out in slow motion, Maximilian Dumars' hand shot out for the Uzi on the worktop. He spun towards Hercules who was in mid-flight towards the workstation. His finger slipped easily around the trigger and squeezed.

A percussive rattle rang out through the lab. Hercules collapsed as his momentum was checked by the hail of bullets. His broken body crashed to the floor and almost instantly a dark pool of blood began to spread around his crumpled form.

Maximilian Dumars vacantly regarded the corpse of his latest victim. Almost as quickly as the light had returned to his eyes for his reflex strike, it faded. For a last time, he looked at the other people in the lab, and uttered the same words he had spoken twice before.

'I'm sorry,' he said. He pushed the button.

* * *

For a moment nothing happened.

The earth stood still. Time froze. Then it began to tear. In the chamber below the ATLAS lab the fabric of reality began to unwind.

Time screamed.

* * *

Bosun Boson watched in horror as the grenade sped towards him. He was dimly aware of another projectile heading for the bridge...

The earth shook. Not the ground. That would have been of little consequence to the *Good Ship* forging across the briny deep. The entire planet rocked on its axis.

The sudden jolt tipped the bosun off his feet. The fire hose slipped from his grasp sending a powerful jet of water snaking through the air. The first arc of the wave caught the underside of the rocket propelled grenade that had been rapidly bearing down on his position. The glancing blow of the jet of water tilted the flight path of the grenade, forcing it into a climbing arc.

The uncontrolled hose whipped back and forth. Its spewing flow met the tail of the second grenade and sent that, too, shooting into the sky above.

The pigeons had not altered their course on account of the minor sea skirmish raging below. There was no reason that it should have been of any consequence to them. They were still powering through the air when the first stray grenade struck the lead bird and exploded.

Lying flat on his back where he had fallen, the bosun saw the explosion. But it was the flight of the second grenade, that was midway through describing a giant loop in the sky, which held his attention. He pulled himself to his feet. One of the deck-hands had had the presence of mind to shut off the valve feeding the fire-hose and its spent coils now snaked limply across the deck like a giant constrictor. The other deckhands noticed the direction of their foreman's gaze and all eyes were raised towards the flight of the second grenade.

On the skiff, Abdullah and his fellow grenade launcher were struggling against the choppy waters to reload their weapons. They could not believe that their first shots had not met their targets. Mercifully, they were no longer being bothered by the spray from the fire-hose.

One of the pirates behind Abdullah shook his shoulder. He looked up in annoyance. The man was pointing to the deck-hands on the container ship, who were all staring up into the sky and pointing. Abdullah's eyes followed the direction they were indicating until he picked out, high above, the grenade that had just reached the apogee of its loop-the-loop and was now beginning to fall back towards the sea in the direction from which it had come.

The skiff was still moving forward through the water, but its entire crew, including the helmsman, were now also fixated on the flight of the second grenade, as it traced its elegant path through the sky. Together, they stood transfixed as the tiny dot grew bigger and bigger in their vision, until the simultaneous realisation occurred that by some marvellous fluke of physics (and the helmsman's failure to have taken any evasive action) the grenade was heading straight for them. In unison, the pirates on the skiff leapt from their boat, just in the nick of time as the grenade slammed into their launch and blew it to smithereens.

* * *

The soldiers and police still left in the cordon at CERN looked at one another in horror and covered their ears at the awful, soul-rending sound emanating from the ATLAS building. It was as if a hand the size of a planet was dragging its fingernails down a blackboard the size of a galaxy.

In the lab itself, the noise was, as if this were possible, worse. This did not stop one of the scientists turning to a colleague and observing, 'Well, we've created scenarios that factored the effects of Dark Energy into the ultimate end of the Universe, but I don't think we can blame ourselves from having failed to predict *this!*'

His colleague had his hands firmly clamped over his ears. He watched the mouthed words without comprehension.

The ground rumbled and shook, and a small dark spot appeared on the floor close to where Maximilian Dumars stood, and Hercules' body lay. The spot was not black – that would have indicated that it did not reflect any light. The spot was anti-black – it didn't merely fail to reflect light. It didn't just suck light from the surroundings. It positively radiated a total absence of light.

The two chairs that were by the workbench began to rattle on their wheels. Then they both rolled together across the short distance of floor towards the dot. When they got to a closer proximity they started to unravel into twin streams of chair particles that were sucked into the void.

The dot was slowly growing in size, and with it, the strength of force that it exerted on its surroundings. The keyboard, monitor and mouse on the workstation, along with a stack of papers that had been left on the desk shortly followed the chairs. Dumbfounded, Maximilian Dumars stood rooted to the spot, watching as Hercules' body was the next object to get sucked into the void. He didn't move or make a sound when he was pulled into the vortex.

Mr John was clearly enjoying himself. He began to dance a little jig around the lab. Unfortunately for him, or perhaps as a deliberate act, in his excitement at the doom he had wreaked on Creation, he strayed too close to the ever-growing chasm of anti-existence and disappeared.

Chaos erupted in the lab. Albertine, the scientists, the remaining members of the Aryan Defence Order/League/Front and the hostages in the adjoining room began to scream and shout, desperately seeking something solid to cling amid the maelstrom as the widening abyss started to suck tables, chairs, papers and computer equipment into its emptiness.

* * *

The second pigeon had been shaken by the explosion that had killed his loft mate, but apart from a few singed feathers, he was unharmed. The same could not be said for Asif's delicate homing device though. The force of the explosion had completely fried the intricate circuitry.

To the pigeon, this was somewhat disconcerting. As his magnetic senses readjusted, his little brain computed that he was no longer a couple of hundred miles from his loft in Yorkshire, but somewhere altogether warmer with a good deal more sea.

Luckily for the little bird, his magnetic senses were not the only means of navigation at his disposal. He could remember his flight path from visual clues as well. As he circled above the sea, he resolved to retrace his journey so far. Blessed also with a supreme sense of smell, he was sure that if he could find his launch site he would be able to track down his owner.

It was what his kind were bred to do.

He was going home.

THIRTEEN

ONCE AGAIN HERCULES found himself collapsed into a single point of existence. The next thing he knew, he was floating in darkness.

There was a dreadful pain in the side of his face. Very carefully he tried to move. Lightning shredded the nerves in his cheeks. He felt himself being pulled backwards, dragged by the source of his agony. He turned, so that he was moving in the same direction that the pain was pulling from. Instantly he felt a respite. He dashed forwards. The pain had been pulling him this way. Maybe he could outrun it.

For a few seconds his plan seemed to be working. He felt nothing as he raced onwards. He could not tell which direction he was heading, whether it was up or down, left or right. Everything was black. He hurtled on, and then…

…He slammed abruptly into a wall of hurt once more. His face exploded in searing agony. Once again he was being dragged backwards. He turned on his heels.

Once more the pain subsided. He dashed forward again. This time he had been travelling for less time when he was suddenly cut dead in his tracks. The process repeated again and again: each short dash for freedom soon cut short in paroxysms of pain.

Hercules became aware that he was slowly being drawn towards a dim glow. Each time the pain slackened he dashed into the darkness. But each time his bid for freedom was halted, he was drawn ever closer to a slowly growing point of weak light. In desperation he thrashed and fought against the force that was drawing him inexorably upwards. But he was growing tired. His efforts had exhausted him. The point of light had grown to a glowing pool that surrounded him.

He was too worn to fight any more. He felt himself being dragged up into the pool of light. The pain in his cheek was unbearable, but he was too spent for all but the weakest of struggles in protest.

A hand reached out and grasped him. Hercules thrashed about in surprise. The hand tightened against his struggles and gripped him firmly but carefully. Hercules stopped struggling and looked around. The hand that held him belonged to an ancient Inuit woman, wrapped in sealskin and furs. She was fishing at an ice-hole through which he had just been hauled. In the background the lights of the aurora danced off the snow-scape and lit the heavens with an eerie glow. The old lady's dark eyes twinkled with the light of a billion stars.

She reached out with her free hand. Hercules realised that she dwarfed him in size. The hand that held him encased the entirety of his body. The other hand reached forward, and the calloused fingers grabbed at something thin and white that was poking out of his mouth. Pain seared through his cheek as the old lady firmly grasped the protrusion. With a swift twist and a tug, she expertly pulled whatever it was from his mouth. As she withdrew her hand Hercules saw that the cause of his pain was a large fish-hook, carved out of some sort of bone. It had been buried in his cheek.

The removal of the hook instantly brought with it some relief from the agony he had been experiencing. As the Inuit stuck her fishing pole into the snow at her side, Hercules had the opportunity to take in the scene before him. The old fisherwoman had already caught a couple of other fish which were laid out on the snow to her right. To her left, looking up at him with saucer-like blue eyes, was the smallest, whitest and quite possibly cutest kitten that Hercules had ever seen. Surrounding the ice hole, a collection of the kinds of potted plants common in office buildings dotted the snow.

The old lady turned her attention to her most recent catch. She smiled at Hercules. He looked into her eyes and saw depths of space beyond time – unfathomable ages.

'Y-Y-You – y-y-you're Him, aren't you?' he stammered.

The old lady's smile broadened. The wrinkles in her face deepened. She radiated good humour.

'Apart from being a "she". Yes, I suppose I AM.'

Hercules gulped. 'If you don't mind me saying, you're not quite what I expected.'

'And what would that have been?' asked the old lady.

'Erm…I don't know really…Just something…else.'

The old lady continued to smile. 'Hercules, I am the Creator. The Alpha and the Omega. The Beginning and the End. You are but a mortal. If you were to see me in my true form your brain would not be able to cope with it. I have taken many forms in my time. I've done animal, vegetable and mineral. It just happens that today I am an old Inuit lady… and you…you are a fish.'

'Oh,' said Hercules. He flapped his gills.

There was a moment's silence. The lights of the aurora continued their mysterious dance across the horizon. Hercules flapped his gills once more.

'I failed, didn't I,' he said eventually.

The Creator stroked her chin. 'Well that all rather depends,' she said. 'What would success have been?'

'I was meant to stop them,' Hercules replied gloomily. 'I was supposed to stop them from using the Dark Anti-Matter.'

'And how were you going to do that? They had help from the Other Side. One of their finest operatives, so I believe. What was your plan?'

Hercules wasn't sure, but when the Creator said "One of their finest" he thought she spoke with as much good-natured warmth as she was showing in her dealings with him.

'I don't really know,' he said. 'I'm not sure I ever really got as far as working that out.'

'No – it would rather appear that you didn't, did you?'

Neither spoke for a while, while they contemplated Hercules' lack of a plan. Eventually the Creator broke the silence. 'But you did try, didn't you?'

'Yes.'

'What made you so sure that I didn't want Creation to end? How did you know I hadn't had enough of it all?'

Hercules thought for a moment. 'I don't think that I was sure,' he said. 'I'm still not sure. After all, they detonated the Dark Anti-Matter, didn't they? I couldn't stop them... *You* didn't stop them... But if you gave us anything, you gave us the ability to choose. I chose to try.'

The old lady beamed at him. The warmth of her smile was too much for Hercules. It burned with the intensity of the full glare of a million suns.

Hercules lowered his gaze.

'Yes, you *did* try, didn't you?'

The small, white and almost impossibly cute kitten mewed softly. The Creator reached down with her free hand and tickled it gently behind the ears. The kitten began to purr at a volume that belied its size.

'You see,' said the Creator – possibly to Hercules, but possibly just to Herself – 'you just can't make life *and* have it perfect.

Heavens knows I've tried. If you achieve perfection, then nothing can change – it can no longer be perfect, or what you had before can't have been. On the other hand, without change, you can't have life. I've heard it a trillion times in people's prayers – "Why, God, did you create a world with so much suffering?"

'The simple truth is – it's *the only* way to create a world. For life to exist you have to allow change to occur. The conditions that create a Universe only exist within a very narrow band of the possible. Trust me; I have aeons of experience in these matters.'

'Couldn't you just make it so that life could exist in a perfect environment? You are the Creator.'

'Yes I am – and good Heavens: No. The way of things is the way of things. You can only work with the materials you have. I have experimented… I have *created*…it all comes down to this one simple truth. *Life* needs change. Perfection, if it exists at all, lies in the fact that life is possible at all.

'It's quite simple, we all have rules to follow – yes, even me. And we must all make choices.

'Some people choose religion as their means of expressing devotion to the mysteries of creation. That is their choice. But there is no *rule* that states that you *have* to be religious to be good. And conversely, some very bad acts have been perpetrated in the name of faith, but not every follower of religion is bad. Morality is less about what you believe than how you act. What I can never begin to understand is how one group of people might think I have chosen *them* above another. I came to the conclusion a long time ago that dogmatic adherence to any set of beliefs is a sure-fire recipe for trouble. I happen to like a little bit of uncertainty.'

'Uncertainty? You?' Hercules was incredulous. 'But surely *You* know everything.'

'I am older than time. I am the Beginning and the End. I have made countless worlds. I am older than Matter, I am bigger than Time. Certainly I know *most* things.' The old lady had a far-away look in her eyes – and far away on her scale of things meant *very* distant indeed. 'But there is one thing that always puzzles me.'

'Really?' asked Hercules. 'What's that?'

'I made everything,' said the Creator slowly. 'But what made *me*? Where did *I* come from?'

'Oh.' It had never occurred to Hercules that the Creator should be bothered by her own existential considerations.

Once more there was silence. The lights of the aurora danced their ghostly dance.

'It's OK,' the old lady said eventually in a kindly tone. 'I find it quite comforting, actually. As you may have heard, I'm really rather fond of the odd paradox. That's why I make rules, so that they can be contradicted.

'I made just such a rule after my boy took it upon himself to take responsibility for the sins of mankind. Oh, he meant well. But we all know where good intentions lead. It didn't take long for people to lose sight of the message and start worshipping the creeds. It never does. So after that, I put a ban on anyone leaving Heaven. For anyone who breaks this rule, there is no going back. Simple. And so it's been for two millennia. Yet *you* saw fit to break this rule.'

The Creator fixed Hercules with a stern look. Hercules opened and closed his mouth. Suddenly he felt very small and helpless. And scaly.

The Creator's face softened. She smiled. 'Luckily for you, I have another rule. If you give your life to help others, you have to go to Heaven. So, if I let you go to Hell, I break one rule. But if I let you back into Heaven, I break the other.'

'You could just let creation be destroyed.'

'And ruin all my hard work?' the old Inuit winked at him. 'I don't think so! Besides – they cheated.'

'So you're not going to let the Multiverse be destroyed?'

'It already has been, and it has already been reborn. That is the bit that Legion and his kind don't get, bless them. Every second is a new creation, a new chance. But every second is also its own loss and destruction. Your time won't end here. Not now, not today. I'll send you back, but it won't be the same Universe. And it won't be the same you. By having made the choices you have made you have changed, and the Universe has changed, too.'

'So what should people do?'

'Be reasonable. Keep talking. Try and see the other person's point of view and work things out as best you can. Oh, and one other thing...'

'Which is?'

'Never, EVER think it's OK to use the excuse that you are doing something in MY name!'

The old lady gave Hercules a gentle squeeze. He felt a ticklish sensation at the back of his throat. He coughed. A bullet shot out of his mouth and landed in the snow at the fisherwoman's feet. She squeezed him again. The ticklish sensation returned. This time when he coughed a shower of bullets joined the one already lying in the snow.

'What happens now?' asked Hercules, eyeing the small pile of metal that had recently been inside him.

'Who knows?' smiled the old lady.

'Er...you do?' ventured Hercules.

'Yes... I suppose I probably do.'

* * *

Hercules found himself lying on the floor of the lab in the ATLAS building. He looked around. He dimly recalled there having been more furniture in the room before.

Albertine was at his side. ''Ercules! 'Ercules! Can you 'ear me?' Hercules felt Albertine shaking his shoulder, gently but insistently. ''Ercules! Wake up!'

Hercules tried to push himself upright. His head was spinning.

'Easy there, not so fast!' Albertine caught him as he slumped back towards the floor, catching him just before he gave his head a nasty whack. She helped him to sit up.

'Wh-what happened?' asked Hercules with difficulty. His tongue felt swollen, and his mouth was dry. A faint taste of metal and cordite lingered on his palette.

'I was going to ask you the same thing,' said Albertine. 'The manic one pressed the button and all 'ell broke loose. Furniture was flying everywhere. People were screaming. This 'ole appeared in the floor and people and stuff started getting sucked in. The leader of that group of nutters for one... and the oddball who grew a new skull... and your body... And all of a sudden the next thing we know it is deadly quiet and you are just lying there on the floor...'

She paused.

''Ang on a minute. This all happened after you got shot. Why aren't you bleeding?... And where did that scar on your cheek come from?'

* * *

Once the pigeons had been sent forth on their mission, Asif had retreated from the coast and directed the Land Cruiser inland. About twenty kilometres from the coast, a low range of dark grey mountains rose from the sand.

Away from the tarmac of the road, the emptiness of the desert filled Asif with a sense of the raw power of nature. He followed a dried-up riverbed that wound between the peaks, weaving around the stunted thorn bushes that eked out an existence by drawing on the memory of waters that once flowed down this course.

He drove on for about an hour without seeing so much as the hint of a sign of another soul. Eventually he felt that he had secured himself enough isolation and pulled the Land Cruiser to a halt. The sun was high in the sky and the shadows were short. Asif set about rigging a tarpaulin off the side of the vehicle to create a bit of refuge from the heat. When this was done, he took out his mat and prayed. Then he laid down in the shade to rest.

The heat made him drowsy, and he must have drifted off to sleep.

He was woken by the sound of wings flap-clapping into landing. This was followed by the scratch and patter of small, sharp-clawed feet across the roof of the Land Cruiser. For a brief moment, there was silence. Asif listened intently. There was a gentle coo and a quick flapping of wings as Asif's pigeon fluttered off the roof and joined him under the tarpaulin. Asif stared in stunned disbelief at the bird; slightly singed, but still wearing its harness and hood.

There was a soft click followed by a gentle hiss.

'Oh… bloody hell!'

Revelations

CAPTAIN HIGGS SURVEYED the busy docks with a sense of quiet satisfaction. Giant cranes had begun the process of unloading the many containers of aid supplies bound for refugee camps inland.

The *Good Ship* had made port at Djibouti in double-quick time. Despite throttling back the engines after their encounter with the pirates, the vessel had continued to surge though the waters of the Red Sea without slowing from the twenty plus knots it had reached during the skirmish. Only with Djibouti looming in the distance did the speed drop, and the Captain had never known a boat of this size to decelerate in such an alarming fashion. But no harm had come to ship, cargo or crew.

It was all some kind of miracle.

There was a commotion on deck as a door to one of the containers swung open while it was being hoisted into the sky. It must have been damaged in the gunfire from the pirates. A sack dropped from the container and onto the deck of the ship, bursting open and scattering its contents.

As the container was lowered back down and the deck hands busied themselves with securing the damaged door, Captain Higgs' eyes were drawn to the figure of the Bosun. He stood on deck, stock still, staring at the pile of spilt grain. While the Captain watched on, Bosun Boson bent to scoop up a handful and stood immobile, staring at the seeds in his hand, transfixed.

* * *

Hercules sipped his coffee, watching in amusement the two figures who were engaged in an argument while at the same time trying to look inconspicuous. He grinned at Albertine and nodded in the direction of the pair.

The figures were dressed in women's clothing. The smaller of the two might have been able to carry this off, but "her" mountainous companion looked anything but feminine.

'I just don't see why we have to go round looking like this,' grumbled the large one. 'People are laughing at us. Besides, this wig's really itchy.'

'Shut up and stop moaning!' snapped his smaller companion. 'People are only staring because you are making such a fuss. We agreed this is for the best. We might still be wanted men.'

Albertine grinned back. 'What do you think? Should we turn them in? Do you think they are still a threat to society?'

Hercules smiled. 'Oh, I think they're probably more of a danger to themselves than anyone else. Besides, they stood up to their boss in the end...'

In the confusion that had followed the ending of the hostage taking, Nick and Eugene had recovered their wits fast enough to slip unnoticed through a side door of the lab and down in the labyrinth of tunnels below. More by luck than by judgement, they had managed to navigate their way to safety – an exit through a building that was beyond the police cordon.

Hercules and Albertine had joined the rest of the hostages as they tumbled out of the ATLAS building towards the decidedly relieved security forces. Hostages, police and soldiers were united in a common joy that they were not currently splashing their way to the far corners of the continent and beyond.

Hercules had done his best to tell Albertine what had happened to him after he had disappeared into the void, but the more time passed, the more it all seemed strange and surreal and the less it felt like anything other than a dream he once vaguely remembered having had. Remarkably he had no wounds from the bullets Albertine assured had struck him. The small star-shaped scar on his cheek remained as the only evidence of his other-worldly meeting.

Taking advantage of the exodus of the civilian population, they had managed to retrieve Hercules' passport and belongings from the still abandoned airport. But people had begun to return to the city as quickly as they had fled, and things were slowly returning to normal.

Hercules looked up at the station clock. It was time to go.

'Are you sure you won't stay?' asked Albertine. 'The Geneva branch of the Monitors could always use an extra pair of eyes.'

'With all the connections you have, I doubt there's much you miss,' said Hercules with a smile. 'Besides, I could really do with just spending a few nights in my own bed and trying to get back to some sense of normality.'

'I doubt that anything for you is ever going to be normal again.' She smiled and held out a hand. Hercules reached out to shake it and Albertine embraced him with a hug instead.

'If you ever change your mind…'

'I'll just wave at the nearest CCTV camera!'

'I will be watching!'

* * *

'All in all, I'd say you've made a total balls-up of things,' said Baalberith. He dropped the heavy report onto his desk contemptuously and glared across the table at Legion.

'Thank you, sir,' replied Legion, cheerfully. 'I'm always happy to do a bad day's work.' He smiled at his boss. His boss continued to glare back.

'Once again you find yourself within a hair's breadth of a promotion!'

Their session of mutual loathing was interrupted by a knock at the door. It was Loki, Chief bringer of Mischief and occasional Messenger to the Underworld. 'Not interrupting anything important am I?' he asked casually. 'Only you two look like you're about to kiss!'

'What is it, Loki?' growled Baalberith, not shifting his gaze from his superior. 'Did you want something?'

'Let's see, there was something. Now what was it? I'm sorry, it's just that seeing you two lovebirds together has just plain made me forget. Oh, yeah, that was it. The Boss wants to see you both. In his office. Now!'

A look of panic swept across Baalberith's face. He scooped up the report off his desk and swept past Loki. Legion hurried after him. Satan was one demon you didn't keep waiting.

As they hurried through the circles of Hell, Baalberith continued to berate Legion. As much to annoy his boss as for any other reason, Legion continued to meet his dressing up with unflinching good humour.

They arrived at the ante-room for the inner circle. A bored looking banshee was sitting behind a desk, chewing gum and filing her talons.

Without shifting her expression, she leant forward and pressed a button on the intercom on her desk. 'They're here,' she said and returned to chewing her gum.

The banshee's announcement was met with a blood-curdling roar from the other side of the door. For the first time in a while, Legion and Baalberith shared a common feeling: they were both glad that they didn't have any blood to curdle. Nonetheless they exchanged nervous glances. The banshee turned her attention to them. 'The Boss'll see you now. Bad luck,' she said, before adding viciously, 'you're gonna need it.'

Baalberith knocked quickly on the door, and they went in.

The inner circle was a huge cavern. In the middle of the cavern was a large desk. In contrast to the atmosphere in the rest of Hell, inside the cavern the temperature was cold. In fact, it was colder than cold. It was glacial. Legion and Baalberith shivered, and their breath clouded in the frosty atmosphere. Behind the desk with his back to them, in a large leather swivel chair, sat the Lord of Darkness, Satan himself.

'So,' he bellowed as he spun to face them. Legion and Baalberith both cringed. 'Which one of you miserable maggots saw fit to try and bring about an End of Days without permission from your inferiors?'

'That would be this insect, your Lowness,' said Baalberith, nudging Legion forward. Legion shot him a daggers look. 'He goes by the name of Legion, your Supreme Evilness. It's all in this report.' He bowed low and crept forward to place the heavy report he had been carrying onto the desk.

The Dark Underlord sniffed contemptuously at the report. He rifled through the pages, without bothering to read them. 'So... Legion is it?' he fixed Legion with his full attention. Legion shifted uncomfortably on his feet. 'What do have to say for yourself, worm?'

'Er...revenge?'

'Revenge?' bellowed Satan. 'What do you mean "revenge"?'

Might as well be hung for a sheep as a lamb, Legion thought to himself. He began to explain in detail the nature of his feud with the Creator and how he had hoped to settle the score by destroying all of His works.

'Hmmm,' Satan scratched his chin when Legion had finished talking. The action generated a shower of sparks. 'Legion, you have displayed a remarkably selfish and not to say incredibly persistent desire for revenge…an unbelievable level of arrogance in believing that your little scheme would be successful…a total disregard for the usual protocols…not to say a total ruthlessness in the way that you plotted and carried out your plan.

'Each one of these is a serious character flaw in itself. Together, they can only add up to one thing. Your behaviour totally merits a demotion!'

'Er, thank you, your Lowness,' Legion was taken aback.

'What was the name of the snivelling maggot that accompanied you here?' Satan asked the question without even looking at Baalberith.

'Er, Baalberith, your Lowness.'

'So what do you say, Legion? Do you want Baalberith's job?'

Legion regarded Baalberith. Baalberith eyed him back with a look of the purest hatred. Legion would have expected nothing less.

'I can't say I'm not flattered, your Supreme Evilness. But if I'm honest, I'm kind of happy with the job I've got.'

'*"If I'm honest"? "Happy with the job I've got"?*' raged the Dark Underlord. Fire streamed from his fingertips. 'What kind of language is that? It's not modesty, is it, Legion?' he roared. 'A demon could find himself on the wrong side of the pits for that kind of behaviour.'

'M-m-modesty? Why, not at all, your Lowness. It's just that I happen to take a great deal of pride in the work that I do. I would hate to miss out on the chance to corrupt new souls because,' he cast Baalberith a contemptuous look, 'I was stuck behind a desk.'

'Ah – pride…Sentiment worthy of a demon. And I daresay we will be needing our very worst operatives out there in the field getting down and dirty. Very well, as you wish, Legion,' growled the Lord of the Flies.

It was clear that the interview was over. Legion and Baalberith began to head for the door. Both of them were glad that the ordeal had reached its conclusion. There was something about spending time with Satan that made even the most depraved of demons start longing for a bath.

As they reached the entrance of the cavern, the voice of the Dark Master stopped Legion in his tracks. Baalberith didn't wait.

'Legion.'

Legion gulped. He turned to face Satan once more.

'Don't forget…From now on I'll be watching you. *All* of you.'

Legion nodded. He was just about to turn to go when he was stopped once more.

'And Legion.'

'Yes, Master.'

'Find out from that useless girl on the desk outside when the air-conditioning engineer is going to get here, will you? It's *freezing* in here.'

Legion nodded in acknowledgement and hurried out of the cavern. Baalberith was waiting for him outside.

'Don't think this means I owe you,' he snarled at Legion.

'Why ever would you suppose that I thought you owed me?' asked Legion in a voice so innocent that melted butter would have reformed into a solid lump in his mouth. The subtext was, of course: 'I won't forget this, Baalberith, and neither will you. And one day, when I really, *really* need a favour…and it will be a BIG one…'

'Yes, well just don't!' snapped Baalberith, fully aware that he was now totally indebted to his superior. He turned on his hooves and slunk off.

Legion stood for a moment, breathing in the sulphurous fumes and listening contentedly to the screams of tormented souls. Life, he supposed, was good. He was actually glad that his plan had failed.

'Er, Mr Legion?'

Legion looked around. He could not see where the voice was coming from.

'Mr Legion, Sir?' the voice repeated, insistently.

Legion looked down. At his feet was an imp. Legion raised an eyebrow.

'Message from reception, Sir,' said the imp. 'And may I say wot a honour it is to be the hw'one to bring it to you, Sir. Your guests 'ave h'arrived.'

A vicious smile spread across Legion's lips. He rubbed his hands together. 'Thank you,' he replied, 'that is h'excellent – I mean excellent – news.'

The little imp bowed deeply and vanished.

Remembering that he had been charged with a message of his own, Legion spent a little while flirting with the banshee before relaying to her as inaccurately and mischievously as he could that her Boss was too warm and had asked for the air-conditioning to be turned up.

As he sauntered away from her desk, whistling casually, he wondered to himself if the reason for the sub-arctic temperatures in the inner circle was not simply the result of generations of demons having played exactly the same prank as he just had. But then you just weren't worth your salt as a demon if, when someone's back was turned, you didn't stick in a knife.

Legion continued to wander through the circles of Hell towards where the new arrivals were being held. He stopped for the odd turn of the wheel on a rack here; the odd twisting of a pitchfork there. He was in no rush. He had the rest of eternity. He was free to take his time and enjoy himself. This was almost the exact opposite of what his new guests could expect.

Eventually he arrived at reception. Here another banshee was sitting behind a desk, chewing gum and filing her talons. Without bothering to look up she nodded towards the corner of the room.

Two terrified figures were perched uncomfortably on seats that were not so much seats as sharpened spikes. They were surrounded by a group of imps who were all armed with tiny pitchforks with which they were taking turns to stab and jab their victims. There was little that the two new arrivals could do to prevent this. They had been bound by an expert in the arts of restraint. Leather straps and handcuffs restricted them to all but the smallest range of movements. They could not look away from their torment as their eyelids had been stitched open with rows of fishhooks. Nor could they protest against their torture as each had a large ball strapped into his mouth.

'Ah...Maximilian...Asif,' said Legion pleasantly, addressing the figures in turn. They both rolled their terrified eyes wildly by way of response. 'How good of you both to join us...' there was a pause, before he added, conspiratorially '...although really being good is something we try to avoid around here.

'Anyway, time to show you to your new homes.' He nodded at the imps. In a blur of activity an imp scaled each of the bound figures and plunged a large hook through his nose – in one nostril and out of the other. Whatever screams were screamed were bounced back into Asif and Maximilian Dumars' throats by the balls in their mouths.

Affixed to the hooks were chains. The imps passed the other ends of the chains to Legion, who took them, nodded his thanks to the imps, and began to saunter away from reception. Pulled by the hooks through their noses, Maximilian Dumars and Asif had little alternative but to follow. Hampered by their bonds, their progress was not, however, as casual and carefree as that of Legion. They hopped, staggered and stumbled behind him, all the time shrinking in fear from the screams of the damned that surrounded them and the occasional shower of burning pitch through which they were led.

Eventually they reached a heavy door. A large key protruded from the keyhole.

'Ah, here we are,' said Legion brightly. 'Home, sweet home.

'Maximilian,' he said, turning to the spirit of Mr Dumars, 'since you showed such an admirable inability to integrate with anyone from another culture while you were alive, we thought it would be appropriate for you to spend eternity with a soul from one of the cultures that you so despised. Better than that, you can share his own private hell.' He clapped his hands together with glee. 'Say "Hell…oh" to your new roomy.

'And Asif,' Legion turned the key in the lock and heaved the weighty door open, 'I believe you planned to spend eternity in paradise in the company of virgins.' He yanked hard on the two chains in his hand and propelled the two damned souls into the cell beyond the door. Around the walls of the cell loitered a collection of the foulest, most disgusting, depraved, horrifying and above all unmistakably, and in some cases monstrously, male demons that Legion had been able to assemble.

Maximilian Dumars and Asif looked at one another in sudden mutual recognition of the significance of their bondage gear. Although it barely seemed possible, their eyes widened further at the total and utter abject terror of the fate that awaited them.

'Well,' Legion was grinning mischievously as he began to close the door behind them. 'We've done our best with the décor, but I'm afraid it might be a little below the standards you might expect in paradise. But as for virgins… well, I can assure you, gentlemen, that none of your new friends here have ever done *THIS* before!'

***

Nore watched the stranger with interest. He had not seen a man like him before. He was sure the stranger *was* a man. He looked like a man. He moved like a man. But there was something that was odd. Even when he was looking directly at him, Nore he wasn't able to make out even the simplest detail of the stranger's face.

The stranger had a simple bag slung over his shoulder. Every few paces as he walked along he would dip his hand into the bag. The bag evidently contained seeds. Each time he had retrieved a fresh handful the stranger would crouch down and press the seeds deep into the soil.

And there was the damnedest thing, thought Nore, as he watched the man's progress up the valley. Each seed that was pushed into the ground had sprouted into a small plant by the time the stranger had walked on a few steps. The accelerated growth appeared to stop there, but for Nore it was enough. He understood. These plants would be left to grow into the mighty trees that had filled the forest before the loggers had come. This time, Nore swore, the tribe would not fail. This time they would live up to their role as the guardians of the forest.

Bosun Boson had a new name.

It was Hope.

About The Author

LIAM STIRLING is the author of The God Particle, the first Hercules Leek adventure which mixes fantasy, science-fiction and philosophy with a liberal sprinkling of laugh-out-loud humour. Liam is currently working on the follow-up The Ivory Tower and has a number of other titles planned for the series. 

Liam began life as a baby, but professionally soon outgrew this calling and eventually moved on to study Zoology at Oxford University. Following a few years as a reseach scientist, he was subsequently a saxophonist in an marvelously unsuccessful reggae band, before the gravity of adult life sucked him into a career in IT.

When not doing the day job, he can be found doing the things that take up all the waking hours of a self-published indie author. But somehow he still finds time to play his saxophone and keep bees.

You can chat with Liam on Twitter @HerculesLeek or visit his website at www.herculesleek.com, where he blogs about writing and gives away free stuff.

Free Audiobook

Your Free Audiobook Is Waiting

* * *

THEY SAY possession is nine-tenths of the law.

Unfortunately for Legion, that wasn't quite how Jesus saw things. Banished to Purgatory, and humiliated by their inferiors, is there no way Legion can avoid spending eternity in their own private Hell?

* * *

Get a free copy of Legion's origin story, narrated by the fabulous James Macnaughton, here:

www.herculesleek.com

www.ingramcontent.com/pod-product-compliance
Lightning Source LLC
Chambersburg PA
CBHW021226190726
48289CB00005B/1192